CODE

OF

CONDUCT

Karen Black

CODE OF CONDUCT

Copyright © 2003
C & K Publishing
144 E. Washington Ave.
Escondido, CA 92025-1814

ISBN: 0-9724449-0-4
Library of Congress Catalog Card Number: 2002095261

DEDICATION

To my husband, Cole Black, and his Vietnam ex-POW buddies, whose combined experiences provided the inspiration for the prison episodes.

ACKNOWLEDGEMENTS

I want to thank several friends whose support and prodding kept me going forward: Terry Badger, a retired Navy pilot and friend; all the members of the Scribblers writing group, who critiqued and encouraged; Sofia Shafquat, who edited and challenged me to do better; and to all those literary agents and publishers who turned down the earlier versions, forcing me to rewrite . . . rewrite . . . rewrite . . . .

FOREWORD

While many POWs came home to broken marriages, the personal relationship portion of this book is purely fictional. On the other hand, the prison scenes are based on actual events that happened to the POWs in Vietnam. The story was inspired by years of listening to the recollections of my husband and several of his Vietnam ex-POW buddies. Time does not seem to have faded their memories of what they went through (although they can now joke about it) and each reunion or get together provided a new tidbit.

My goal is to present an accurate depiction of the horrendous prisoner-of-war experience and the resulting shattered personal lives in the format of a novel to attract a group of readers who might have overlooked some of the non-fiction books that have been written by several of the returning POWs. For more information on the POW experience, see the bibliography page.

PROLOGUE

<u>February 14, 1973, Miramar Naval Air Station,</u>
<u>San Diego, California.</u>

Commander Matt Tillet pushed his forehead flush against the small window searching for familiar landmarks as the C-9 circled the field waiting for clearance to land. Except for the patches of development creeping ever closer on three sides, Miramar hadn't changed much. But, that rain drenched runway had never looked better!

Matt vividly recalled, as if it were yesterday, the last time he had taken off from here in November, 1965. He had kissed his wife and children goodbye and climbed up into the cockpit of his sleek single-seated F-8 Crusader. With a farewell glance over his shoulder at his family, he and Johnnie Agnatella taxied to the end of runway 24, powered up, checked the gauges, released the brakes and selected afterburner. About an hour later, Matt caught the number three wire on the rolling deck of the USS Hancock.

Matt's second back-to-back eight-month West Pac cruise had been a long and memorable deployment! But now it was over. He was almost home.

Was this plane ever going to land? Matt exhaled long and slow, leaned back in the seat and surveyed his fellow officers. Their sunken eyes and hollow cheeks attested to their years of deprivation and mistreatment. That was in the past. Now they were coming home! Matt's face felt flushed, his eyes stung. His heart raced uncontrollably. He was about to realize his seven-year dream; he was about to hold his wife, Bobbie, in his arms once again.

Bobbie, with an outwardly calm Debbie and an obviously excited Hank by her side, waited uneasily and fearfully for the big airplane to land. The roiling dark storm clouds matched her mood. This was indeed the moment of truth. Matt was coming home after more than seven years, but not to what he expected.

****

CHAPTER 1

<u>June 1, 1966, South China Sea, Cruising off the Coast of Vietnam.</u>

Lieutenant Commander Matthew Allen Tillet sat up in his bunk at the sound of the alarm, ran his fingers through his short cropped brown hair, and stared glumly at the big red circle on the calendar. June 1st. His eyes darted to the framed snapshot of his family.

"Well, Sugar, we're going to miss another one, but I'll figure out some way to make it up to you," he promised the petite blonde woman in the picture. "Maybe you and the kids can meet me in Hawaii." As the red circle so graphically reminded him, their 14th wedding anniversary was just another in a long list of anniversaries, birthdays and other special occasions that Matt and Bobbie Tillet had celebrated separately. A couple of days in Hawaii would be good for all of them and it would be fun for Hank to ride the ship back to San Diego since the Hancock was planning a Tiger Cruise this year.

Rereading Bobbie's latest letter, with its usual pledge of her abiding love, Matt momentarily savored the mental image of her small nude body encased tightly in his arms. An electrifying thrill shot directly to his loins. But a glance at the alarm clock forced him to switch gears, to return the memory to its hidden spot, and focus instead on the task ahead.

Just as Matt and his assistant maintenance officer, Roy Roberts, entered the intelligence briefing room, Jack Hayes, the air wing commander, rapped for attention. The intelligence officer displayed

3

a map of North Vietnam showing the most recent photos of the target, a bridge north of Haiphong, and pointed out the nearby flak sites.

Commander Hayes addressed the leader of Foxtrot flight, "Matt, your fighters will be flying escort. Our route will be north toward the China border." He drew an imaginary line on the map. "We'll hug the north side of these mountains until the last minute when we'll pop over this karst, hit the target, then retrace our course and proceed east to feet wet. You are to position your fighters here, above my A-4s, between the target and Kep Airfield." Again, he pointed to a specific location on the map. "Any questions?"

Matt nodded his understanding. After the aerographer filled them in on weather and visibility, Matt and his crew headed to the squadron ready room to review the flight profile and emergency procedures.

"Okay, guys, listen up," Matt began. "Bingo fuel to the ship is twenty-eight hundred pounds; to the refueling tanker is eighteen hundred pounds, and to punch out feet wet will be one thousand pounds. Let's keep our eyes open for MiG action. Enemy aircraft have been sighted on recent flights. We'll be flying low to avoid being spotted on radar any sooner than necessary."

Matt briefed his flight about two other squadron missions. "Jonesy will be flying escort for Lou West, who will be conducting photo reconnaissance on the northeast railroad, and Dan White will be escorting another photo recce driver shooting the road from Hongay to Haiphong." He paused, looking around at his three squadron mates. "Any questions? . . . No? . . . Okay, let's suit up."

"Pilots, man your planes," blared over the ready-room intercom just as Matt finished zipping his torso harness. He grabbed his hard hat.

He, Roy, Johnnie Agnatella and Edward "Frenchie" French rode the escalator to the flight deck and scurried to their assigned F-8s. Matt visually checked his aircraft and ordnance, climbed into the seat and waited for his plane captain to help strap him in. The distinctive smell of jet fuel permeated the area. At the Air Boss's command, "Jet Pilots, start your engines," the flight deck turned into a crescendo of noise and feverish activity. Jet engines spooled up and pilots and crews completed pre-launch checks, while waiting for the carrier to turn into the wind. Matt's plane captain rapped on his canopy. Holding up four fingers of his left hand, he motioned thumbs down with his right. Matt nodded his understanding: Frenchie's plane was down. He scratched #4 off his kneeboard check list.

The slower, heavy, bomb-laden A-4s launched first. Then, shortly after 1200 hours, Matt pushed on full power and gripped the t-bar, checked his gauges, positioned his head into the head rest, saluted the catapult officer, stuck his right elbow in his gut and cradled the stick. The carrier's nose rose on the waves. Out of the corner of his eye, he saw the Cat officer's hand go forward. Immediately, the jolt of the steam catapult's power gripped the plane, hurling it from a dead stop to 200 knots in 220 feet. As soon as he was free of the catapult bridle, he raised the wheels and executed his clearing turn. The two remaining members of Foxtrot Flight were catapulted within seconds of each other. All three joined up on assigned TACAN radial, fell in behind the bombers and headed north toward the China border.

Streaking low over the Gulf of Tonkin in his sleek, supersonic Crusader, Matt warily recalled the saying in the fleet that a pilot could find his way to Hanoi by simply following the wreckage of F-105s, the Air Force fighter-bombers based in Thailand that were involved in many previous bombing missions. He hoped none of Commander Hayes' A-4s would contribute to that metallic highway. Maybe the Navy was lucky to approach from the sea.

At their coast-in point, the flight turned inland.

Rising out of the ravine where the bridge had been, Commander Hayes reported, "Eagle One, off target. Outbound."

Matt signaled thumbs up to his wingmen. But Foxtrot Flight had little time to enjoy the success. Over the guard channel they heard Jonesy's excited warning, "Falcon, Falcon, you've been hit! You're on fire! Get out! Get out!"

Matt keyed the microphone, "Eagle One, this is Foxtrot One. We're going in to see if we can spot the pilot." In trail, Foxtrot Flight turned north.

Commander Hayes acknowledged, "Roger, Foxtrot One, we'll orbit ten east. Report downed pilot's status."

With the A-4s circling to the east, Matt called to the recce escort pilot, "Falcon Two, Foxtrot One. What state?"

"Twenty-eight hundred pounds."

"Rog. Head out. I have smoke from the recce in sight."

Matt, Roy and Johnnie made one sweep through the hilly area where the plane had augured in, taking care to avoid a nearby flak site off to the right. Just as they crossed a ridge, Matt saw the emergency flare. "There's Lou's flare. Let's make one more pass to see if he comes up on Guard channel."

Flying low, hoping to pick up Lou's transmission, the trio made one final pass. Silence. Just as they were pulling up, Matt heard Johnnie's excited yell, "Tally Ho, guys. MiGs. Two o'clock."

Matt twisted his head in time to see four MiG 17s coming from the direction of Kep, the big North Vietnamese air field nearby. His mind raced. The MiGs were flying in formation as if they hadn't sighted Foxtrot flight. Each of his aircraft still had a full bag of sidewinders and 20 mike mikes. If they could maneuver in behind the MiGs unnoticed, it would be a duck shoot. His hand tightened on the stick, his whole body tensed at the prospect of his first kill.

He pulled his long, flexing Crusader in a steep climb to the right, pushing the power up. They had to fall in behind the MiGs before they were spotted. Suddenly, the sky exploded in front of him like a 4th of July fireworks spectacle, with him right in the middle of the show. "Oh, shit. Forgot that damned flak site." He stroked the burner and the big jet jumped past the zinging fragments like the old mare on the farm when she was whooped on the rear, then sputtered. He heard Johnnie's call, his voice neither low nor calm, "Foxtrot One, you've taken a hit. You're blowing smoke, and there is a MiG on your tail."

Matt spotted the MiG coming in at four o'clock at about 500 knots. "Sonofabitch. Where'd he come from?" This had to be a different MiG; the other four hadn't had time to turn around to get behind him yet. Matt pushed the stick to the right and pulled back, at the same time applying right rudder. He had to turn into the oncoming fighter.

"What the hell?" The plane wasn't responding to his commands. The MiG started firing.

"Holy shit!" Choking bile rose in his throat, as he fought to control his aircraft. He rolled the stick, nothing happened. The plane's lateral control was gone. The enemy was closing in. His personal panic indicator was on red. Desperately, he yanked the nose up. The MiG zipped by just below and yoyoed high. Matt let out a long, audible sigh as the North Vietnamese pilot, probably low on fuel, turned back toward Kep.

"Now, what? How do I get this baby home?" Spooked and jittery, Matt tried to mentally plot a course, while weighing his options. "If I can reach that scattered layer of clouds above me and level the wings by using rudder control, I might be able to ride the plane out to the ocean for a pick-up." He checked his instruments. His primary hydraulic system was gone, and the hydraulic failure light was on, but there was no engine fire warning light. He wasn't out of the woods yet, but he still had a chance.

Suddenly the F-8E Crusader pitched forward violently. The control stick which normally responded with the sensitivity of a Lamborgini, now behaved like a Sherman tank gone off its tracks. The plane gathered speed as it spiraled out of control, plummeting toward the ground.

Matt's heart thumped wildly. The negative G's slammed him up against the canopy, pinning his arms above him. He fought to grasp the overhead face curtain, the primary ejection device. The G forces held him taut. How much time? Panic-propelled adrenalin surged through him. He willed his arms to move—just enough—he felt the handle, and yanked savagely. The canopy left the aircraft.

"Jesus," he shouted in frustration, his stomach feeling like a kite in a twister. The ejection seat had not fired. He was still strapped in. The curtain had blown around to the left leaving his face and upper body fully exposed to the biting blast of the pounding wind stream. Only seconds remained. Only seconds before . . . . It appeared hopeless. But his survival instinct was stronger than the seducing temptation to just give up. In a frenzy, he exerted all the strength he could muster. The seat fired.

Suddenly Matt was free, a human missile rocketing through space. Almost simultaneously he saw the fireball, heard the roar and felt the concussion and heat as his plane exploded like an Oklahoma thunderclap only a few hundred yards away.

The clumps of bamboo on the ground loomed larger and larger. Now he could make out the contours of the terrain. "I'm going in. This is it." Wrapping his hands in front of his lowered face, tightly shutting his eyes and gritting his teeth, he braced himself for the inevitable deadly impact.

Whoosh. He felt a sensation like floating in air, as if suspended. *So this is how death feels.* He'd seen the drawings, where the spirit ascends from the body of someone who has died. Strange. He hadn't felt the impact when he hit the ground. There had been no pain, as he had expected and feared. Just then, he opened his eyes and squinted. No body, just that same green carpet of grass, but much closer now. The sting of the shroud lines cutting into his neck brought him back to reality. He wasn't dead after all. His body swung half an arc backward, then slammed into the ground, feet-first and hard.

For several seconds Matt gasped for air, lying where he'd landed, dazed and disorientated, fighting faintness and nausea. From his prone position, he could see his wingman had reversed course and was headed toward Kep in hot pursuit of one of the MiGs. The F-8's missiles fired with deadly accuracy just as the planes disappeared over the ridge. *At least we got that SOB*, he noted with some small measure of satisfaction. Although it seemed like an eternity since he was searching for cloud cover to ride to the ocean, his unplanned sky dive actually had taken only a few seconds.

He closed his eyes, wiped the sweat from his face with his sleeve, inhaled a deep breath, then slowly exhaled, totally drained. He rolled over and raised to a crouching position on his hands and knees. Dropping his head between his arms, he muttered, "What the hell did those geniuses in Survival School say I should do next? If I'd have thought I'd end up here, I'd have paid more attention." He recalled the instructions: first hide your parachute; then look for a means of escape. "Escape! Hell," Matt scoffed.

He tried to stand, wobbled a bit, dropped back to his knees and steadied himself with one hand on the ground. His internal gyro was still fluctuating wildly.

After the adrenalin slowed down to warp speed, Matt turned his attention to his predicament. He touched his torso—didn't feel like any ribs were broken. On the second try, he made it to his feet.

Gotta remember to thank that parachute rigger if I ever get home, Matt made a mental note as he fumbled briefly, then un-latched the parachute's fasteners. Gathering the billowy material into his arms, he started running up the hill toward the high, grassy area he had spotted. That would afford at least some measure of cover until he could get his bearings and dispose of his excess gear. What was his next move?

Reality hit him like a kick in the gut. What was left of Foxtrot Flight already had turned for home, their fuel state precariously low after the dogfight with the MiGs. A helicopter couldn't be sent this far north for a rescue attempt. The sea, which might have offered a reasonable chance could he have reached it, was more than 100 rugged, enemy-infested miles away. He couldn't avoid detection that long, even if he went in the right direction and not in circles, the more likely course. The prospects seemed bleak, but he had to try. He needed rest, he needed water, he needed time to sort things out; he wasn't thinking straight right now. He had to hide out for awhile and develop a plan. He was, by some miracle, still alive, but he had a lot to do if he wanted to stay that way.

Just as he reached the edge of the tall grass, something moved up ahead. He stopped dead in his tracks, crouched down, waiting, watching. Had it been the wind? Had it been his imagination? His eyes probed the terrain. He heard something; something that sounded distinctly like a gun being cocked. He stiffened.

Two Vietnamese militiamen rose up from their hiding place in the grass directly in front of him. Both held rifles pointed threaten-ingly in his direction.

Matt inhaled sharply, involuntarily whistling through his teeth as he stared into the business end of two large weapons. He quickly sized up the situation. There was no chance to go for the .38 still strapped in its holster across his chest. That would be an irrational act. He hadn't survived being shot down to now commit suicide. For the same reason, he did not give in to the urge to run. The inescapable truth was that he lacked a safe place to go, even if his suddenly jelly-filled legs could have responded.

The taller of the two men approached Matt, and motioning with his rifle, ordered, "Han Up."

CHAPTER 2

June 1, 1966, Vietnamese Countryside, Northeast of Hanoi.

Matt clutched the bundled parachute tightly to his chest to shield his palpitating heart from his captors while he pondered his dilemma. *If I drop the chute to raise my arms, it's going to expose the .38 strapped across my chest. That might get me shot. On the other hand, if I don't follow their orders, that might get me shot too. Easy, pal, and you may live to tell about it.*

Very slowly, very deliberately, he spread his arms up and away from his chest so that his hands were high in the air when the chute dropped.

The smaller of the two Vietnamese men, no more than about 20 years old, warily eyed the weapon as he circled around and cautiously approached Matt from the rear. Keeping one finger on the trigger of his own weapon, as if expecting Matt to turn and pounce at any minute, he leaned over Matt's shoulder, and with his other hand seized the revolver, and darted away. From a safe distance, he lowered his own weapon, and stroked the barrel of the .38. At a sharp command from his buddy, he reluctantly relinquished the gun, and resumed stripping Matt of his other belongings: his survival gear, torso harness, helmet and boots. When he got down to the G-suit, out came his knife.

"Oh, shit," Matt cried aloud in alarm. Holding his hands high and far apart, he frantically shook his head back and forth, "No! No! I can do it." His captor stepped back, eyed Matt skeptically, then motioned with his gun and nodded in apparent acquiescence.

Cautiously, so as not to cause alarm, Matt lowered one arm until his fingers located the waist zipper, his eyes focusing on the militiamen for any ominous reaction. Grasping the toggle between his shaking thumb and forefinger, he slid the zipper downward, toward his upper thigh, until it stuck, stopping before it was completely unfastened. He gave it a gentle but determined tug, and the top part of the suit flopped down around his legs. Still holding one hand in the air, he bent over and unzipped both legs. The G-suit fell to the ground.

Using the laces from his boots, the militiamen bound Matt's hands behind him, attached a short rope they had with them, and started up the hill. Ever so fleetingly Matt recalled how he used to lead the team of horses back on the farm in Nebraska when he was a boy.

Cresting the hill, Matt could see a small group of shacks in the valley below, about three-quarters of a mile from where he had crashed. He hadn't noticed the village, just over the knoll in a clump of trees, as he came down, not that he'd had the leisure of checking his surroundings during his short and swift descent. It hadn't exactly been a sightseeing excursion. But, what had appeared as uninhabited grassland and forests from the cockpit, he now realized was a series of small villages.

As the trio started down the hill, a large group headed up. Matt's thoughts raced to rumors he had heard on the ship of downed pilots being beaten to death by the villagers who had captured them. He had also heard that the peasants in the countryside were rewarded for turning over live prisoners to the Vietnamese People's Army, the VPA. He could just picture his face on an old-fashioned "Wanted" poster. Was he worth more dead or alive? If he was lucky, the fact that he hadn't just bombed the hell out of their village might keep him alive—or it might not matter at all.

The groups converged. Matt couldn't control the shaking or stop the spontaneous shudders that seized him despite the tropical heat. The cluster of pajama-clad humanity pushed forward, surrounding him, suffocating him. Their high pitched voices sounded like shrieking birds of prey swooping down for the kill. He swallowed nervously. His throat and chest tightened in fear. They were closing in, wrapping him in an ever tightening human cocoon . . . tighter and tighter.

Out of the corner of his eye, he saw it—a fist. Instinctively, he ducked.

But it wasn't a blow. He was being touched, just touched, not aggressively, not painfully, just inquisitively, like the baby ducklings used to do when he held grain in his hand. After several minutes, but what seemed like hours, their curiosity satisfied, the crowd slowly started to open up, giving him breathing room. His claustrophobic feeling slowly diminished.

A tall lad, with a noticeably pock-marked face, lingered a few feet away, staring at him. Matt kept turning his head away, trying hard not to stare back, but antsy. The young man seemed so intense, and he just kept staring. The other villagers chatted among themselves, leaving Matt almost alone. Finally, the lad approached, tentatively at first, then purposefully. He stopped directly in front of Matt, hesitated a moment, then clutched the green Marine fatigue shirt on either side, and pulled it over Matt's head, forcing his arms up at the same time. He was stymied when he couldn't get it over Matt's bound hands. The gun-toting captors displayed renewed interest when they saw the boy approaching their prisoner, and now they giggled like schoolgirls at his plight. Embarrassed, he turned away and moved back into the crowd. Still laughing, one of his captors untied Matt's hands, stripped off the shirt, and with some fanfare, awarded the trophy to the flustered youth. The lively crowd clapped with enthusiasm, as if the pock-marked lad had just won some sort of contest.

Matt exhaled slowly as his icy tension ebbed. It didn't look like they were going to kill him. In fact, these people didn't seem that different from the farmers in his home town in Nebraska when the whole community got together for a town picnic on a holiday, or at the end of hay-baling season. Maybe catching an American pilot gave these villagers a similar reason to celebrate.

An elderly villager, his leathery face withered from too much sun and his few remaining teeth blackened from the betel nut he chewed, pushed his way through the crowd. Standing squarely in front of

Matt, he whispered hoarsely in clear, crisp English, "War is hell," then turned abruptly and was soon swallowed by the crowd.

Matt stared. *Old man, you must have been reading my mind.*

The trek down the hill resumed. No one even bothered to retie Matt's hands. This was almost like a late afternoon stroll in the park. Except that he had been stripped of his belongings and his freedom, he was marooned in an enemy country where be couldn't speak the language, and they didn't speak his, and he knew that he probably wouldn't see his own family again for many months, or even years. No, this wasn't Nebraska; it wasn't the end of hay-baling season, and he'd gotten himself in one hell of a lot of trouble. In his excitement to get a kill, he'd committed the ultimate "pilot error." He'd flown right over a previously identified flak sight. He knew in his own mind that's what got him. He'd already been hit before the MiG started firing. *Stupid, stupid. After more than a hundred flights over this very area, you knew better than to pull a dumb shit stunt like that.* He pursed his parched lips and grimaced.

Their destination was a small, thatched-roof, mud-covered hut in the middle of the village at the bottom of the hill. Following the lead of one of his captors, Matt stooped low to squeeze through the narrow four-foot-high door into a pen-like room. Paneless windows framed a courtyard enclosed by a high bamboo stake fence.

A sudden stabbing sensation in his foot forced Matt to sink wearily, groaning, into a hay pile in one corner of what had to have been a pig pen. In his eagerness to find a hiding place, he had forgotten the momentary pain he felt when he hit the ground. Now, the throbbing in his previously ignored injured foot forced him to remember. He heard a sharp authoritative male voice, and a small boy hurried off.

Within minutes, a lanky young man entered the shack carrying a pouch decorated with a red cross. After a cursory, unenthusiastic examination, the medical corpsman sparingly applied some Merthiolate to the parachute shroud burns streaking down Matt's neck, then pointedly tossed the bottle back in his bag.

"I need something for the pain," Matt called.

The medic, now near the door, puckered his lips and wrinkled his nose as he glanced toward Matt's shoes, his squinty eyes following

Matt's pointing finger. He looked like someone who had Limburger cheese stuck under his upper lip. Unfortunately, it seemed to be his normal expression. It also seemed to fit his personality. Knitting his brow in an even deeper scowl, Mr. Congeniality tossed his head arrogantly and left.

"Thanks a lot, Asshole," Matt muttered under his breath.

Slowly the other villagers drifted out of the hut and courtyard, until Matt was finally alone. He spread the straw into a makeshift bed, and closed his eyes, hoping against hope that when he opened them, this would all be a bad dream, and he would be back in his stateroom aboard the carrier.

Matt sensed someone's presence, and sat up abruptly, disoriented and startled at the sight of an emaciated young woman kneeling beside him. Using hand signals, the girl asked if he wanted something to drink. Remembering where he was, and why, he enthusiastically nodded his head up and down, and rubbed his salt-encrusted arms for emphasis. With a nervous, shy smile, she rose, bowed slightly, and backed out the door.

A few minutes later, another wrinkled-faced old man entered the shed. He handed Matt a goat-skin flask, motioning for him to drink. Nodding first to show his appreciation, which seemed to be the acceptable custom, Matt placed the canteen to his lips, tilted it upward, and greedily gulped its contents. Instead of water as he had expected, it was warm, dark, slightly pungent-tasting Vietnamese beer. It didn't matter what it was, he was so thirsty, he could have drunk urine if they boiled the piss out of it first.

After Matt emptied the container, the weather-beaten old man motioned for him to follow. Hobbling behind his guide, past several shacks, they came to one of the better houses in the area, possibly his host's own home. Like most in the village, it consisted of a thatched roof atop bamboo poles lashed together with bamboo leaves. He was led into one small room of the shack, containing nothing but a frame, about the size of a double bed, covered with a woven mat. A six-inch square piece of wood was neatly placed at the end near the wall, like a pillow.

At the old man's direction, Matt dropped to a sitting position on the mat. It would never replace a Beautyrest or the old featherbed he slept on as a kid, but it sure as hell beat the mud floor in the pig shed.

Matt lay down at his host's urging, but sat back up almost immediately as people started coming into the room. Several peered through the open window. Soon the small room was jammed with children and bare-breasted women, many nursing naked babies. Matt no longer felt any fear from these villagers, but right now he was uncomfortable, a little self-conscious; he wasn't used to being on display, or to having so many nearly naked women running around so casually in front of him.

One small boy, no more than ten years old, nude except for a loin cloth, made his way through the crowded room and bravely sat cross-legged beside Matt. Poking him lightly on the chest with one skinny finger, he asked in halting English, "from Sheena?"

Matt shook his head no.

The youngster extracted a pad and pencil from a small pouch he was carrying and carefully printed "Vienam," omitting the "t." Proudly pointing to himself, he announced, "Me from," as he showed his pad to Matt.

Matt grinned, nodded his head in approval, pointed to the pad, and enunciated very slowly, "Very good. You write well."

Puffed out like a young bantam rooster, the lad happily rejoined his impressed and envious playmates, and they ran outside, yelling in excited voices. Others followed and soon the room was empty.

Matt watched until the youngsters had disappeared from his sight. They had different features, they wore different clothes, and they spoke a different language, but, oh, how much they were similar to the grade-school children in his neighborhood in San Diego. They had the same innocence, trust, playfulness, eagerness to learn, curiosity—particularly curiosity—as Hank. He could just see Hank boldly walk up to a stranger and try to communicate.

He lowered his head and rubbed both hands across his forehead and his burning eyes as he pictured his mischievous, bright-eyed son. What was going to happen to him? His heart felt very heavy.

What would happen to Bobbie? How was she going to handle this? How was she going to make it alone? She depended on him for just about everything. She needed him, the kids needed him. Who would be there to help them? Would the Navy look after them? Thankfully, he'd signed all the paperwork to allow Bobbie to receive half of his pay if something like this happened to him. But, was that enough? He should have prepared her better, he should have at least planned for this risk. He usually marveled how she got through a six-month cruise, it was going to be absolute hell for her if he didn't return for several more months, or years—or ever.

His mind drifted back to his son. Hank was just at that age when he needed a father. Who would provide guidance for him? Certainly Bobbie wasn't good at discipline, and Hank was already a handful. Who would teach him to play ball, take him fishing, take him to the beach? Bobbie was an excellent homemaker, but she must have been born with two left feet when it came to athletics.

What about Debbie, just going into her teens? Who was going to warn her about men and what most of them wanted? Who was going to teach her to drive? Bobbie? A smile flickered across his face as he thought about Bobbie's driving. She drove by feel, when she felt something immovable in front or back of her, she stopped. That's why the car had a few too many small dings. But teenage girls needed their fathers—and Debbie wouldn't have one.

Damn. Damn. Damn. I should have realized the consequences to my family. How could I have thought I was invincible? He just wanted to go to sleep, to blot out the picture of his family, and the pain his captivity was going to cause them. His own predicament was less of a concern to him at this point. These villagers, except for the corpsman, had been almost hospitable, treating him to some degree like a guest. This was not what he had been led to believe. If the stories about how the prisoners were treated out in the countryside were so wrong, perhaps the stories of torture were exaggerated too. He felt more hopeful now than at any time since hearing his wingman's cryptic warning. He rested his head on the wooden pillow and drifted . . . .

A loud noise roused Matt from his near sleep. He sat up abruptly, filled with ominous misgivings. From the sound of the engine, he was pretty sure a large vehicle had stopped near the house, most likely military. *I bet this means they aren't going to turn me over to the Red Cross.* He no longer felt relaxed.

Three armed men in military uniforms burst into the room. One of them, who appeared to be in charge—a sergeant, he surmised—motioned both with his head and his rifle in a way Matt understood to mean "Stand up." Matt rose to his knees. Using the wall for support, he lifted himself to a standing position, balancing on his one good foot. The other two men searched him and his belongings, which apparently had been placed in the room while he slept. From his wallet they removed his Geneva Convention card, two crisp new $20 bills and some miscellaneous Philippine money, all of which quickly disappeared into the pocket of the senior man, who then motioned toward the door and grunted something. Matt didn't understand the language but the message was unmistakable.

He struggled into his flight boots, wincing as the injured foot slid into place. Growling to display his impatience, the sergeant grabbed Matt roughly by one shoulder and shoved him out the door. At the end of the lane, on the outer edge of the hamlet, across the small, shallow creek that ran through the village, Matt saw the vehicle. It wasn't as large as he'd imagined, sort of a cross between a Jeep and a pick-up truck.

One of the two armed guards blindfolded Matt, tied his hands tightly behind his back, and pushed him roughly into the rear of the Jeep. Their boots made a crunching noise against the pebbles as they walked away.

A few minutes later, he heard the villagers cheering in the distance, no doubt receiving their "reward" for turning him over. This pretty well sealed it; he was a prisoner of war. As he waited for the soldiers to return, that sobering realization forced him to think about what that meant. What did he know about being a POW? Not a hell of a lot. A two-week survival training course at Warner Springs, up in the hills outside of San Diego. Two weeks—ah—if only this could be so limited. They'd thrown him in a cell, roughed him up a bit, and made him stand with his hands in the air for hours. Primarily the short survival training course concentrated on how to live off the flora and fauna of the region. It was designed to teach escape and evasion. At this point, there wasn't much chance for either. Unlike most aspects of his Navy training, for this he just hadn't received much practice. Guess that was about to change. He was about to receive some on-the-job training.

In addition to escape and evade, they'd also taught him one more thing: the American Fighting Man's Code of Conduct, the rigid guidelines of how military men should conduct themselves if they were captured. He tried to remember it all; he was going to need it now, but could only recall the essentials: the American chain-of-command remained in effect, even behind prison walls; prisoners were to continue to resist by all means available, they were to give nothing to their captors but their name, rank and serial number.

He'd heard the words; they'd registered in the abstract. Now, he realized ruefully, he was going to have to live by them, up close and personal.

His heart rate ratcheted up when he heard the heavy footsteps returning. He swallowed hard, forcing the bile back down into his gut. Despite his apprehension, he couldn't help but think of the irony of his situation. He was a man who liked order, a place for everything and everything in its place. He liked everything planned out to the nth degree, no surprises. He always had a Plan B in case Plan A went awry. And he was a man in charge of almost every part of his life, and his family's.

You really planned this one, didn't you, pal? No, he hadn't planned to fly over that stupid goddamn flak site, or get his plane shot full of holes; he hadn't planned to nearly die trying to eject; and he hadn't planned to get caught by the North Vietnamese Army. All of it had been a total surprise. Where in the hell was his Plan B? And right now he wasn't in charge of anything, probably not even whether he was going to live or die.

He tried to mentally prepare himself for what probably lay ahead. He must not appear weak. He must uphold the Code, uphold his honor. He'd been in tight spots before, he could handle it. He'd demonstrated his mettle many times. He was confident he could take whatever they dished out. He would probably be taken to the former French prison in Hanoi, where it was reported most of the American prisoners were being held. They'd probably throw him in a cell, make him spend a lot of time with his hands in the air, maybe they'd even smack him around some, but primarily he'd probably spend the rest of the war locked up, hopefully not alone. *Oh, please give me someone to talk to.*

It wasn't a pretty picture, but he was sure he could handle it. He breathed deeply several times to calm his nerves. It wasn't so much that he feared the unknown, he just didn't like not being able to control his own destiny.

The noisy old truck lumbered shakily into gear. It was close to midnight by Matt's best estimate when they finally drove out of the little village, twelve hours since he flew off his ship on what he anticipated was to be a routine mission. It had certainly been an unforgettable twelve hours. "Happy Anniversary," he muttered sarcastically, the roar of the engine drowning out the sound of his voice.

CHAPTER 3

June 2, 1966, Vietnam, North of Hanoi.

The Jeep bumped and bounced along, locked in unholy combat with the rocky, rutted dirt road. Struggling to remain upright, Matt attempted to keep track of time and figure out which direction they were heading. It helped distract him from his ominous misgivings about what lay ahead. And, if by some slim chance he could escape, or was rescued, it would be useful intelligence.

By his calculations they had been traveling for about two hours before mercifully grinding to a halt. One of the soldiers untied the blindfold, pulled Matt out of the vehicle, and removed the ropes. Matt rubbed his hands and arms to restore some circulation. As his eyes adjusted, he spied his parachute and what appeared to be one wheel from his airplane in the back of the Jeep, near where he had been sitting.

The sound of voices drew his attention to a small group of people assembled near a building that at first glance in the dark looked amazingly like his old one-room school house.

An old man, dressed in civilian clothing, approached the Jeep and addressed Matt in broken English. "You tell us your name, please."

"Matthew Allen Tillet."

"What is your military rank?"

"Lieutenant Commander, United States Navy."

"Your serial number, please."

He recited his serial number, intrigued at the carefully scripted questions. They were asking exactly what he was allowed to answer. Everyone seemed to be following the rules of the game, but unfortunately the game was war.

Writing the information on a piece of paper in English, the elder spokesman passed the paper to Matt. "This is correct, please?"

Matt nodded. The delegation seemed pleased, judging from their collective smiles. The English speaker motioned with his arm, and a particularly attractive young Vietnamese girl and an equally hand-some young boy, each wearing military-type uniforms and carrying rifles, stepped forward, and stood, on either side of Matt. They must have been hidden behind the building as he had not previously noticed anyone other than his guards in military uniforms. These two looked liked teenagers.

It was clear who was in charge, but of what? Why had they stopped here in the middle of nowhere, in the middle of the night, and who *were* these people? The uncertainty was maddening.

The girl gently placed her hand on Matt's shoulder and motioned for him to move straight ahead. He hesitated. Straight ahead was a heavily wooded area. Even with the lights from the Jeep pointed directly into it, the growth was so thick Matt could see only a few feet ahead. Why in the hell would they take him in there? At a second tug on his arm, he reluctantly moved forward.

"Oh, shit," he uttered apprehensively under his breath as the light from the Jeep grew dimmer and then faded away entirely as the trio proceeded deeper into the woods. *This is it. They're probably taking me out into the jungle to shoot me. So now what do I do?* This seemed the only logical explanation to what was going on. His mind was racing. He wouldn't have any trouble taking care of these two. But why on earth would they send these kids to do this? Maybe it was an initiation of some sort. *If I kill them or knock them unconscious, I can probably hide, given the thickness of this place, during the night, but by morning they'll have the whole North Vietnamese Army looking for me. But if they're going to shoot me, I'm going to take some of them with me.* He was weak, but his arms were free; he would be able to strangle the girl before the guy knew what was happening. Then . . . .

He jumped. The slight pressure on his arm startled him from his thoughts. In the darkness he could barely make out the forms of his escorts. The young lady turned him around and he could see her finger motioning him to follow once again.

"What in the hell is going on?" he asked aloud. They were retracing their steps.

Emerging from the woods, at the same spot where they entered, Matt was momentarily blinded by the bright lights aimed directly in his eyes. He squinted, lowered his head and shaded his eyes with his hands. The lights, he finally figured out, were coming from several large flashlights and the headlights from a couple of vehicles.

What was that sound? He raised his head, still shielding his eyes, to look around. It sounded like—yes, it was—the whirring sound of cameras. Now he understood. He was a friggin' movie star. This was the re-enactment of the capture of the American air pirate by the young, heroic Vietnamese patriots. He remembered seeing a similar propaganda sketch in a briefing on the ship. Now it made sense why the two at his side were so attractive. He was reasonably certain none of the camera gear had been in the Jeep, so obviously the stage and the cast had been imported just for this purpose. Considering the number of Air Force and Navy pilots that had been captured these past few months, this crew must be kept pretty busy.

Their filming complete, most of the lights were shut off, and the cast and crew stood around in small groups, talking among themselves, and drinking from porcelain cups set up on a white linen tablecloth. Matt stood off to one side, marveling at the surreal scene being played out in the eerie dimness. Who'd have ever thought he would find himself in this situation? It was simply mind-boggling. Except for that one wrong move, he could be in his bunk on the ship, fast asleep. Since he hadn't eaten in almost 24 hours, it had to be a mixture of emotions that stirred up the dull ache in the pit of his stomach.

The young actress interrupted Matt's remorseful thinking, offering him a cup of whatever they were drinking. He dipped his head slightly to show his appreciation, took the cup and downed the liquid; this time it was tea. She stood beside him, touching the fragile rim of the teacup with long, sensitive fingers, watching him with the faintest hint of a shy smile. She was a pretty Vietnamese girl;

her thin, angular features would even be attractive by American standards.

The sergeant, irritated at the girl's modest demonstration of kindness, grabbed the cup, shoved it back into her hand, splashing its remnants on her uniform, and yelled for the other guards and driver. Binding Matt's hands behind him and wrapping the blindfold tightly around his head, he pushed Matt into the back of the Jeep. The other guards scrambled in just as the Jeep moved out with an uncharacteristic surge of power.

Up yours too, Buddy. Matt complained silently, acutely aware that as little as a combative look could bring down the wrath of his obdurate captor, and probably his gun butt as well. Yet, with the exception of a few bullies, like the Army sergeant, and there was always one in every crowd, the people seemed not that different from farm folks in Small Town, USA. This perception was still surprising to him, for he had been inclined to paint them all with the same broad black brush. That was one of the advantages, or possibly disadvantages, of being a pilot in this game of war. He rarely got close enough to see the faces of the people he was shooting at. That allowed him to think of them in more abstract terms, not as individuals, just collectively as "the enemy." He tried to push the troublesome subject away.

Trussed up as he was, it was impossible to sleep, despite his exhaustion. The constant jarring caused by the Jeep's unrelenting demolition derby with the road, didn't help either. The amazing thing was that the crate was still in one piece. Oh, what he would give to be in his bunk on the ship . . . .

They stopped again, and again the ritual of unloading and removing his blindfold was repeated. This time, they left his arms bound. They were in a graveled clearing between several buildings. Matt could hear lots of loud, belligerent voices. He tensed. Now what? Maybe not everyone was so friendly. The guards led him into the nearest brick-like structure, shoved him down on a bench, then left.

The highly excited voices drew closer. Matt's eyes darted quickly around the dimly-lit, nearly barren 20 by 30 foot room. There was no place to hide. As the first of the angry group entered, shaking an upraised fist and yelling loudly, Matt clenched his teeth, swallowed nervously and stiffened. Sweat broke out all over his body, mixing with the salty residue on his arms, causing them to glisten eerily in the dim light.

Soon the room was filled with an ugly, agitated, screaming mob. Many circled around the bench like hungry animals. Others stayed outside, but through the paneless window, he could see their gestures and hear their roar. Their mood steadily grew more threatening. What would they do? How far would they go? How much damage would they be allowed to inflict before the soldiers returned? Or—would they return in time? He tried to assure himself that this was just as staged as the recent filming episode. Would they have documented his capture and then allow him to be killed by a mob? Wouldn't it be politically more acceptable to be able to report he was killed in the crash? That rationale gave him little comfort. He struggled to calm himself. Once again he remembered the grim reports from the ship. Even if unintended, he might be dead before the guards could intervene if the crowd really got out of control.

He endured the verbal abuse resolutely, determined not to give them the satisfaction of seeing his growing fear. Someone spit on him—a black, sticky, smelly spittle—right in his face and eyes. It burned. He blinked repeatedly, but otherwise sat almost at military attention.

An elderly woman weighing no more than eighty pounds, screeching hysterically, attacked Matt with a wooden club. With his hands tied behind his back, but his feet free, he was able to bob and duck, dodging her largely impotent blows, most merely glancing off his shoulder. Others in the group finally restrained the frenzied woman, who continued to scream belligerently as she was dragged away. Despite his own predicament, Matt couldn't help feeling sorry for the scrawny old lady; she seemed genuinely more upset than the others; perhaps she had lost a son, or other loved one, in the war. If not, she was certainly one of their better actresses.

Again, time was playing tricks on him. It seemed this attack had lasted hours, but he knew it had been only a few minutes. He breathed a sigh of relief when the soldiers returned. They were unfriendly bastards, but at least they were more predictable than an aroused mob. As quickly as it had appeared, the crowd dispersed. The show was over, and Matt was again alone with his military escort. At last, they untied his hands, allowing him to reestablish some circulation. After two cups of tea, it was back in the Jeep, tied and blindfolded. The uncomfortable gymkhana continued.

As best Matt could figure, they were heading basically southwest, toward Hanoi. He had seen reconnaissance photos of the road that ran alongside the Northeast Railroad. This was probably it. His blindfold rode high on his face, permitting him a brief peek if he raised his head just so. There was lots of foot traffic, mostly women, hundreds and hundreds of women, supporting shoulder poles attached to baskets. Because of the darkness, he was unable to see what was in the baskets, but he could discern the form of the people and their poles. Some appeared to be road crews, using the cover of darkness to rebuild the roads and bridges the bombs had destroyed. The Jeep proceeded slowly now, a welcome relief, stopping several times to allow the road to clear in front of them. While the guards engaged in conversation with the workers, Matt could feel their eyes boring in on him. He was an easy target if they wanted to even the score.

As they neared Hanoi, Matt was conscious of increased vehicular traffic, lots of trucks and other heavy machines. They passed over several bridges, some no more than rock fords across the water; crossed what felt like railroad tracks; and at another point, had to wait about fifteen minutes for a train to pass. Everywhere, Matt caught glimpses of people scurrying about, bent over from the weight of their heavy loads.

Dawn was just breaking when they reached what was apparently their final destination. The first thing Matt saw after they removed the blindfold was that they were in a high walled courtyard. He turned his head just in time to see the huge, double-door iron gate closing behind them. It made a loud metallic thud. It was a forlorn sound, almost as dismal as the idea of where he undoubtedly was— Hoa Lo prison in Hanoi.

The sergeant motioned for him to remove his boots, but his right foot was so swollen, he couldn't pull it out. He couldn't stifle a yelp when the sergeant impatiently yanked it off. Now barefoot, Matt was led across the cobblestones to the building directly in front, and into an austere, green, lumpy-walled room. Responding to the motions and grunts from the sergeant, Matt climbed onto a high, backless stool in front of a large beat-up desk.

A pudgy, beady-eyed man in a plain khaki uniform with no insignia sat on the other side. "You are a prisoner of the heroic North Vietnamese People's Army. You are a war criminal. You are to obey all orders of the guards and the interrogators. Do you understand these instructions?"

Matt nodded, surprised to hear English spoken so well in this place. "Yes, I understand."

"What is your name?" he asked, scribbling something on the paper on the desk.

"Matthew Allen Tillet."

"Your rank?"

"Lieutenant Commander, United States Navy."

Matt gave his serial number to the question that followed, comforted that this "interview" was following the same scenario as before.

"What was the name of your ship?" His adversary raised his piercing eyes to meet Matt's, a thin malevolent smile on his lips, confirming he knew he had just upped the ante.

Startled at the inappropriate question, Matt responded in a restrained voice, "I cannot answer that question."

Ignoring Matt's refusal, the interrogator continued brusquely, "What air wing were you with?"

"I cannot answer that question. International law states that a prisoner of war is required to give only his name, rank and serial number."

The man across from him repeated his initial statement in a voice that was strained and harsh. "You are a war criminal. You have killed innocent women, children and old folks. Your country has not declared war; therefore, you may not rely on the Geneva Convention. You must answer the questions put to you. Now, do you understand?"

"I do not agree, but I understand what you have said."

"Tell me the name of your ship."

"I cannot give you that information."

Raising his voice, the examiner pressed, "What air wing were you with?"

"You know I cannot give you that information."

Jumping from his chair, his face contorted in rage, the interrogator screamed at Matt and for the guards. Immediately, the heavy vaulted door swung open and two guards ran in, one carried a rifle pointed menacingly at Matt; the other carried a sinister-looking long bar with manacles. The force of a fierce open-palm blow caught Matt completely by surprise, knocking him to the floor. The other guard crammed Matt's ankles into the two U-shaped metal clasps positioned in such a way that Matt's legs were spread slightly apart. The clamps had been intended for much smaller limbs, and they pinched and cut into Matt's ankles and it hurt like hell when the guard forced them shut, forcing him to flinch. He bit his lower lip to keep from crying out. He couldn't show weakness. He'd been through this type of show before, twice at least. They'd probably try to bully or intimidate him into doing something dishonorable, but if he didn't break, they'd have to leave him alone.

Before Matt knew what was happening, one of the guards wrapped a one-inch wide manila shroud line just above one elbow, knotted and tied it and yanked Matt's arms savagely behind his back. He wrapped the line around the other elbow, and Matt could feel the line being pulled tighter and tighter. The pain was becoming unbearable. He cried out. As the guard worked feverishly, Matt tried to clear his mind. What in God's name were they doing? Fear seized him. If this was for show, it was too damn realistic.

The heavy-fisted guard applied pressure with his feet to Matt's back and pulled on the rope, forcing Matt's elbows closer and closer together until they were touching behind his back. Matt screamed in agony. This was unbelievable. These rotten bastards were serious. The shipboard rumors of torture were true. He struggled to keep his chest inflated, so that when they eased off he would be able to breathe, but his powerful torturer simply placed his foot in the middle of his back and tugged and pulled harder, drawing the line tighter and tighter. Matt's breaths now came in short, shallow gasps. His back cramped, his shoulders felt like they were being pulled out of their sockets. The pain was excruciating. He was screaming, and couldn't stop, but they weren't through. The guard passed the line around his neck and tied it behind his hands, so that if Matt leaned forward, or fell, he could choke. He felt pure panic. This couldn't be happening. Were they going to kill him? Were they actually going to torture him to death?

The artist, John McGrath, was a Navy lieutenant when he became a Prisoner of War in North Vietnam on 30 June 1967. He sketched this drawing upon his return home in 1973. It appears in John M. McGrath, Prisoner of War: Six Years in Hanoi *(Annapolis, Md.: Naval Institute Press, 1975) and is reprinted with permission of the Naval Institute Press.*

The beady-eyed interrogator grabbed Matt's hair, lifting and rotating his head upward in one sharp jerk. Matt's neck cracked loudly, and he gasped as the rope cut off his already inadequate air supply. Leaning down so close Matt could feel the heat and smell the stench from his breath, the officer snarled, "When you are ready to talk, we *might* let you up again." He shoved Matt's head downward, causing him to gag momentarily as the rope choked off his meager air supply. From a final push, Matt fell sideways, landing on his right side. Gasping for breath, he numbly heard the door clanging shut and the bolts being rammed into place. His stomach was churning, and he swallowed with difficulty to keep from vomiting.

Lying on the cold floor, Matt writhed in agony, sweat flowing from every pore. Minutes passed in slow motion, each lasting an eternity. Spasm after involuntary spasm racked his body as he surrendered to uncontrollable panic. With each contraction, he let out an ear splitting shriek until he had screamed his throat raw. There was no way to stop the pain, no way to ease it. If only he could pass out, experience blessed nothingness, but he'd probably choke to death if he did, so he fought to stay conscious. His air passages felt like they were stuffed with cotton. His next gasping breath might be his last. His body quivered. Retching sobs racked his body until his cries were nothing more than guttural whimpers.

After a pain-filled eternity, a guard loosened the rope around Matt's arms. Throbbing pain shot through him as the blood flow resumed like water through a just-unkinked hose. He stared in disbelief and horror at his lifeless limbs, deathly black, dangling limply at his side. All the skin had been rubbed off in the crook of his arms, exposing the white tendon sheathing. He tried to rub his fingers and thumb together. He couldn't feel anything. His heart sank. "You sonsabitches, I'm going to lose the use of my hands. If I live, I'm going to be a cripple."

The interrogator, his half smirk making him appear even more demonic, hissed at Matt's outburst. "We will reduce you to a dog. You will not be able to use your arms; you will not be able to eat with your hands; you will have to eat out of a bowl like a dog."

A guard forcibly propped Matt onto the stool. He vainly struggled to sit upright, but lacking the strength, his head slumped on his chest, his body hung like a limp dishrag. With no feeling in his hands, he could not stop his fall, crumpling to the floor like a puppet when the strings are cut.

The interrogator, glowering down contemptuously snarled, "Now you must tell us your ship, your air wing and your squadron."

"Why don't you just kill me and get it over with?" Matt was certain at this point that death would be more honorable and more merciful.

His inexorable abuser grinned fiendishly. "Death would be too easy. Living is difficult. You will learn just how difficult living can be for a war criminal."

Matt felt powerless to resist further, humbled by being helpless and dependent. Had other prisoners endured this without giving in? How could they? How could anyone? But the notion that he might not be alone brought little solace. It meant violating the Code of Conduct.

The interrogator repeated his demand, this time more emphatically "Now tell us the name of your ship."

Matt dropped his head to hide the shame he felt as he muttered, "USS Hancock, CVA-19."

"What class of carrier?"

"It's a twenty-seven Charley."

"What was your Air Wing ?"

Matt cringed. "Carrier Air Wing 3."

"What was your squadron?"

With each question, he wanted to crawl away and hide. "VF-211," he mumbled.

"I cannot hear you. What squadron did you say?"

"VF-211."

With a toothy smile, which displayed his gold dental work, the interrogator pressed on. "Now tell us the name of the skipper of your ship."

Matt shook his head. Asking the names of units or ships was one thing, but compelling him to give the name of other Navy personnel was unthinkable. "I can't give you that information. You have no right to ask that."

Almost instantly, the ropes were wrapped around his arms again. And though he hadn't thought it possible, they were viciously pulled even tighter than before. With each violent jerk on the rope, Matt screamed uncontrollably. Another furious tug of the rope, and the last thing he heard was his own piercing cry.

When he came to, he was alone. His shoulders felt like hot coals had been jammed into their sockets.

Several times his torturers returned and loosened his bonds, sending a new surge of searing red-hot poker pain each time the ropes were relaxed. Each time he was sure he would not survive. The straps cut deeper and deeper, exposing the muscle, tearing tendons and blood vessels and cutting off all circulation to his lower arms. Matt drifted in and out of consciousness, only dully aware of what was happening. He didn't know how long he had been there. He didn't know what day it was, or whether it was day or night. He found solace in forgetfulness.

Although not a particularly religious man, Matt turned to prayer. "Please make them stop. They've got to stop. I can't stand any more. If there is a God, make them stop."

At first he prayed just to get through it. But he wasn't sure he could. So he prayed for another kind of strength. "If I can't make it, let me die bravely. Let me die like a man." He didn't want to die dishonorably, but he was afraid of what it would cost to live.

Others must have gone through this. Had they been stronger? Was he weaker than his fellow officers? Maybe they wanted to drive him out of his mind. Pain could do that. He would have welcomed a quick, clean shot to the head, but they had made it clear that death, if it came, would not be that easy. They were like lions toying with their prey throughout the infinite night, postponing the inevitable until they were hungrier. He realized the futility of further resistance. That realization only compounded his misery. But if he gave them the information they wanted, he would have to divulge the names of some of his senior officers. What would they do with that information? What danger did that knowledge pose to those men? Would the Vietnamese somehow target those guys? And, as they had already demonstrated, that wouldn't be enough; they would want more. Did he know things he could be forced to reveal that could cause death or this living hell for others?

No other experience in Matt's life had prepared him for this ordeal. He was a fighter. He hadn't thought the word surrender was in his vocabulary. He remembered his last high-school wrestling match—the championship. Six days he had wrestled and he had won six bouts. In the last bout, the score was tied. He got his opponent in a half nelson and a head lock. The thought running through his mind was that if he gave it his all, and didn't hold his competitor for three seconds, he wouldn't have anything left if the guy got away. But he had persisted. Once he got the man's shoulder down to the mat and tried to hold it, he felt his opponent go limp. "Fuck it," he heard him say, "it ain't worth it." Matt won because the other guy quit. Who knows if that would have been the result had he just fought a little harder.

Now the tables were turned. To resist further was futile. They had his shoulder to the mat, but they weren't going to let him up. They were prepared to leave him here like this as long as it took, or until he died. It was not his nature to give up, but these were not sane, rational enemies.

The next time the guards came in and loosened the bonds, a new wave of sharp pain exploded, triggering another shriek. Between screams Matt gasped, "Okay, okay, I'll tell you what you want to know." Never in his life had he felt so totally defeated.

The straps came off. Again, his blackened arms hung uselessly, unfeelingly at his sides.

"Tell us the name of the skipper of your ship."

"Captain Donald Martinson."

"Tell us the name of your squadron skipper."

"Commander Paul Lance."

How many airplanes are on the ship?"

Matt fudged as best he could. "There are fifty or sixty, I think."

"You lie," shouted his tormenter angrily.

Matt cowered, expecting they would put the straps back around his arms. Instead, he was ordered to sit on the stool again. Numbly, he struggled to climb up. Impatiently, the guards grabbed him by each arm and lifted him onto the stool. He swayed unsteadily, barely able to hold his head up. He didn't want to fall again. The man across the desk smirked maliciously as he removed a book from his desk drawer. Although it was difficult to focus his eyes, Matt could make out the front of the cardboard cover of the book — "USS Hancock, CVA-19."

Matt listened in utter disbelief as the pompous snarled-toothed devil started to read. He had the name of the ship, the ship's captain, the name of the air wing commander; he knew the name of Matt's squadron skipper, and he also knew the names of most of the pilots in the squadrons. "Your squadron, VF-211, has twelve, single-seated, high-performance, supersonic F-8E Crusader jet fighters and twenty-two pilots. There is a second fighter squadron that has twelve F-8C aircraft. Both squadrons are based at NAS Miramar, in San Diego, California."

The interrogator paused, jubilantly noting Matt's astonished look. Much like a college professor reciting the day's lesson, he continued, "In addition, the Hancock carries three RF-8 Photo Reconnaissance planes from VFP-63, stationed at Miramar, two attack squadrons from NAS Lemoore, California, each with fourteen A-4 Skyhawks, and one squadron of four E-2s from NAS North Island. The E-2s are propeller-driven early warning aircraft, equipped with sophisticated radar for detecting ships on the surface and other planes. Additionally, there is one A-3 tanker, known as the Whale, to provide in-flight refueling."

The bittersweet realization hit Matt like another seizure. All this had been totally unnecessary to acquire any military information. The sole reason for this torture had been vengeance, or as he thought despairingly, "to break me to lead." Because he knew that in the future, at least until he had recovered from this ordeal, if indeed he ever would, he would have to tell them whatever they asked.

It's incredible. He didn't ask me for a damn thing he didn't already know or hadn't already dragged out of some other poor son-of-a-bitch in probably the same way. He didn't need to torture me to get this information. These were monsters who took pure, unadulterated pleasure from savagely destroying another human being. These weren't soldiers; they were thugs. Matt recoiled at the realization, trembling in fear and rage.

His enemy just gloated, as if he could read the thought going through Matt's mind. A powerful emotion like a shot of numbing anesthesia surged through Matt's body, so strong he momentarily forgot the pain. He could think of no other way to describe it. Hate—a strong loathing, fierce repugnance for the beady-eyed, diminutive monster across from him. Hate, yet at the same time, terror, because he sensed that this degenerate would take great pleasure in repeating what had just occurred, or worse, if given the slightest provocation or opportunity.

"Oh, by the way," the interrogator sneered superciliously as he walked past Matt, cracking his club across his open palm, "that criminal you tried to help—he's dead." With an evil laugh, he strutted out of the room.

CHAPTER 4

June 1, 1966, San Diego, California.

After the children went to bed, Barbara Jean Tillet poured herself another cup of coffee from the second pot of the day, opened a fresh pack of cigarettes and dropped into the worn, overstuffed recliner. It was the first piece of furniture she and Matt had purchased when they bought the house in Oceana, and it was still her favorite chair, even though the frame had been tweaked in the move to San Diego. It leaned a little "toward starboard," Matt had teased.

The light from the muted T.V. provided the only illumination in the den. Oblivious to the images flickering in the gloom, Bobbie gazed intently at the red glow from the cigarette. The familiar twinge of guilt started creeping over her. Matt didn't like her to smoke. He did everything he could think of to make her quit—from threats to bribery. She avoided smoking in his presence, but somehow she couldn't give it up entirely. It gave her something to do with her hands at squadron functions, or at wives-club meetings, occasions when she didn't really feel comfortable. Despite several years of practice, she had never become as totally immersed in the Navy community as many of the other wives. The Navy was her rival, and Matt devoted entirely too much time and energy to his naval "mistress." The only good thing about the cruises was that she could openly smoke in her own home without being chastised, except for that soft, nagging voice in her ear.

Staring at her bare feet beyond the ashtray she had placed in her lap, she wiggled her toes back and forth, side to side, as her thoughts again drifted to Matt. Generally, when he was away on a cruise, she tried not to think about him. It made it much easier to get through the lonely seven or eight months. But she could sense his condemnation as strongly as if he were in the next room. Why tonight? It wasn't like this was the first cigarette she had smoked since he left. Suddenly she realized the reason: it was their 14th wedding anniversary. She had totally forgotten.

What a twist. She used to feel sorry for herself when Matt wasn't there for special occasions. Husbands were supposed to be shining knights who brought flowers and candy and made mad, passionate love to their cherished damsels, particularly on birthdays and anniversaries. At least they did in the romantic novels she read. Matt, on the other hand, had to be reminded to send a card. Gradually, over the years, she had resigned herself to his utterly unromantic behavior. It was Matt's way, and she wasn't going to change him, but still it hurt, almost as much as his priorities, which left her and the kids somewhere below flying, duty, football and wrestling.

Anyway, she didn't fare very well in arguments with him. Only once had she really stood up to him and won. She had not wanted a gap of almost ten years between her children, but for several years after Debbie's difficult birth, Matt had adamantly refused to discuss having another baby. He was quite content with one healthy child, and he wasn't about to take another chance on "losing his wife." It was only after some careful planning, and just a hint of manipulation on her part upon his return from a cruise that forced him to finally give in. It worked out fine. She didn't have any problems with her second pregnancy or Hank's birth. Matt had even reluctantly agreed, admittedly after she nagged and pestered him all last summer, that they could try for another baby when he came home this time.

Thinking of Matt and another baby, she was filled with a powerful sense of urgency for his return. While he might not be the ideal romantic lover, he certainly looked the part: good-looking in a rugged, masculine, square-jawed sort of way, sexy by most women's standards, still trim as the day they were married, broad shoulders, narrow hips and flat stomach. Just thinking of him now in this way caused a sensation in her groin. She downed the last of the now-cold coffee, turned up the volume on the television and adjusted the recliner as far back as it would go. Perhaps the "boob tube" would help her relax.

The doorbell rang, rousing Bobbie from near sleep. Her eyes darted to the ship's wheel clock above the T.V.—10:30. Who on earth would come calling at this time of night? Peeking out the big picture window in the living room, she spied a black sedan under the street light in front of the house. Two Naval officers stood under the porch light, holding their hats in their hands. Both their heads were bent.

She felt herself turning cold. As a Navy wife, she had a pretty good idea what this meant. Trembling, she opened the door. The uniformed men entered silently.

The base Chaplain from Miramar spoke slowly and sadly. "We're very sorry, Mrs. Tillet. Very sorry . . . but we've received word that your husband has been shot down."

Bobbie inhaled sharply as her internal elevators descended a floor or two. She covered her mouth with her hands. "Is he alive?" she whispered, her voice trembling.

Chaplain White twisted the brim of his hat. "I'm sorry, Mrs. Tillet, we really don't know. At the present time we can only report that he is missing."

Blackness, punctuated by darting little white spots, enveloped her. The room started to move, and she felt her knees buckling. As she began to slump forward, Dr. Morse rushed to her side.

She was numbly aware of being carried across the room and gently placed on the couch. The Chaplain and the doctor were talking. She could hear their voices, but not their words.

She groped through the mental fog. This can't be true. This must be a bad dream? Are these men really here? There's some mistake. Matt wouldn't do this to me. We had so many plans for this summer. Matt, where are you? Please come home. Show them how wrong they are.

"Is there anyone we could call, someone who might be willing to come stay with you?" Chaplain White was standing over her, gently shaking her shoulders.

Bobbie shook her head, tears blurring her vision.

"Don't worry, Mrs. Tillet, you're doing fine." Dr. Morse handed her a glass of water and two small pills. "Is there anything else you would like?"

"A cigarette, please," she mumbled, pointing toward the den.

Dr. Morse retrieved the pack, lit one and handed it to her.

"Kathryn Roberts," she said absently.

"I beg your pardon," inquired the Chaplain.

"Kathryn Roberts. I could call Kathryn Roberts. Her husband is in Matt's squadron."

As Kathryn entered, Bobbie lifted her head and attempted to stand.

"Don't get up, honey, I can sit right here." Kathryn quickly sat down beside her.

Gratefully, Bobbie dropped back onto the couch, and accepted a hug from Kathryn. Her eyelids weighed a ton. She wanted to speak, but she couldn't form the words. It took all her concentration just to hear some of the conversation around her.

"Mrs. Roberts," Chaplain White was saying, "Dr. Morse gave Mrs. Tillet some pills to help her relax and put her to sleep. As you can see, they're already taking effect. Will you be able to stay until the children wake up? I think she's going to need some help telling them what has happened." The sounds and things around her became a blur.

Awakened by a noise, Bobbie sat up abruptly and looked around. She was in her own bed, still dressed. *How did I get to bed last night?* In the back of her mind she knew there was something she should remember. She shook her head to clear the cobwebs. Where were her house shoes? She needed some coffee and a cigarette.

"Good morning. How do you feel this morning?"

Bobbie gasped sharply and jerked her head up, exhaling quickly as she recognized Kathryn. Then the events of last night flooded back: the Chaplain, the doctor, and the reason—Matt. She rubbed her head, pushing her hair away from her eyes, "I'm fine, I guess," and after a pause, "under the circumstances."

"I didn't mean to startle you." Kathryn sat beside her on the bed and placed her arm around her shoulders. "Honey, I'm so sorry. I feel so helpless. Is there anything I can do to help?"

Bobbie buried her head on her friend's neck and leaned against her, welcoming a comforting arm around her shoulder. After a few minutes, she pulled away, sat up and inhaled deeply, then slumped over, hiding her head in her hand, her elbow resting on her leg.

Kathryn stood and patted her on the shoulder, "Dr. Morse made a fresh pot of coffee late last night and it was pretty good. Why don't I just heat it up?"

"That's fine. Please just make yourself at home. I'm going to take a shower."

Kathryn was caressing a cup of coffee and gazing absently out the window when Bobbie entered. She turned and smiled. "Boy, what a difference."

"Thanks. It's amazing what a shower, a comb and make-up can do." Bobbie smiled lamely as she walked around the bar and took a seat on a stool at the counter. She rested her head in her hands and sighed, "Oh, Kat, I just don't know what I'm going to do. Debbie is going to be so upset."

Bobbie reached for a pack of cigarettes and tore off half of the top. She absently fumbled with the pack as she tried to remove a cigarette. "She was really looking forward to Matt coming home this time. She had the whole summer planned. I had even agreed to let her skip Vacation Bible School this year."

She removed a lighter from her pocket, lit the damaged end of the cigarette and took a long drag, slowing blowing out the smoke. "Matt was supposed to be home in July and the program didn't end until August. When he left, he promised we could do something special when he got back from this cruise. We haven't had a family vacation since he started Post Graduate School, before Hank was born. I just don't know how to tell her."

They heard the bathroom door close, and Debbie walked into the kitchen. She raised her eyebrows in obvious surprise. "Hi, Mrs. Roberts. What's going on, Mom? How come you're already dressed? You guys going somewhere?"

Bobbie slipped off the bar stool and walked slowly around the cabinet, put her arms around her daughter, and pulled her close. "No, Sugar, I'm not going anywhere. Something very bad has happened. You're going to have to be very brave."

Debbie jerked away and stared with sullen anger at Bobbie. "What's happened to my dad?" she demanded, an accusing look on her face.

Bobbie tried again to pull her close, but Debbie twisted away. "Yes, honey, it's about Daddy. He's been shot down."

Debbie glared defiantly for a few moments, then, flinging her arms around her mother, broke into sobs. They remained locked in each other's embrace for several minutes.

"Honey, I'm so sorry. I'm . . . ." Bobbie couldn't finish. Her whole world was crumbling around her. She should be comforting her thirteen-year-old daughter, but she didn't know how, she couldn't figure out the right words. Matt should be here at times like these. *Oh, how stupid of me, of course he's not here, that's why this is happening.* She dropped to her knees, her whole body shivering.

"Mom, Mom, everything's going to be okay. He'll be okay. You know how tough Daddy is, he'll be okay. Mom, don't cry. Mom, we'll get along okay until he comes home; you'll see, we'll be okay. Mom, please don't cry."

The schnauzer barked and scratched at the patio door. Bobbie rose from her knees, patted her daughter's damp hand. "Sure, Honey, you're right, everything will be fine. Go on, Ludwig needs something."

Bobbie exchanged a sad glance with Kathryn as Debbie slid open the door, scooped up the dog, clutched him tightly to her chest and disappeared around the side of the house.

"Well," Bobbie exclaimed, exhaling a long, nervous sigh, "Debbie handled it better than I expected, don't you think?" She picked up the pack of cigarettes, then tossed them back on the counter, realizing she already had one lit.

"Yes, she's a very grown up young lady, Bobbie. I'm sure she will be a lot of help to you in the next few days and weeks."

"Oh, don't say weeks, I don't want to even think about it being more than a few days. Did they tell you anything last night after I . . . after I passed out?"

"You didn't pass out, Bobbie. Dr. Morse gave you a couple of sleeping pills, and they finally took effect. You fell asleep in the living room. He carried you to bed before they left. I found myself a couple blankets in the hall closet and slept on the couch. It's quite comfortable."

"Thank you. But what did you do with your children? I really hate to impose on you this way." Bobbie appreciated everything Kathryn had done, but she wished she would leave. She just didn't feel like talking with anyone right now.

"A neighbor is watching them. And, don't you even use the word, 'impose.' It's not an imposition to help another squadron wife in times like these. You'd do the same thing, and you know it."

"Well, thank you very much anyway." Bobbie silently sipped her coffee and massaged her forehead with her free hand. There was so many things to consider, so much to do, she didn't know where to start.

"You know, I think I'll call Mom and Dad before Hank gets up. I'm not anxious to discuss the subject in front of him. I'm just going to tell him that Daddy is still away and won't be back for a while. At four he wouldn't understand anyway. I think that's a better way to do it, don't you?"

"You'll have to tell him sooner or later."

"Better later." She dialed the phone and was crying as she hung up.

"My folks would like for me to bring the children and come back to Oklahoma, but I can't leave now. I have to learn more about what happened. I don't know if Matt is dead or alive. I want to be here when the ship gets back so I can talk with the guys who were flying with him. I need to be where the Navy can find me right away in case they hear anything. The best place for me is right here in San Diego, don't you agree?"

Kathryn was slow to respond. "I suppose, but it would be nice to have your family around though. Can they come out here?"

"Dad said they would try to get reservations for Mom to come out today, or at the latest tomorrow. Poor Mom, she doesn't like to fly, but she's going to because it would take too long to come by train."

"Oh, that's great."

"Kat, I think you should go home too. I'm okay, truly I am. You have been wonderful, but I don't want to impose—sorry—inconvenience you—anymore. Go on home to your own children." She stood and started toward the door.

Kathryn looked skeptical, but picked up her purse and followed.

"I think I can handle things better with Hank if you're not here when he gets up, and Mom will be here in a day or two."

Kathryn nodded and stepped outside. "Be sure to call if you need anything."

Just as Bobbie closed the door, she heard Hank calling, "Mommy!"

CHAPTER 5

<u>June, 1966, Hoa Lo Prison, Hanoi.</u>

Matt slumped over, exhausted. Numbness engulfed him, not just in his arms and hands, but in his mind seeking refuge from the assault of shame, guilt and humiliation that was eating at his very core. His eyelids drooped almost shut, blurring his vision. As his hunched body wobbled unsteadily, he realized he was about to fall; it shocked him awake. He'd have plenty of time for self-recriminations later, when he was able to think straight, but right now he had to figure out how to get off the damn stool, preferably without doing further damage.

He looked down; the legs of that stool appeared at least ten feet high. It hurt like hell when he fell before, and he was going to fall again if he didn't figure out how to dismount. His hands were touching the edge of the seat, but he could feel nothing.

"Shit," he grumbled. The likelihood of being a cripple added measurably to his already fathomless despair. He tried to lift himself; he had no strength in his arms, they wouldn't support his weight. Twisting his aching body first on his right cheek, then on the left, he butt-walked to the edge of the stool. Stretching downward with his feet as far as he could, he took a deep breath, clasped his arms in front of him, grimaced in anticipation, and slid his rump off the stool. His manacled feet gave way immediately, and he collapsed in a crumpled heap.

A cursory examination revealed no further injuries. He exhaled in relief, and then squirmed about to find the least painful position.

His eyes burned from lack of sleep; his muscles felt as if they had been tenderized with a meat mallet.

A shiver ran through him as he lay on the pissed-on, puked-on, shit-on, blood-encrusted, cold floor. What was going to happen next? When? Why had they broken off the questioning without asking for some new intelligence? Certainly he wasn't in a position to refuse.

He heard the door bolt creak. Damn. They were coming back—they did want more. He inhaled sharply and his trembling intensified. He couldn't stop shaking.

A guard set a cup on the desk, and without so much as a look in Matt's direction, walked out and rammed the bolt shut. God, he hated that sound. Realizing he had been holding his breath, Matt exhaled audibly. Using his aching stomach muscles, he pulled himself into a sitting position, then scooted over to the desk. Twisting and turning, he forced his manacled feet behind him and knelt. Leaning against the desk, he looked into the cup. Water. How long had it been since he'd had a drink? Two, three, or was it four days? Time was a blur. He really couldn't remember, he was a prisoner of lost time, lost hours, lost days. But how was he going to drink? How could he get the liquid from the cup into his mouth without spilling it all?

Gripping the cup with his teeth and using his upper arms to steady himself, he carefully tipped the container forward, catching most of the precious liquid in his mouth, savoring every drop.

Before he could sleep, one other little problem required attention. He had to take a leak. The idea of just lying there and pissing on himself was distasteful. Who knows when he'd get to wash. He didn't need a good rash to go with the rest of his injuries. Matt called, *"Bao Cao."* Silence. He didn't know what it meant, but it usually evoked a response. "Bastard" or "sonofabitch" would convey his feelings, but he was reasonably sure that wasn't the translation.

He yelled again, louder. *"Bao Cao."*

A guard shoved the door open and peered inside. Using primitive sign language, Matt explained his problem. The guard tittered, amused at Matt's gestures, then motioned with his rifle barrel toward the door. Matt laboriously crawled out to some bushes while the guard stood nearby, smoking a brown cigarette and watching nonchalantly.

You asshole, would it kill you to give me a hand? Matt silently cursed. But taking a leak was turning into a time-consuming and difficult chore.

First he had to unbutton his fatigue pants. That was certainly easier said than done without any feeling in his fingers. After fumbling around for several minutes, he felt the top buttons give way. "Jesus," he exclaimed in frustration as he tried to remove his penis from his shorts with his numb fingers. *It's a good thing I wasn't in a hurry.*

After relieving himself, he pulled the trousers back up around his waist; he didn't try to button them; he couldn't have even if he had all night. Well, come to think of it, he did have all night, but leaving them undone would make the next time easier. He dragged himself back into the green-walled hell hole, closed his eyes and tried to blot out his strange new world.

A creaking sound awoke Matt from his fitful sleep. It was dark. *Now what?* Two guards were unfastening his leg irons. They half-dragged, half-carried him to a cell in another building across the prison yard, laid him on the dirty concrete deck, shut the door and left.

The dimly lit room had no windows, no skylights, no connection to the outside except for slivers of light that snuck under the cracks around the door and through the guard's peep hole. The low watt naked light bulb near the ceiling cast an eerie glare that aggrevated Matt's already burning eyes. He just wanted to close them and shut out the dismal sight and stench of the cell, to withdraw into darkness so he could better hide his shame. He crawled upon one of the "slabs," and curled up in a ball, using the leg irons that were bolted to the slab as his head rest.

As best he could figure, he had arrived at the Green Room at dawn on June second. He was pretty sure they had tortured him for three days. It could have been four; he really didn't know how long he had been unconscious. It was however long it took to descend into the fiery depths of hell. He was certain that if he now died and went to hell, it could be no worse, only longer perhaps. In his wildest dreams, he could never have imagined that people could act in such an unspeakably brutal fashion toward another human being. If their goal was to reduce him to an animal, as the interrogator had boasted, even animals shouldn't be treated this way.

Deep down, Matt knew it wouldn't have mattered if he were the meanest bear that walked the woods, after what he'd been through, even the best of 'em would have caved in. At least, he rationalized, he hadn't told them anything they didn't already know. But, it gave him little consolation; the interrogator was a mindless savage; he would want more. It was just a matter of time.

What about Lou West, the recce pilot? The interrogator said he was dead. What could have happened? He'd seen the flare, so Lou was alive when he landed. Did he die of his injuries? Was he killed by angry villagers, or had he been tortured to death? He'd probably never know for sure. He brooded at the irony—it was trying to help Lou that got him here in the first place, and it was all for naught.

The squeaking door startled Matt from his thoughts. A guard set a bowl of some kind of soup with a small loaf of bread draped across it and a cup of water on the opposite slab. Matt eyed his first food since arriving unceremoniously and unexpectedly in the Democratic Republic of Vietnam probably four days ago. He was too sore and depressed to have any appetite, but he had to eat something; that much he remembered from survival training. The important thing in a situation like this is to keep up your strength. Of course Matt had never believed he would be in a situation like this. He'd said as much to Tom Finley less than two hours before his last memorable flight. As Matt's roommate, Tom would probably be tasked with returning his belongings to Bobbie. Poor Bobbie. This was going to be so hard on her. She needed help. Who was going to be around to help her? *Dumbshit. You should have thought of that before.* But, how does one really plan for something like this? He'd made sure she would receive enough money, she wouldn't have to worry financially, but Bobbie's needs went well beyond someone to help balance the checkbook, and he wasn't going to be around to take care of them. She could barely take care of herself; how was she going to take care of the children? Hank. What a handful he would be.

He had to stop thinking about home. That would drive him nuts. He eyed the water—that was what he really wanted.

Just then, three little mice crept out on the slab and started nibbling on his bread.

Kicking vigorously with his feet, Matt yelled, "Get away! Get away! That's mine!"

Immediately, he dropped to the floor, and, sticking his face into the bowl, lapped up the sticky swill. It tasted a little like stale dishwater smelled, but at least it didn't gag him—well, not completely. It wasn't likely to be served at the finer restaurants in San Diego, but it was the most expensive item on the menu here, and he had certainly paid one hell of a price for it. He completed his first "dining in" by gnawing a few bites off the end of the soggy bread opposite where the mice had started, and drinking the water, the best part of the meal, notwithstanding the fact that it was warm and dirty brown in color. Luckily, he'd been blessed with a strong constitution and could eat just about anything put before him. That was obviously going to come in handy if this was an example of the chow.

Ignoring his somewhat rebellious stomach, Matt climbed back up on the other slab. He hadn't quite fallen asleep when he heard the door opening again. This time the guard brought clothes. He removed Matt's dirty, bloody shirt, lifting the injured arms gently, as if he were trying to avoid further pain. Matt was grateful. The guard looked no more than twenty; he was a soldier and he was doing what he was told. That's what soldiers do. Maybe they didn't *all* get their kicks from abusing things that couldn't fight back, like the goose-stepping goons in the Green Room.

The guard helped Matt into a clean tee shirt and some dark-blue loose-fitting pajamas. The cotton-like material was the same kind that had been on the table in the interrogation room. He placed a mosquito net and a thin blanket on the slab, picked up the food dish and started toward the door.

"Guard." Matt held up his arms. "I need medicine."

At the sound of Matt's voice, the guard glanced at Matt's still bleeding, raw, dirty limbs, wrinkled his brow, grimacing, but before Matt could say anything more, walked out, ramming home the lock in the door. They all seemed well-trained in that maneuver. His earlier hopeful assessment of the guard's good character vaporized like the smog off the San Diego coast in the path of a strong Santa Ana wind.

Damn it. I need medicine. I'm going to get an infection. Matt examined his blackened lower arms. At the sight of what would pass for ground hamburger where the ropes had eaten away the skin, he felt sick. He forced his hands together. Nothing. He couldn't feel a goddamn thing. "I'll bet that sadistic little bastard knew exactly what I wanted, he just doesn't want to be bothered." With a weary sigh, Matt wrapped his precious agony in his newest creature comfort—the small, thin blanket—and collapsed.

The grating sound of his cell door opening awakened Matt again. It was morning. To his surprise, he had slept the entire night on that cold hard slab. Most of his anatomy still hurt, but it was amazing what a night's sleep can do for the mind. Daytime made little difference inside the cell, it was still dimly lit by that little light bulb, but as he waited for whatever came next, he took a better look at the austere six-by-eight-foot cubicle that was apparently going to be his new home. Bare concrete slabs, two to three inches thick, about eighteen inches above the deck, with heavy leg manacles that could be operated only from outside, were built into each side of the cell, separated by a narrow passageway in between. The thick iron door had a peephole, but it could not be opened from the inside. Matt shook his head as he thought, *Our pigs lived in better quarters, certainly more comfortable. At least they had some straw to lie on. I guess this is what they call solid comfort.*

For the next six days, morning and afternoon, he was escorted back to the Green Room where he was grilled on targeting, airplane performance, and number of missions flown by each squadron. During one session, Vietnamese Air Force officers accompanied the interrogator. They were polite, more military in their demeanor, but firm. They were particularly interested in fighter tactics used by the American pilots. Matt avoided giving helpful information whenever possible, but with each renewed threat to use the straps, he answered obliquely and evasively until they were satisfied.

"What is the location of the next target?"

"I don't know." Matt's truthful answer infuriated the interrogator. As the straps were brought in, Matt quickly conjured up a feasible target; he couldn't handle the rope treatment again—not right now.

"It's the bridges." After the hundreds of attacks by the American Navy and Air Force pilots on the bridges in North Vietnam, it should be no secret that they were targets generally.

His inquisitor's anger subsided, apparently satisfied by this hastily made-up answer. They continued.

"How fast does the F-8 fly?"

"One thousand mph."

"What ordnance does it carry?"

"The sidewinder and twenty millimeter cannon."

"How many missions did you fly?"

It seemed like the questions would never end.

Back in the dingy solitude of his cell, Matt thought about the events that brought him to this place. With a deepening sense of resentment, he seethed about the limitations placed on the American fighting forces: destroy the bridges but don't hurt any of the people; don't go beyond this point; don't go past that river. If they would just let the military do its job, if they could "bomb them back to the Stone Age" as one Air Force general had advocated, they could have this thing wrapped up in no time. But, he was going to be here for a long time, given the way the politicians were screwing up the war. And "here" was a place he'd rather not be.

To maintain his sanity, pass the time and break the endless monotony, Matt traversed the gravel roads and sparkling rivers of his memories, vividly reconstructing a chronology of times past—events in his life, going back to the days on the old farm in Nebraska.

To this day the old two-story frame house where he was born still lacked inside bathrooms and hot running water. Dad inherited the 100-acre farm located about eight miles outside the little town of

Hoyt, population, 4386. This did not exactly qualify it as one of the top 25 metropolitan areas in the bustling state of Nebraska.

As a kid, Matt liked to lie in his bed and watch those grand winter snowstorms. The snowflakes would gather on the window sills, first a fine coat, then a deep plush carpet of white, eye-squinting brilliance during the day, shimmering jewels in the moonlight. But winters also brought temperatures down to 25 degrees below zero. To keep warm they had to huddle around that one big old oil heater in the living room or the wood cookstove in the kitchen. They finally hooked up to electricity about the time Matt started high school. It sure made it easier on his eyes when he had to study at night after football practice and the chores were done. Yet, as he recalled, those kerosene lamps threw out more light than the dim bulb in his cell.

Mom and Dad never owned a car when Matt was growing up, so he, his younger brother, Melvin, and their sister, Bonnie, usually walked to grade school down at the corner about a mile from their driveway. When he was in high school, he caught the school bus that stopped on the main road about a quarter mile down the lane. Several of the town's businessmen took turns taking the farm boys home after sports practice. During football and wrestling seasons, Matt was a recipient of their generosity. Dad finally purchased an old clunker the summer after Matt's graduation, just before he left for the Navy.

A pressing problem forced Matt back to the present; he had to answer the call of nature. With some effort, he made his way to the back of his cell to his "honey bucket."

Later, back on his concrete slab, the rusty pail reminded him of the facilities his family and most of their neighbors used back in Nebraska. Nearly everyone who lived in the farming areas had an outhouse. Most were two-seaters. Matt never could figure out why those things were designed with two seats. Taking a crap wasn't exactly the social event of the season. Maybe one hole was "Men," and the other "Women." But, then, he'd never thought of inviting a date either.

He chuckled as he recalled several incidents involving those out-houses and some mischievous teenagers, including one when his brother threw the cat down the hole, and Mom had to make him get it out. He couldn't think of home without thinking about some of Momma's good home cooking. Here, he received the same meal twice a day: two cups of water, a dish of soup with something floating in it, a small loaf of bread and a side plate of something that resembled a green vegetable. It was often difficult to identify the "somethings." Even aided by his best imagination, Matt still couldn't turn it into fried chicken, corn on the cob, mashed potatoes with cream gravy, Momma's fresh-baked baking-powder biscuits and cherry cobbler. Jeez, even a greasy hamburger and fries would be a feast about now.

His world had narrowed to this small, sweaty cell, and time passed so slowly it hardly seemed to be moving at all. After that first night when he was more unconscious from exhaustion than asleep, it was impossible to lie more than a few hours at a time on the hard concrete slab, and inside the cell, it was hard to tell day from night. It didn't really matter anyway, since he wore the same pajama-like clothes all the time, and his calendar was reasonably free of appointments.

The imminent threat of torture seemed to have lessened somewhat, and his biggest problem was learning how to deal with the endless reservoir of time. At home, he'd never had enough of it to go around, not enough to play football, wrestle, study, keep up his grades, and later fly and still spend any time with his family. With a start, he realized that it was his family who usually got the short end of it, and added guilt to his other miserable feelings.

His injured arms prevented anything more than jogging in place in the fifteen inch space between the two slabs, but all forms of exercise were forbidden. If he couldn't do calisthenics, at least he could work out his mind. It became his mental gymnasium outside the prison walls, where he was free to move about at will.

Over the next several weeks, he managed to reconstruct most of his early life, year by year, and play it back like a movie, in which he was the star. It allowed him to escape, if just for a few hours, from his Communist prison and his state of turmoil, both intolerable locales.

As soon as he started high school, Matt discovered competitive sports. He was strong for his size, having worked in the fields from the time he was old enough to toddle, toting heavy hay bales and chopping hundreds of cords of wood for cooking and winter heating. That toughness helped him make the football team and earn a spot on the wrestling squad even as a freshman. His competitive spirit was rewarded when he was elected captain of the football team his junior year. Then, re-elected his senior year, he become the first player in recent memory to have served as captain two seasons. To his knowledge, the '49 Tigers were still the only undefeated team in the school's history.

As a wrestler, what he lacked in stature, he made up for in sheer determination and brute strength, and he won consistently in his weight class. Shedding those fifteen or so pounds from football to wrestling sometimes proved challenging. He'd spent many hours in the sauna sweating off those last four or five pounds to meet his 165-pound weight the day before the match, but he'd put them all back on at the training table dinner after weigh-in. As he recalled, the sauna was about the size of his cell, but, come to think of it, a hell of a lot more comfortable.

His grades, which qualified him for the National Honor Society, coupled with his prowess on the mat, and a lot of help from his coach, landed him a scholarship to a small college in Iowa. It was the only way he was going to college; his folks certainly couldn't afford to send him.

But fate interceded. During that summer, right after graduation, the Navy recruiter came to town. In his well-pressed uniform, shiny shoes and brightly gleaming medals, the black chief petty officer described a whole new world of adventure. He talked of travel and excitement, and he spoke of one other thing—education. Not only education, but a trade—something a young man could use to get a good job after the Navy. He described jobs working with airplanes, repairing complicated equipment, training that would prepare the Navy man to get a good paying job later. "Youse guys won't have to use a mule's tail for a compass no mo," he had teasingly promised in his exaggerated black southern drawl.

So Matt, Buddy, Teeter and Hawk, who had grown up together, played on the same football team, and not one of them having ever ventured more than a hundred miles from home, joined the Navy together. Each, in his own way, wanted to get away from his perceived confinement of the small town, from the guaranteed boredom of following in his father's plow row, or working in his dad's corner drugstore or hardware store, of going nowhere, of being nobody. Instead they wanted, as the posters and the recruiter promised, to "see the world."

Matt visualized in his mind the photo of the four of them taken on their first pass after reporting to boot camp at Great Lakes, Illinois. Spiffied up in their new Navy jumpers, they were all wide-eyed and full of anticipation for the exciting things to be done and the interesting places to go. Chicago was the biggest, busiest place they'd ever seen. And the girls! Wow, they never had anything like that down on the farm. He could still remember with utter amazement the maze of neon lights, bars and brothels. Anything was available, even for a boy of seventeen.

After boot camp, they had gone in separate directions. Buddy had been killed in Korea; Teeter put in his time, got out and returned home to help his dad run the drug store; Hawk got out, married a girl from back east and was living somewhere in Connecticut; and Matt, well he'd seen a lot of the world all right. Right now he'd happily trade the "confinement" of a small town for his current six-by-eight-foot cell. Amazing how easily one's perception can change. If he'd gone to that college in Iowa, he could probably be coaching at some small town high school now, maybe even at Hoyt, not an unappealing trade.

As the picture of the four friends flashed through his mind, Matt felt an overwhelming sense of futility. Would he, like Buddy, never make it back home? Pondering his fate, he suspected that Buddy's death, which had come quickly from a sniper's bullet through his head, had been easier than his would be. In retrospect, it may have been a mistake to pull that face curtain. It might have been better to go in with the plane than to have survived for this. It would have been painful for his family for a time if he had been killed, but maybe that would have been better than them waiting and waiting, and never knowing what is going to happen.

Stop it! Shaking his head, he jumped up and started jogging in place with a fury.

****

Finally, the inquisition seemed over. The Vietnamese apparently had obtained all the information they thought he could give. But, they had one final humiliation in mind.

"You must now write a confession. Here are examples of what it should say. These have been volunteered by other criminal pilots."

Matt reviewed some of the "confessions." He knew how they had been obtained—exactly the same way his was—after days of torture, and weeks of fear and coercion. But, they confirmed that he wasn't the only American pilot who had "violated the Code." It gave him some small measure of satisfaction. "I guess that old saying about misery loving company has some basis," he mused bitterly.

To save face, he put up some token resistance, but he was so weak from the ravages of the fever that further resistance was impossible. At the first threat of the straps, he admitted he had violated Vietnamese airspace; had probably killed Vietnamese people, including women, children and old folks; that it was an aggressive war, and that he disagreed with it. At the bottom he scrawled his name illegibly.

For almost two weeks, Matt had appealed daily for medical attention. Red streaks, resembling rays of a sunburst breaking through a cloud, were shooting up and down his arms. His small ration of water was scarcely enough under normal circumstances; it was totally inadequate to alleviate his fever thirst, but pleas for more went unheeded. His eyes burned and itched unmercifully. Finally, after he signed the "approved" statement, he was taken to a medic who cleaned out the maggots, dumped sulfa into the pus-oozing black holes and covered his arms with clean used bandages—just something to hold the medicine.

Later that night, under cover of darkness, the guards once again came to his cell, bound his painful arms behind him, and led him, barefoot, to the back of a Jeep. He was thrust into the seat at one side of a guard. On the other side was the first American Matt had seen, although he had heard other prisoners crying out. A threatening look and word from the guard restricted them to nothing more than eye contact during the almost hour ride. Still, it gave him a boost just being in the company of another American; he had felt so alone, so forsaken, these past few weeks.

As he was being led to his cell, Matt quickly inspected the new camp, counting at least ten buildings located around the perimeter. Then, just before he entered his cell, he caught a glimpse of bare feet behind the cell next door. *Great. A neighbor.*

As soon as the guards left, Matt lay down on the floor and stuck his face very close to the crack in the door nearest the other cell.

As loudly as he dared, he whispered, "Is someone there?"

Silence. He tried again, a little louder. "Who's there?"

This time he heard noises. Was it the guard returning? If he were caught, he'd be punished for trying to communicate. It was forbidden.

His temples throbbed, rhythmically like a drum, loud enough, he was sure, to be heard outside the door. He lay perfectly still, hardly breathing, waiting. Waiting. Nothing. He mentally kicked himself. If he'd reacted quickly enough, he could have stood up and moved away from the door and be out of danger by now. Still nothing. Maybe it wasn't the guard after all.

Then, from the next room he heard a voice. Again he put his mouth right next to the crack, and speaking softly, asked, "Who is there?"

From the other door came the distinctly American voice, "Lou West, Lieutenant, U.S.N."

CHAPTER 6

<u>San Diego, late June, 1966, Ship Returns.</u>

Bobbie was just finishing the breakfast dishes when the doorbell rang. It was Chaplain Kennedy and a young officer. She invited them in.

"Good morning, Mrs. Tillet. I wanted to introduce you to Lieutenant Bob Nelson who will be your CACO—um—your Casualty Assistance Calls Officer. He's your official point of contact with the Navy, and part of his job is to help you with the financial matters."

"Thank you, Chaplain Kennedy. Your timing is very good if the size of my checkbook balance is any indication." She laughed half-heartedly, trying not to reveal the degree of her apprehension. With no clue what was going to happen financially, she had asked her mother, before she returned to Oklahoma after a week's visit, for a loan. Although Mom had been generous, it was embarrassing for a grown married woman to be asking her mother for money.

"Well, that's exactly what Lieutenant Nelson can help you with. I'm going to leave you in his capable hands now, but if there is anything at all that you need, you have my number. Be sure to call."

"Thank you for everything."

The young officer stepped forward and smiled hesitantly. "Mrs. Tillet, I'm really sorry about your husband."

"Thank you." So was she, but what else could the poor guy say?

"I'm looking forward to working with you. Do you have any questions about the finances?"

"Are you kidding?" she asked incredulously. "I have nothing but questions." She immediately felt bad seeing the young officer's flustered look. He was there to help, he hadn't caused her problem. "I'm sorry. I didn't mean to snap."

"Oh, Mrs. Tillet, don't apologize. This has got to be really tough on you."

He seemed so young to be handling this sort of thing.

"I remember Matt saying if anything ever happened to him, I'd be taken care of, but frankly, I never inquired into the details. How does it work?"

"Well, you will continue to receive your husband's regular pay until the paperwork is processed. After that, a portion of it will be paid directly in your name. The balance will go into a savings plan. The amount you receive will depend on what percentage your husband selected. You'll continue to receive that unless it should be determined that he is, um . . . uh . . . unless he is declared killed in action. If that should happen, then you will receive his service insurance."

"You mean if he's dead, I'll get ten thousand dollars, isn't that the amount—and that's it?" This time Bobbie felt like she had been punched in the stomach.

"Yes, ma'am."

"Wow. I guess I really *didn't* understand the rules."

"Well, try not to worry, Mrs. Tillet. I'm sure things will work out. Now, if you have any problems until they change things over, here's my number. If you need anything at all, call me."

After he left, Bobbie walked to the kitchen counter, poured herself another cup of coffee—her third or fourth one—and grabbed for her cigarettes. Her hands were shaking. "Jesus," she moaned, emitting a long sigh. *How are we going to get by if Matt is dead?* He had always said they couldn't afford any other insurance, the rates were so high because he was a pilot. She had not realized how little security she had if anything happened to him. "Damn you, Matt Tillet." Her sudden anger was exceeded only by her feeling of desperation.

<u>Early July, 1966, Hancock returns.</u>

The 11 o'clock news profiled the huge welcoming celebration as the Hancock pulled into North Island.   Bobbie had purposely avoided the 6 o'clock news when the children were up.   She didn't want to deal with their questions.   She wasn't sure if Hank would understand that this was Daddy's ship, but she wasn't ready to find out.   Now, they were asleep and she could postpone the inevitable no longer.

Suddenly, she felt terribly alone, abandoned and cheated, like a bride jilted at the altar.   Most of the aircrew would have flown into Miramar the day before, but no one from the squadron had called her yet.   None of Matt's precious Navy buddies had even taken the time to express their condolences.   Then, recognizing the unreasonableness of her resentment, she chastised herself.   If the men had just gotten in yesterday, they were surely entitled to a day or two with their own families.

Part of her wanted to turn off the T.V. and shut out the happy scene, but she couldn't.   She felt compelled to watch as reality gripped her tightly and forced her to face what until now her mind had tried so hard to deny.   Her husband should have been home now.   She and Debbie and Hank should have been at Miramar yesterday to greet him.   Last night, she should have been able to snuggle into his big, strong arms.   He should be here to take care of them.   They needed him.   But the ship was back, the squadron was back, and no steadfast, dependable Matt was going to come walking through the door.   No, Matt wasn't coming home, not today, probably not in a month, and maybe never.   For all she knew, he might already be dead.   How could he desert her like this?   Why was this happening to them?   It all seemed like a terrible dream.   Tears welled up in her eyes.

"Oh, Matt, where are you?   How could you have put us in this position?   You knew this could happen.   Why didn't you warn me?"   Deep down she knew his answer would be that he didn't want to worry her.   But the truth was, he didn't want to deal with the fuss he knew she would have made.   He didn't want to get out of the Navy, pure and simple, and he alone had made the decision to subject all of them to this risk.

Gradually her distress turned to raw anger. How could Matt so smugly have excluded her from decisions that were so directly going to affect her? Her outrage at Matt was only slightly overshadowed by her own self-flagellation. Why hadn't *she* been more insistent on an equal partnership? Why had she left all those important decisions to Matt? Why was she such a damn pantywaist?

She fixed herself a drink to steady her nerves and went to bed. But sleep didn't come easy as she reran the dockside scene over and over: the flowers, the "Welcome Home Daddy" signs, the hugs, the kisses, the band's patriotic music. And she kept asking over and over the questions Matt should have discussed long ago without her having to ask. But, she should have asked! A second strong drink allowed her to start to relax and silence the voices.

Roy Roberts called early the next morning. "Bobbie, would it be convenient if I stopped over for a few minutes?"

"Oh, of course, Roy, I'd really love to see you and talk to you." Last night's petulance was submerged. Roy would know what happened. He was one of Matt's best friends in the squadron; he would be able to tell her Matt was okay.

She checked on Hank, who was busily engrossed with his toys in the sandbox in the back yard, then changed from her robe to a summer dress. For the first time in weeks she noticed her drawn reflection.

Addressing the image in the mirror, she admonished, "You need a haircut and color. Those roots are definitely too dark. And look at your nails. There is no excuse for you looking like this." Bobbie resolved to go to the beauty shop as soon as she could get an appointment. Just because Matt wasn't home was no excuse to let herself become sloppy.

She ran down the sidewalk to greet Roy as soon as the car pulled up.

"Oh, Roy, you don't know how glad I am to see you," she bubbled, throwing her arms around him. Then looking toward the car, she inquired, "Kat didn't come with you?"

"No, she thought maybe we would rather talk alone. Besides, we just got back yesterday; Kat and the kids flew out to meet me in Pearl Harbor and Tim rode the ship back. Kat and Tammy stayed a couple extra days in Hawaii after the ship left, and they didn't get back until yesterday, so she had quite a few things to do at home."

"Oh, how exciting for the kids. And Kat, too." A frown danced briefly across her face, but she hastily converted it into a smile. She would have loved to go to Hawaii to meet the ship—and Matt. "Kat has been such a great help to me, I don't know what I would have done without her. She is such a dear." Taking his hand, she started toward the door. "Come on in. I've got some fresh coffee made, and I want you to see Hank; you won't believe how that child has grown."

Roy followed Bobbie to the patio door. Hank was running about the back yard, flying imaginary airplanes while the dog chased behind. "You're right. He's grown a foot since last summer. My God, he looks just like Matt. He's even built just like him."

"I know," she admitted, momentarily biting her lower lip. "Just like a fire plug."

Roy laughed, "Yeah, that or a bull." Roy turned back to the patio door. "He certainly seems to have adjusted nicely."

"Oh, he really doesn't know anything about what happened. We haven't discussed the situation in front of him. He just thinks Daddy is delayed and won't be home for a little while yet. To a four-year-old, time is so vague. He talks about Matt a lot, but he doesn't seem to be disturbed."

Roy's brief scowl and betraying flicker of his eyelids did not escape her, but he said nothing.

They watched in silence as Hank's imaginary plane dipped and swooped across the length and breadth of the back yard.

"How's Debbie doing?" Roy inquired.

Bobbie gave a last look at Hank, bit her lip, shrugged her shoulders and turned around. "How about a cup of coffee?"

"Fine. Black." He walked over to the dining room table and pulled out two chairs.

Bobbie brought the coffee and donuts. Before sitting down, she picked up her cigarettes and lighter from the cabinet. Lighting a cigarette and motioning to the pack, she remarked, "Matt would die if he could see how much I'm smoking." Then she stopped, realizing her choice of words, "I mean . . ." she stammered, and her voice trailed off.

Roy smiled and patted her hand, "Yeah, Bobbie, I know what you mean."

She doctored her coffee with cream and sugar and absently stirred it.

Controlling her curiosity no longer, she blurted, "Roy, can you tell me any more about what happened to Matt? Who was he flying with? Maybe I can talk to them. Do you think he's alive? I have so many questions, and I don't know who to turn to." Her words sounded rushed.

Roy was quiet for a moment. He swallowed and raised his eyes. "Bobbie, Johnnie Agnatella and I were flying with Matt when he was shot down."

Bobbie's eye's opened wide in surprise, but she remained mute as Roy continued.

Roy took a sip from his coffee, then went on. "We were escorting a flight of A-4s on a bombing mission. The bombers had done their job and we were ready to head home when we heard that a recce pilot on another mission nearby had been shot down. The air wing commander asked us to check on his status. Matt sighted his flare and wanted to go in for one more run to see if we could raise him on the radio. That was when we spotted the MiGs. In the course of the battle, a MiG got behind Matt. Either the MiG got off a shot that damaged his plane, or he was hit by ground fire. We had been under attack from a flak site right in that area, and we could have gotten too close when we went after the MiGs. We know he wasn't personally hit, because he didn't even know he was on fire until Johnnie told him. A little after that, Matt reported that the plane wasn't responding and that he was going to have to get out."

He hurried on. "Neither of us saw Matt's parachute." Noting her startled look, he continued quickly. "Now don't get me wrong, that's not because there wasn't one, it's just that we were both in the middle of a dog fight with the MiGs, and it took us out of the area where Matt ejected. We think Johnnie shot down the MiG that was firing at Matt, but by that time we were both almost out of fuel and had to head back to the ship. We were too far north for any rescue attempts.

"Bobbie, my best guess is that Matt ejected from the plane safely and was picked up on the ground. We know there were North Vietnamese in that area. My personal opinion is that Matt was captured and is a POW. That may not be much consolation, but that's the way I see it."

Bobbie sat quietly throughout Roy's story, fascinated by the description of what may have happened to her husband. She tried to think back, to Matt's accounts of his experiences after the first cruise; and was surprised that she really hadn't any idea how dangerous it was. He was not the type who brought his work home; that was clear. It would have been his way of "protecting" her, or at least that would have been his explanation.

Roy was quiet. She waited for more, but when Roy seemed finished—seemed, in fact, to have momentarily left her—she placed her hand on his arm and smiled. "Thanks, I really appreciate what you've told me. It makes me feel good to know that you were flying with him. I know that nothing more could have been done to help him, or you would have done it. I've been so desperate to hear what happened to him. I feel better now to know he probably wasn't killed."

Suddenly the enormity of what Roy had said really registered: the daily dangers that her husband faced without ever mentioning a word; the terror he must have felt on that last flight, and now the reassurance that he was probably alive! Her entire chest heaved as she breathed in deeply and then slowly exhaled. She covered her mouth with her left hand, slid her fingers up across her nose and rubbed the indentation between her eyes as she digested this information, then raised her head, squared her shoulders, and addressed Roy tentatively. "Do you really think he's alive? I've been so afraid to even hope . . . I mean, ... Well, you know . . . the Navy is very noncommital."

Roy nodded. "Well . . . I suppose . . . um, I mean Matt wasn't hit . . . so . . . ."

Bobbie read Roy's hesitation as confirmation. She clapped her hands and continued, beaming. "Oh, this is wonderful news. Just wonderful. How long do you think it will be before he's released?"

"Bobbie, I don't know . . . it might not be . . . ."

She interrupted again. "I guess I just sit tight now and wait. It will probably just be a matter of time before the North Vietnamese notify our government that he is a prisoner." She lowered her hands to her lap and looked expectantly at Roy.

"Well, I don't want to give you false hope. The North Vietnamese haven't released any information as far as I know, on any of the prisoners."

"Oh," she said flatly.

Roy patted her hands. "Now don't worry."

"Well, I guess we'll just have to get used to his being gone for awhile. I'll just treat each month like the first month of a long cruise. That'll work, won't it?"

"Kat was right, you're handling this better than I expected. I know it takes a lot of courage. Matt would be very pleased."

She smiled as he held her hand. *You mean surprised.*

"Oh, by the way, Johnnie said to give you his love. His wife went back east to stay with her folks on this cruise, so he flew back there just as soon as we got in. They're going to drive back out, and he said tell you he would call when they get back."

"Oh, that's nice. I'd like to congratulate him on shooting down that MiG."

"Bobbie, how is Debbie?" Roy repeated his earlier question.

She shook her head, pursed her lips together and shrugged again. "I really don't know. At first she was angry at me, as though it were all my fault; then she became very loving and comforting, almost protective of me."

Bobbie dropped her head, swallowed with difficulty, and cleared her throat as Roy simply looked at her, his eyes encouraging her to continue.

"She doesn't mention her father unless it is absolutely necessary. But she has changed so much; she seems to have aged five years in five weeks. She doesn't act like a thirteen-year old anymore. It's like she's missing her adolescence. I . . . um . . . ."

Again Bobbie hesitated, searching for words, not really wanting to share her concerns, but not wanting to appear evasive. Roy sat quietly, occasionally patting her hand. She felt compelled to explain.

"Don't get me wrong, she doesn't give me anything to complain about, she's no trouble whatsoever. She almost makes me feel like I'm the child and she's the adult. It's kind of spooky. I guess the thing that bothers me most is that she seems to have buried Matt, put him totally out of her mind, as if he didn't exist anymore. I, um, I suppose we all handle things like this differently, but I don't believe she's as strong as she appears. I think she's in her own personal little hell, and I can't reach her to help her."

Roy nodded, but before he could say anything, Hank burst in from outside, stopped at his mother's side and looked quizzically at the stranger.

Bobbie, glad to have the uncomfortable discussion interrupted, kissed him on the cheek. "Don't you recognize Lieutenant Commander Roberts, sweetheart? Remember, he came to see us several times last summer."

Hank studied the man for a moment. His eyes brightened in recognition. "Oh, yeah, he's a friend of my daddy's, isn't he?"

"Yes, honey, he is. Now remember your manners and say hello."

Hank stuck out his hand, and in his best big-boy fashion addressed Roy, "How do you do, sir?"

Roy shook the little hand. "I'm fine, thank you. You have certainly grown since the last time I saw you, Hank."

"Yes, sir, I'm a big boy now," Hank assured Roy matter of factly. Turning to his mother, he asked, "May I go down and see if Alan can play?"

"Okay, but don't go anywhere else, and don't be gone too long."

"Sure, Mom. Bye, Mr. Roberts." In a movement Hank was out the door, the screen slamming behind him.

"And stay on the sidewalk," Bobbie called after him.

"What manners for a four-year old," Roy said.

"Oh, thank you. You know Matt was always very firm that the children should be polite."

Roy rose to leave. " Bobbie, I probably better get home. I'm sure Kat has a whole 'honey-do' list ready for my attention."

Again Bobbie frowned momentarily. Matt always repaired things as soon as he got home. Once again, she repressed the thought. "Roy, I really do appreciate your coming over and telling me about Matt. It has helped a lot."

"I hope so. Oh, before I forget it, Matt's roommate on the ship, Tom Finley, will be getting in touch with you. He has all of Matt's personal belongings packed up, and he'll give you a call and bring them by when it's convenient."

She fumbled with her wedding ring, her mind transported to another place, another time. Covering her face with her hands, and fighting back tears, she mutely acknowledged Roy's goodbye kiss on the cheek and his words of comfort.

When she regained her composure, she once again felt the anger creeping in. She took a long drag off her cigarette and fiercely crushed it out in the ashtray. "Matt Tillet," she exclaimed out loud, "you better be alive, because I'm going to kill you when you get home."

CHAPTER 7

<u>Cu Loc Prison (The Zoo), July 1966.</u>

The clanging noise from two trash can lids being banged together awoke Matt. Time to rise and shine. He stood up, shook his arms and legs, and paced around his cell, then quietly ran in place. He had to keep active; couldn't give in to the temptation to hibernate.

Shortly after the morning meal, Matt met the Vietnamese official in charge of his cell block. "The first thing we need is your biography—where you were born, what your parents do, if you are married, if you have children, your education and where you have been stationed."

Matt raised his damaged arms toward his jailer. "I am willing to do as you ask, but I cannot hold a pencil."

"Very well, then, you may take these to your cell and write your biography when you are able, but do not try to fool me." His don't-screw-with-me tone implied that he was not to be messed with.

Matt smiled inwardly. Although his excuse was valid, it still felt like a victory. He had gotten out of complying with an order, even if only temporarily. As he left the room, a guard handed him the pencil, paper and some reading material. Atop the stack, the face of a weary, very subdued American pilot stared out from the front page of the English version of the Vietnam Courier. Matt studied his photograph carefully, and read the glowing report of how the valiant militia up north had captured another "American war criminal." He recognized the photo as the one taken when they filmed his "capture" en route to the prison. The young lady had photographed well.

****

In early July, the turnkey gave Matt a pair of makeshift shoes fashioned from old truck tires, the soles cut in the shape of a foot, with straps made from old inner tubes to hold them on. Odd. Why was he being given shoes? He'd seen other prisoners through the crack under his door as they were marched past his cell on their way to the bathing area or to the interrogation room. None wore shoes.

The following morning, another turnkey took one of Matt's two sets of blue pajamas and left a long-sleeved khaki-colored set with numbers stenciled on the back of the shirt. Even odder.

Just after sunset on July 6th, Matt heard a large truck drive into the compound and stop not far from his building. A guard opened the cell door and made a chopping motion with his right hand on his left wrist. Matt had come to know this meant put on the long-sleeve shirt. He felt a brooding uncertainty. Something big was in the works; he knew it, just not what it was. A few minutes later, the guard returned, ordered him to put on the thongs, tied the blindfold, cuffed his hands behind him and led him outside.

Matt could hear feet shuffling, then someone bumped into him. There was a lot of coughing, men clearing their throats. They were deep husky sounds of Americans. But, why? Was it possible they were going to be released? A burst of adrenaline shot through him. Just as quickly, his elation turned to cold fear. Not likely. To be shot perhaps.

An English-speaking guard ordered, "Do not talk or you will be punished."

Matt stumbled around blindly with the other American prisoners. He felt a number of taps on his arm, but didn't dare respond. What *was* going on? The gnawing in his gut grew in intensity. He could feel his heart pounding. *Breathe deeply. Get a grip.*

A voice called for attention. The Camp Political Commissar spoke over the public address system. "War criminals, we have work to do, and you must show good attitude."

Matt sneered inwardly. Good attitude was the Vietnamese euphemism for doing what you were told unquestioningly—usually something despicable.

With a guard on either side, Matt was led up a ramp into the back of a big truck and seated on a bench along one side. He felt someone on his right, then someone sat down on his left. If only he could just see a little. He turned his head up and down, back and forth, lifted his forehead and eyebrows and clenched his jaw; his blindfold was too tight.

Despite the hot, muggy temperature, Matt felt chilled. Where were they being taken? What he wouldn't give to talk with another American, but he best not try, not in the truck anyway. But would he have a chance later? After what?

When the truck stopped after a short trip, Matt could hear voices, lots of cheering voices. It sounded like they were at some huge sporting event. In the distance, he heard what sounded like male cheerleaders, yelling through bullhorns.

An English-speaking guard warned, "American criminals, you must show humility, you must bow your heads; you must not show hostility toward the Vietnamese people or you will be shot."

As soon as they started unloading the prisoners, he heard a commotion, as if someone had fallen, followed by a loud angry American voice. "Ouch. Dammit. How in the hell are we supposed to get off this goddamn truck blindfolded? We're going to break our fuckin' necks."

When it was Matt's turn to alight, the guard slipped the blindfold down around his chin. Matt quickly glanced around, looking for a familiar face. He didn't see anyone he knew. He watched as men seeing each other for the first time as prisoners, greeted their buddies.

"Hey, when did you get bagged?"

"Who won the World Series last year?"

"I heard Smitty bought the farm."

"Yeah, say, has anyone seen CAG?"

71

Matt used the time to assess their surroundings. They were in a small park area at the end of what appeared to be one of the major streets in downtown Hanoi. It was made of cobblestones, and wider than those leading away. Most of the side streets were dirt. As far as Matt could see, literally hundreds of thousands of Vietnamese, crowded shoulder to shoulder, lined the streets. He had never seen so many people crammed into such a small space. The center of the street was clear, with soldiers stationed at intervals, holding back the surging crowds.

The light dawned. Another "show." The American pilots were going on display for the crowd. His mind flashed back to a movie he saw once: Christians being led to the arena to fight the lions while the crowd watched and cheered in bloodthirsty anticipation, ultimately deciding the fate of the would-be warriors by the turn of their thumb.

This was too much like the "sporting event" from the movie to suit Matt. *Oh, shit. How do we get out of this one?*

As speakers addressed the crowd in Vietnamese, the guards handcuffed the men two by two and lined them up in two separate groups. Then, the prisoners were allowed to sit on the sidewalk.

While their guard was distracted by the speakers, Matt introduced himself to the American officer with whom he was hand-cuffed. "Matt Tillet, Lieutenant Commander, US Navy."

"Captain Randy Wright, USAF." Wright leaned close and whispered, "The SRO has passed the order to look proud and stand tall."

Matt raised his eyebrows. "Passed the word? How?" How was a senior officer getting that message out; they had just been told to show humility and bow a few minutes ago.

Wright nodded his understanding. "Haven't you learned the tap code?"

Matt shook his head. "What is that?"

Before Randy could explain, the guard returned, pointed to the grassy area and gestured as if unzipping his pants.

Randy interpreted, "I think he means if we need to piss, we'd better go do it."

By now Matt had the program figured out. They were going to be center stage in a public castigation. The cadre of political agitators were provoking the crowd against what they called "the criminal American pilots." They were succeeding—too well. The throng of people lining the streets was highly agitated. Matt felt another chill. He had already received a preview of what a small, unruly crowd was capable of, and this was anything but small. "I wonder if the guards will be able to keep those bastards away from us," he whispered as he practiced his deep breathing, trying to relax.

Randy just shook his head. "I sure as hell hope so. But listen, I need to tell you about the tap code."

A guard poked Randy in the ribs with his gun barrel. "Silence."

Matt was desperate to hear about this code, but Randy was under the guard's watchful eye. "Later," he whispered as they were told to assemble.

Matt and Randy seemed to be the last pair in the first group. As best Matt could determine, there were 22 or 24 prisoners in front of them and a like number behind, but with a larger space between them. Matt's still partially numb right hand was manacled to Randy's left hand. Although his arms were starting to heal, he had little feeling in his hands, and was still unable to grasp anything with his fingers. While the swelling had gone down, his foot had never been treated, and it still hurt when he walked, forcing him to limp a little.

The march began. One guard was assigned to each two prisoners. They lined up on alternate sides. Matt yelled to Randy, "What is this tap code?"

Randy, his head turned to the right eying the mob, couldn't hear above the din, but the guard grabbed Matt's hair, pulling his head down, grunted and pointed toward the street with his trigger finger.

Two flatbed trucks drove alongside, providing protection, acting as a buffer between the men and the agitated horde. Two large spotlights were mounted on each truck, illuminating the prisoners and the street. Cameramen and television equipment filled the beds of the trucks. Everywhere he looked, Matt saw people taking pictures. Even ragged, shoeless peasants had cameras and were recording the spectacle. Matt started to feel a little more comfortable. Maybe this would turn out to be just another "staged" event like the others.

When the streets narrowed, Matt realized his complacency was premature. The trucks could no longer continue alongside the men. Instead they dropped in behind the second group, leaving him and Randy and those in front of them in near darkness. Without the trucks as a buffer, the frenzied crowd could get up close and personal. Too close and too personal. The shellacking intensified—sticks, rocks, bottles, whatever they could get their hands on. The guard on their right speared a woman's heavy purse with his bayonet just before it hit Randy. Periodically, Matt caught a glimpse of the political agitators working the crowd. He could see as well as hear the excitement of the crowd building.

Matt and Randy's position was particularly vulnerable. Rabble could dart into the gap between the groups and strike them before the guards could intervene. As more and more prisoners were injured, the disorderly crowd became bolder and more violent in its attack—like wild animals after wounded prey.

Just then, Matt took a sharp blow to the back of the head. His knees buckled. He could feel himself going down. "No!" he yelled, struggling, grasping with his free arm for something to grab on to. He willed his feet to keep moving. He could feel his adrenaline pump kick in. Randy, deflecting punches himself, somehow managed to hold him up until he regained his balance. They exchanged frantic glances, Randy's eyes showing the same panic Matt was feeling. Each recognized they could be torn apart by the crazed mob. All it took was one incident. No way those few guards could stop it. The mob was more riled up than even the Vietnamese could have anticipated. The guards, even in hard hats and with bayonets now fixed to their rifles, couldn't maintain control much longer.

The nightmare continued through ever-narrowing, dimly lit streets and an increasingly savage pack. Matt and Randy, like the prisoners in front of them, had lost their shoes and were struggling barefooted and bloody over the rough, rocky, streets.

Matt returned Randy's earlier favor, supporting him as he reeled from a vicious smash to the back of his head. They were leaning on each other almost constantly for support, knowing if one went down, they were both goners.

Matt didn't see who or what hit him, but he received a terrific whack above his left eye. He almost blacked out. Blood spurted from the wound, obscuring the sight in his left eye. Shaking his head vigorously to clear his vision, he concentrated on staying upright. He couldn't fall, he just couldn't. His adrenaline pump was working overtime. To say he felt panic would be an understatement. He and Randy would be the first to go, but it would also be the end of most of the guys behind them. There was no doubt they would be beaten to death if they went down. He staggered blindly, sagging against Randy who wrapped his right arm around Matt's waist, while Matt hung on desperately. They continued like two wrestlers locking horns for a couple of blocks, until Matt once again regained some of his equilibrium.

As the pandemonium continued, Matt could feel his legs trembling and growing weaker. He was becoming too exhausted to protect himself or fend off the pelting. He sensed the same in Randy and could see the sagging, stooped shoulders of those in front of them, and their feeble attempts to protect themselves. If this spectacle didn't end soon, they were all going to be killed. What might have started as a big propaganda ploy by the Vietnamese Army was totally out of control. The prisoners had been under this constant barrage of kicking, shoving, gouging and pounding for the better part of an hour, and they couldn't hang on much longer.

Frantically, the guards motioned for the prisoners to close ranks and turn off onto a side street. As they rounded the street corner, Matt saw large gates that appeared to be the entrance to a large, enclosed stadium. The crowd had surged into the street, forming a human barricade, almost impenetrable. Beleaguered guards formed a wedge around the weary prisoners to fight their way the last several yards. Fortunately, the mob was so tightly packed that none among them was able to land any serious roundhouse punches. Finally inside the stadium, Matt and Randy collapsed onto the cinder track and watched anxiously as the exhausted guards slammed the large gates shut against the crush of the onrushing crowd. The second group was not yet inside. They fearfully waited. Every few minutes the guards would open the gates just a little to allow another pair to enter. After at least fifteen minutes the last of the worn-out prisoners struggled inside.

Matt, astounded but bordering on elation that they were still alive, turned to Randy, "I wonder if we're allowed to go on these parades often?"

Randy snorted and shook his head in disbelief, "Are you shittin' me?"

"For a minute or two there, I thought we might be outnumbered."

Randy laughed again, then turned somber. "Listen up. You gotta learn the tap code. It's how we communicate through the walls, and I won't have much time." With one eye on the guards, Randy quickly instructed Matt how it worked. "This code employs the alphabet, minus K, in a five by five format: A through E on the first row; F through J on the second line, no K, L through P on the third line, and so forth. The first tap is the row, the second series of taps is the column. So your name, Matt, is: M—tap, tap, tap for third line, hesitate, then tap, tap for the second letter; A—tap, hesitate, tap for first line, first letter; T—tap, tap, tap, tap, hesitate, tap, tap, tap, tap. That's the fourth line, fourth letter. Since the second T isn't sounded, it's disregarded. Remember that, and practice whenever you get a chance."

Randy barely finished his briefing before they were unshackled and separated, and Matt was led out to a grassy area in the middle of the stadium away from most of the prisoners, where a medical attendant was treating some of the more injured.

For over an hour he sat by himself in the darkened arena remembering what Randy had said, visualizing the matrix in his mind, using his left palm as an imaginary blackboard. Occasionally, the raucous shouts and clamorous protests of the angry pack outside the gates intruded briefly on his concentration. He had to learn this new way to communicate with his fellow Americans. Then it dawned on him. This was why he had been touched earlier. Guys were trying to communicate with him. This was a godsend; he had to learn it quickly.

Finally, he was placed in a jeep with two other battered prisoners. "It's about time they got us some medical attention," one of them proclaimed indignantly.

But after a short ride, Matt found himself back in the dreaded Green Room of Hoa Lo Prison. Staring in revulsion at the blood-stained floor, he felt a sudden chill, his muscles tensed and he started shivering. He quickly pressed his hand over his mouth when he felt his stomach churning. He wasn't going to receive medical attention, he was going to be interrogated, perhaps tortured again.

As the minutes ticked on, the green, lumpy walls started closing in. He was suffocating. His stomach muscles cramped as if trying valiantly to disgorge their meager contents. Then, with a silence-shattering blast, the door flew open and the same pompous interrogator sauntered haughtily into the room. Matt jumped to military attention. Only his wide eyes betrayed his inner nervousness.

"You are going to meet some high-ranking officials of the Vietnamese People's Army tonight. If you wish to continue enjoying our lenient and humane treatment, it is well that you do what they say." Looking a little like he had been cornstarched in arrogance, the interrogator strutted out, cracking his baton across his open palm as before.

"Lenient and humane treatment, my ass." Matt's sudden anger had a calming affect on his anxiety.

The interrogator returned with three VPA officers. "Sit on the stool."

Matt climbed upon the familiar stool. The trio sat on the other side of the table, while the interrogator stood behind them. A guard brought a tray with three glasses of beer and a pack of cigarettes, and placed it on the desk in front of the officers. Matt stared longingly at the beer, swallowing the saliva that involuntarily formed, then looked above the glasses to the men across from him.

The senior VPA officer inspected Matt, lifting his eyebrows in aloof contempt or scorn. Matt couldn't blame him, he was probably a pretty grizzly sight. The filthy rag that had served as his blindfold was tied around his head, but it had not stanched the flow of blood from the not-insubstantial gash over his eye, and he could stick his tongue through the hole in his upper lip. But, understandable or not, it made him ill at ease to be the object of their attention, to be a specimen under their microscope.

"Do you now understand the determination of the Vietnamese people?" the senior officer asked in reasonably good English. For some reason he couldn't quite understand, it always surprised Matt when they could speak English.

"Yes, it looked like they were determined to kill us. I thought it was about the most outrageous display I have ever seen. I can't believe in our modern society a shameful thing like this could happen. It's the type of barbaric action you would expect from a backward, primitive people, not the Vietnamese." Matt's bravado belied his simmering tension.

The interrogator turned red, his neck muscles noticeably taut, his long pointed nose twitching like a rabbit testing the early morning air, but the VPA officer merely gave Matt a patronizing smile, "You must realize the determination of the Vietnamese people."

"Do you know anything about low-altitude combat tactics?" the older of the three asked.

"I've not heard that term," Matt lied. "I was a fighter pilot. Maybe it has to do with bombers."

The men conferred briefly, then the three VPA officers stood to leave. The senior officer paused in the doorway, turned to Matt and asked, "Do you like Vietnamese beer?"

"Sure, I like your beer."

"You may have it—and the cigarettes."

Matt didn't wait for a second invitation; he jumped off the stool and gulped down the liquid in each glass before anyone could take it away. Then he stuffed the cigarettes into the band of his pajamas. He didn't smoke, but it might come in handy for a buddy, and he had learned not to turn down anything usable that was offered.

The interrogator was incensed. "We want a statement from you. You know that your country is waging an aggressive, illegal war. You know that you have killed many innocent Vietnamese people. You must urge your government to get out of our country and let our people settle their own differences. You must write this, American criminal, or you will be severely treated." Then, as if he just noticed Matt's injuries, "When you have finished, we will provide treatment for your bruises."

Matt was annoyed that he would have to "perform again" in order to receive proper medical attention, but not surprised. This seemed to be standard operating procedure. He attempted to duplicate his previous "confession," grasping the pencil in his fist.

Repeatedly he wrote his condemnation of the war. Each time the interrogator "suggested" changes or corrections. Throughout the night, Matt wrote about the heroic Vietnamese people, about how the brave gunners stood up to the cannon fire and bombs. He tried embellishing his confession with blandishments; the Vietnamese liked that sort of thing. Sometime during the night, Matt became aware of someone in the next room, no doubt going through the same ordeal. Again, it was comforting just to know another American was near. They might both be shot at first light, but it would be easier to face with a countryman.

The sun had risen before the interrogator informed Matt that his statement had been accepted by the VPA high authority. Matt silently breathed a sigh of relief. At last he would receive some medical attention for his eye, which was still oozing blood after all this time. The guards brought breakfast—a bowl of rice and some watery soup. Although Matt had little appetite, he ate.

The interrogator returned. "Because your confession is not very legible, you must read it into a tape recorder."

Matt's heart sank. His "confession" would be heard on next week's Voice of Vietnam. Dejectedly, in a dull monotone, he repeated his written words, purposely mispronouncing several, and placing the accent on the wrong syllable in others.

A guard brought the afternoon meal, just like the previous: a bowl of rice and some watery soup, but still no medical attention. After more than 30 sleepless hours, Matt had to sleep. He lay down on the detestable floor encrusted with the body fluids of many a brave but broken man. It was dark again when he was awakened by a guard and led to a different section of the prison.

As soon as the guard left, the prisoner next door whispered hoarsely through the walls. "Do you know the tap code?"

Matt whispered back, "I just heard about it. I need to practice."

"Me too. I'll try to tap you a message."

Once they started tapping, they found there were other prisoners in the cellblock, and soon the cellblock sounded like a group of woodpeckers at a hickory-wood barbeque.

Within a couple of days, the area above Matt's eye scabbed over and quit bleeding and his blurred vision returned to normal even without medical attention. But, the punctured lip was taking a little longer; it presented such a natural attraction for his tongue.

On the afternoon of the third day at what the prisoners referred to as the Heartbreak Hotel section of the Hanoi Hilton, Matt was finally allowed to wash his face. Later that evening, after it turned dark, he was again blindfolded and loaded into the back of one of the jeep-like trucks. By peeking under his blindfold when they stopped, he knew he was back at his former camp.

A new camp commander and an interrogator Matt had not seen before met the truck. He braced himself for a new set of demands and the usual lecture on camp regulations.

To his surprise, the commander greeted him almost cordially. "I want you to tell me everything that happened to you on the march through Hanoi. Please also describe your injuries."

As Matt related his story, the camp commander made notes in his book. At the conclusion, he repeated the familiar question, "Now do you realize the determination of the Vietnamese people?"

Matt swallowed and bit his lips together, but said nothing. No need to piss this guy off just for the hell of it—at least not yet.

Observing Matt's blood-crusted, dirty clothing, the camp commander asked solicitously, "Would you like to wash your clothes?"

"Yes, I would."

"If you wish, you may bathe also."

"Thank you."

Matt waited for the customary guard to come to escort him to his cell. No one came.

Noting Matt's hesitancy, the camp commander motioned, "Go on to your room." This was highly irregular. For the first time, Matt walked alone through the camp grounds to his old cell. It was dark except for a few dimly lit lamps.

The door was open, but no one was around, so he rested his back against the outside wall, and savored a rare look at the heavens. The stars looked like glistening holes poking through a black blanket. The sight triggered the old familiar ache. Could Bobbie be looking at the same sky? The ship should be back in San Diego by now. How was she dealing with his absence?

Much too soon, the camp commander and a guard appeared at his door. "Bring your things and follow me."

Matt grabbed his clean underclothes and fresh pajamas and trailed along. They headed toward a different area than Matt had used before, a little shed with a shower nozzle at one end and a bare light bulb dangling from wires in the center of the room. The only way to turn on the light was to touch the two bare wires together. Cautiously, Matt started toward the bulb, but the commander stopped him and called the guard. Matt watched in disbelief as the guard, standing in a puddle of water, attempted to connect the two wires. Sparks flew, the guard jumped back, then as if embarrassed at his failure, tried again. To Matt's utter amazement, on the next attempt the guard pieced the two wires together without being electrocuted.

He bathed and washed his clothes as best he could, drying himself with his small square cloth that served as both washrag and towel, then stepped outside.

The camp commander was waiting. "You may go to your room now."

Feeling somewhat like a small boy sent to his room by the headmaster, Matt obeyed.

A few minutes later the commander appeared at the still-open door. "Do you have water?"

Matt looked around the cell. "No."

The commander ordered the guard to bring a pitcher and water, and then turning to Matt, he smiled and offered him a cigarette. Matt accepted it, thanking the commander as he did so.

Nodding his head to show his apparent satisfaction, the commander smiled at Matt and departed. The cell door clanged shut behind him.

Matt sat quietly on the slab, rejoicing in having survived what could easily have been a death march, his clean clothes, clean body and improving health, and marveling at the unusually humane treatment he had just received. With his new communication skills, life might be almost tolerable.

He warily rubbed his eyes and forehead as his thoughts returned to home, remembering their last 4th of July squadron family picnic at Miramar. Bobbie looked so radiant in her white shorts, her small body beautifully tanned. *Bobbie . . . Oh, honey . . . .*

CHAPTER 8

<u>San Diego, July 1966.</u>

Although Tom Finley and Matt shared a stateroom on the ship, they shared little else and never became close buddies, never close enough to go on liberty together, to share their personal thoughts or feelings. Tom didn't dislike Matt, in fact Matt was rather likeable in a square sort of way. He was a terrific roommate, the neatest and most considerate guy Tom had ever bunked with. He was just too straight-laced and proper, too much the over-achiever to suit Tom. The truth was, Tom just didn't think Matt was much fun. Matt was very much married, and acted that way, and Tom was a rabid party animal, and acted that way. They simply didn't share the same interests. But the Skipper asked him to return Matt's personal belongings to his wife.

As he cleaned out Matt's desk, Tom recalled that prophetic discussion with Matt the morning he was shot down. Tom had just finished his morning jog around the flight deck, and was lying on his bunk, engrossed in a paperback novel. He raised his eyes and mumbled a greeting when Matt returned from his morning maintenance meetings, then returned to his book while Matt went about his work quietly. Tom's attention was drawn to Matt when, in preparation for his flight, he removed his wedding band and class ring and placed them in a tray in the drawer of his desk, along with the papers he had neatly stacked there.

"You really believe that if a guy gets shot down, the Commies will cut off his fingers just to get his ring?" Tom had propped a pillow behind his head and was watching Matt's oft-repeated ritual.

"Well, that's what they say. S'pose it could be true, but that's not the main reason I don't wear mine when I'm flying. When I was a kid on the farm, I saw a lot of accidents caused by jewelry getting caught in machinery. One guy lost a finger in a tractor, and another guy lost his whole arm in a hay baler. Neither one would have happened if they hadn't gotten their rings caught. So I've always made it a practice to take them off when I'm working around moving equipment."

Tom rubbed his unshaven chin thoughtfully. "Yeah, I guess that would make you kind of careful. I'm a city boy, never really thought much about it until that briefing. Hadn't even considered the possibility of getting shot down. Have you?"

"Not really. I mean, I don't dwell on it, but I suppose it could happen. The Gooks' aim is improving."

"Whatta ya mean?"

"I was here last year on the Bonnie Dick and just a few pilots had been lost, both Navy and Air Force. This cruise the numbers are a lot greater. I think the last I heard was close to a hundred that they think are prisoners. That's in addition to the ones who've been killed."

"Do you believe those stories about torture?"

"Wouldn't surprise me. Otherwise why wouldn't they let the Red Cross into the camps? It's happened before. Look what the Germans and Japanese did in World War II."

"I can tell you one thing," Tom quipped, "If I get caught, the Gooks aren't going to have to torture me for information. They'll have to muzzle me to shut me up."

"You're full of shit, Finley." Matt laughed, closed the drawer and headed toward the ward room.

They got word later in the day that Matt and Lou West had been shot down.

Tom stroked the wedding band Matt had carefully stowed before that last mission, slipping it on. Matt had big fingers. He took it off, feeling suddenly self-conscious. He didn't particularly relish the idea of going to visit the grieving wife or widow, or whatever the hell she was, but he didn't see how he could gracefully say no. So, he loaded a box of Matt's stuff in his little sportscar and headed to Miramar.

After settling into his BOQ room, he picked up the phone. He might as well get this over with. While he had never met Mrs. Tillet, he would recognize her from the picture on Matt's desk, which he studied while he waited. Matt Tillet's wife was undoubtedly a very prim and proper Officer's Lady, a little too wholesome-looking to be his type, but certainly attractive.

A soft, young-sounding female voice answered the phone.

"Is Mrs. Tillet at home?"

"Just a minute, please. Mom, phone for you. It's a man."

A short pause, then he heard a female voice that sounded as smooth as sipping whiskey. "This is Bobbie Tillet."

"Hello, Mrs. Tillet. This is Tom Finley. I was your husband's roommate on the ship. This is a little awkward, but would it be convenient for me to drop off a few of his things today or tomorrow?"

A slight pause, then he heard an audible sigh. "Of course, Commander Finley. Roy told me you'd be calling. I'll be home both days, just pick a time that's convenient for you."

"Well, look, I have a few things with me in my locker here on the base, but most of it is still on the ship. How about I bring these things over now; then I'll go pick up the rest of his things and bring them another time." Maybe this wouldn't be so unpalatable after all. He had half expected to be greeted with tears or some other annoying display of emotion. But then, that might not come until she saw Matt's things.

"That would be fine. Do you have the address?"

"Yeah, I can find the place. See you in about an hour, Mrs. Tillet."

It was Thursday. Tom could get this all handled quickly and have his weekend free to do some serious skirt chasing. When the ship was in port, San Diego's beaches provided an excellent locale for his conditioning exercises, which he quite easily combined with girl watching. Admittedly, "watching" didn't exactly describe the extent of his activities.

Having checked the map before leaving Miramar, Tom drove directly to the Tillet home. It was about what he had expected from old Matt. A neat little ranch house in a neat little neighborhood with two cars in most driveways and a parcel of kids playing on the sidewalks and in the streets.

"Yep," he concluded cynically, "I didn't figure Matt wrong—Mr. Solid Citizen, USA. Borrrrring."

A petite blonde in a crisp white sundress that accentuated a lovely tan greeted him at the door. "Lieutenant Commander Finley, I presume?"

He nodded and smiled. "Call me Tom, please."

"Thank you. I'm Bobbie Tillet. Please come in."

Motioning toward the couch, she invited him to sit down. "It was kind of you to bring Matt's things."

"Oh, it's no trouble, Mrs. Tillet, or may I call you Bobbie?"

"Bobbie's fine. Well, thank you anyway, Tom. Perhaps it's a little early, but would you care for a drink or a beer, or I still have some coffee left?"

"I could go for a cold beer, if it's no trouble."

When she disappeared into the kitchen, Tom examined the living room. It was impeccably neat—everything where it was supposed to be. Shades of Matt, no doubt. What he could see of the house was furnished nicely, not expensively nor elaborately, but in good taste and it looked comfortable. Maybe Matt wasn't so dumb after all. This was certainly preferable to the BOQ, and Mrs. Tillet's picture, it turned out, did not do her justice.

She returned with his beer.

"Nice touch," he grinned as he lifted the tall iced mug.

For the first time she smiled. "Matt usually drinks beer, so I keep some glasses in the freezer."

As she sat down across from him, her white dress contrasted with her bronzed shoulders. Tom mentally noted her trim figure and large blue eyes. He had a special mental database for just such information. "You must spend a lot of time at the beach. You have a beautiful tan."

"Oh, thank you. Actually it comes from sitting in the backyard a lot while Hank plays. I don't have much else to do." She paused reflectively. "The children love to go to Pacific Beach or La Jolla, but without Matt around, I don't take them very often."

He heard the hint of sadness in her voice. Oh, what the hell. He could put his serious skirt chasing on hold for a while longer. He owed Matt that much. "How would you like to correct that tomorrow? Why don't I pick you and the children up around noon, and we'll go to the beach. All it'll cost you is a picnic lunch, and I'll even bring the hot dogs."

Bobbie hesitated. "That's very kind, but I'm afraid it would be a terrible imposition. I mean you must have things you want to do with your own family, just getting back and all."

"Listen, it wouldn't be any trouble. In fact, I'm looking forward to it. I'm one of those aberrations called a bachelor officer, and I didn't have anything special planned. A day at the beach would be fun."

"I hate to admit it, but I've neglected to include some 'fun' things in our activities. I tend to do that when Matt's gone on cruises, but, . . . I guess I can't count on him to . . . ." Her voice trailed off, then after a moment, she smiled again. "The kids would love it, if you're sure we're not intruding."

"It's settled then. I'll be here tomorrow around noon." Then, remembering his reason for coming, "I hope this won't be too upsetting, but I have some of Matt's things in the car. Would you like me to bring them in?"

Her smile faded and she quickly turned her head and stared blankly out the window. Then, drawing a deep breath, she nodded.

Tom returned with a couple of boxes. "Most of this is his personal papers and jewelry. His ring is in a little box on top."

"His ring?" She looked startled.

"Yes, I think it's his wedding ring. It was in his desk drawer."

She picked up the box, opened it, then quickly shut the lid, a frown on her face.

Tom understood her unasked question. "Oh, now don't you get the wrong idea about that ring." He then described their conversation just before Matt's fateful flight.

She stared at the little box for several moments, then closed her fist around it and looked up, the hint of a sad smile on her lips. "Yes, that sounds like Matt, all right. Thank you."

Tom felt a tug of sympathy for the grieving widow. Well, maybe not exactly a widow, but close enough. Tom considered himself, above all else, a realist. If Matt hadn't been killed in the crash, or the landing, the chances were damn good that the villagers had done him in. After all, the Americans had been bombing the hell out of that area regularly, and those people weren't likely to be friendly toward the American pilots who had been killing their families and friends. If, by some slight chance, Matt had become a prisoner of war, a prisoner of the North Vietnamese Army, then, in Tom's opinion, it would have been more merciful to have died in the crash. He was pretty confident that the intelligence reports were correct; that the North Vietnamese didn't play by the rules; that the American prisoners were being tortured, some even killed. But he didn't want to tell Bobbie any of this.

He patted her hand solicitously, took the box and placed it back on top of the papers and set them on the table. He could feel her eyes watching him, following the trail of her husband's ring. How was she going to make it alone? He didn't like thinking of what lay ahead for her, she looked so lost. He felt a sudden urge to comfort her. When he put his arms around her, she leaned against him, her head just reaching his chest.

Tom felt something inside stirring; he liked how she felt in his arms; liked in it a way he shouldn't. *Finley, you've been away too long.* Reluctantly he removed his arms. "I better go now, but I'll see you all tomorrow."

Bobbie stepped aside, but attempted another smile. "Thank you again."

At noon on Friday, Tom, showcasing his bronze-tanned athletic form in an open-neck shirt and shorts, called on Matt's family. Hank, as rambunctious as any four-year old eager for an outing, greeted Tom as if he were an old friend, then crawled into the small back seat of Tom's sportscar. Debbie, polite but reserved, inspected him carefully, and after a moment's hesitation climbed in beside Hank.

Hank spent most of the afternoon constructing, occasionally with Tom's assistance, a gigantic sand castle. It could have been completed sooner, but the waves kept coming in and tearing down parts of it, which Hank would immediately start to repair.

Sensing Debbie's coolness, Tom, spotting a volleyball game on the beach, set about to win her over.

"Hey, Deb, do you play volleyball?" He motioned toward the group.

"Yeah, a little."

"Wanna' join that game over there?"

Debbie hesitated, watching the game, then looking at Tom. "You know them?"

"Nah. But that's not a problem. I've been watching them, and they could use a couple good players. Come on."

Debbie hung back as Tom walked over to net. He spoke with a couple of the players, then motioned to Debbie. "Come *on*."

Debbie was a decent player, quite good at set-ups, and Tom spiked the ball for several points. Debbie's reserve melted like a forgotten ice cube in the hot afternoon sun as their side won handily.

You know how to wow 'em, boy, he thought smugly to himself. *You just have that way with women, even thirteen-year-olds.*

At the end of the volleyball game, Debbie encountered some of her school friends, and, after thanking Tom profusely for the fun afternoon, disappeared down the beach. Tom helped Hank reconstruct his castle for the umpteenth time, waded out into the ocean to wash off the sand, then returned to the grass mats where Bobbie was sitting, seemingly lost in thought. He intentionally shook water all over her, which got her attention, then sprawled out beside her.

They spent the next several hours getting acquainted. Tom found himself willingly sharing personal information and feelings, much of which he hadn't shared with anyone before. "My dad was career Navy. He encouraged me to follow in his footsteps. He also encouraged me to marry the Admiral's daughter when I was in college. He thought it would be a 'good connection,' since I hadn't gone to the Academy. I was too young to take on the responsibility of a wife, she was too immature, and more than a little spoiled and used to having her way, and we quickly decided not to let our folks dictate our lives, and mutually agreed to part company. We didn't even celebrate our first anniversary. Luckily, we didn't produce any offspring either. I've been pretty determined not to get married again, at least until I think it's right for me."

Tom listened intently as Bobbie talked about growing up in Oklahoma, her Mom and Dad, her job, her life before Matt. He found himself wishing he could have known her back then, before Matt.

What Tom had perceived a few days ago as an unpleasant chore was turning into something quite unexpectedly intriguing. Mrs. Tillet was a very easy lady to talk to, very warm, genuine and trusting.

"If I had my way, my husband would have a regular job, come home every night and never have to go away on these long cruises. But, I really don't have a right to complain. I could have married the bank officer I dated some before I met Matt. He would have given me that kind of security. Matt was in the Navy when I met him. I knew him well enough before we were married to suspect that he would make it a career." Bobbie seemed very relaxed talking about her very personal feelings. In some ways he felt like a trusted confidant, pleased that she felt comfortable to be so open with him.

"It's not only the long separations that I hate. When Matt's home, he does just about everything, from paying the bills to repairing anything and everything that breaks. My role, and I do it rather well, even if I say so myself, is to keep the house neat, prepare his meals, take care of his children and be there when he needs me in the bedroom."

At this point, she was being so direct that Tom felt a little like an intruder, but she continued, unabashed. "I'm not very military in my bearing, you may have noticed, and I'm not very good at filling in when Matt's gone. And, I'm really not that much of a social animal. I'd frankly like for just the two of us to go out to dinner and a movie. But Matt loves to go to the club and to all the squadron functions. For some unknown reason he wants me to go too. For the life of me I don't know why, because I never see him from the time we enter the front door until I pull him out of about the eighteenth re-hashing of that week's flight exercises. You pilots seem to eat, sleep and breath airplanes, don't you?"

She didn't seem to be complaining, just stating, brutally and honestly, how it seemed to her. Tom found himself wishing the afternoon wouldn't end so soon. Bobbie Tillet was having an unnerving effect on him.

Acutely aware of the inappropriate feelings that were creeping in, lurking in fact, since the first day he met her, Tom stood up, reached down and offered his hand "Let's go walk in the water."

Bobbie looked up and smiled, their eyes locked for a brief heartbeat, causing her to blink and quickly look down.

After brushing the sand off her suit, she rose to her knees and accepted his hand.

"I wonder if Hank has finished his castle," she commented as they approached her son.

Tom laughed. "Part of it is half way to Hawaii by now."

It was dark by the time they left the beach. Hank fell asleep in the back seat on the ride home, so Tom carried him inside and followed Bobbie down the hall to the last door on the right. He carefully laid the sleeping Hank on the bed after Bobbie turned down the covers.

"He should have a bath, but I hate to wake him. I'll just wash him and the sheets tomorrow."

When they returned to the living room, Debbie was waiting. "Tom, thank you very much for a lovely day. I really had a great time. I hope we can do it again." She approached Tom and slightly brushed her cheek against his. "If you'll excuse me, I'm going to bed now. I've got another big day planned tomorrow."

Tom wrapped his arm around her shoulder. "Glad you enjoyed it. We'll do it again real soon. And, hey, you ain't too shabby at volleyball."

Debbie giggled, blushed ever so slightly, kissed her mother, and disappeared down the hall.

Bobbie vanished into the kitchen. Returning to the living room, she handed him a beer, "I thought you could use one after a hot day at the beach. You look as bushed as I feel."

"Bobbie, I can't tell you how much fun it was today. I guess I never realized the pluses of being married and having a family. I used to pity Matt and some of the other 'really married' guys. Now I think I should have envied them."

She reddened. "Tom, that's a very nice thing to say. From what you've told me about yourself, it sounds like maybe you've just been looking in the wrong places for a nice girl. I'm sure you'll find her someday, and I know you'll make a wonderful husband."

Tom downed his beer, chuckled and shook his head. "I can't even believe I told you all that stuff about myself. You're sworn to secrecy, you know. I have an image to maintain." He winked and she smiled broadly.

Then, after an awkward pause, "I better be heading back to the base. I know you're tired. It was fun, and I hope we can do it again."

"Tom, I really do appreciate the attention you've shown my family, but I don't want to intrude on your personal life. I understand that it's not uncommon for squadron mates to help out the family in times of need, one of the *good* parts of the Navy, and this certainly qualifies, but you've been out to sea a long time. I know what that means." She reddened a little again.

"Bobbie, let me be the judge of what intrudes. I'm a pretty plainspoken guy. If I don't enjoy something, I'll say so. Spending the afternoon with you and the kids was fun. In fact, I can't think of anything that I have enjoyed more in a long time. So, forget the idea that I'm fulfilling some duty. You aren't an obligation. And, as far as the other thing, well, bar hopping and girl chasing aren't as important to me as you may think. Let me see what's happening during the next week, and I'll call you."

She cocked her head and raised her eyebrows, her eyes betraying her disbelief then shaking her head slightly, she smiled again. "Okay. Give us a call if you *really* want to."

****

When Tom first started dating after his divorce several years ago, he often ended up with nothing more than a goodnight kiss at the end of a costly evening. He didn't particularly mind spending money, didn't mind taking the girls to nice places—he preferred that himself. Nor was it that he particularly expected sex in repayment for every date. But at times he felt he was being played for a chump. Some girls seemed to consider it great sport to let a guy take them out for dinner—the more expensive the better—flirt and tease and give unspoken promises throughout the evening, and then right-eously protest that they didn't go to bed on the first date. After several costly dates and too many cold showers, Tom grew bolder and more up-front in his expectations. Now, he seldom wasted an evening on a girl who wasn't "cooperative." He enjoyed living up to the sailor's reputation—having a girl in every port, sometimes two or even three.

At first it had been a challenge to see how many different girls he could take to bed. Now, it was almost boring. The girls chased him, and he needed only to pick and choose.

He knew some of the guys in the squadron accused him of being rather crude in his approach. He accidentally overheard one young lieutenant's take on his dating technique. "Tom's approach goes something like this: 'Hi, I'm Tom Finley, jet pilot extraordinaire, wanna' screw?' If she's game, she's treated like a queen. If she says no, she is politely dropped while Tom ferrets out easier prey. You have to admit, even though he gets his face slapped a lot, he also scores a lot, and the chicks are always lookers. And he must be good in bed, because those who accept keep saying yes as long as he asks."

Tom dismissed these attacks as envy; the other guys hadn't fig-ured out how successful the direct approach could be. Besides, he didn't mislead anyone. He never promised a steady or continuing relationship. He was always quite clear, right at the onset, about his intentions to stay unencumbered. He wanted neither a steady girl-friend nor a wife. He wanted no responsibilities. Usually before the first evening was over, he would lay out, so to speak, the ground rules: no commitments, no promises, no nothing. He wanted a warm body for the night, and he was willing to show the girl a good time in exchange. No pressure. If the lady wasn't interested under those conditions, she could leave with no hard feelings.

The amazing part, in his opinion, was the number of girls who accepted him on those terms, and who continued to show interest even after he lost it.

His success with women was nevertheless a constant subject for the squadron, at parties or whenever the subject of women came up, an enigma that many tried to explain. Sometimes it was openly talked about in front of him, often as if he weren't the subject of the discussion.

At one squadron party last summer before the ship left, he happened to walk into the bar just in time to hear one of the older married officers giving a group of younger single officers assembled around a table in the back of the room his explanation. "Tom's a challenge to them. Each one thinks she will be the one to tame him. Underneath that crude but extremely good-looking, well-built, studly exterior, they see a soft, sweet lovable guy—once they change him—and they do think they can change him. Some women just never learn. That, and then you know what they say about a man in uniform."

Just then one of the officers spotted Tom, watching from a distance, an amused smile on his face. "Bogie, two o'clock." The group fell into an embarrassed silence.

"Hey, you shitheads," Tom laughed as he joined the subdued group. "You assholes act like you disapprove of my tactics, but I notice I'm never lonesome for company. And, don't tell me it's because you like me so damn much. You opportunists are there to pick up my crumbs. You have to tag along with the head tomcat in order to find a little pussy."

The group relaxed. Tom poured himself a glass of beer from their pitcher and lifted it in a salute. "Drink to Tom, you neutered cats, and come along and watch 'em purr."

He downed his beer while the group debated the subject near and dear to their hearts—women, and variations thereof. "You jackoffs just don't know that honesty is the best policy. My way is much fairer—laying, no pun intended, my cards on the table. I like variety, and I'm not bashful about admitting it. I may have missed some of the 'nicer' girls, but given the choice of being a gentleman or getting a piece of ass at the end of the evening, I know which I prefer, and you shitheads are baldfaced liars if you say you don't agree. Right now, I'm hungry."

With good-natured shouts of "asshole"—and other less endearing terms thrown in his direction, Tom topped off his beer from their pitcher, and moved off to the dining room to partake of the baron of beef and peel-your-own shrimp.

****

Now his smug shell had been cracked. *You dumb son of a bitch, get hold of yourself. You're not about to fall for a married woman, or widow, or whatever the hell she is, and with two kids yet. You can't afford those feelings. Besides, there are too many chicks out there for you to concentrate on one who comes with all the strings attached.*

Tom drove directly to the BOQ. He showered, changed and walked across the block to the "O" Club. It was late and the place was dead. All that remained were some senior officers and their ladies who had been attending a private party in the back of the club. Tom ordered one drink at the bar and listened to the third-rate band playing in one corner.

"Jesus," he complained to the bartender, "this is terrible. No wonder no one is here." It was too late to drive back down to the beach. The truth of the matter was he really wasn't in the mood for the glitzy, superficial atmosphere or the phony, insincere game-playing, so he walked back across the grassy area to his room. Loneliness was a new emotion for him.

By the next morning, Tom was sure he had reached the right decision. He was going to deliver Matt's stuff from the ship and forget about Bobbie Tillet. She would only be trouble. He just didn't need that. Besides, he probably was just feeling sorry for her. That's what it must have been. Life was going to be tough for her and those kids, but they weren't his problem. Shit happens.

After breakfast at the Club, Tom put on his uniform and drove to North Island, loaded Matt's steamer chest into his car and headed for the Tillet house. He wanted to get this over quickly, and get on with finding a cooperative chick. Certain of his muscles had not been exercised for entirely too long.

Tom walked up to the door and rang the bell. Debbie smiled radiantly. "Oh, Hi, Tom."

"Hi, Debbie, is your mother home?"

"Oh, yeah, she's out back with Hank. Would you like to come in?"

"No, thanks. I just wanted to drop off some of your dad's things."

Debbie expression turned to one of alarm. "Hey, I don't think Mom wants Hank to see that stuff. We haven't told him about Dad's . . . accident; he just thinks Dad, well . . . that he hasn't come home yet." Pointing toward the garage, Debbie continued, "Why don't we put them in the garage, and then Mom can sort it out and put it away when Hank's asleep."

Debbie opened the garage door. The young lady's composure and maturity were impressive.

Bobbie appeared at the front door. "I thought I heard the doorbell. What are you doing in the garage?"

Debbie and Tom stepped around from in front of the garage.

"Oh, hello, Tom. I didn't realize it was you. What are you doing here?" She was smiling as she approached them.

"Is Hank still in the back yard?" Debbie asked.

"Yes, why?"

"Well, Tom just brought over some of Dad's things, and I didn't think you'd want Hank to know, so we were going to put them in the garage."

Bobbie's smile disappeared. Spotting the chest in Tom's car, she stopped walking, then turned her head away, swallowing noticeably.

Tom felt a surge of pity and caring propelling him toward her, but he stood very still.

"I'm sorry," he said apologetically. "I should have called. I hope I haven't created a problem. I was on my way back to the base, so I thought I'd drop these things by. You said you would be home today."

She walked on down the sidewalk. "Oh, no, it's no problem"

She was standing so close now he could reach out and take her in his arms. Did his feelings show? He couldn't think what he should say next. The silence was broken only by the thunderous pounding of his heart.

"Mom, I was just heading over to Patty's. Okay if I go ahead?" Tom's chest heaved as he let out a sigh, welcoming Debbie's interruption.

Bobbie patted her daughter's arm. "Sure, honey. You have a good time. See you at supper."

"Sure thing. Nice to see you, Tom. And thanks again for the great time yesterday. I hope we can do it again."

Tom and Bobbie watched as she disappeared around the corner. Bobbie bit her lower lip and rubbed the back of one hand.

Tom shuffled his feet. "Look, I'm sorry. I know this is not very pleasant for you. I'm really not very good at this sort of thing."

Bobbie touched his arm. "Tom, I understand. Let's just put them there in the garage. I really don't want to deal with them now."

She cleared off a spot on the workbench, and Tom carried the chest from the car and set in down.

"Hank's out back. Would you like to come in and say hello?"

"Thank you, but . . . I . . . I think I'd better go."

She nodded and started walking with him toward his car. "Tom, thank you again for spending the day with us yesterday. I think it's the first time I've laughed since I learned Matt had been shot down. I'd like to echo Debbie's sentiment. I hope we can do it again, too."

Tom felt his jaw clinch. Then, with a muttered, "Sure, I'll call you . . . soon," he jumped in his car and sped away, not daring to look back.

****

Tom drove faster than usual as he headed back to the base. "Damn it." he hissed aloud. "Why does that woman affect me this way? What is it about her that gets under my skin? And why in the hell did I say I wanted to see them again?"

It was Saturday and most of the pilots were away for the week-end. Tom changed into his swim trunks, threw on a pair of shorts and a shirt and walked over to the "O" Club pool. It was almost empty. He swam lap after lap in the Olympic-size pool until he was physically exhausted. Then he lay down on a lounge chair and fell asleep.

Although his watch said it was almost eight o'clock, it was still light when he awoke. Finding none of the other bachelor officers at the Club or at the Q, he showered, changed into slacks and a sport shirt and headed to his favorite Shelter Island hangout.

Making his way to the bar, he ordered a scotch and water. "Make it a double," he added.

Slowly, his eyes adjusted to the dim light. On the stool to his left was, from what he could see from this angle, a sexy-looking blonde. *Hot damn!* She had her back to him and was busily engaged in conversation with a rather plain-looking brunette.

He leaned his right elbow on the bar, his cheekbone resting on his hand, and as the blonde turned slightly, he asked, "May I buy you ladies a drink?"

She turned to face him. Click. Like a camera, he captured the image. Her hair was bleached, but well done. She obviously used the services of a good stylist. Her low-cut, off-the-shoulder dress daringly revealed her ample bosom. Except for the big boobs, she was almost on the skinny side. Yep. She would do very nicely.

The blonde bent her head and lifted one eyebrow, "Well, thank you," she drawled in a put-on, sexy Southern accent.

Tom ordered, "Mac, another round here." Circling with his finger, he pointed to the girls and another for himself.

"I'm Tom," he spoke softly so she had to lean toward him. "And you're . . ." he ran a finger lightly down her bare arm.

She tilted her head down, looking at him from an oblique angle. "And I'm Denise." She lowered her eyelids and slowly ran her tongue over her upper lip.

The band started to play a slow song. Tom touched her ear with his tongue and whispered, "Dance?"

She slipped easily into his arms. On the dance floor her movements were very suggestive. He felt her pelvis swaying with exaggeration, pressing against his thigh. Her breast rubbed against his chest.

"Where do you live?" Tom murmured in her ear.

"Point Loma," she replied sweetly, adding, "I have my own apartment."

"Terrific. What about your girlfriend?"

"What about her?" she purred. "She has her own car."

"Well, then, how about getting rid of her, and you and I go to your apartment?" he suggested.

Her eyebrows arched upward in mock surprise. "Wow. You don't waste much time, do you?"

"Not when I see something I like, and I've seen something I like." He pulled her even closer. Their bodies, swaying to the rhythm of the music, were locked together.

She nestled her face in his neck and ran her tongue around his earlobe, inserting it in and out of his ear. "I hope you perform as well as you talk."

"Baby doll, I've been out to sea for seven months. You better believe I'll perform." He leaned back and surveyed her one more time. "You can count on it."

They floated off the dance floor back over to the bar stools where Denise consulted quietly with her friend.

"See ya later, Dennie," the brunette said as she left.

Tom wrapped his arm around Denise's waist, and the two of them glided over to a little table in a very dark corner.

Three strong drinks later, Tom was feeling no pain.

"Wanna dance, Bob—I mean Denise?"

"Sure, honey." She thankfully hadn't noticed his slip.

They stood up unsteadily, but Tom fell back down into the chair. "I think we ought to blow this joint, the room is starting to spin."

It was around midnight when they slithered out of the bar, giggling and leaning against one another for support. They collapsed into the front seat of Tom's car. Tom laughed at the possibility that he might have lost his keys, but after several minutes, he found them—right there in his pants pocket. But finding them didn't solve the problem. The damn ignition kept moving around. When he finally succeeded in starting the car, he unsteadily followed Denise's directions to her apartment.

"How about that," Tom exclaimed as he pulled into the parking lot. "We made it."

"Come on in," Denise invited. "I'm gonna change into somethin' more comfo . . . more com . . . fort-able."

Tom howled as Denise wormed her way down the hall. She was slurring her words; she sounded drunk. Then he quit laughing. *She better not conk out on me now.*

He fixed the two of them another drink from her small bar and sipped from his as he waited. All of a sudden he felt dizzy, his vision blurred, and he broke out in a cold sweat. Hurrying down the hall, he found the guest bathroom just in time. Drooping his head over the rim of the stool, he threw up.

Tom vaguely heard the concerned cries of his companion, but he just couldn't raise his head. The room was spinning, and if he tried to move, it kicked off another round of retching.

He could hear his hostess through the fog, "Tom, are you all right?"

Then the door opened slowly, nudging his limp prone body.

"Christ, what a mess. Look at my new fur rug." Denise didn't sound too pleased with him, but there wasn't a thing he could do about it at the moment. He hung his head over the rim and upchucked again.

"Yuck. Oh boy, Hot shot." she sneered disgustedly, "that was some performance." The last thing he heard was the slamming of the door. The last thing he muttered was "Damn you, Bobbie."

Dawn shining through the bathroom window woke Tom. He untangled himself from his totally ruined fur cocoon, and examined himself. His clothes were caked with vomit, his mouth tasted like someone had shit in it; in short, he and the room were a mess. Quietly, to avoid waking his understandably pissed-off hostess, he washed his face and hands, rinsed his mouth with a good dose of Listerine, cleaned the floor, dried it with paper towels, and threw the once fluffy, now matted rug into the kitchen trash. He scribbled a note apologizing for the damage, attached a hundred dollar bill to the note, laid it on the kitchen counter by the coffee pot and let himself out into the cool morning air and located his car parked at an odd angle in two parking spaces.

CHAPTER 9

<u>Zoo Camp, July 1966.</u>

Matt slowly adjusted to the prison routine. He discovered that Sunday was different from the other days. On Sunday they got two meals, and that was it. The rest of the week he was allowed out of his cell for about ten minutes to dump his crapper and wash his body and clothes. Going back into that solitary cell was the last thing he wanted to do, but, of course, he had no say in the matter.

Still restricted, both physically and by camp regulations, Matt continued re-running his version of This is Your Life. His soliloquy transported him back to a happier time.

After boot camp he had gone to Naval Air Station in Norman, Oklahoma, for an eight-week introductory aviation-rating prep school. He had finished high enough in the class to choose a field, and he had selected electronics. Continuing with his pattern from high school and boot camp, Matt divided his extra time between wrestling and football.

But life in Norman didn't turn out to be all electronics or sports. One Friday evening in late July, 1951, Mike and JoJo, a couple of his classmates, called out, "Hey, Matt, wanna share a cab downtown?"

"Where you heading?" Matt, at 19, was too young to get into the bars in Oklahoma, and Oklahoma, unlike Chicago, tended to enforce the law.

"To the USO."

"Sure."

As soon as they entered the huge high-ceilinged room, they spotted three girls standing against the far wall. "C'mon, lets catch those three before someone beats us to them," JoJo called over his shoulder, already zeroed in on his target.

Shy and embarrassed, Matt tagged along. This girl stuff was still pretty new to him. When the next dance started, Mike and JoJo grabbed two of the girls, leaving Matt and the third girl awkwardly staring at each other.

"Would you like to dance?" Matt asked hesitantly, "I'm afraid I'm not very good."

"I'd love to," she smiled and moved effortlessly into his half-extended arms.

Barbara Jean Simms fit the Nebraska farm boy's idea of the typical "Southern belle"—a graceful, soft-spoken beauty, fragile like porcelain. She had shoulder-length light brown hair, bright blue eyes that sparkled like stars, and a waist so tiny he was sure he could encircle it with one hand. She danced smoothly. In contrast, he felt clumsy and inept.

"You're a very good dancer. I'm sorry, but I seem to be spending more time on your feet than the floor."

She laughed. "Oh, you're exaggerating. You're doing fine."

After a couple of songs, Matt maneuvered her to the balcony. "Tell me about yourself. What do you do?"

"Well, I'm twenty. I work as a secretary at a bank downtown, and I still live at home with my parents and younger sister."

"Do you come here often?"

"Once in a while. I like to dance and it's a nice place to meet people."

During the rest of the evening, Bobbie managed to coax Matt back on the dance floor a few more times. He had never understood why people thought dancing was so much fun. But, as he held Bobbie close, lights started flickering. He liked the way her body felt in his arms, and he enjoyed the newly discovered sensation he was experiencing. Perhaps there was more to dancing than he had imagined.

All too quickly the evening was ending. If he didn't do something, he might never see her again. Overcoming his bashfulness, he blurted, "Could I see you again sometime? Maybe next Friday night, here?"

To his astonishment, she accepted. She even seemed pleased.

The following week Matt experienced something new; he couldn't get Bobbie off his mind. No girl had ever interfered with his concentration before. He eagerly anticipated Friday. It was an extremely slow week.

Matt arrived early; she wasn't there yet. Eight o'clock. The band started playing and the crowd swelled. Still she didn't show. She was late. Maybe she wasn't coming at all. He paced. Quarter after; half past. Exhaling heavily, he started toward the door. He had been stood up. It was probably just as well; he couldn't afford to spend another week like this past one; he had to pay more attention to his studies. Still . . . .

Then he saw her. She spotted him at the same time, waved, and headed his way, smiling. In her pale-yellow cotton sun dress, she was even prettier than he remembered.

"I'm sorry I'm late," she apologized as they met, "I had to finish a report for my boss."

They started to dance. What a difference a day, or in this case, a week, makes. In just seven days, Matt had acquired quite a taste for the slow, close dances. By the end of the evening, he knew what he wanted. "Would you like to go to a movie sometime next week?" Her affirmative response was quick and enthusiastic.

As they waited for the last bus back to the base, Bobbie issued her own invitation. "Matt, Dad's fixing hamburgers on the grill this Sunday. Would you like to come over?"

December, 1951 was decision time—the end of "A" School. Matt's wrestling coach had a suggestion. "Matt, I'd really like you to stay in Norman with the team. You have the grades to qualify, so you could go to instructor school here, then stay on to teach electronics, probably for a year or two. I also want to look into getting you an appointment to the Naval Academy. You know, Matt, they could really use someone with your ability and determination on the team. With proper coaching such as they have at the Academy, I think you could be an Olympic wrestler."

He thanked his coach. "I'm honored that you would even consider recommending me to the Academy. I'll think about instructor school."

Matt weighed his possibilities. He wasn't exactly sure he wanted to be an instructor, but if he stayed, he could continue on the football team and the wrestling squad, and it would mean another year or two years in Norman. He wanted that extra time with Bobbie. He wasn't ready to think about marriage yet—it was too big a step—but neither was he ready to go off somewhere and risk never seeing her again. In the end, his internal struggle was resolved in favor of instructor school.

In matters of the heart, Matt was a novice. His limited sexual experiences had not prepared him for what he felt for Bobbie. Before, they had all been one-night stands, easy pick-ups from the bars around boot camp and one here in Norman. In Chicago, on his first pass, he had learned the meaning of the term—"screwed and tattooed." He had gotten his first of both. But with Bobbie it was all different. He wanted her as he had never wanted anything in his life. At the same time he didn't want to hurt her. He had to protect her, even from himself if necessary. She was so innocent, so sweet, so warm and tender, but oh, so loving. Over time their petting grew more intense, more passionate. He took more liberties, touching previously forbidden areas. Each time, he went a little farther, she did not protest.

Only when he crushed his body so tightly against her that she could feel his sexual excitement through her skirt did she push him gently away, warning, "Matt, we shouldn't."

Once they came very close. Lying on the floor at her parents' home, locked in each other's arms, he was sure she wanted him as much as he wanted her. Her family was away for the day, they had lots of time and plenty of privacy. He raised her skirt, kissed her thigh, caressed her hips with his hands. Then he started pulling down her underpants. Above his wildly beating heart he could hear her rapid breathing. She hugged his head to her body and stroked his naked back with her fingers. Slowly he raised himself over her and kissed her lips. With one hand, he started to unzip his trousers.

She took his head between her hands, smothered his face with kisses, and whispered, "We can't do this here. I'm a virgin and we'll probably make a mess all over the carpet."

Matt went limp as quickly as a pin-pricked balloon and the drive that had almost united them cooled like a hot coal tossed out in the snow. Her revelation shocked him back to reality. *A virgin!* What had he almost done? Sitting up abruptly, he pulled her skirt down over her knees and helped her sit up.

"Bobbie, I'm so sorry. I wasn't thinking straight. I better get back to the base, I've got to prepare for tomorrow's class." He muttered "I'll call you," and darted out the door.

Over and over those next few weeks, he thought about what she had said. She must really love him to give herself for the first time. Did he love her equally? Physically, he wanted her more than any girl he'd ever known. The thought of marriage had flittered through his mind before, but he had dismissed it. Did he really love her, or was he merely consumed by this overpowering physical desire? Was he ready to make a lifetime commitment? He really didn't think so, so he'd have to keep a tight rein on his passion.

Shortly after he became an instructor, Matt was promoted to third class petty officer. With his raise, he could finally afford to buy his first car, a 1947 Ford. That night they celebrated by going to a drive-in movie. As they petted and kissed, ignoring the screen, Matt was ready to explode. The warmth of her body, the soft smooth skin under her sweater, left him electrified. He wanted to crawl into the back seat and show her what she was doing to him.

From that day in her house until this moment, Matt had consciously held his emotions in check. But now his desire was so strong; his body, controlled for so long, trembled, crying for relief. His mind hurdled past the arguments against what he wanted to do.

Gently he had laid her body across the front seat. The bottom half of her legs dangled over the edge. He pulled her skirt up around her waist. Slowly, deliberately, he lowered his taut, straining body to hers, supporting her head with one arm, while he explored her entire body with his free hand.

She offered no resistance, her big blue eyes meeting his as he kissed her. As if to assure him she was willing, she placed both her arms around his neck, and hugged him close. "Matt, it's okay, I love you," she whispered.

Matt, half sobbing, torn between his intense desire and his puritan sense of morality, buried his face in her neck and cried, "Oh, Bobbie, I love you, too."

Then, as tenderly as his pent up passion would permit, Matt took her offered love and her virginity. She was right, it made a mess in the front seat of that old Ford. Afterward, as he raised up to kiss her lips, he could feel the tears on her cheeks. The tension slowly drained from his body as they shared a lingering, probing kiss.

"Oh, Matt," she cried, "I do love you so much."

Matt's eyes were damp as he recalled that night. "And I love you too, darling," he whispered aloud.

Those words did not come easily to Matt. He couldn't remember using them very often after they were married, although she often told him of her love, and always when they made love.

Occasionally she would ask, "Do you love me?"

His reply was always the same, "Of course," but at times he could detect a change in her mood: more subdued, more reticent. Now, suddenly, he realized the reason: she had wanted him to say those three important little words.

They were married on June 1, 1952, a few months before his twentieth birthday. Bobbie was in the first few weeks of her pregnancy, but she hadn't started to show. It was a small family wedding in the base chapel with her parents and a few of his teammates and coaches in attendance.

They spent their weekend honeymoon at a hotel in Oklahoma City, then moved into a small furnished one-bedroom apartment close to the base. Bobbie continued to work at the bank; they needed the money.

In September, Matt's wrestling coach called Matt into his office. In his hand he held a brown manila envelope. He looked troubled.

"Matt," be began slowly, "you remember my telling you I was going to try to get you an appointment to the Academy so you could wrestle and play football on the Navy teams? Well, what I have here is a request for information on you so the Bureau can cut you a set of orders to Prep School. Now, I'll have to tell them that you're married, and you won't be able to go. Sorry, son." He handed the letter to Matt and laid the envelope on his desk.

Matt stood rigid, silent, his throat suddenly dry, a knot forming in the pit of his stomach, grinding his innards like pumice.

"I think you could have made it to the Olympics with your tenacity and ability and the proper coaching. Sure wish we'd have gotten this before you went and got yourself married."

Matt was still too stunned for words. Coach Lazaro had mentioned the Academy before, had said that he thought Matt could be a top collegiate wrestler, might even go to the Olympics. Coach had said he thought the Navy could use him, but Matt had never believed it was possible. Not that he doubted Coach's sincerity, he just didn't expect him to be able to pull it off. They didn't take dumb little farm boys like him at Annapolis. Yet he had just been told, provided he could pass the prep school course, he would have been sent to the Academy. Passing prep school would have been a piece of cake. Matt had been an honor student in high school and had finished near the top of all his schools in the Navy.

"Well, I'll be damned," he finally stammered, suddenly feeling nauseous. For him, going to the Naval Academy would have been the biggest thrill of his life. It was still difficult to believe it had even been possible. Yet Coach had made it happen, had believed in him more than he had believed in himself, and Matt had blown his greatest opportunity by getting married just three months too soon.

"Well, Coach, I don't know what to say," he swallowed, bent his head to avoid the coach's eyes, and swallowed again. "I really didn't think it would ever happen. I don't know how to thank you for going to bat for me like that, and I really feel bad about letting you down. Believe me, if I'd have known it was coming through, I'd never have gotten married, but I guess there's nothing to do about it now. I think it's probably better not to say anything about it to Bobbie. She'd feel real bad if she knew it was because we got married that I couldn't go to the Academy."

The Coach nodded his head in agreement, patted Matt on the shoulder and walked away, leaving Matt alone with his misery, caught in an undertow, pulled under by a maelstrom of conflicting emotions.

"Shit. Why couldn't you keep your damn pecker in your pants?"
Shit.

Matt said nothing to Bobbie, preferring to keep his loss to himself. There was nothing to be done about it now, anyway. Besides, getting married had been his idea, she hadn't forced him into it. Of course as soon as she told him she was pregnant, he hadn't considered any other alternative. It was better to forget the whole thing. The door to Annapolis was closed forever. He spent a lot of time over the next few weeks jogging and working out in the gym, pounding out the demons of wallowing self-pity and resentment still threatening to suck him down.

A couple of months later, Matt received word that he had passed his second-class petty officer test. He peevishly placated himself with the knowledge that he was advancing quite rapidly within the enlisted ranks, but the loss of the opportunity to go to the Academy to become an officer and wrestle in the Olympics left him with a galling sensation of inconsolable regret.

By the fifth month of her pregnancy, things weren't going so well for Bobbie. She had trouble keeping food down, she was weak much of the time, and she was spotting now and then. The doctors advised her to stay in bed as much as possible and to avoid strenuous activity. She had to quit her job at the bank, and the loss of the income put a crimp in their already tight budget—a crimp that wasn't sufficiently offset by Matt's promotion.

Shortly after he made second class, Matt received new orders - as a crewman in HU9, a helicopter rescue squadron at Ream Field, just south of San Diego. That evening he broke the news to Bobbie. "Just like the recruiter promised, we're about to travel and see the world." He tried to sound upbeat. It would be a good job, just not . . . the Naval Academy. He mentally shoved the thought into its bitter resting place.

"Oh, Matt, San Diego sounds so exciting, but it's so far away. I was hoping Mom could be around when the baby's born."

"Maybe she can come out. Talk to her. You better check with the doctor about traveling, too." He suddenly realized that she might not be able to go with him.

A few days later, Bobbie happily announced, "Mom says she'll come out as soon as the baby and I come home from the hospital."

"What did the doctors have to say about you making the trip?"

"Well, they're concerned about me riding all that way in an automobile at this stage of my pregnancy, particularly with the problems I've been having. But, I explained that we simply couldn't afford for me to go any other way, so they just warned me to take it as easy as possible. They said you need to stop every hundred miles or so, and that I should get out of the car and walk around for several minutes. I'll have to check in with the doctor in San Diego as soon as we get there."

Matt breathed a silent sigh of relief.

After a tearful farewell between Bobbie and her parents, they headed north to Nebraska where Bobbie met Matt's family for the first time.

As soon as they arrived in San Diego, Matt headed to the housing office. "I'm going to run in and see if they have anything; want to go in with me?"

"No, I'm going to walk around the parking lot for a little while."

He opened the door and helped her out. "Can I get you a Coke or something?"

"No, I just need to get the kinks out." She stretched and rolled her shoulders.

Bobbie was leaning against the open car door when he returned, grinning, dangling a key. "They had one furnished one-bedroom house in Navy housing in Chula Vista. It's ours for forty-eight bucks a month. Here's the key, let's go check it out."

Though assigned to the helicopter rescue squadron at Imperial Beach, Matt's reputation had preceded him, and he was invited to play football for the North Island Skyraiders. His executive officer, after some behind-the-scenes arm twisting, reluctantly agreed to allow time off for practice and games. Thus, Matt spent a lot of his time at Ream Field and North Island and little at home. As a result, he was only scarcely aware of Bobbie's problems with her pregnancy.

In early November, the Squadron XO called Matt to his office. "Petty Officer Tillet," he began rather formally, "it seems that your enlistment is going to terminate this month, on your twentieth birthday."

"But, I don't understand. I haven't been in four years yet."

"I know. You're under what's called the Kiddie Cruise Program, because you were under eighteen when you joined."

Then the XO's attitude changed. "We—I mean the Navy—hates to lose someone like you. You've had an outstanding record, and," he grinned, "I hear you're a damn good football player. I'd like to ask you to consider reenlisting. There's a pretty good bonus in it if you do."

"Thank you, Sir. I'll have to discuss this with my wife, but we have a baby due in a couple months or so. I don't think I have much choice. When do I have to let you know?"

"Let me know as soon as you can. I think you can go far if you decide to stay, but either way, I can handle all the paperwork."

Lying in bed that night, rubbing Bobbie's aching back, Matt outlined the problem. "Honey, I don't know how we could pay for the baby outside the Navy. I didn't know I'd have to make a decision until next summer, after I had four years."

"But, if you stay in, you'll have to go on a cruise soon. You might not even be here when the baby's born."

"I know, but what in the hell do you want me to do? I don't know what kind of job I could get on the outside, how much I could earn, or how long it would take to find a job. And we'd have to move out of Navy housing. We certainly couldn't find anything this cheap anywhere else." He also liked playing football. He'd already been told they wanted him to wrestle with the squad there after football season was over. If he didn't stay in, he'd have to drop out of football right in the middle of the season, and he'd miss wrestling completely.

Bobbie sighed in resignation. "I guess we really don't have much of a choice, do we?"

So Matt signed over. They bought a brand new '53 Ford with the bonus he received. It was a beautiful car, but a real gutless wonder.

A few days later, the electronics shop chief motioned to Matt, "Tillet, you have a phone call."

Dottie Young, their next door neighbor who was supposed to drive Bobbie to the hospital for her OB-GYN appointment that day, sounded very excited. "Matt, get over to Balboa right away. Bobbie started hemorrhaging and they're going to take the baby. Now."

"My wife's in the hospital," he yelled to his division officer as he rushed out the door. Demanding of his underpowered Ford all it would deliver, he raced to the Naval hospital, fearful of what he would find. The baby wasn't due for at least a couple of months, so something must be terribly wrong.

Matt alternately paced around the small fathers' waiting room or sat slumped over in the uncomfortable plastic covered chair, holding his head and rubbing his temples. He jumped up when a green-robed doctor appeared. "Petty Officer Tillet?"

"Yes, sir."

"Congratulations. You have a baby girl. We had to deliver her by C-section because your wife had some problems, but both seem to be doing fine now.

"The baby is pretty small, three-and a-half pounds. That's because she's about six to eight weeks premature, but I think she has a very good chance of surviving."

Surviving! Matt gulped. It really was more serious than he had thought.

"How about my wife? How is she?" The muscles in his neck were taut.

"We'll just have to see how things go. We were really lucky your wife wasn't very far from the hospital when this happened. She was losing a lot of blood. It could have been a real problem if someone hadn't gotten her here right away."

If his words were meant to be encouraging, they weren't doing the job. Matt let out a breath with a shudder.

Noting Matt's agitation, the doctor continued, "Look, everything is okay now. We've given your wife a transfusion. We'll have to watch her carefully for a few days, but barring any unforeseen complications, she should be fine. We'll want to keep her in the hospital for at least a week, and we'll want to keep the baby perhaps a little longer, depending on how fast she gains weight. If all goes well, you should have both of them home in no more than ten days."

"Can I see her now?" Matt asked timidly.

"As soon as they take her to her room. That should be in about an hour. But," he cautioned, "don't stay more than a few minutes today. She really needs the rest. I'll ask someone to let you know as soon as she's ready."

When the doctor left the room, Matt numbly sat down and dropped his head into his shaking hands. He had come very close to losing his wife, and that knowledge left him dazed and scared. "Oh, God," he pleaded quietly, "don't let anything happen to her."

It was after eight o'clock when the nurse told Matt that Bobbie was in her room and he could go up. "Just for a few minutes, please, she needs her rest," the nurse said, echoing the doctor's warning.

Bobbie's face looked like she had been dusted with talc. An intravenous line was hooked into one arm. Her head was turned away from the door. He bent over and lightly kissed her forehead.

"Oh, Matt," she murmured hoarsely, lifting her free hand, "we have a daughter. Have you seen her?"

"No, honey, not yet. They told me it would be better to wait until tomorrow. She needs a lot of care tonight. How do you feel?" He took her hand and held it.

"Okay, I guess, a little woozy." Her voice was thick and hesitant, her words slurred.

"Sugar, you need to get some sleep. Don't talk, just lie there quietly. I'll sit here 'til you go to sleep. Then I'll be back first thing in the morning when you're feeling better."

"Okay." She was struggling to keep her eyes open. As he started to turn away, she pressed his hand with hers, and in a barely audible voice, mumbled, "Matt, I love you."

He squeezed her hand tightly and smiled down at her, "I know, honey, and I love you too." *Sometimes you don't realize how much until you almost lose it.*

For the first few days following Debra Ann Tillet's birth, Bobbie struggled to regain her strength. She tried to nurse the baby, but it wasn't gaining weight as it should. After a few days, the doctors decided she would have to switch to a formula. Bobbie was allowed to go home in six days and Debbie followed three days later. Bobbie's mother arrived on the train the next day.

Bobbie thrived on motherhood. Daily she grew visibly stronger, but Matt was haunted by the picture of his wife lying so close to death on that hospital bed. He didn't want her ever risking her life that way again.

For the next thirteen months, Matt racked up the miles as he commuted between Imperial Beach and North Island. He completed the 1953 football season, and was about to start working out with the wrestling squad when his Executive Officer intervened.

"Look, Tillet, I know you're good, and I know the coach wants to keep you, but I think you have had enough time off for football and wrestling. There weren't any billets for right guard or wrestler second class the last time I checked. I can't approve any further time away from this squadron. We have to send a detachment out to the Tulsa in about four months, and you'll be one of the crewmen. We're going to get involved in some intensive training starting next week, and I just can't excuse you—even for a few hours. When a guy is out there in the drink waiting to be picked up—he isn't looking for a football jock. He needs a guy who knows how to get him into that helicopter. I'll inform the coach."

Matt started intensive rescue crew training the following week. But he never made it to the Tulsa. The Admiral at Litchfield Park, near Phoenix, Arizona, needed a second-class electronics technician immediately. Over the strenuous objections of his infuriated XO, Matt received orders to Phoenix. About the same time, he received notice that he had passed his first-class petty officer test.

"First class and he ain't even got a hash mark yet," one of the salty old chiefs complained enviously.

In the spring of 1954 Matt loaded Bobbie, a now healthy, hearty, bouncy Debbie and their meager possessions into the gutless wonder and headed to Phoenix. The dry, hot climate seemed to agree with both Debbie and Bobbie. They both tanned a golden brown and Bobbie regained that special sparkle in her eyes. She seemed to have completely forgotten her narrow escape. Matt had not, and he was constantly on guard for signs of renewed problems.

He was particularly determined she should not get pregnant again, "Bobbie, you must promise me you'll use your diaphragm."

Matt was at Litchfield only a short time when his department head called him into his office. "Matt, they're giving a test for members of the fleet in a few weeks, for Officer Candidate School. You're qualified, you ought to go for it."

Matt signed up, took the test and later went in for the oral interview. Everyone was very non-committal. The Navy would let him know in due time if he were selected. After several disappointing months, having heard nothing, thoughts of OCS were buried. Then, in the spring of 1955, out of the blue, he received a set of orders directing him to report within sixty days to Newport, Rhode Island.

"Well, it isn't the Academy, and I won't be playing football or wrestling, but at least I get a shot at becoming an officer." He'd had trouble putting that loss behind him, so this opportunity lifted a heavy weight.

It meant another move across country, but everything they owned still fit in the feckless Ford.

In September, just before he was to be commissioned, Matt read the notice posted on the bulletin board. The Navy needed pilots due to the losses incurred in the Korean War. The flight program would be open to any new OCS graduate who could qualify.

He rushed home to tell Bobbie. "Honey, I'd ten times rather fly airplanes than ride around on one of those tin buckets. I'm expecting orders to a destroyer, but I'm going to apply for flight school."

"If that's what you want, fine," Bobbie agreed.

Matt received his "Wings of Gold" in Pensacola, Florida, in the spring of 1957.

Photo school followed, also in Pensacola. Then came his first operational squadron and another move, this time to Oceana, Virginia, where they bought their first home.

Matt wistfully envisioned that cozy little place in Oceana as he looked around his current dingy quarters, the walls decorated with fly-speck artwork and the floor carpeted lavishly with droppings from the pet-sized rats who shared his humble abode.

While they were in Oceana, he made two Mediterranean deployments, the first with a Cougar detachment on the USS Roosevelt.

Between cruises he transitioned into the new F-8E Crusader, and made his second Med cruise with an F-8 detachment aboard the USS Intrepid. Matt was somewhat surprised that Bobbie made it through both cruises with no major mishaps. Somehow he hadn't thought she could get along very well without him. She knew how to keep the house nice and clean, but he had to do just about everything else.

He lay back on his slab and sighed. Those early cruises had been good training. No telling how long she'll have to handle things on her own now. It'll be even harder with two children. Matt's mouth tensed into a straight line as he thought of his family, then he relaxed and smiled, remembering how she had persuaded him to let her have the second baby. Actually, persuaded wasn't exactly what she'd done.

Several times when they were in Pensacola, she hinted it was time for another baby, but he had insisted it be put off until later. He needed to concentrate on his flying and his studying, and a baby would have been very disruptive.

Right after they arrived in Oceana, she started again. She wouldn't stop pestering him. One night, just as they were about to make love, she blurted out, "Honey, I want a baby."

His hard-on deflated like a tire gone flat. Lifting his body off her, he complained, "Dammit, Bobbie, why do you do this?"

She tried to pull him back down. "Honey, I'm sorry I mentioned it. Come on."

"Oh, shit, Bobbie, you know how I feel about this. If you didn't want to, just say you have a headache." He lay back down on the bed and turned his back to her.

"Honey." She rubbed his back, and tugged on his shoulder. "Come on, I want to."

"Go to sleep."

"Matt, please don't be angry with me." She sounded hurt.

"Go to sleep; I'm not in the mood any longer." He couldn't bring himself to relent; her nagging about a baby really pissed him off.

After that, she didn't bring the subject up again before his first deployment.

Between cruises, she became more insistent. "Matt, I don't want Debbie to be an only child. We certainly can afford a second baby now. Besides," she reminded him, "when you get back from this cruise, you'll be due shore duty, so you'll be around to enjoy a new baby."

"Honey, I'm concerned about your health. I haven't forgotten how sick you were before." He always fell back on that argument.

This time she was defiant. "Oh, dammit, that's a crock and you know it. You know perfectly well that I'm as healthy as a brood mare. Every doctor I've seen for the past four years has said I was healthy and there was no reason for me not to get pregnant again if that's what we wanted."

Matt was shocked. She never used strong language like that. He also knew that she was right, at least about the report. He had talked to a couple of the flight surgeons personally, but still he wasn't convinced. He couldn't rid himself of the memory of her lying so near death on that hospital gurney. Why? Was it just a manufactured excuse because he wasn't sure he wanted all the disorder a new baby would bring? Partly true, perhaps, but the thought of losing her terrified him, and that was for real.

He didn't think Bobbie would intentionally deceive him by not using birth control, but maybe it was better to try another approach. Instead of flatly objecting to having another baby, he bought a little time.

"Let's wait until after this next cruise, and we will see what orders I get. If I'm going to be on shore duty for awhile, maybe we can talk about it then." He purposely avoided making a firm commitment, but it was enough to satisfy her. He was relieved when she stopped harping about it, and he was sure now that she wouldn't try to trick him. He'd just have to figure out a new argument when the time came.

The time did come. After the second Med cruise, he was headed to Post Graduate School in Monterey. The Navy, in all its wisdom, decided that its line officers should have more than a high-school education. That meant about three years of shore duty.

Bobbie also knew what it meant, and she didn't waste any time. On his first night home, she greeted him with a bottle of chilled champagne. "To welcome you home, and to put you in the proper mood."

Matt gathered her in his arms, lifting her feet off the floor. "As if I need any help getting in the mood." His lips interrupted her next remark. It struck him as slightly odd that after a seven-month cruise she would even consider he needed any additional stimulation. Already his desires were making themselves noticeable.

Bobbie wriggled free and started tearing the wrapping off the bottle. "But this is a very special night, not just your first night home," she laughed. "It's even more important."

Matt caught the teasing twinkle in her eyes and took the bottle from her hands, carefully easing out the cork and pouring the bubbly liquid into the two glasses she had removed from the cupboard.

"Okay, I'll bite. What's more important than my first night home after a long, lonely cruise?"

Raising her glass high in a toast, she announced, "It's not every night a man has a chance to become a father." She started sipping her drink, watching him carefully over the rim of the glass.

Matt stopped, his hand in mid-air, stunned by her pronouncement, and genuinely annoyed that she would choose this very night to renew that old argument.

"Oh, Bobbie, dammit, not tonight. Don't start in on that. I told you we could talk about it when I got home, but can't it wait until we sort of get things squared away? There are several things to consider, lots of things to discuss, and I don't particularly want to spend my first night home talking. We just can't go rushing into a thing like this."

Bobbie was adamant. "Matt," she said sternly, her eyes blazing, "No more. I want another child, and I want it before Debbie is grown. And I doubt that you want me to shop for another father. Eight years difference is already too much, and it's hardly 'rushing.' We are going to California for probably three years while you're in school, so now is the time." She emphasized her last words with a finger stabbing into his chest.

Matt was surprised and taken aback by her fierceness and intensity. What had happened to her? Give the woman a little authority and look what she turns into. Could this be the same sweet, gentle, submissive Bobbie who always deferred to his wishes? In all their married life, she had never opposed him so vigorously.

She sat her half-empty glass on the cabinet, and said coolly, "Matt, you can do what you want, but if we make love, I will not be using anything to keep from getting pregnant—and neither will you," she added pointedly. She turned on her heel and walked out. He stared after her as she disappeared down the hall into the bedroom. Momentarily dazed, he contemplated the abrupt turn of events while sipping his champagne. Were his fears for her health justified? The doctors all agreed she should have no problems, and he had to admit she hadn't been ill a day since Debbie's birth. Was he just being selfish? Bobbie was a good mother, Debbie was certainly evidence of that. It was always Bobbie who was there to help her, to teach her, to solve her problems, and to give her encouragement. He had contributed very little, except to establish the rules of behavior and administer the discipline when needed. Bobbie had wanted another baby since Debbie was only a year old. It was pretty obvious she had made up her mind on this issue. He could continue to oppose her and spoil his homecoming or . . . . Slowly his objections melted away. If Bobbie was so determined that she would resort to blackmail on his first night home, maybe he really didn't have sufficient reason to say no. Besides, he wouldn't mind having a son. He could teach him to fish, to wrestle, to play football. Maybe he'd even become a pilot like his old man. She was right, they shouldn't wait any longer.

Refilling his glass and topping off Bobbie's, he carried them into the bedroom. Bobbie was sitting on the edge of the bed in her sexiest black lace nightgown. He caught a tantalizing whiff of his favorite perfume. She was pulling out all the stops he noted with amusement.

Matt placed the glasses on the night stand beside the bed, sat beside her and took her hands in both of his. They were cold. She looked up with apprehension.

He put one arm around her and slowly nudged her onto the bed, pushing his chest roughly against hers. When he kissed her, he could feel her body respond, her nipples tighten into small knots. Their tongues explored each other. Between kisses, she muttered his name softly under her breath.

He pulled away, raised himself to one elbow, and looked into her eyes. Shaking his head in mock admonition, he asked, "Well, mother-to-be, are you ready to get your program started?"

A look of astonishment crossed her face. Then wrapping both arms tightly around his neck, she was more bubbly than the effervescent champagne, "Oh, Matt. Oh, darling. Thank you. Thank you."

Henry Matthew Tillet was born, without incident, nine months later.

Matt licked his lips as he savored the memory of that night. He could almost taste the champagne, their sweat, her salty tears.

CHAPTER 10

August 1966, The Zoo, North Vietnam.

Matt was starting to get his health back. He could hold some things with his fingers and his eye was almost healed.

But after weeks of solitary confinement and torture, he would just about give his left testicle, figuratively speaking, to have another human being to live with. Solitary was the pits. Being in the company of other Americans during the march through Hanoi, even with all its danger, had really given him a lift. Being able to communicate with the tap code, however slow, helped some, but solitary was still solitary. Other prisoners were starting to receive cellmates. But as much as he wanted one, he dreaded the cost.

In early August he was summoned to the interrogation room.

"We are going to put you with another American criminal," the camp commander announced. Matt's spirits soared, but he maintained a noncommittal expression. He was quickly learning how to suppress his emotions, to deny the enemy any satisfaction.

"You must show good attitude. You will write a statement condemning the U.S. criminal action."

Damn. He should have known. His immediate reaction was that he wasn't going to write anything. But, after reviewing several "samples" written by other prisoners, and with the full realization that if the V really wanted the statement, he would eventually be forced to write it, he decided to comply. What the hell, it was nothing different than what he'd already written two or three times.

He tried to word it carefully, writing that he did "not agree" with the U.S. policy, but his "literary editor" changed that to "condemned." When at last his statement was completed to their satisfaction, Matt was returned to his cell. No one else was there. *Dammit. Why am I so gullible.* They'd done it again.

The next morning, the guard opened the cell door and made the familiar circular motion with both hands around one another, which Matt knew meant "roll up your bedroll and follow me."

"What now?" Matt asked aloud, though not expecting an answer. What type of "concrete acts," as the Vietnamese called the propaganda statements and other actions they coerced out of the prisoners, would they extract today? *Maybe I'll just tell them to go to hell.* If only he could.

As soon as he entered the Head Shed, he spotted another bedroll and blanket lying on the floor. Could it be? Were they really coming through with what they had promised?

A few minutes later, a tall, husky man with a casted broken leg hobbled into the room between two guards.

"Bring your things and follow me," ordered Dumb Dumb.

"Oh, damn," Matt swore under his breath, "not him again." Yet not even the reappearance of Matt's detested first block commander could dampen his euphoria at having, at long last, a cellmate.

As soon as they were left alone in their new cell, Matt violated camp regulations. "Matt Tillet, Lieutenant Commander, United States Navy." He offered his hand.

"Major Lee Wilson, U.S. Air Force." Lee shook Matt's hand.

"So what did you fly?" Matt asked quietly.

"F-101 Voodoo driver. I was shot down July sixth near the Chinese border while some of you guys were in Hanoi, frolicking about on your first day of liberty." Lee grinned. "Did you get to participate in that outing?"

Matt grinned. "Yeah, that was some liberty. Everybody loves a parade. Sorry you missed it." He wrinkled his forehead. "How did you hear about it way up there?"

"Well, they weren't exactly consulting with me, you know, but I figured it out. Those province leaders were saving me for a ticket out of there if things in Hanoi got out of hand. If any of you guys had been killed, they were quite apprehensive about what the U.S. would do. They thought I might be a good bargaining chip if the U.S. decided to take Vietnam apart. That, among other things, was why it took six days to get me to Hanoi."

"Six days. Wow. Why so long?"

Lee explained, "I was the subject of two condemnation rallies. You know, I bet a lot of our guys never made it to Hanoi because of those side shows. Some of those village people were out for blood—mine."

"I had a similar experience: stopped to socialize with some of the locals, they made me a movie star, just the usual sort of stuff, but they crammed it all into one day."

Matt motioned to Lee's cast. "Who set your leg?"

"Russian-trained Vietnamese woman doctor. She was assigned to Regiment headquarters, which I think is like the state capital for all these various little territories we'd been going through. She set my leg and put the cast on. Did it all by feel—no x-ray, no fancy equipment—no anesthesia."

"Ouch," Matt winced.

"Yeah, just her and a couple frail little women helpers. They pulled on the leg until she was satisfied it was back in place; then she cast it. Damn good job too, don't you think?" he asked, displaying the handiwork.

Matt examined the cast with greater interest. "Hell of a job. You're damn lucky it was taken care of before you reached Hanoi. Probably wouldn't have set it here, and probably would have damaged it more as a means of 'indoctrination.'"

"Thank God for small favors. I'll probably be able to walk upright, with both feet facing forward, thanks to that lady. Actually, I think she was a pretty good doctor, just primitive conditions."

A gong sounded.

"What's that?" Lee asked.

"That's our cue to sleep," Matt explained. "I'm anxious to hear more about your trip here, but we've got all day, all week—and then some. So let's take a nap. We get in lots of trouble if we disturb the guards during their quiet time."

When they awakened, Matt pressed for more information. "So did you stay there with the doctor for several days?"

Lee responded, "No. I was in and out of that area in a matter of hours. But they had to carry me on a litter to get out of the back areas. One really curious thing. You know I used to think of the Vietnamese as little guys. Well, there are some tribes out in the hills that are over six feet tall, and they can run like racehorses. Four of them lifted me up, each grabbed one end of a pole, and they lit off like they were running from a fire. Damnest thing. Smooth ride too; they'd get in a stride, and away they'd go."

"I'll be damned. Like you say, I thought they were all fairly short."

Lee continued, "Once we got out of the hills, down where there were some regular roads, I was turned over to the Vietnamese Army. During the trip to Hanoi, I was tied up with wire and forced to give information about my flight. I arrived in Hanoi at the big prison on the eleventh. I assume from looking at your arms that the welcome here is about the same for everyone. I'm ashamed to admit it, but after a couple of days, I spilled my guts."

"Don't feel like the masked man on the white stallion," Matt exclaimed.

Lee seemed not to have heard Matt's assurances. "I just arrived here at this camp this morning and I've already had to write some damn condemnation statement."

"Like I said, you aren't the Lone Ranger. For over a month, actually until I saw the other guys at the march, I was afraid I was the weakest sonofabitch in the United States Navy. I couldn't dig a hole deep enough to crawl into, I felt lower than a snake's belly."

"That's exactly how I felt." Lee seemed pleased. "So, how did the march change that?" he asked.

"Actually, I had a hunch before, when I was shown some of the 'confessions' the other men were supposed to have given 'voluntarily.' But I still didn't know if they had resisted longer than I had. But on the march I saw a bunch of gaunt, hollow-eyed emaciated men who looked a little like they were shell shocked. It was obvious every one of them had been on the same trip to hell and back that I had. You could see the scars from the rope treatment, I saw broken bones that hadn't been set, which is why I said you were lucky. But seeing the guys convinced me this is SOP. The V seem to have this need to break us. It really doesn't matter, at least not to me anymore, whether it took some guys one day and another guy two or three. We all have different scare levels. Some people can be scared with just yelling at them, and others you have to half kill them, but the V pushed everyone to their breaking point. "

Lee seemed puzzled. "Do they just beat the hell out of us so they can get some goddamn stupid statement that anyone listening to will know wasn't voluntary?"

"It sort of seems that way. So, two good things happened on that march: I had confirmation that I hadn't done something for which I might be court-martialled, and I learned the tap code. It made that near-death experience almost worthwhile."

"What can you tell me about these luxurious quarters?" Lee inquired, looking around the grungy cell.

"Well, I know a hell of a lot more than I did a month ago." Matt responded. "Using the tap code and talking through cups, I've gotten all sorts of information. The prison is named Cu Loc, but we call it 'The Zoo.' The reason for the name will become obvious after a few days. It's either in or at the edge of a large military complex. We've given each building a descriptive nickname. Since arriving here, I've lived in the 'Office' and just before you came, I was in the 'Barn.' This building is very aptly called 'Pig Sty,' and we are in, let's see, this would be Cell eight. Your quarters, sir, are what's known as a double, with a semi-private bath."

"Oh, I see, you mean two concrete slabs and one honey bucket." Lee interpreted, snickering.

"Oh, yes, but *very* elegant, you know—the latest in French decor." Matt pointed to the manacles.

Just then the guard shoved in the afternoon meal.

"And room service twice a day," Matt whispered.

After the guard removed the bowls, Lee continued his questioning. "What about the Vietnamese command structure? I haven't seen any insignia on any of them. How do we tell who's an officer and who's not? In those drab little green uniforms, they all look the same."

Matt explained what he and the other prisoners had managed to piece together. "At the top is the Camp Commander and his staff. Then there's a group of block or building commanders, like our prized leader, Dumb Dumb. By the way, he's nastier than a sack full of assholes. He's responsible for administering punishment or securing information. Each cellblock also has at least one gun-toting guard and one or more, depending on the number of cells, who carry no guns. These 'turnkeys' perform most of the work detail, supervise the peasant women who prepare the food, take us to and from our baths or interrogations, and supervise the dumping of the honey buckets and cleaning of the cells. You'll be able to figure out who's who fairly quickly. Just watch and you'll see who says 'Froggie' and who jumps."

"Ahh, sounds just like a normal military organization." Lee grinned.

Matt laughed quietly. "Uh huh. Shit runs downhill in this man's army, just like our own."

Then he knitted his brow. "By the way, is that an English accent I detect?"

"You can tell, huh?" Lee chuckled. "Yeah, I was raised in England. My mother, who's American, married an English horseman when I was five or six, and we moved there. He later had a bar, and we lived above it. I'll have to tell you sometime about living in London during the bombings. *Raaather* exciting."

"So how did you end up in the U. S. Air Force?" Matt asked, surprised.

"When I turned eighteen, I had to choose between the RAF or going back to the States." Lee paused thoughtfully. "For some reason—which at this moment appears to have been a bad choice—I decided to go back to the States and join the Air Force—and—here I am."

After a couple of days of almost non-stop talking during their waking hours, Matt suggested it was time to get down to business. "I need to teach you to communicate."

"Okay, I'm all ears." Lee sat down on the slab, sticking his casted leg off to one side.

"There are two or three ways, depending on the situation."

First Matt explained the tap code. "Now, that's the basis for a lot of communicating—tapping on walls, on pipes, on cups, on arms, but it can also serve for hand signals or using some object that can be seen, like a stick or a light. So it's important to get it down as quickly as possible. It's slow, because at first you have to spell out every word. There are some short cuts, but that'll come later. Just practice. I think I was tapping in my sleep those first few days." Matt grinned as he recalled his dedication to learning the code right after the march.

"Let me show you how it works. Go stand by the door and keep an ear out for the guard. If you hear him coming, get the hell back on your slab and poke me. If we get caught communicating, we get thrown in irons."

Matt stood over by the common wall with the other cell, and started tapping.

After several minutes, he told Lee, "I just tapped, 'What is your name?'"

They heard taps. Again, after several minutes, Matt translated, "He says, 'Hal Tracy, but call me Pop.'"

As he tapped, he interpreted for Lee. "What—your—shoot-down—date?".

Matt listened to the reply, then jerked away. "Hey, Lee, if I heard right, this guy says he was shot down in 1944."

"Oh, couldn't be. Ask him again. One of you needs more practice."

Matt repeated, "What your shootdown date?"

Again the reply came back, "1-9-4-4."

"Holy shit. That was twenty-two years ago." Lee calculated.

Matt tapped again, this time slower, "Did you say 1-9-4-4, twenty-two years ago?"

They could hear noises in the next cell, like laughter, then the message came back, "1944—first time, over Germany; 1965 the second. I'm a two-time loser."

Matt breathed a sigh of relief. "At least he hasn't been *here* for that long."

When they finished, Lee crawled back up on his slab. "It's a good thing we aren't in a hurry. That isn't exactly like talking on the telephone, is it. That little exercise has killed at least an hour."

Matt shrugged. "Got anything better to do?" Then he added, "We'll improve. Tomorrow, I'll show you another method."

The next morning Matt instructed Lee in "cup talk." "First I signal to get them to come near to the wall or maybe use the cup to say it, but it's more risky to use the cup than to tap. So, we only do it when we're pretty sure the guards are not in the building, or during their quiet time, when they're supposed to be sleeping. We have a standard signal, a loud thump, like rabbits do to warn of danger, that anyone who knows a guard is around is supposed to give, so we try to keep the guys in the cellblock aware that a guard is present."

"Hey, this is some system. Why wasn't I taught this?" Lee asked.

Matt shook his head, "Good question. Let's ask someone when we get home.

"Okay, here's how we use the cup. One of us stands guard at the door, the talker takes his tin cup here, you can wrap a piece of clothing around it, or just use your hands, cover as much of it as possible, put the bottom of it on the wall, put your face into the opening, and speak directly into the cup." Matt demonstrated with his hands.

Lee examined it carefully, and nodded as if he understood.

"Now, it's important in order to hear on the other side of the wall that the cups be aligned as close to opposite each other as possible, so when I tap on the wall or call them to the wall, we've decided that we'll come back from the front wall six feet, and since most of us are about the same height, we use about 5'10" high off the deck. Here, you try it."

Lee took the cup, surrounded it with his hands, placed the bottom against the wall and spoke, "Just testing."

"Okay, now to listen, turn it over, and put your ear to the bottom of it." Matt showed him now.

Lee listened, then turned to Matt, beaming "They said 'heard you loud and clear.' How about that? Sure is a lot faster than tapping out each letter."

"Yeah, but a lot more chance of being caught." Matt cautioned.

For the next several months, Matt and Lee's mental recollections gave way to recited stories. Lee described in precise detail his life as a boy in England during the war, watching the buzz bomb attacks on London, and being thrown through one of the walls of his stepdad's bar.

"I used to stand in the doorway of the bar when the sirens were sounding. You could hear those buzz bombs coming. As long as you could hear them, it was okay, when they quit making a noise, that's when they were coming down, and you took cover or went to the shelters."

Matt was curious. "So if you knew when and where they were going to fall, how did you get blown through the wall?"

"Damn clever Germans came out with a new version, radio controlled or something. They continued to make a noise, even when they were coming down. I was standing in the door watching the explosions off in the distance, and one went off in the park directly across the street. I was blown clean through the pub and out the back wall. I wasn't hurt badly, just some bruises and a few cuts from flying glass. But this old lady had been in the park walking her dog, and that bomb must have landed right were she was standing. There wasn't anything left."

"That must have been some experience. I don't remember that it was that rough back home. A couple of my relatives fought in the war, and one uncle was killed. I remember going to his service; another cousin got hurt, was always a little slow mentally after that. But except for the food rationing, it didn't affect us that directly. I guess people on the farm had it easier than town folks, since we raised most of our own food."

By mid-October Matt and Lee had established pretty good communication with the cell next door, which held four guys, including a severely injured Air Force Captain. Usually they were very careful. One of them would watch at the door for the guard while the other communicated. One day they got careless. They were so involved in sending and receiving the messages that neither one watched for the guard, who popped open the small door flap, catching them right in the act. That was a serious violation of camp regulations.

Dumb Dumb was furious. "You must confess."

"We were not communicating," Matt insisted.

"We were not communicating," Lee claimed.

The guys next door denied they were communicating.

"You lie," Dumb Dumb shrieked. "You must confess."

Each day, they and the other four men were ordered to the Head Shed to confess. They refused.

Matt and Lee discussed the situation in hushed tones.

"Dumb Dumb isn't going to wait much longer, " Matt predicted. "He's losing patience."

"So, what do we do?" Lee scowled.

"We continue to deny."

Finally, on the seventh day, Dumb Dumb turned up the heat. "You will stand with your hands in the air from the time you get up until you go to bed at night until you admit you were communicating," he announced. "Will you confess?"

The all repeated their denials.

Back in the cell, Matt whispered, "This isn't as bad as what I expected; we should be able to handle it, don't you think?"

"It's a hell of a lot better than being in irons," Lee agreed.

From six in the morning until about eight at night, except for time out to eat, bathe and dump their honey buckets, they stood nose and toes to the wall, hands in the air. Each day they were hauled, one at a time, to the Head Shed.

"Will you confess?" Dumb Dumb asked.

"No," each replied.

Back in the cell, Matt complained, "I never realized how tough it would be to just stand around with my hands in the air, but my arms feel like lead weights."

Lee concurred.

At the end of the second week, Dumb Dumb tightened the screws. "You will continue to stand with your hands in the air, *and* you are forbidden to bathe or shave or empty your honey buckets."

"'Oh, shit,' I think would be the proper expression," Matt said, trying to make light.

"I don't know about you, pal, but this is getting to me." Lee dropped his arms and slumped against the wall.

Matt also dropped his arms and shook his hands.

A guard peeked in, shrieked something unintelligible, motioning for them to lift their arms again.

Within a few days, they were exhausted and completely miserable. Lee sat down on the slab and rubbed his leg that had been cast. "It aches, and I itch like I've got poison ivy."

Matt wiped the sweat from his forehead, and scratched several places. "Don't ever tell me your shit don't stink, because now I know better," he grinned.

"Hey, asshole, I don't get all the credit for that repulsive odor. That's 'alf and 'alf, as they say in jolly ole England," Lee explained.

Finally, on the tenth day, one of the men in the other cell tapped a message to Lee and Matt. "Captain Watson can't hack it any longer. Can barely stand. We're going to confess. Think we can convince them it was just our two cells?"

Matt tapped back, "Roger. We agree. Say we were just checking on Watson's health."

Major Holmes, the senior officer in the other cell, composed a statement that admitted they'd been communicating, but just with Matt and Lee.

When Matt and Lee were called in before Dumb Dumb, they each agreed to write a joint statement of apology to the Camp commander.

Dumb Dumb wasn't through. "You will write an article on war crimes." He assigned each of them a specific topic, gave them writing materials, and sent them back to their cells. Matt rolled his eyes and snorted as he reviewed the handouts.

"This is absurd," Lee complained.

They tossed the materials in a corner, and lay down for some much needed rest.

By Christmas, Lee and Matt had whispered and quietly talked their way through several of their lifetime experiences. "You know, I probably know more about you than your wife does," Lee noted.

"Yeah, you're probably right. But then I've never been locked up with my wife for six months with nothing else to do but talk. And, come to think of it, if I were locked up with my wife, I wouldn't spend all my time talking anyway." Matt declared a bit wistfully.

Christmas was memorable only insofar as the meal was different. Dinner included a piece of turkey, a richer than normal soup, a cup of coffee and a first—a piece of candy.

Matt cleaned his plate. "That was actually pretty good," he remarked. "This is the first time in almost seven months that I have gotten enough to eat. Unfortunately, it's still served in this same stinking hole. I sure as hell hope we don't have to stick around for another year before we get another decent meal."

Lee interrupted, "I hope we don't have to stick around here for another year, period. Hopefully, we'll spend next Christmas at home."

Matt shook his head. "Lee, I don't think that'll happen, not unless our government changes the way they're waging this war. It isn't going to be over in a year."

"You're too damn pessimistic. I give it six months."

"You have a very optimistic outlook on life, my friend, for no good reason."

****

In May, 1967, in an attempt to disrupt the prisoners' increasingly well-organized communication effort, the Vietnamese relocated many of them. To their delight, Matt and Lee were not moved. They did, however receive a new cellmate—Lieutenant Commander John Billings—a tall, lanky recent shootdown.

Matt and Lee introduced themselves, including the usual information.

"Tell us about yourself, John," Lee invited.

"I was flying an A-4 off the Kitty Hawk, got bagged over by Haiphong."

"What squadrons you with before?" Matt asked.

"I was a test pilot at Patuxent River before joining VA-22 ," John replied.

"Test pilot. Um. . . ." Lee raised his eyebrows. "I'm impressed."

"Family?" Matt inquired.

"Yeah, two sons, eight and six, and a daughter, age four. Married ten years, met my wife when I was at the Academy. She's a nurse. You guys?"

Matt described his family. "Lee's got an interesting story. He was with the U.S. forces stationed in Germany at the end of World War II and met his wife there. She couldn't speak English and he couldn't speak German, so they had to take her sister on their dates, so she could translate." He laughed. "Can you imagine having a wife that can't talk back?"

Lee grinned. "That didn't last long."

During the next several days, while John recovered from his recent initiation at Hoa Lo, Matt and Lee took turns briefing him on the camp routine.

Matt explained, "Each morning about 0530, while it's still dark, we are awakened by the sound of someone pounding on a trash-can lid. That's the Vietnamese version of an alarm clock. We are expected to get up, fold our blankets and mosquito nets, and then sit quietly for the rest of the day on our bunks. It's kind of like when you're in the hospital and they wake you up to give you a sleeping pill. We have to talk like this, in a whisper, even in the same room, because noise is forbidden. As little as the clanging of a fork against a plate irritates the guards.

"And, speaking of forks, we receive two identical meals a day. The first is served between 1000 and 1100 hours. The afternoon meal, a duplicate of breakfast, is brought in between 1600 and 1700 hours. We're still trying to figure out what kind of soup they serve us, but my best guess is it is boiled sweaty-socks, a delicacy in this part of the world, I believe. I'm pretty sure I've seen them preparing the fixings in the laundry room."

Lee laughed, and picked up the indoctrination. "Most of the guards nap during quiet time, from 1200-1400 hours. You'll find it's almost impossible to sleep more than four or five hours at a time on these hard slabs, so we often sleep during this time as well."

"There's two slabs and three people." John cut in. "So what are the sleeping arrangements?"

Matt pointed. "See that door leaning against the back wall? Just before they threw you in here, they threw that in here first. My best guess is that is your bed. We'll lay it on the floor when we all want to try to sleep. We'll take turns on the slabs at other times."

"I'm going to sleep on a door on the floor?" John wrinkled his nose.

"Well, actually, it's probably softer than our concrete slabs," Matt suggested.

Lee chirped in, "Yeah, our slabs are just like the floor, just fifteen inches higher, and maybe not *quite* as dirty."

John examined the door slab and shrugged. Lee continued with the indoctrination. "The Vietnamese encourage us to sleep when they do, because they always suspect we're up to no good if we're up and about."

Matt laughed. "I'd say that's one of the few things they get right."

Matt continued. "Every day, except Sunday, or unless it's denied as punishment, you'll be allowed about ten minutes to bathe and dump your honey bucket. We've never seen two prisoners out at the same time.

"Exercise is not permitted, but we've been caught before. The guard just orders us to stop. When he leaves, we do whatever we were doing before, just quieter."

"You may be doing nothing more than walking around inside this damn, cramped cell," Lee interjected, "but if the guard sees you, he motions for you to sit down. It's really easy, because of the silence and nonactivity, to become lethargic. That is, for some guys, but not Lieutenant Commander Tillet. This guy makes you tired just watching him. Ever since his arms healed, he does so many push-ups and sit-ups that I lose count. I'm talking hundreds, maybe a thousand or more, in a day."

John interrupted again, "It all sounds fairly boring. Isn't there anything else? What do you do with all your time?"

Matt and Lee looked at each other and shook their heads.

Matt rested his head on his hands, both elbows grinding into his thighs. He rubbed his eyes, his forehead, and scratched his head, then snorted. "Sounds boring? Shit, John, it *is* boring, boring as hell. What in the hell did you expect? You simply cannot imagine how boring it is to have absolutely nothing to do for twenty-four hours a day, seven days a week, week after week confined in these four ever-shrinking walls. I thought I'd lose my mind before Lee moved in."

John squirmed a little. "Hey, take it easy. I'm just asking. I've never been a prisoner of war before."

Matt stood up and paced the back wall. "Yeah, neither had we," he countered edgily. Then, relaxing some, he added, "I've discovered some things to do, though. Whenever possible, I use the Camp's 'library' to read the English version of the Vietnam Courier. Each issue usually contains a picture of an American pilot that has been captured. I have committed the names to memory. If I ever get out of here, I want to be able to identify every man who had been in the prison system. I'm afraid a lot are going to turn up missing."

"Boredom, however, is preferable to the alternative—torture," Lee added. "Every day, through the communication network, we learn of some prisoners still being tortured. We've received reports of men being kicked; others beaten on the head and face with a piece of garden hose; and some have been slapped so hard they've had their eardrums broken. In one instance, the V is reported to have used electricity as a punishment technique."

Matt stood up and stretched to ease out some of the kinks. "I have seen the guards touching bare wires to little animals just to watch their reaction, so I wouldn't be a bit surprised if those reports are true. Another favorite form of persuasion is to aggravate a man's existing injuries. You're lucky you weren't hurt getting out of your airplane, or by the villagers. If a new prisoner arrives with serious injuries, the V can inflict a great deal of pain by twisting his already injured arms or legs, or hanging him by his broken arms. Several guys are probably permanently crippled or deformed because of this. And the sad fact is most of the injuries would easily have mended or at least could have been treated satisfactorily."

"So what does one have to do around here to avoid being tortured?" John asked.

Lee answered, "Well, you've already gone through the worst treatment, at least that we've seen so far. Everyone goes through the initial 'Green Room' indoctrination at Hoa Lo."

"Yeah," John interrupted, "that's the first time I've ever been eyeball to eyeball with my asshole."

Matt and Lee nodded in agreement.

Lee continued, "Later, as a general rule, when you get the dreaded summons to the interrogation room, it can be for anything from explaining some obscure camp regulation or requiring some written propaganda statement to inflicting punishment. Unless you just refuse to do what you're told or you get caught communicating, the use of force usually depends upon how quickly and how badly the V, that's our tap code designation for the Vietnamese camp officials, want some specific information. Generally, they just resort to petty harassment. They don't let us have any light in the room, or we're not allowed to bathe, or we can't dump our honey buckets, or—our own personal favorite—you have to hold your hands in the air from the time you get up until you go to bed. Matt and I have already gone through that. I can tell you, it gets pretty damn uncomfortable."

"Ssh! Guard coming." Matt warned. He heard the door to the next cell opening.

Matt and Lee were sitting on one slab and John was lying on the other when the guard opened the door and pushed three bowls of soup with a roll on top, and three cups of water through the open door.

John looked at his bowl, stuck one finger in the soup, tested it and wrinkled his nose. "This is it, huh?" He moved his tongue around as if taste-testing a fine wine. "Yep, Matt, I think you're right, Sweaty Sock Soup it is."

"Bon appetit, my friend." Lee said as he raised his cup of water in one hand and gnawed a piece off the roll he held in the other.

Later they resumed their camp discussion.

"You guys said you got some punishment—holding your hands in the air. What did you do to earn that?" John asked.

They repeated the story of how they were caught communicating. "The Gooks like joint statements better than just from one or two men, you know, so we figured when all six of us agreed to confess that would make them ecstatic." Matt laughed; it was kind of humorous now, but it hadn't been very funny when it happened.

"What did you have to write?" John asked.

"Dumb Dumb wanted us to write some damn article on war crimes, and gave us a sample of the Vietnam Black Book on War Crimes, published in the DRV, describing every war crime that had ever been committed by anyone throughout history. As far as the Vietnamese were concerned, we American aggressors have committed them all," Lee responded.

"As I recall, my subject was napalm bombing," Matt interjected. "I was to describe how Americans bombed innocent Vietnamese with napalm. Lee, do you remember your topic?"

"No."

"So . . . . What the hell happened?" John asked, frowning with impatience.

"Both of us could barely sit up, so, since Dumb Dumb hadn't given us a deadline, we weren't in any hurry. About a week later he asked if we had our reports ready, and we said they weren't finished yet." Lee paused, then grinned, "In fact, they weren't started yet, but he didn't bother to check."

"Then, three or four days after that, the gun-toting guards came into the room on a routine inspection, found the pen and paper and book on war crimes, and confiscated them, since prisoners aren't permitted writing material. We figured we had a pretty good excuse if Dumb Dumb asked, but, he must have forgotten, because nothing more was ever said."

Matt added. "I've said it before, but at times the goal seems to be just what my first interrogator told me: to make us live like animals. But Lee's right, usually it's just degrading or humiliating or a pain in the ass. We've decided that the only good attitude is a bad attitude by Vietnamese standards. If a prisoner agrees to do what is asked, without resistance, the V asks more and more. But, if he refuses, if he forces them to torture him to get compliance, often times the V either don't need the propaganda badly enough, or they figure they can get it easier from someone else. The senior officer's instructions are to resist."

"But," Lee pointed out, "if they want something badly enough, and if you continue to refuse, out comes the goon squad and the straps. The old comic line about 'we have ways to make you talk' is not funny here, and don't forget it."

"What's the big deal about communicating?" John inquired, raising his eyebrows.

"The Vietnamese are paranoid about our communicating with other prisoners," Lee explained. "The penalty if we're caught is to be thrown in irons from one to two weeks, or until you apologize to the camp commander for breaking camp regulations. But we have to take the risk. It's very important to establish contact and give encouragement to the new arrivals, and to teach them the tap code. No one, to our knowledge, has escaped that initial Green Room torture and humiliation.

"Sometimes a new man will be reluctant to communicate. The person on the other side of the wall could be a Vietnamese guard trying to trap you. So, we've developed special call-up codes to reduce that danger. The standard call-up is to tap 'shave and a hair cut,' followed by some special brushing sound, or an additional letter, something unique to identify the persons in the next room that you communicate with regularly."

Matt expressed his frustration. "You'd have thought we would have been taught some method of communication in survival training, a code or some system that we'd already know how to use."

John agreed, "Yeah, you'd have thought so. When we get out, we'll have to bring that to someone's attention."

Matt's skepticism surfaced again, "You mean—*if* we get out."

"Come on. Cut that out. Six months, remember, six months."

"You said that six months ago." Matt countered. "You know, I read an article on the ship a week or so before I was shot down about a guy that had just been released from a Chinese prison, an American or a Brit, I don't recall. He had been there over twenty years."

John moaned, "Oh, shit. I don't even want to hear it. Tell me about this communication system."

Matt explained, "As our communication system has improved, with the help of the tap code, so has our military organization. We've established which officers are senior, from the senior officer in camp right on down. Each cellblock has a senior officer, and each cell has a senior officer. Messages, directives and questions of policy are passed up and down this chain of command. What's your date of rank?"

"Why?"

Lee explained, "Since the Air Force carried out the initial strikes—as usual—there are more Air Force officers here than you Johnny-come-lately Navy pukes, and particularly since the more senior officers are Air Force, our designation—Senior Ranking Officer, SRO—has been selected. So, what's your date of rank?"

"Um, let's see." John scratched his head in thought, "I guess it was July 1966."

"Well, that means Matt is still the SRO in this room," Lee noted.

"Oh, damn. I guess I'll never get my own squadron," John complained.

"Hey, buddy, let me tell you, here you get none of the benefits of command, but all of the burdens." Matt shot back. "The Vietnamese refuse to acknowledge our military structure. Remember, we're war criminals, not prisoners of war. So they pointedly refuse to deal with the senior officer in any chain of command situation. But . . . if someone breaks camp regulations and is subjected to punishment, the SRO of that group nearly always receives additional punishment, just for good measure. He may not have had anything to do with the disobedience. So, watch what you do. I don't want to take any crap for your screw-up."

"I'll try not to get caught," John quipped, a devilish grin on his face.

CHAPTER 11

San Diego, Summer 1967.

Bobbie had put off telling Hank as long as she could. It had been a year since Matt was shot down, and there had been no encouraging word; in fact there hadn't been any word at all from Matt. Even the Navy was conspicuously silent since they had shown her the photo of him taken on the Hanoi march, confirming he was a POW. There was no hiding the truth any longer; Matt wasn't going to be released soon. It was going to be a long war. In February another friend, Craig Hansen, a neighbor of the Roberts, had been shot down, and his wife Janice still didn't know if he were dead or alive.

Hank was becoming more aware that something was wrong. He would find out sooner or later, and it would be better if it came from her.

So when he asked, "Mommie, when is Daddy coming home?" she decided the time had come.

Kneeling down beside her little son and trying hard to maintain her composure, she confessed, "Honey, I don't know when Daddy is coming home. Some very bad people are keeping him over in Vietnam and won't let him come back to us the way he wants to. I didn't want to tell you until we knew when he was coming back, because I didn't want you to be sad."

His demeanor immediately changed. Almost in slow motion, his face went through a tortured contortion, his lips tightly compressed in a downward frown. He started sniffling and his eyes quickly filled with tears. "I want my Daddy," he whimpered, his face distorted in grief.

She put her arms around him. "I know, sweetheart. I know." He broke into loud sobs. "Honey, don't cry . . . we'll . . . ."

He broke free and ran into his room, throwing himself on the bed, and burying his head in his pillow.

She sat on the bed and rubbed his back until his convulsive sobs subsided.

"Sweetheart, everything's going to be okay." She tried to give him a hug, but he pulled away.

"No," he screeched. "I want my Daddy."

Before she could stop him, he ran out of the room and out the front door, letting the screen door slam. Bobbie sat on his bed, biting her lips and shaking her head.

By the end of June, they were back from their trip to Oklahoma and Nebraska. She always hated to leave her parents, but visiting Matt's folks was a trying experience. The still had outdoor toilets. She was glad to be home. Debbie was already dressed when she came into the kitchen. "Mom, okay if I go to the beach with Patty and some of the guys?"

"Sure, honey, have fun. Please be home before dark."

Hank was also ready to go. Bobbie stopped him as he passed the kitchen, headed for the front door.

"Honey. I have to go to the Commissary. I can't leave you alone. Come with me, then you can go play when we get back."

"No!" he shrieked, "I don't want to go to the store. I want to go play with my friends."

"Hank," she pleaded, but before she could say more, he yelled, "I don't want to go with you, and you can't make me!" He stomped his foot and crossed his arms.

Bobbie covered her face with her hands and turned away. *Damn. There he goes again.* She clenched her fists, and considered the situation silently. *Why does he have to be so rebellious and so disrespectful? He is turning into a real hellion when he doesn't get his way.* What was she to do? She couldn't keep him locked in the house, and if she forced him to go to the base he'd make a scene, embarrassing her.

As she had done so often recently when he threw a tantrum, Bobbie shrugged and gave in. "All right, but only if it's okay with Alan's mother." With some misgivings, she took Hank across the street.

Mrs. Posten was delighted to see Hank. "I'll be here all day. Take all the time you need. It'll be a relief to have him here. Alan almost drove me crazy while you were gone."

Bobbie, leaving a now happy Hank already busily engaged in play, was relieved that a crisis had been averted, but disturbed by his obstinate behavior. He was only five and already she seemed to have lost control. Why wouldn't he mind her? He wouldn't get away with this kind of behavior if Matt were here. But if Matt were here, he probably wouldn't be acting up so much. Her anger resurfaced. *Damn it!* He shouldn't have put them in this position.

She moved mechanically through her chores, while her mind actively analyzed the current situation. As she thought critically about her marriage, for perhaps the first time, she realized some things about Matt really troubled her. She'd just never let it come to the surface before. He wasn't very supportive of her emotional needs, and she was often hurt by his insensitivity. She wished he were more romantic, warmer, more affectionate and demonstrative. She would like to be the very center of her man's world, but she was acutely aware that she had never been the center of Matt's.

Even before he became a pilot, there had been other things that stole his time. First it had been sports. When football season was over, there was wrestling. She didn't even like to watch sports! His choice of activities were things that excluded her, yet he refused to learn the things she enjoyed, like playing cards or dancing. She couldn't lure him to a movie, and he fell asleep if they watched a show on television. Yet he could go to a squadron function and talk football or wrestling, and later flying, with limitless energy, ignoring her for hours.

On an intellectual level, she understood and even admired his dedication to his profession, but it didn't make it any easier from an emotional standpoint. There was something inside Matt that forced him to try to excel. He liked the challenge of flying a jet, of living on the edge. No matter what he was doing, he strove to be the best—except, she sadly realized, as a husband. He seemed to take her for granted.

When she did receive his attention, it was often negative. He criticized her smoking, he wanted the house kept just so, she didn't make the kids behave properly. It was so hard to please him; he wanted everything perfect.

Yet, in fairness to Matt, she knew in her heart that he did love her. For Matt, the word had a different meaning. It meant providing for her material needs. To his way of thinking, she should be happy; she had a nice home, a reliable car, plenty of food on the table, and all the bills paid. He probably wouldn't even understand if she tried to explain that for her something was lacking, that she had other needs he didn't fulfill. He would accuse her of being ridiculous, childish. Was she? Were her expectations of marriage unrealistic, or was he selfish?

Several times when they were dating, she could sense that Matt felt the same powerful desire for her that she had for him, but he always kept it under control. Many times, she had wanted him to be more insistent, to sweet-talk her into submission. But he always stopped. That is, until that night in the drive-in. His emotions were at a fever pitch. She wanted Matt, wanted to feel a part of him, wanted him all to herself, wanted to know that she could set him on fire, that she could put a dent in his control. When she professed her love, that was all the encouragement he needed.

That first time hadn't been exactly ecstasy for her. It was over very quickly. The front seat of that old car was not designed for that purpose, and the experience was painful. She had given him the gift of her virginity, but it was not at all what she expected—no bells, no shooting stars, just a sharp pain and a big mess.

Once the barrier had been broken, Matt demonstrated a hearty appetite for sex, and they made love as often as they could arrange privacy. She didn't know how to get any protection; she certainly couldn't talk to her mother or to the family doctor, and she was too shy to ask Matt to take any precautions. When she suspected she was pregnant, she told Matt right away. At first he appeared dazed, a little stunned, but a few days later he proposed marriage. Would he have married her otherwise? Reviewing his reaction in retrospect, she wasn't sure. Maybe that was the problem; maybe Matt really didn't love her; maybe she was just a commitment and Matt was a man who took care of his responsibilities.

After they were married, even on their honeymoon, with rare exception, Matt never seemed to "let go" like that first night; his lovemaking never reached the intensity she desired. He was always considerate and strove to please her, but always seemed very much in control of his feelings. She wanted it to be so much more—a spiritual thing, an emotional experience, a shared intimacy. It seemed like it was just sex, a physical thing, to him. As she thought about it, it was hard to describe, but their love life lacked something and she couldn't quite put her finger on what.

Maybe she was unrealistic. Maybe the excitement, the intoxication, the abandonment, even the kind of orgasm she yearned for existed only in books and on the screen, or maybe just in her imagination. She had never had any other experiences; she almost wished she had. Without anything to compare, she couldn't be sure, but she always had a feeling there could be more, should be more between a man and a woman in love.

What did all this mean? Had their marriage been a mistake? Did Matt really love her? Did she still really love him? Maybe they were just too different. She was romantic; Matt was too practical. She was spontaneous; he was deliberate and everything had to be planned to the *nth* degree in advance. She wanted hugs and kisses, wanted to hold hands and be touched; Matt considered that to be in bad taste in public, but he didn't do enough in private either. When her feelings were hurt, Matt either didn't notice, or didn't care. If she were depressed or blue or lonesome, he showed little understanding or compassion. Once, when she had the flu and was feeling really down, she had suggested he could at least show a little sympathy. He had jokingly responded, "Honey, you'll find sympathy in the dictionary between shit and syphilis." So she always tried to hide her disappointment.

Certainly she shouldn't blame Matt entirely for their less-than-ideal marriage. She rarely expressed her real feelings or complained to him. For all she knew, he was totally unaware of her unhappiness. For that matter, how could he have known how she felt? She hadn't even acknowledged it herself until now. Well, that wasn't exactly true. There had been things she'd consciously resented before. Perhaps she should have said something then and there, but she didn't like unpleasant confrontations. It was easier not to make waves, to ignore her feelings, to let Matt do things his way.

If—no, correction—_when_ he came back, things would be different. She had grown rather fond of not having to account to Matt, not having to justify even minor expenditures. She didn't have to worry if the house wasn't spic and span all the time or if the table wasn't properly set with the just-so-correct dishes and silver. Life was freer, less restricted. It was fun to go out to dinner when the mood struck her, or stay up until midnight to watch an old mushy movie without feeling guilty because it disturbed Matt. But how was Matt going to react to her new-found independence?

In many ways it had been rather pleasant this past year without Matt, once she got over the initial shock and settled into a routine of her own choosing. Except for the loneliness. She hated not having his warm body to cuddle up to. His hard, strong body was comforting and reassuring, made her feel safe and protected, and she missed that terribly. She also missed the sex. Even without the bells, it was a lot better than celibacy. And, she had to admit, there had been a tinkle now and then.

And the children . . . they needed him terribly.

As she completed her preparations to go to the base, she suddenly thought of Kathryn Roberts. She would like to see her before the squadron returned from this latest cruise. Although Kat and Roy had tried to include her in several activities last summer, she felt somewhat like a fifth wheel alone in the company of all married couples. And, even though Tom Finley had volunteered to go with her, for some reason she just didn't feel comfortable being seen with him, particularly after he'd told her he sort of felt something for her. And while he had continued to take her and the children to the Zoo, Wild Animal Park, Sea World, even down to Rosarita Beach for lobsters, he had never mentioned his feelings or acted at all improperly after that one night. But, if they showed up together, people in the squadron might talk, and she didn't want that.

Nevertheless, Tom had been the one she called after the Navy confirmed Matt was a prisoner. He had rushed right over to be there while she adjusted to this new reality. He truly had been her best friend last summer. She wished he were here now. He would understand, and help her deal with her newly discovered feelings.

Kat wouldn't understand. She and Roy had an entirely different marriage, and Kat would think she was being disloyal and cruel in view of Matt's imprisonment. No, she'd have to keep her feelings private, but it would be good to visit with her friend anyway.

She dialed Kathryn's number. The phone rang several times and Bobbie was just about to hang up when she heard Kathryn's voice on the other end.

"Hi, Kathryn, this is Bobbie. The kids and I just got back from visiting Matt's family in Nebraska and my Mom and Dad. I have to come out to the base to do some shopping today. I was hoping we could have lunch, or at least a cup of coffee. It's been ages since we've gotten together."

There was a long silence on the other end. Bobbie waited, wondering if for some reason Kathryn didn't want to see her. Had she offended her in some way? Finally Kathryn spoke. Her words came very slowly, and she sounded depressed. "Thanks, Bobbie, but why don't you just come over and have a cup of coffee at the house? I don't really feel much like getting dressed and going out to eat."

Something was wrong; she had never heard Kathryn sound so down. "Kat," she inquired, "is there something wrong?"

She heard Kathryn inhale deeply. "I guess you haven't heard." There was a pause. "Well, no, you wouldn't if you've been out of town. I'm sorry, Bobbie." Again she paused as if searching for the right words. "We just got word this past weekend that Roy has been shot down."

****

Driving home later, after a wrenching visit with her friend, Bobbie wanted to shut out the unpleasantness. Kat had been there for her, and it made her feel guilty for being so useless for Kat. One consolation—at least Kat knew that Roy had landed safely. The hardest part—for her—had been those weeks of not knowing whether Matt was dead or alive. Now Roy and Matt were both prisoners. Would they be together? She tried to envision where they were, what their day was like. She couldn't. Why hadn't she heard from him? Despite the caution from the Navy, she wasn't sure she shouldn't be writing to him. But, where would she send it? She didn't even have an address. How would it be delivered? She had been told the Vietnamese weren't allowing the Red Cross into the prisons. Was that Intelligence Officer right? Would Matt be forced to do something bad to get it?

Matt. As much as she wanted him home, the more she thought about it, the more she was convinced that she couldn't go back to the way things had been. Would Matt accept the changes? Was it too late for them even if he came home soon?

"Oh my God!" Bobbie gasped as she realized she was seriously considering the possibility that her marriage might be over, or at least in critical condition.

What about Tom Finley? What would he be like as a husband? He certainly seemed to be more understanding of her emotional needs than Matt. He has shown her more compassion than Matt had ever demonstrated. They spent more time talking with each other last summer, in those four months, about anything and everything, than she and Matt had in the last two years before he was shot down. Tom actually seemed to solicit *her opinion.* As far as she knew, Matt didn't think she was entitled to one.

Recalling Tom's arms protectively around her, comforting her while she struggled with the news of Matt's imprisonment, she wondered what it would be like to make love to him. He'd know exactly what to do in bed. He should, from what he'd told her— he'd had enough experience. Suddenly, she imagined his cold blue, lustful eyes penetrating into hers, and his steel-like arms encircling her, pinning her beneath him, and the sensation sent ripples of excitement through her.

As she pulled into her driveway, she snapped back to reality, ashamed of her prurient thoughts about Tom Finley, and guilty about

her not-so-happy assessment of her marriage. Before she went to pick up Hank, she fixed herself a stiff drink and tried to blot out her troubled feelings.

CHAPTER 12

<u>DRV, June 1967.</u>

U.S. planes were bombing the DRV day and night. The men in the Pig Sty could hear the guns firing. Although they weren't supposed to watch, Matt, Lee and John took turns standing on each other's shoulders to look through the ventilation hole near the ceiling.

"What can you see?" Matt asked as he steadied John on his shoulders during a raid.

"Without a doubt it's a flak site right outside the fence. I can see guns and people scurrying about," John responded in hushed excitement. "They must be militia. I can make out an assortment of uniforms."

"What kind of guns?" Lee whispered loudly from his position on the floor near the crack at the bottom of the door, listening just on the off chance one of the guards had failed to seek refuge in the bomb shelter.

"They're pretty well camouflaged."

After the bombing stopped, John offered, "Hey, Matt, wanna change places?"

"No. I'm okay. You're not that heavy. Go ahead. Tell us what you see."

"They've cleaned the guns and they're pointing the barrels up in the air to dry. They look like they're 57- and 85-millimeter cannons."

Lee jumped up, "Down, boys. I hear a guard!"

Matt moved away from the wall and John dismounted quietly. All three were sitting innocently on their slabs when the guard popped open the flap in the door.

"Wonder what he thought he'd find?" John asked, looking about as wide-eyed and innocent as a ten-year old caught smoking in the closet. Matt and Lee laughed.

The next day, after another attack, John climbed atop Matt's shoulders and glued his eyes to the hole. "Hey, you know what. Those guns must be mobile. They aren't in the same place they were last night. I'll be damned. They're mounted on trucks."

Matt said, "I bet they move them after each raid to try to confuse the flak suppressors."

"Yeah, probably, but we're definitely close to a target of some kind, because they haven't been moved very far."

After yet another bombardment, their new cellblock officer, called the Rat because of his small beady, closely-set eyes and long pointed nose, stopped by the cell.

John brazened a question. "I've noticed some colored balloons in the sky above the back wall. What are those?"

The Rat seemed pleased to have an opportunity to boast about the Vietnamese defense system. "We use a barrage balloon to measure elevation for our flak sites; different colors indicate different heights. When a plane comes in level with a red balloon, the gunners set their flak to go off at that altitude." Then, in a rare display of pride, he puffed up like a blow fish and bragged, "Those balloons are tied to the ground with very strong cables. Should any of your airplanes hit one, the steel cables will shear the wings right off."

A few days later, during another raid, Matt looked out of their peephole to see an F105 smoking by at about 600 knots. Draped over the wing of the plane was a deflated balloon. Describing what he saw to the others, he commented, "Well, so much for the strength of those cables."

The men scurried for cover when a plane roared right over the camp several days later. The pilot laid a whole stick of cluster bomb units right on top of the gun site behind the Pig Sty. As the thunderous noise of the climbing jet's afterburner disappeared, Lee whispered, "Listen!"

John and Matt lay quietly for a few seconds. "I don't hear anything," they said in unison.

"That's what I mean. I don't hear any guns firing."

A few minutes later, the Rat ran down the sidewalk outside their cell. He was crying.

Lee observed, "I bet a lot of those gunners were his buddies."

John chirped in, "'Were' is the operative word here, pals. They *were* his buddies." His mood was almost buoyant.

For the rest of the day and into the night, they sat in darkness and listened to the wailing scream of ambulances. The bomb had knocked out the electricity in the whole area.

With his meager water ration, John proposed a toast to the unknown pilot. "I'm convinced the target is a military installation right near here. The guy who dropped those CBUs was probably a flak suppressor just doing his job. And a good fuckin' job at that. I wish I could shake his hand."

Lee had a better idea. "I'd like to be there to buy him a nice steak dinner and a drink tonight when he gets back to Udorn."

Matt licked his lips. "Just the thought of a nice steak dinner makes me salivate. This weight loss plan they have us on is working—I've already shed at least twenty-five or thirty pounds."

Lee pulled his pajamas tight, "I've lost about the same—but I needed to."

"It's the lack of beer." John teased.

Again Matt felt saliva forming. "A steak *and* a beer. Oh, God, that sounds good."

****

As the summer wore on, they could still hear the American jets flying over, but there hadn't been much activity near the Pig Sty. The Vietnamese hadn't replaced the guns destroyed in the earlier raid. Things were actually pretty routine. Then, without warning, a guard hauled Matt out of the cell.

At the Head Shed—the building used for quizzes and interrogations—he was confronted by the Rat. "You are to write your name, rank and serial number, date of birth and native land."

"What's this for?" Matt asked.

The Rat ignored his question. "Write," he ordered.

Matt knew they were looking for some sort of propaganda, but as usual it was nothing new, so he wrote what they asked.

Once he had complied with the instruction, a guard brought in a tape recorder. "Now you will read what you have just written into the tape recorder."

The SROs had decided that they were not going to make any more tapes for the Vietnamese without resisting, so Matt flatly refused.

"If you do not do as I say, you will be punished."

"No." He was led out to the Coop, a cage used for punishment.

Once again the Rat commanded, "You must speak into the recorder."

"No, I will not do it."

The leg manacles were brought in, and his hands were tied loosely behind his back. "You have one more chance to show good attitude."

"No."

The manacles were locked in place, pinching and numbing his ankles immediately. The straps were lashed tightly around his arms, peeling off all the skin underneath. His elbows were forced together behind his back with his wrists turned inward. A searing electric shock-like pain surged through Matt as the strain threatened to pull his shoulders out of their sockets. His chest shot forward spontaneously as he gasped for short spurts of air. The muscles in his upper body quivered. He had been down this road before, and would have to give them what they wanted eventually if they persisted.

Matt stoically endured the pain. He had withstood this type of punishment for longer periods in the past, and he knew what it did to him. But as the minutes slowly turned into hours, it became clear they weren't about to turn him loose until he made the tape. The directive from the camp senior officer was that the men were to resist every attempt to use them for propaganda, but only up to the point of avoiding permanent injury and preserving their sanity.

He decided he had pursued his resistance long enough. They wanted this piece of propaganda, and they meant to get it, one way or another.

When the Rat returned, Matt conceded through clenched teeth, "All right. I'll read into your damn tape recorder."

The ropes came off. "Repeat the information you wrote on the paper."

He read his serial number as one complete number, instead of with the two breaks normally used. He also used the term "native land" instead of city and state, hoping these deviations from normal usage would be sufficient evidence to any American hearing the tape that this was not a voluntary act.

After Matt finished, the Rat chided, "You are stupid. Major Holmes from the room next to you, gave us the same information willingly." He then played the tape of Neil's voice.

"Yeah, sure, and I'm an astronaut," Matt gibed. He knew he risked further punishment, but he couldn't resist. The Rat smirked, then merely flicked his fingers, a sign for the guard to return Matt to his cell.

He briefed Lee and John. "Well, they're back at it again. The first part of that tape was probably some condemnation against the war and the U.S. involvement that we're supposed to be endorsing. I guess Major Holmes got the same treatment."

"So what's the plan?" John asked tensely.

"Force them to put you in irons before you give them what they want," Matt instructed.

After three days, neither Lee nor John had been taken to the Head Shed. They debated the reasons, at the same time unable to hide their relief.

A couple of days later, Matt held out his ulcerated arms, "Why in the hell am I the only one that gets this?"

John examined Matt's foul smelling wounds. "Hell, they're already starting to heal. You'll live."

"Yeah, probably, but let me tell you what can happen. When I first got here, after the Green Room treatment, I went so long without medical care I got maggots in the wounds."

John made a gurgling sound, and Lee groaned.

"They're actually good little critters. They only eat the dead and decaying matter, but I gotta tell ya, it's pretty tough watching those little suckers chomping away."

John puckered his face, "Oh, shit, shut up. That's an image I can do without."

Matt had to laugh in spite of the pain. Served John right for being so flippant.

A few days later, all three were led out to the yard and ordered to dig foxholes.

"We are to refuse to perform any kind of military work and to cite the Geneva Convention," Matt whispered to the others.

Addressing the guard, he said, "We will not dig any foxholes."

The guard left, returning a few minutes later with the cellblock officer.

"You must dig the foxholes," the Rat commanded.

They all refused. Although Matt's arms by now had started to scab over, they were still numb and basically useless for digging. That didn't seem to matter. He was dragged away and thrust into the Coop. Lee and John were returned to the cell.

"You will dig!" The Rat was adamant.

"Under the Geneva Convention, prisoners are not required to do military work." Matt hit the first volley in the tournament of wills.

The Rat dismissed him. "You are criminals. You have no rights. You have a few minutes to reconsider. I will return."

Later, "You will obey and dig now?"

"No, we will not do it."

The familiar ritual resumed. In came the goon squad with the manacles.

The Rat gave Matt one last chance. "If you do not dig the foxholes, it will be necessary to administer heavy iron discipline."

Matt unswervingly stuck by his refusal. They brought in the same straps as before.

The Rat asked, "Now will you dig?"

"No."

They placed the manacles on his ankles, causing Matt to wince.

"Will you dig?"

"No."

They put the straps around his arms and drooped them over his shoulders.

"Will you dig?"

"No."

At that point, Matt was knocked to the floor and tied up again. He yelped as the scabs from his previous treatment were ripped off. He had decided he would resist this time only to the point of making them tie him up.

"Okay, I'll dig one friggin' foxhole, but no more."

Immediately, he was released.

Nodding toward his bleeding arms, Matt protested, "But I can't lift a pencil right now, let alone a shovel."

"Very well. You may wait until you are healed, but you must apologize to the camp commander for refusing the orders of the camp guard."

"Yeah, okay, I can handle that."

"And you must order your roommates to dig also."

Matt was free again and some of his defiance was restored. "No, I will not order them to do it. They won't anyway; it is dishonorable."

"You must order them," the Rat insisted.

"No," Matt repeated with equal determination.

John was led into the room.

"Order him to dig."

Matt shook his head.

Disgusted, the Rat ordered that Matt be returned to his cell.

As he was led away, Matt whispered to John, "Pursue it until they threaten to put you in irons. Agree to dig one."

John blinked his eyes to show his understanding.

During the noon quiet time, they contacted the cellblock SRO for instructions since Lee had not yet been called.

They received the response later in the day. "You handled correctly. Lee, force them to put you in irons before agreeing to do same thing."

Matt added, "Agree before the interrogator leaves. Left to their own devices, the punishment detail can be really mean and unstable."

Several days later, a guard entered the cell and gave the chop-chop sign with his right hand against his left wrist and ankle.

After changing into their long shirts and trousers, Lee was the first to be called out of the cell.

Upon returning he whispered, "Matt, they're taking pictures. Roll up your sleeves to expose your arms."

Having received no medical treatment, Matt's blood-encrusted arms were swollen and feverish with bright red streaks again running up toward his shoulders and down to his wrists. It hurt when the shirtsleeve rubbed the rotting and decaying skin, so he willingly complied.

The photographer's face registered shock at the sight of Matt's disgusting-looking, putrid-smelling wounds. The guard moved to cover them, but the photographer motioned him away. When he finished, he spoke in a voice that oozed irritation. Contritely, the turnkey trotted off, returning almost immediately with the camp medic.

After a redoubtable reprimand from the photographer, the medic sprang into action, but his pathetic efforts produced no noticeable results. The formidable man with the camera issued additional orders. This time Matt was taken to the camp clinic where his arms were properly cleaned and sulfa applied, as usual, without any painkiller. He gritted his teeth, determined not to yell.

Later in the afternoon the photographer stopped by the cell and personally examined Matt's arms. All the while the guard stood nervously at attention.

"He must have been someone important," Matt theorized. "I bet he's VPA; they certainly followed his orders in a hurry. Whoever he was, I owe him. Now I won't have to perform some humiliating act to get medical attention."

With the help of the sulfa, Matt's arms healed, and the three of them dug one foxhole, placed, at the insistence of the guards, in a low spot. Before it was even completed, the hole started to fill with water.

With a Cheshire-cat grin, John quipped, "Almost makes it all worthwhile, doesn't it?"

****

As they had learned over the past several months, boredom was often relieved by something even less desirable. This time it was Lee's dysentery. After a few days, he couldn't make it to the honey bucket, and most of the time he was too weak to even move off his slab. He soiled all his shorts and splattered the wall behind him. The cell was doused with a fetid aroma.

"Jesus," John complained, "that smell is bad enough to gag a maggot."

"We need to rectify his rectal problem." Matt called the guard, who stuck his head in the door, made a face and quickly left to fetch the block commander.

The Rat, twitching his nose in remarkable impersonation of his namesake, reluctantly entered the cell. "What's the matter?"

"Major Wilson needs medicine. He's getting very dehydrated and weak, and that mess has to be cleaned up. In this heat, the smell is unbearable."

The Rat cautiously approached Lee's slab, warily eyeing the wall behind. "What's wrong with you, Wilson?"

Lee, too sick to raise his head or speak, merely reached under his slab, withdrew a pair of his stinking shorts and stuck them directly under the block commander's nose.

The Rat jumped backwards and shrieked.

John guffawed at the look on the Rat's face, delighting in having a laugh at the V's expense.

The Rat was not pleased at being the brunt of a joke. Turning slowly to John, he smiled his mirthless grin, and asked sardonically, "You think this is funny? Good. You should really enjoy what comes next."

With that, he threw all of Lee's fetid shorts in John's face, and ordered him to wash them. "In addition, you will clean up the bunk, and you are to clean up your friend."

It was now the Rat's turn to laugh at the expression on John's face as he gingerly carried the pungent garments out the door toward the wash area. John's nose was more than offended by the foul smell; it was clearly out of joint. Humble pie was not something he easily digested.

CHAPTER 13

San Diego, August 1967.

The cruise on the Bonhomme Richard was the most costly, in terms of losses, of Tom's three Westpac tours. Two of his squadron mates had been killed and Roy Roberts had been shot down, now probably a prisoner of war.

Thinking of Roy reminded Tom of Matt, and Matt reminded him of Bobbie. In fact, just about everything reminded him of her. No matter how hard he tried, her memory kept returning like a boomerang.

On the trip home, Tom debated what he should do. Long before they arrived in San Diego, he made his decision. He had to see her at least one more time. If she told him to get lost, he'd have to deal with it and move on, but, he had to tell her how he felt. It had happened quickly; it had simply taken him almost a year to understand his feelings and what they really meant.

The previous summer had been a difficult one, primarily because of Bobbie Tillet. He wasn't used to wanting a woman he couldn't or shouldn't have. Not that he hadn't had his share of women. Despite his one disastrous encounter with Denise and her furry rug, he had not suffered for lack of female companionship, attacking his game of conquest with a vengeance and a greater intensity than ever before. But it wasn't the same. His weekly visits with Bobbie and the children were the highlight of his summer. He'd never realized how satisfying it was to be needed, to do things with someone that really mattered.

Another reason for his discomfort had been his indecision about staying in the Navy. Although he had already been in more than ten years and could look forward to a good retirement after twenty, three tours in Vietnam left him questioning that choice. Many of his fellow pilots delighted in the intoxicating high they experienced in aerial combat, but for Tom the excitement of battle had long ago vanished. Even though he rarely saw the death and destruction on the ground, he could imagine it, and he didn't like being a part of it. He'd never realized before how much politics impacted the waging of a war. Politics in this case was keeping the military from winning the war and ending it quickly. It wasn't worth the lives of so many good young Americans.

But flying was the only thing Tom was trained to do, so last summer he had mailed applications to several of the commercial airlines. Shortly before the squadron deployed in late November, he received a promising response from West Coast Airlines, based in San Diego. He had immediately called the personnel manager.

Mr. Chasteen painted a rosy picture. "We're going to experience some phenomenal growth in the next few years and I can promise a bright future for any pilot who joins us. Lieutenant Commander Finley, we'd certainly be happy to discuss the possibility of you joining us if you decide to leave the Navy."

While Tom had not actually been promised a job, he felt confident enough to turn in his letter of resignation before departing for Vietnam. He was going to trade in his F-8 Crusader for a passenger airliner, if all went according to plan.

Toward the end of August, the Bonnie Dick neared the coast of California. A day ahead of the ship's arrival at North Island, the squadron pilots flew their planes back to Miramar. Tom's first phone call, even before he checked into the BOQ, was to the personnel manager at WCA. They set up an appointment for Monday morning.

It was Friday afternoon. Should he call Bobbie or just drop by the house? It was really no contest—he wanted to see her.

Bobbie spent Friday morning shopping for school clothes. Hank would be starting kindergarten in September, and Debbie was always in need of something. At noon she had lunch with a friend, and listened to her former neighbor's diatribe about her soon-to-be ex-husband and the unfairness of the California divorce laws. After a couple of drinks, she was feeling warm and relaxed, in anticipation of a quiet afternoon alone. Debbie had taken Hank to a baseball game at the stadium. Hopefully it would go into extra innings.

She had just started to unload her packages when a vaguely familiar car pulled up out front and a tall, well-built man stepped out. For a split second, she did not recognize him; then she gasped aloud. Tom Finley! Her face reddened, her mouth suddenly felt full of cotton, and her pulse raced uncontrollably.

Tom walked up the driveway and nodded to the assortment of packages and boxes in her car. "May I help you unload these?"

"Tom." She hoped her voice did not betray her discomfiture. "How good to see you. When did you get back?"

"The squadron just flew in this morning, ship will be in tomorrow. Here, let me have those packages."

Picking up the last small box, she kicked the car door shut and headed for the front door, chattering nervously. "Gee, I'm so glad you came over. I missed our weekly outings. But I figured you'd moved on when we didn't hear from you."

He walked beside her toward the front door. "I started to write a couple of times, but I'm not very good at that. And it was a bitch of a cruise. I guess you heard that Roy Roberts got shot down."

She nodded, frowning. "I visited with Kat right after she found out. It was really sad."

Bobbie put her packages on the couch, and turned to face him. She almost seemed as nervous as he felt. Dropping the packages he had been holding into the chair behind him, he pulled her into his arms. Before she could say anything or pull away, he blurted out what he had been trying to figure out how to say.

"Bobbie, there's something I've got to tell you. I tried to stay away, but I couldn't. I had to see you. All this cruise, I've thought of nothing but what it would be like to hold you, to kiss you and to make love to you. I know you're married, and I know I'm a fool, but my feelings are what they are. I can't explain it any other way, except to say I guess I love you."

She stared at him, her eyes wide, her body rigid, her surprise evident.

"I'm sorry if I've made you uncomfortable. I wouldn't blame you if you slap my face and tell me to go to hell, and if you do, that's okay. I'll understand and go away, but . . ." he spread his arms. "Oh, shit, Bobbie, say something. I missed you more than I ever thought possible, and right now I want to kiss you so much I can taste it."

Slowly, as if in a trance, her body relaxed and she moved closer, and laid her head on his chest.

"Oh, Tom, I missed you too."

His arms closed around her savagely, forcing the breath from her body. "Oh, baby, that's what I hoped you'd say." He relaxed his grip, lifted her head and kissed her softly. When he looked into her face, her eyes were wet.

"Oh, sweetheart, I'm sorry. I've done it again. I didn't mean to make you cry," he whispered, rubbing one finger gently across her cheek.

"It's not your fault. You want to hear something really funny. I've thought about you these past few months almost as much as I've thought about Matt. I missed you. I missed having you to talk to. I missed just having you around. I thought it was just because you were such a good friend. But, when I saw you in the driveway, my first reaction was to run to your arms and kiss you. It was definitely not 'good friend' feelings. But I feel so guilty and embarrassed, so confused, for feeling that way."

Tom wrapped his arms around her again and held her tightly, unable to believe what he heard.

Suddenly she pulled out of his arms. Before he had a chance to stop her, he heard voices outside. The door flew open and Debbie and Hank burst into the room.

Upon seeing him, they stopped short, then smiled in recognition and yelled his name. Hank came running over and threw his arms around Tom's legs.

"Hi ya, pal," Tom laughed as he lifted Hank off the floor. "My goodness, how you've grown."

Hank giggled with delight. "Hi ya, Tom," he imitated, slapping Tom's shoulder with his small fist.

"You remembered my name."

He put the other arm around Debbie and pulled her against him. "And you've really grown too, Debbie," he declared. "You look, what? Not so much taller or bigger, I guess you look . . ." he searched for the words to describe the charming change in Debbie, "more mature. And prettier, too," he added admiringly.

"Thank you, sir." She gave him a light kiss on the cheek. "Did you just get back?"

"As a matter of fact, yes, just this morning. The ship will be in tomorrow morning. But I couldn't wait to come over and see you." He looked directly at Bobbie.

"Hey, you guys, do you have any plans for dinner? Maybe we could all go out and get something to eat to celebrate my homecoming. Mrs. Tillet, are you hungry?"

Debbie extricated herself from Tom's embrace. "Aw, gee, I was going to spend the night with Patty." After a slight pause, "But that's okay, I'd rather go out to eat with you."

"I have a better idea," Bobbie suggested, "Why don't we fix some hamburgers in the back yard? You can invite Patty to join us, and if you'd like, you can still spend the night with her."

"All *right*." agreed Debbie excitedly.

Tom looked at Hank. "Well, pal, is that okay with you?"

"Yeah." Hank started wriggling to get down.

Bobbie turned to Debbie. "Why don't you take Hank and go over to Patty's to see if she can come over. Tom and I will go to the store and get what we need for supper. Then we'll all meet back here in about an hour or so."

Debbie wasted no time. Grabbing Hank's hand, she ordered, "Come on, shrimp, let's go." Hank followed.

Tom and Bobbie were once again alone in her living room. They stood silently for several moments, their eyes locked. He hesitated, unsure of his next move, then started toward her across the room. At first she seemed stuck to the molding of the door, using it for support, but when he reached out his arms, she stepped toward him and into his open arms. As he pulled her close, she raised her head for his kiss, wrapping her arms around his neck and pressing her body close. Her kisses were seeking, passionate, hungry; her breathing fast and irregular.

Tom's desire was becoming very evident. Instead of moving away, she squeezed even closer. The silence yielded only to the thunderous pounding of his heart. He lifted her into his arms. "Where's the bedroom?"

She pointed toward the hallway, warning, "Better lock the door."

Laying her gently on top of the covers, he started to unbutton her blouse, kissing her neck, her chest and then her breasts. Her nipples hardened. She unbuttoned his shirt and eagerly pulled his bare chest down to hers, at the same time wrapping her arms around his neck, seeking his mouth. Her tongue probed deep and a low moan escaped from deep within her throat. He could feel her hips moving ever so slightly beneath him.

The late afternoon sunlight snuck around the edges of the curtains, casting a golden glow on their naked bodies. He ran his fingers deftly across her silky figure, softly caressing her erect nipples. She held out her arms, summoning him nearer while her body swayed in an enticing rhythm. He lay across her, supporting his weight on one elbow. Her body was now in perpetual motion, her breasts rubbing against his chest, her thighs against his. Within seconds he entered her and she went wild, kissing him, biting, scratching his back and buttocks as she strained to pull him even deeper inside, all the time murmuring his name in a deep, throaty voice. Her aggressiveness and eroticism fanned his own flaming desire.

He tried to slow the pace. "Easy, baby, I won't last long like this."

She moved even more rapidly. "Who's waiting?" She pulled his lips back down to hers.

He had never suspected she was capable of such fiery emotion, such unbridled passion. As much as he had wanted her, her intensity surprised him. Her desire exceeded his own. With every thrust she grew more excited, her breathing labored, a low deep continuous moan escaping from her lips. Tom felt an urgency, then a tremendous release as he pressed hard inside her, only to find her own body unyielding, pressing against his. She cried out as her emotions surged like a breaking dam. For a moment he was afraid he might have hurt her, but as the tension slowly ebbed from her body, she relaxed beneath him.

He looked down into her half-closed eyes. "Darling," he whispered hoarsely, "that was wonderful."

She blinked and lamely tried to lift her head, then let it fall back limply on the crumpled pillow, a half smile on her lips. Suddenly her face reddened.

"Hey, what's the matter?"

Bobbie turned her head sideways, avoiding his gaze. "Oh, Tom," she cried, "I don't know what got into me. I'm ashamed of myself. I've never acted that way before. Please don't look at me."

Roughly he forced her head back around to face him. "Look," he scolded, "There is nothing to be ashamed of. I love you. I told you. I'm going to keep on loving you. And, do you know what? I think you just told me you love me, too."

She quickly averted her gaze, bit her lip and exhaled slowly.

Tom cupped her chin and kissed her. "I can't explain because I simply don't understand what has happened. If anyone had told me a year ago I would fall in love with you, I'd have suggested they needed to call the little men in white uniforms. I certainly didn't intend to fall for a buddy's wife, particularly one that's a POW. But it happened, and I think it must have happened to you, too."

She squirmed beneath him and turned her face to the right, trying to shied her face with her hand. He stroked her cheek and pushed a lock of hair away from her eyes. He could see the anguish in her eyes.

"Oh, Tom, this is crazy. Yes, I think I do love you. I thought about you a lot. But don't you see how hopeless this all is? I must really be a terrible woman. While my husband is a prisoner of war, I've jumped in bed with the first man who shows me any attention. I've been lonely, but that doesn't make it right." She sobbed uncontrollably, her whole body trembling.

"Sweetheart, what we just shared was beautiful, it's the way love should be between two people. So don't let me ever hear you say you are ashamed of loving me, do you understand?" His eyes were blazing.

She sobbed louder.

He pulled a tissue from the box on the nightstand and gently wiped the tears. "Honey, I don't know how things are going to work out, but as trite as it sounds, we'll work it out together. You're not alone anymore."

She took the Kleenex, wiped her eyes, blew her nose and smiled meekly. Using her free hand, she ran her fingers through her hair and pushed it out of her face. Then she closed her eyes and started crying again.

Tom tried to relieve her guilt. "You know, I'm not exactly the world's nicest guy either. Basically, I've always been a bastard where women are concerned. And I'm still a bastard, at least as far as Matt is concerned, but not with you. You may not believe this, but I have never felt about a woman the way I feel about you. I don't understand it myself. I guess I've just never really been in love before."

The gushing tears stopped, but her repressed sobs shook her upper body. She inhaled slowly, cleared her throat again, and spoke timidly, "Oh, Tom, I don't know what to do. I want you so much, but I feel so . . . ."

He interrupted her with a tender kiss and started to raise himself off her small body. She caught his hips with her hands, hugging him close.

"Hey, lover," he chided, "I don't think you want those children of yours catching us like this, do you? And we still have to go to the store."

She turned her head toward the bedside clock. "Oh, my goodness!" Immediately she released him, grabbing for her clothing.

Standing up, he offered his hand to assist her, then gathered her close. She was so fragile, so vulnerable. She needed him more than he had realized, and he silently vowed that he would be there for her. What to do about Matt? They would just have to face that problem later. He kissed her gently once more.

"Say, why don't I run down to the store and get the food, while you clean up—and don't forget to make the bed," he added mischievously.

"That won't be necessary." Her panicked look was gone and in its place a teasing look. "I have everything we need in the refrigerator. You want to shower with me, or alone?"

Smacking her bare bottom with his palm, he grabbed her hand and headed toward the bathroom, "I'm a conservationist," he quipped, "You know, save water—shower with a friend. Come on, friend, last one in gets a cold shower."

The bed was made, the hamburger patties were on a platter and the beans cooking in the oven when Hank, Debbie and Patty arrived. Finding the door locked, Debbie rang the bell. A flustered Bobbie rushed to the door. "Sorry, guess I forgot to unlock it when we got back."

Debbie shot her mother a questioning glance.

Tom quickly interceded. Addressing Debbie, he asked, "You want to watch the hamburgers, or help your mom in the kitchen?"

Debbie piped, "We'll do the hamburgers. Come on, Patty."

After dinner, Tom joined Debbie and Patty in a game of Monopoly while Bobbie washed the dishes. Hank watched the game for a little while, tired of it, "helped" his mother a little with the dishes, tired of it too, and finally ambled off into the den to watch TV.

When Bobbie entered the living room, Tom complained loudly, "Jesus Christ. This kid's a whiz. She's ruthless. She owns three quarters of the properties, and she's driven me straight into bankruptcy." Patty laughed gaily.

Debbie agreed, "Yeah, she beats me *all* the time. I gotta find a new game."

After polishing off the last of the potato chips and Cokes, Patty and Debbie were ready to head over to Patty's house. "Don't forget, Mom, we're going to the beach in the morning from Patty's, so I won't be home until tomorrow evening. That okay?"

"Okay, but be careful."

After the girls left, Tom picked up a half-asleep Hank from the chair in the den. "Okay, Little Buckaroo, it's bedtime for you."

Hank started to protest, but Tom interrupted, "If you go to bed now and get a good night's sleep, I'll ask your mother if we can go to the beach tomorrow. We haven't done that since last summer."

Hank assented sleepily.

Alone at last, Tom had a chance to pass on his exciting news. "I have a surprise, which I think you might like. I'm getting out of the

Navy, and if everything goes well Monday, I may become a pilot with WCA."

"Oh, that's wonderful." Her eyes sparkled. "Does that mean you won't be going off on any more six- or eight-month cruises?"

"That's what it means."

"When does all this happen?"

"My resignation has already been accepted effective the end of September. If I get hired by WCA, I can take terminal leave for most of next month. I have about thirty days on the books, and I can start training whenever WCA gives me the green light. Keep your fingers crossed for me, baby."

Bobbie's eyes clouded, her smile turned upside down, and she took a slow, deep breath as she sank into the sofa chair. "Oh, Tom, what's going to happen to us? I want to be with you like this all the time. I've been so lonely this past year. This evening was so pleasant, and the kids enjoy having you around too. But I can't possibly let them think there's anything going on between us. I am still married to their father, and they would never forgive me. I know they wouldn't. I just couldn't risk it."

The subject had never been far from his thoughts all evening. Here he was, Mr. Love 'em and Leave 'em, actually wanting to settle down permanently with a married woman and her two kids. He liked Debbie and Hank; they were good kids; and given the opportunity, he could be a good father to them. If only Matt were here so she could get a divorce, then the four of them could be a regular family. He wanted that. It would be the best for everyone, even Matt. Matt would never be happy with a wife who didn't love him, with a wife who had cheated on him. He wasn't the type who could forgive that kind of transgression. Tom was willing to accept the major share of blame for this situation, particularly in view of Matt's imprisonment, but there must have been problems already, for her to so easily fall in love with another man. Suddenly, he knew what they should do.

"Bobbie, I want to marry you. I want to help you raise the children. You need someone around to help you, you need a man, the children need a father, and I don't think Matt is coming back for a long time. Look, I don't know what it takes, but perhaps there is some way you can get a divorce even with Matt over there. I can check with the legal office at the base."

She froze, her face registering her alarm. "No, Tom, no! I couldn't do that, and I don't want you talking with anyone at Miramar. You might as well advertise in the paper what we've done."

It was hard to miss the sarcasm in her voice. "Did you hear what I said?" he asked, perplexed. "I said I want to marry you. I want to marry you *now*—not in five or ten years, when and if Matt finally gets home. I don't want us—you, me and the children—to waste those five or ten years. By then it might be too late, certainly too late to make a normal home for Debbie and Hank, a real home— with a mother and a father. Too late for another baby like you said you wanted."

"Oh, Tom . . . I . . . ." Her voice trailed off; she wrung her hands and chipped at her fingernails.

"No one knows," he pressed, "least of all us, when those guys will come home. But I can tell you one thing, that war isn't going to end in another year or two. You can't throw away our chance for a life together just so you can tell Matt in person that you were in love with someone else while he was gone. Is that your idea of fairness?"

She dropped her head, rubbed her eyes and covered her face with her hands. After what seemed like hours, she looked up and spoke softly. "Tom, you don't know what you're asking me to do. It sounds so simple the way you say it, and I wish I could believe you're right, but I could never send Matt a 'Dear John' letter while he is in prison. I just couldn't live with myself if I did something like that."

All the while she spoke she was wringing her hands. Suddenly she dropped her head again, her shoulders stooped as if under a tremendous weight. For several moments she stared at the floor. She was shaking her head when she faced him.

"I'm so confused. I just don't know what to do. I want you so badly, and I want to do what's right for us and the children, but I don't want to hurt Matt. I'm so afraid of how the children, particularly Debbie, would react; she'd hate me for deserting her father."

"I think you're wrong. I think Debbie would understand perfectly." He put his hands on her shoulders, forcing her to look him squarely in the face. "Do you love me?"

"Yes, I think so . . . yes, I love you, but . . . ."

"No buts, Bobbie. For Christ's sake, be realistic. Do you really think you would be doing him a favor to let him think for five, six, ten years that he has a loving family waiting for him to come home to, that he has a loving, devoted wife waiting for his return, when you know that can never be again? Do him a favor, send him word as soon as you can, ask him for a divorce. Let him use his time over there to get used to the idea, instead of letting him come home full of hope, only to find his world shattered."

She continued to slowly shake her head, and press her lips together, staring at some imaginary spot out the window.

"You can't be sure it wouldn't be better to wait. What if because of my letter he did something foolish, or just gave up and let them kill him? Do you think we could possibly base a marriage on something like that?"

Now it was Tom's turn to shake his head, "You know Matt even better than I do, and I haven't any concern whatsoever that Matt will do anything foolish. He is not going to react violently; he's too practical, too sensible, and I think, perhaps too unemotional." He appended the last description, given what he knew about Matt, thinking that was most likely one of the problems with their marriage.

"Look, you think about it. We can't do anything right now anyway. I am going to ask some discreet questions, no one will know what is going on, if that's what you want, but I'm going to find out just what you can do. For the time being, we'll just play it cool." Pulling her against his chest, he added, "But, lady, remember what I said. You can't get rid of me now, now that I know you feel the same way about me as I feel about you."

She buried her head in his chest and leaned against him.

"How can we possibly work this out?" Her voice was muffled.

"I don't know. I really don't know. But, somehow, we'll figure it out."

He once again lifted her into his arms and carried her toward the bedroom. Without a sound they undressed in the darkness and lay down together on the cool, inviting sheets. This time they came together slowly, deliberately, as he expertly coaxed her into a tremendous climax, and then a second, and a third.

Afterward, he lay on his side, stroking her hair, listening to her slow and irregular breathing as she slept fitfully, her head on his shoulder. For the first time in his life, as far as he could remember, he felt an emotional fulfillment like he had never experienced before. "Bobbie, I love you," he murmured, and started to drift into sleep.

"Mommie!"

Tom and Bobbie both awoke with a start. She jumped out of bed and grabbed her robe. "Stay here," she whispered hoarsely, then closed the bedroom door behind her as she rushed toward her son's bedroom.

She returned after a few minutes, where Tom was sitting naked on the edge of the bed. "Thank God. It was just a dream. He's still asleep. You've got to leave. They mustn't find us together like this—ever." She was handing him his clothes as she spoke.

There was no point arguing. She wasn't ready to admit her feelings publicly, or even to the children. It was a mistake. He was sure the children would not only accept their relationship, particularly if they got married, but would probably welcome it. He would just have to give her more time. He dressed quietly and quickly. "Honey, I'll come by tomorrow and take you and Hank to the beach. While he's playing in the sand, we can talk some more. I'll stop by about twelve or one because I'm going to look for an apartment first thing in the morning." Playfully he pulled her back into his arms. "Since you aren't going to let me move in here, I have to find a place to live. Perhaps it will give us more privacy, and a chance to be together more. I suggest you develop an interest in bowling or something else that will get you out of the house a couple of evenings a week."

"You really are devious, aren't you?" Her mood was more relaxed. "You already have everything figured out."

"Well, not everything," he conceded with a twinkle. "But when it comes to ways to see you, that I'll figure out." He deftly untied the belt of her robe, exposing her breasts, bent down and kissed each nipple roughly. She squirmed with the slight pain. He continued kissing her navel, running his tongue teasingly around her belly above her pubic hair.

Catching his hair in her fist, she yanked upward. "No you don't, not again, you sex fiend."

He kissed her on her nose and both cheeks. With one last long, lingering kiss, he released her and went out into the night air, checking to make sure the door was locked securely behind him.

CHAPTER 14

<u>San Diego, late August 1967.</u>

On Saturday morning, Tom rose early, bought a newspaper and walked over to the "O" Club for breakfast. After reading the classifieds, he decided to look at a new "Adults Only" complex near Mission Bay, just down the hill from Bobbie's house, not more than a five-minute drive.

He selected a large, bright two-bedroom unit. Located on the far end of the complex, away from the swimming pool and tennis courts, it was perfect. Bobbie could park just outside the enclosed patio, and come in and out the side door with little chance of being observed.

Tom caught himself as he realized what he had just been thinking. He did not like the idea of Bobbie sneaking in and out of his apartment, preferring to announce to the world his love for her. How would the men in the squadron react if they knew? Big, bad Tom falling in love with a married woman, with two children yet. Oh, there would be plenty who would disapprove because it was Matt's wife. Maybe announcing it to the world wasn't the best approach, not just yet. But what the hell, they'd know sooner or later. His friends would understand, and the others wouldn't matter.

Tom put down a deposit on the apartment, with the lease to start the following weekend. He would need at least that long to buy some basic furniture and linens. With a little bit of luck, Bobbie might change her mind, and, married or otherwise, he'd move into her house.

His apartment hunt concluded, Tom headed straight to Bobbie's. After a quick check to make sure Hank was occupied in the back yard, she snuggled into his waiting arms. Tom's reaction was instantaneous.

Restraining his mounting passion, he released her with a sigh and held her at arms' length. "I've found an apartment. I think you're going to love it. It's right down at the bottom of the hill, and it's very private. Since I'm a little early, how would you like to drive over and take a look before we go to the beach?"

"Sure. I'll get dressed." Bobbie hurried off to the bedroom. After a couple of minutes, Tom walked down the hall, and watched, unnoticed, as Bobbie wiggled and tugged at her swimming suit. As she started to pull the straps over her shoulders, she raised her head and spied Tom, leaning against the door, arms folded, a twinkle in his eyes.

"Get out of here." she sounded stern. "What if Hank walks in?"

"Then I'll just be coming out of the bathroom." He motioned to the door next to hers in the hallway, while continuing to let his eyes roam over her semi-nude body.

She shook her head. "You're impossible."

"Hey, lovely lady, I'm only admiring the scenery," Tom responded, shrugging.

He was still blocking the door when she finished slipping into her wrap-around dress.

"Well, I'm ready," she said, trying to move past him.

"So am I, but I guess this isn't the time or place." He pulled her close and kissed her roughly. "Do you suppose we could get rid of the kid out there for an hour or so?"

She rested her cheek against his chest. "I repeat, you're impossible." She pulled away, laughing. "Come on, let's get Hank and go see your new apartment."

Tom found a guest parking space in front of the rental office, went in and addressed the tall, attractive lady who had earlier rented him the unit. "Would it be okay if I show the apartment to a friend?"

The resident manager smiled and handed him the key. "Of course."

She was waiting when they returned several minutes later.

Spotting Hank, she began nervously, "Mr. Finley, did I fail to mention this is an adults only complex? If so, I'm . . . ."

He interrupted her in mid-sentence. "No, you didn't. I just wanted to show this place to my, uh, sister and nephew."

"Oh . . . uh, good." He caught the uplifted brow and smiled. They obviously weren't very good actors.

On Monday morning, Tom dressed in one of his two civilian suits and drove to the employment office of WCA, near the airport. Walking into the large, richly furnished reception room, he approached a strikingly beautiful brunette behind a desk.

She glanced up through mascaraed lashes. "May I help you?" she asked pleasantly.

"My name is Tom Finley, and I have an appointment with Mr. Chasteen. Have I come to the right office?"

"Oh, yes, Mr. Finley." She broke into a friendly smile. "Mr. Chasteen is expecting you. It's the first office on the left down this hall." She motioned to a hallway leading away from her desk. "How do you take your coffee?" she called as he headed in the direction indicated.

"Black, with a little sugar, thank you." He heard the receptionist announcing his arrival to someone on the other end of the phone line. As he neared the first door, another charming young lady with shiny black hair appeared.

"Mr. Finley, please walk this way. She smilled. "Mr. Chasteen is in the conference room. He's expecting you."

As Tom followed behind the gracefully swinging hips, he decided he couldn't walk that way, but he was content to watch while she did.

The raven-haired beauty opened an ornately carved wooden door at the end of the hall, exposing an oblong walnut conference table surrounded by plushly-upholstered chairs sitting on an opulent carpet. On the inside wall was a large screen and podium; two corners of the room were filled with tree-size plants. This definitely was not your run of the mill, standard-issue, drab-Navy gray metal.

A big man, taller and heavier than Tom, rose from one end of the table. Tom's perception that his interviewer might be a little soft from the desk job was inaccurate if the strength of the handshake was any indication. "Tom, Larry Chasteen. Here, have a seat. The girls will be bringing in some coffee in a minute."

For the next hour, Larry questioned Tom about his flying experience, his family situation and his interest in joining WCA. Apparently satisfied, he rose and shook Tom's hand. "Marcie will escort you down to the medical offices."

After Tom finished the physical, he returned, as directed, to the executive offices. Within minutes, Mr. Chasteen called him back into his office. "Well, now, how soon before you can report for training?"

Tom spent the rest of the day filling out papers and signing contracts. It was after five when he finished, so he drove straight from the airport to Bobbie's house, anxious to share his good news. He couldn't wait to see how she would react. Suddenly, he understood. Until he met Bobbie, he had never gotten excited about sharing anything with a woman, except a bed. *It really must be love.*

Pulling up in front of the house, Tom jumped out of the car and burst through the front door. "I got it, Baby, I got it! I start training with WCA on the fifteenth of the month."

When Bobbie appeared from the direction of the den, Tom grabbed her and gave her an enthusiastic kiss. Then he released her and stepped back, studying her carefully. Something was wrong. She seemed disoriented, her eyes weren't focusing. Glancing inside the TV room, he noted an empty bottle on the small coffee table, and a half-empty glass. "Bobbie, have you been drinking?" Tom was appalled. "What in the hell do you think you're doing?"

"Oh, Matt, umm . . . Tom, I'm sorry." She started to cry. Leaning toward Tom, she lost her balance and stumbled. He caught her before she fell.

"Jesus Christ! Let me get you to bed, then I'll make some coffee." Tom carried her down the hall to her bedroom, where he unceremoniously dumped her on the bed, the same bed·they had so passionately shared just a few days before. He stormed back up the hall to the kitchen and searched for the coffee. To his amazement, he was shaking.

While he watched the slowly dripping water, Tom fumed. What on earth caused her to get sloppy drunk at this time of day? The coffee finally finished brewing and he poured two cups. Walking back to the bedroom, he noticed Hank's open bedroom door. It was after six and Hank wasn't home. He stepped into Bobbie's room.

She lay huddled in a pitiful heap, crying. With difficulty, her eyes focused on Tom. "Oh, please, Tom, please don't be angry with me."

Ignoring her plea, he asked gruffly, "Do you know where Hank is? It's late and he's not home yet. Is he with Debbie?"

Bobbie sat up in bed, struggling to concentrate.

He sat down beside her and held the coffee. "Here, drink this."

"Hank is across the street," she finally remembered. "He's, . . . he's going to eat dinner with his friend, Alan." After another long pause, she leaned her head against Tom's shoulder and added, "Debbie and Patty went to the beach."

Gradually his anger dissipated, and he gently slipped his arm around her. "Bobbie, what in the devil were you thinking about?"

She started to cry again, burying her head in his shirt. "Oh, Tom, I'm so mixed up. I didn't think I was such a terrible person. I've never done anything really bad before. I didn't always go to church as a kid, and Matt and I hardly ever went, but I have a certain idea about right and wrong. There are certain things you just don't do— you don't kill, you don't steal and you don't commit adultery." She shivered as she uttered the words.

Tom tried to interrupt.

"No. Let me finish. You asked why I'm drunk—well, I'm trying to explain. Tom, I'm a married woman, my husband's alive. I know he's alive, and what's worse, he's in a Communist prison. Heaven only knows how he's being treated. If I were a decent wife, like Kat or Janice, I'd be waiting faithfully for my husband to come back. I'd be keeping the home fires burning." She continued quickly, denying him a chance to respond. "Instead, in less than a year I'm in another man's arms, sharing Matt's bed and oh, Tom, I behaved shamefully. I've never acted . . . you know . . . that way . . . not even with Matt. I don't know what came over me. I'm so embarrassed, I just want to die. I can hardly look you in the eye. But even worse, I can't face myself in the mirror. I don't like the person I see. But I've come to one decision. I'll just have to live with the guilt I already feel, but I don't have to face you again. I want you to leave, and not come back. Maybe God can forgive me, but I'm not sure I can ever forgive myself for acting like such a slut, and I know if Matt ever knew, he wouldn't forgive me. So, please, just go away." Tears ran down her cheeks as she clung to him for support. He sat silently for several minutes, holding Bobbie against him.

When she stopped sobbing, he stood up, pacing as he spoke. "I've heard of Bible Belt morality, but this is ridiculous. How can loving me make you a wicked woman? How can my loving you be evil? I suppose you can call it adultery, if you want to get Biblical about it, but we could correct that—by getting married. This isn't some sleazy back street affair."

She sat on the bed, nervously wringing her hands.

"Bobbie, this is no good. I can't leave you like this. I can't leave you feeling this way. Don't you see what it's already done to you? Do you want Hank to come home and find his mother passed out on the floor? Or Debbie for that matter? Is Hank supposed to take care of himself while you sleep it off? He's only five years old. Bobbie, don't you see that drinking will only wreck your life and maybe your kids' too?"

She sobbed loudly now, the mention of danger to her children causing her even more pain and guilt. "Oh, Tom, what am I going to do? What am I going to do?"

He cradled her in his arms and pulled her close. "Sweetheart. That's what I came to tell you. I've been hired by WCA; I'll be based right here in San Diego. I'll be gone no more than one or two days at any time. I start training in a couple of weeks. By the end of the month I'll be out of the Navy. I won't have any contact with people who knew Matt. We can see each other without any of Matt's friends knowing. We can do it your way. We'll wait till Matt comes back, if that's what you want, and we'll face him together. Honey, you can't go on feeling guilty over one of the most beautiful feelings in the world—our love. What you expressed the other night was your love for me. It was beautiful and you have nothing to be ashamed of. You forgot some of your inhibitions and let your heart speak. That's the way it should be between two people when they love each other. I love you, and you love me. You can't deny that, can you?

"I don't know. Maybe I was just . . . ."

He interrupted her, kissing her lips.

She clung to him, responding eagerly to his kiss. "Oh, yes, I do love you. Yes, I really do."

"Okay, then, that settles it. That is the only thing that is important. Now I don't want any more of this stupid drinking. It doesn't work. I should know. I used it to try to forget you, and you were in the bottom of every bottle. Honey, we're going to work things out. Don't ask me how, but we will—together. Together, sugar. Just remember, you aren't in this alone. We're together, all the way."

Bobbie wept until she fell asleep. Tom held her, rocking her in his arms until he heard the front door. Laying her head gently on the pillow, he walked into the living room, closing the bedroom door behind him. In the living room, a slightly perplexed Hank greeted him.

"Hi, partner," he said cheerfully.

"Hi, Tom, where's Mom?"

"She's taking a nap. But I'll stay here with you 'til bedtime, or until Debbie gets back, if that's okay with you. You've had dinner, right?"

"Yeah. Wanna watch TV?"

When Debbie arrived, Tom explained to both of them that Bobbie was not feeling well, and he tried to explain why.

"With your father gone, it's very hard for her alone, and even though she's being very brave, sometimes she gets depressed. Try to understand if at times she seems unhappy. She needs your help, too." He was sure Debbie knew exactly what he was taking about, having eyed the empty bottle Tom had neglected to throw away.

"Look, I want to be your friend, and your mom's friend. I'm going to be living not too far from here, so I'll be close if you need me." Tom waited for their reaction.

Debbie appeared grateful and relieved.

At the mention of his father's absence, Hank fell sullen. "I want to go to bed now," he sniveled.

Tom helped Debbie put Hank to bed, checked on Bobbie, who was sleeping like a baby, and then returned to Debbie. "Here's my telephone number. Call if there is any problem you can't handle."

She fingered the card for several seconds, then raised her head and looked straight into his eyes. "You're in love with Mom, aren't you?"

Tom stopped dead in his tracks. What could he say? Her question wasn't an accusation, it had been stated matter-of-factly, just as if it were perfectly logical. Obviously he and Bobbie hadn't been as skillful at hiding their feelings as they thought. Well, Bobbie might not give her the same answer, but he wasn't going to lie to her. "Yes, I am." Then, when she made no comment, he asked, "What do you think about that?"

She studied him pensively for several seconds, then raised her eyebrows, shrugged her shoulders, and looked away.

He turned to leave, adding, "Debbie, it'd be better if you didn't ask your mother that question."

"Yeah, I know."

Driving back to his BOQ room, Tom struggled over the turn of events in his life. It was going to be a difficult, painful process, no matter what happened, and he had a hunch there was a long, rough road ahead. Would Bobbie feel differently about getting married if she could have heard his exchange with Debbie? Maybe it would only make her feel worse. He decided not to share it for the time being.

It would be better for him if he could just walk away from this situation. He was in for a lot of heartache and trouble if he stuck by Bobbie. But, remembering their lovemaking, the way she felt in his arms, he knew he really had no choice. It was actually very simple. He had, at long last, fallen in love. Maybe it was only fair that he was so inextricably involved with a married woman. The "Love God" must be getting his revenge.

CHAPTER 15

Zoo Camp, North Vietnam, late 1967.

Without explanation in the fall of 1967, security grew much stricter. The guards entered the cell one night and directed Matt, John and Lee to sleep so that their heads were visible from the door. For a month, they were forced to sleep in leg irons. Punishment for communicating was swift and severe. If they were caught, they were immediately tied up and tortured. For no apparent reason, the SRO of the cellblock, Commander Mason, was beaten savagely, locked in wrist irons with his hands behind his back and left that way for several weeks.

Eventually, through the prison communication system, they started to learn what had prompted this harsh treatment.

Commander Mason's cell passed on the first information.

"Two prisoners from Dirty Bird prison attempted to escape," Matt relayed to his cellmates.

"What and where is Dirty Bird prison?" asked John.

"It's another camp south of here on a river near a bridge. Rumor is that it was located in that spot so that if the bombers missed the bridge, they would hit the prison," explained Lee.

Slowly the story of the escape circulated through the prison. During the night, two men got out of the camp, slipped into the water and let the current carry them downstream. They took refuge in a crevice when it started to get light, intending to hide during the day and travel by river at night until they reached the Gulf of Tonkin. There they planned to commandeer a boat and use it to find the American destroyers located somewhere off the coast. They had agreed to attempt this escape, at least up to the point of stealing the boat, without violence. When they were discovered quite by accident by an old fisherman and his wife, they allowed themselves to be recaptured rather than harm the old couple and risk the additional violence that fleeing by day would involve. When they were caught, they were returned to the prison and punished, but apparently they managed to convince the V that no one else had participated in or even knew in advance of their plan, which was true. They told the V they figured they were going to die in prison anyway, so they had nothing to lose by trying to escape.

"God. That was ballsy." John's voice was full of admiration.

"Risky too," Matt cautioned. "And it affects more than just the guys going over the wall. Look at the shabby treatment we've all been getting."

"I'd gladly spend a few weeks in irons if it meant a couple guys got out of this joint," John argued.

Lee joined the discussion. "I agree with Matt. There would be hell to pay if someone escaped, and I mean hell—a lot more than a few weeks in irons."

John continued to disagree. "I can tell you, if I get the chance, I'm outta here."

Lee and Matt looked at each other and shrugged. Resignation rendered them quiet. They had come to learn it was difficult to win an argument with John.

Prison life gradually settled back to its normal, monotonous routine. Utilizing a cup to transmit their voices through the wall, they became complacent and failed to post a lookout. A guard caught them. Jumping up and down and flailing his arms, he ordered them to stand in the center of the room. Then he disappeared.

"We've got to agree on the same story," Matt whispered. "We might be able to bluff our way through without involving others if we can come up with something believable. But what?"

Lee pointed to the foxhole in their cell. "We were trying to catch the cockhopper."

Before they could perfect their explanation, the block

commander appeared. John and Lee were led out of the room. The Rat interrogated Matt. "Who have you been communicating with?"

"No one."

"Why have you broken camp regulations?"

"I was not communicating." Pointing to the bomb shelter in the center of the cell, a hole about six feet long, two feet wide and five feet deep, Matt explained, "This *thing* lives in that hole. At night it comes out and we are afraid it is going to bite us. It looks like a large cockroach, but it jumps around like a grasshopper. We call it the 'Cockhopper.' We have been trying to catch him. Today we saw him, and in my excitement, I yelled to the others that we must catch him."

"And the cup?" asked the Rat, eyeing Matt with disbelief.

"Just before we saw the creature, we were getting ready to go out and get our morning meal, and the cup was on the hook where our clothes were hanging." The story sounded absurd, but it was all they had.

"You must stand against the wall with your hands above your head."

Lee was brought back into the room. In the brief second before the Rat walked back in, Matt whispered, "Go with the cockhopper story."

The Rat strolled back into the cell. "Write everything that has been going on in your room."

Lee wrote basically the same story Matt had told.

The Rat read it, raised his eyebrows and threw one hand into the air. With a snort, he marched into the next room where John was being held.

After a few minutes, John was brought back in. The Rat lined the three of them at attention. "You must apologize to the camp commander for making undue noise in the room." They all agreed. As he left, the Rat peered hesitantly into the hole, looked back at the three, executed one of his famous nose twitches, glanced again at the hole and walked out.

As soon as they heard the guard's steps fading into the distance, Matt, John and Lee let out a quiet whoop, each giving a raised-thumb gesture.

"So what happened with you?" Matt asked John.

"Well," John mimicked the Rat's demeanor, "he marched in and said, 'Your roommates have confessed to everything. They have told me how they were communicating, and what you were doing in the cell. Now you must tell me how you were communicating and what you were doing with the cup.' I considered the situation for a few seconds. I figured not enough time had passed for you to have been tortured, and you would not have confessed otherwise, so I stuck with the cockhopper story."

Later that evening, Matt observed, "I think there's a message here for us. It's better to have even a ridiculous lie than nothing at all. I think the V need some way to save face when a camp rule has been broken. Even that stupid story gave the Rat an out."

John imitated the Rat, "Confess, quickly, so I can forgive you. It must be a religious thing."

"John, you missed your calling, you're a thespian," Lee laughed.

****

Zoo Camp, North Vietnam, 1968.

Within the prison system, any big shake-up was usually preceded by several smaller moves. In February 1968, the men in the Zoo started to notice small changes. Matt, John and Lee were moved from Cell 8 to Cell 6, nearer the dishwashing facilities. Several new men were brought into Zoo Camp and placed in Cell 11.

They tried to contact them. The men in the room on the other side of 11 also tried to reach them. Over time, they obtained the names of the new prisoners but were told that their SRO, a LCDR Corbett, did not think it was safe to communicate. All efforts during the next several weeks were met with silence.

The anticipated big move came in early May. Matt, John and Lee were moved from the Pig Sty to Cell 1 in another cellblock the prisoners dubbed "the Stable," acquiring another cellmate in the process. The men from Cell 11 were placed in a large cell next door, along with several men who had been brought from other locations.

The potential impact of the move weighed heavily on Matt and his cellmates.

John was the first to express their shared apprehension. "I don't like this at all. This building is under the control of that depraved Cuban."

Lee agreed, "I don't either. I've heard a lot of bad things about Fidel."

Their new cellmate, Major Bill Collins, USAF, a recent shoot - down, was shocked, "You mean there's a Cuban guard here?"

Matt explained what they knew. "There are three we know of. Fidel's a perverted asshole with a quick, violent temper, and a drinking problem. His two Cuban henchmen, Chico and Pancho, are just plain mean. One of Fidel's favorite tricks is to break both eardrums at once by slamming his open hands against a prisoner's ears."

John added, "He doesn't even want the men to do anything in particular; it just gives him sadistic pleasure to injure, maim, or degrade us. When a prisoner finally bows, Fidel just laughs and sends him back to his cell."

Lee warned, "I've heard he wants to prove to the Vietnamese that he knows how to make the Americans crawl."

Bill, still suffering from a broken leg, asked anxiously, "Does that mean he's our building commander?"

"I don't know. It seems he's in charge of only certain prisoners," Matt replied.

John voiced their shared concern. "I sure as hell hope we aren't in his section."

Matt was the first to be summoned by Fidel.

"Be careful," warned Lee.

Matt nervously shifted from one foot to the other while he waited. The man in the Castro type green fatigues with his back to him was tall, over six feet, and weighed at least 190 pounds, with broad shoulders and slicked-back black hair. When Fidel turned to face him, Matt was jolted by the black flashing eyes that bore into their target like a shot of cold carbon steel. The Cuban had a swarthy complexion, sharp nose and pointed facial features, giving him the appearance of a B-movie tough guy, except he was fit, with no gut. Fidel seemed to be sizing him up too.

After several minutes of visual sparring, Fidel asked some general questions. Matt let his guard down a little.

"How many men do you think are in camp?" It was an interrogator's trick—the unexpected, deadly question dropped in the midst of neutral chatter.

Matt's answer was deliberate and cautious. "I think there are between one hundred and two hundred." This was the number he actually thought was in their camp. This line of questioning was probably to determine if the men in Zoo camp knew about the camp on the other side of the high fence behind the Garage and the Barn, almost directly behind the Zoo. It had taken almost a year, around the middle of 1967, before the men in the Zoo learned there were more prisoners in a previously unknown camp. Communication between the Zoo and what they dubbed "the Annex" was difficult and cumbersome, but contact was finally established and the men in the Zoo were aware of who was in the Annex.

Fidel fixed Matt with an unrelenting stare for more than a minute. The stillness was maddening. Finally, he continued, "How did you come up with that number?"

Again Matt carefully considered his answer. "The men in the cell and I have now washed dishes in three different cellblocks. We know how many men are in each block."

Fidel arched his bushy eyebrows, his eyes glowering from their deep-set sockets.

Matt felt compelled to give a more detailed explanation. "In addition, some of the guys lived in other blocks before they came to my cell, so we just added it up, and that's what it looks like to us."

Apparently satisfied, Fidel turned away. Matt hoped the interrogation was over.

Suddenly Fidel jumped directly in front of Matt, his menacing face less than an inch away. "Have you ever been tortured?"

Matt jerked his head back and turned to avoid the foul cigar breath, and the evil, piercing eyes. "Yes."

Fidel sneered, "What do you mean you've been tortured? You still have all your fingernails."

Matt followed Fidel's gaze to his hands, but said nothing.

"Have you ever been kicked in the balls?" Fidel spun around on one leg, like a martial arts expert, his other steel-toed boot crossing precariously close to Matt's crotch.

"No." Matt jumped backward, sweat covering his brow.

"Well, then, you haven't been tortured," Fidel crowed.

Matt swallowed, then swallowed again, trying not to betray his anxiety. A gloating Fidel dismissed him with a wave.

A few days later, they heard a loud commotion outside their cell.

They took turns watching through the slit in their cell door as the Cubans lined up all the men from the cell next door in the courtyard. Each was forced to kneel in front of the Fidel while he administered three strong licks to the head with a thick rubber hose. The room SRO, Commander Ward, was given his three, plus an equal number for each of the 11 men in the cell.

As soon as the men returned to their cell, Matt contacted Commander Ward, "What's up?"

The tapped response, "Punishment is because Corbett refuses to bow to guards."

Since moving into the Stable, the men next door had acquired a new SRO and had started communicating. Little by little, over the past several days, Matt and his crew learned what had been happening when the men were first brought to the Pig Sty.

Lieutenant Commander Corbett had been brutally beaten and tortured before he arrived at the Zoo Camp in February. As a result of his injuries, he was practically unable to care for himself. The three younger officers fed him, bathed him and generally cared for his wounds. But, in spite of his debilitating injuries, Corbett remained defiant toward the Vietnamese. He steadfastly refused to bow to the guards, despite repeated beatings.

"Corbett thinks he is resisting in superior fashion," tapped Ward. "I think he is unstable, irrational; his mind affected by horrible beatings. We all agree he's mentally ill. He's suspicious of us; thinks some of us are Russian spies."

Throughout the day, with the others watching for the guards, Matt received the rest of the story and repeated it to his cellmates.

"Corbett refuses to do anything they ask him to do. He won't bow to the guards, won't bathe, doesn't exercise. He just lies in his bunk all day long, staring into space. Even though he's physically capable, he refuses to eat; thinks they're trying to poison him. They're having to force feed him."

"How are you doing that?" asked John.

"It's pretty complicated; takes seven of them to do it. Two hold down his legs; two hold his arms, one cradles his head and holds his nose shut; one spoons in the food, and the seventh shoves it down his throat and holds his mouth shut until he swallows."

"I don't get it. What's the big deal about bowing to the guards?" Bill asked, grimacing as he pictured the ordeal just described.

Lee explained, "We are required to bow to the guards, even when they just open the peephole in the cell door. It's the Vietnamese way of making us feel subservient. Under the Geneva Convention, military officers who are prisoners of war are not required to salute or bow to any enlisted troops. But the Vietnamese claim we are criminals, not prisoners of war. In order to force us to bow, those who refuse are usually beaten until they acquiesce."

Matt continued recounting Commander Ward's message. "It seems to them that forcing Corbett to bow has become an obsession for Fidel. He personally beats Corbett a lot. While the men in the cell watch helplessly, Fidel knocks him down with a backhand blow, picks him up and knocks him down again. Corbett just rises up, dizzy and bleeding but still refuses to bow. Even when he's being battered in the face with a hose or an old fan belt, he just stands there, unblinking and unbending."

"Jesus," Bill declared, shocked. "Isn't there anything we can do?"

Matt shook his head. "No. If anyone can do anything, it's Ward and the men in that cell. Hell, we're not even supposed to know what's happening. If any of us said anything, they'd know we'd been communicating. Fidel would have a field day with all of us, and it would not help Corbett."

For once, John agreed with Matt. "There may be nothing anyone can do in this case."

The standoff continued over several weeks. Matt reported Ward's messages. "Ward has tried several times to intervene with Fidel. He's insisted that Corbett is sick and needs treatment. But

Fidel just rejects his protests with a smirk and hits Corbett in the face again. He says that Corbett is just being obstinate, and he intends to make him bow."

One day the men in Cell 1 heard noise next door. They watched through the slit as guards burst into the cell, dragged Corbett out and threw him into a nearby cell by himself. Several times during the next several days, they were assaulted with his agonized screams as he was relentlessly beaten and tortured.

One minute he was yelling loudly as before, then they heard an eerie, soul-wrenching screech, a wheezing death rattle, followed by deafening silence.

"Jesus Christ! They've killed him," John exclaimed in a hushed tone.

The others shook their heads in stunned agreement.

Later in the day, they received a surprise message from Ward. "Corbett just brought back. Hell beaten out of him, but he walked in. Like a zombie; hasn't uttered a sound. Think his mind is gone. Fidel finally succeeded in driving him crazy."

Daily Matt received the update from Ward to pass on to the building SRO, and Cell 6. "Not only are they having to force feed and bathe Corbett, if someone doesn't help him with the honey bucket, he just goes without removing the lid. When he's finished, he doesn't even pull his trousers back up, just stumbles back to his bunk, with his clothes down around his ankles."

"Are they still torturing him?" John and Bill both asked.

"According to Ward, Corbett's incredible. He says you'd have to see it to believe it. He doesn't flinch or blink, even when they stick needles clear through his arms, yet that SOB Fidel still claims he's faking."

A few days later, John, whose communication skills were improving, received an urgent message from one of the men next door. His voice was excited as he relayed the latest information. "Ward finally convinced the V that Corbett is sick. Fidel has been dismissed from his position and all the Cubans have been expelled to Cuba."

They couldn't contain themselves. In unison, they cheered and raised their fists in a victory salute.

John motioned. "There's more." Lee took up the guard watch while John received the rest of the message.

"The Rat told Ward they couldn't blame the Vietnamese for what the Cubans did."

Lee jeered, "Like hell."

John continued, "Ward told him they were responsible for bringing that bastard Cuban here in the first place."

Bill nodded, "Right on."

A week later, Ward tapped and Matt reported as it was received, "V trying to undo harm caused by Fidel. Are administering electric shock treatments to Corbett. When he returns from hospital, can see burned places each side of his head. Sometimes he appears better. He's eaten and walked around a little. Trying to convince V they need to remove him from prison environment. Each time he's thrown back in cell, reverts to old behavior within days. He's in bad shape. Don't think he's going to make it."

A couple of days later, Ward sent another message. "Corbett not returned. V won't tell me where he is. I'm sure he's dead. Pass message up the line."

CHAPTER 16

San Diego, California, Fall 1967- July 1968.

When he wasn't flying, Tom usually spent at least one day of the weekend with Bobbie and the children. At her insistence, they saw each other alone only on the sly.

One evening, she snuck in through the patio. "Close the door, quick. I thought I saw someone I know." Bobbie was really shaken.

"Bobbie, I hate it when you reduce our love into this cheap back-alley relationship, afraid to be seen with me, afraid to go out with me," he complained. "We can't go out to dinner, we can't go out to a movie, the only time you're seen in public with me is at the beach with the kids, or when we go down to Mexico."

"Tom, please, let's not argue over this again. It's important to be discreet for the sake of the children. I just can't flaunt that I am sleeping with another man while their father is a prisoner of war. And you know if we were seen together, people would talk and it would get back to Matt somehow." She dismissed his arguments as she always did.

"There's always the option of your getting a divorce and we get married. Lord knows I've asked you enough times."

"You know that isn't possible. I haven't heard a word from Matt, I don't know how to get in touch with him, and I'd be afraid to write even if I could, for fear he'd read between the lines. Please, *please* let it go for now. I just couldn't face the children's scorn."

Should he tell her about his earlier conversation with Debbie? It probably wouldn't make any difference, anyway—she was so damned concerned about appearances.

Shortly before Christmas, Bobbie announced, "My folks will be out at Christmas. You mustn't come near the house while they're here."

"What?" Tom frowned. "I have been looking forward to meeting them."

"You *cannot* come over while my folks are here. I'll try to get away for a few hours and come to your place."

"But I want to spend the holidays with *you*," he protested. "I want to meet your parents. Honey, they're concerned with your happiness. They'll want what's best for you. Let's show them how much better it would be for you and the children if we were married." If he could win them over, and he was confident he could, that just might be the key to breaking down Bobbie's resistance

"No way! Tom, I don't want you to come near the house. Is that clear? I know my folks. They're old fashioned. Marriage is forever, for better or for worse. Remember those words? They'll expect me to wait like a good little wife until Matt gets home. On top of everything else, I can do without their condemnation, thank you very much."

Tom's face hardened. "Bobbie, you're making a big mistake."

"Promise me. Promise me you won't come near the place," she pleaded as she prepared to leave.

"Oh, shit. . . . Sure, why not." He shrugged and threw his hands in the air. "Enjoy your Christmas." He shut the door hard after her.

He didn't want to spend the holidays alone in his apartment, so he volunteered to fly extra trips over the holidays so the married pilots could stay home with their families.

What little time he was home, his thoughts were up the hill. How could they deal with her guilt? It was becoming abundantly clear that no matter how much he loved her or how good their lovemaking might be, Bobbie couldn't get past the big red flashing "ADULTERY" sign. It was as though she couldn't help loving him or making love with him, but in so doing, she was committing a terrible sin for which she should be punished. With no one else around to do it, she punished herself. Since her binge in August, he could tell she was being careful not to get drunk, but her alcohol consumption had increased significantly. Being in love was not turning out to be what he had expected.

A couple of weeks later, she stopped by Tom's apartment, and announced excitedly, "Guess what, I got a job."

"Hey, that's good news." *That'll cut down on her drinking time.* "Tell me about it."

"It's an insurance company. The office is over in the Clairemont Mesa area. They had an opening for a steno in their sales office and needed someone four hours per day. The pay isn't very much, but they are willing to train me. They have free parking and it's only about a ten-minute drive. I start Monday."

For awhile Tom noticed an improvement in Bobbie's drinking. Her work was good therapy. Then, in May, just before school was out, Bobbie announced she was quitting her job. "I can't work while the children are home for the summer."

Once again, when she came to his apartment, Tom could smell the alcohol on her breath.

****

Summer, 1968, North Vietnam.

Matt returned to the cell after a meeting with the block commander. "Guess what. The Rat said I can write a letter home if I want to. I wonder if I should?"

"How long has it been since you wrote?" Bill asked.

"I haven't. About six weeks after I was shot down, I turned down the only other chance I've had to write home. I was suffering from the Green Room treatment, and it was right after the Hanoi march. I had already violated the Code of Conduct, but I knew they wouldn't let me write a letter unless I gave them more. I was also afraid that a letter might be used for propaganda purposes, either by the Vietnamese themselves, or by some of the peace groups that had been coming to Hanoi. All I could think was that those anti-war activists would bother Bobbie or my folks, or might demand something in exchange for delivering the letter. I didn't want them to pay money or be forced to say or do anything improper, something that might unintentionally support the anti-war effort. As much as I wanted to let Bobbie know I was okay, I refused to write."

"What happened?" Bill asked, puzzled.

"When I declined, they tried to force me to write a letter, if not to my wife, then to a congressman. I knew if they wanted me to do something, it was probably not in my best interest, so I continued to refuse. They didn't resort to physical torture, and after a few days of pressure they dropped it. But, just as I suspected, those who did write letters at that time were then forced to tape record them, and those letters were read on the Voice of North Vietnam, as propaganda."

John added, "I think by the time I got here, the V were just not letting any of us write. I've never had a chance, but I've heard some of the guys have gotten mail, so the V must be relenting."

Bill expressed his shock. "Before I was shot down, the C.O. told our squadron that if we ended up in prison it was okay to write letters home. I haven't been allowed to yet, but if I get the chance, I intend to."

Still Matt was hesitant. "I know some people are receiving mail. Some of the letters aren't stamped. Doesn't that mean they aren't going through normal postal channels? I don't want Bobbie to have anything to do with any of those peacenik groups that have been poking around over here. She shouldn't have to deal with scum like that."

John agreed. "A lot of good men have been beaten and tortured to force us to meet with some of those visiting sonsabitches. You remember when some of the guys weren't allowed to sleep for four or five days until they agreed to see that loud-mouthed Hollywood broad, Jane Fonda, or the former Washington big-shot politician, Clark or whatever his name was, to report on the 'kind and lenient' treatment we were receiving. I don't blame you, Matt. They aren't the sort of people I would want to entrust with a letter to my wife either, but—if you want to let her know you're okay. I imagine after two years she'd welcome a letter, no matter how it got there."

John draped an arm around Matt, "If I'm given the chance, I'm going to write to Sharon."

Bill shook his head; staring in disbelief. "Do you mean you guys haven't received any mail at all since you've been here? Matt, does your wife even know you're alive? What about your folks?"

"Oh, I'm sure one of my wingmen must have seen my chute, so Bobbie and my folks should have been notified. If they didn't see my chute, there were numerous photos taken during the Hanoi march. Some of them had to have made it back to our guys."

Again Bill shook his head, stunned. "Write her a letter," he urged.

Lee added, "Yeah, I agree. I'm just waiting for the chance to write Brigette."

John nodded his head in agreement.

Matt reclined on his bunk and fell silent. He so wanted to hear from Bobbie. Was she okay? How were the children doing? More than anything he wanted to let her know how much he loved her. With so much time on his hands over these past two years, so many hours alone in a prison cell, he had plenty of time to reflect on his life. In many ways he could have been a better husband. When he got home, if he survived, he was going to make up for a lot of things he should have done before. He would even get out of the Navy if that was what she wanted. She had never been particularly thrilled with military life. He just wanted, somehow, to let Bobbie know that she was the most important thing in his life, even though he had done so little to show it before.

They were right; there really wasn't any choice. He needed to get his message to Bobbie.

The Rat gave him a small scrap of paper. "Write your letter. It will be submitted for approval. You may not write anything that suggests you are in bad health or that you have lost weight. You may not ask for vitamins or food, and you are not to mention dates or places."

The censor made some minor changes. Matt reviewed the corrected version. It still said basically what he wanted to say—that he was okay and how much he loved her. He neatly printed his precious message on a small, clean single sheet.

****

San Diego, August 1968.

In August, Tom returned about noon after a late evening flight with a layover in San Francisco, and called Bobbie's house from the airport as soon as he landed. The phone rang several times, before it was finally answered by Debbie.

"Hi, Deb, this is Tom. How's everything going?"

There was a hesitation on the other end. Tom sensed a problem. "Is something wrong?" Silence. He raised his voice, "Debbie, I can tell something is wrong. Now tell me what it is."

Her answer was low and controlled. "Maybe you ought to come over if you can."

"Debbie, where is your mother?" He sensed there was a problem with Bobbie.

"She's here. She's in bed right now, but she's here," she replied woodenly.

"In bed. It's one o'clock in the afternoon. What's she doing in bed? Is she ill? Has there been an accident?" He didn't like the growing feeling of impending disaster.

Hesitantly Debbie answered, "Well, yes, she's okay. She's just not feeling well. I think it would be better if you came over."

Now he was really alarmed. This wasn't like Debbie to be so mysterious and it portended something serious. "See you as soon as I can change clothes." He had a premonition of what "not feeling well" meant, having used it himself to describe the condition he feared Bobbie was in. But why? She was going to have to get some help for her drinking, that was all there was to it. For the first time he began to question their relationship. As much as he loved her, perhaps it wasn't good for them to stay together, particularly if he was the primary cause of her drinking. But would she quit if they stopped seeing each other, or would her guilty conscience continue to haunt her and drive her to do something rash? Once he believed that if he loved her enough, maybe—just maybe—she would come around to his way of thinking. But, he noted glumly, in the year they had been lovers, she had gone steadily downhill. It was time for him to take a good, hard look at the situation. He still loved her, that he was sure of. He wanted to take care of her and the children, and they needed him desperately. But as fine and noble as that sounded to him, it seemed to have the opposite effect on her. Perhaps he should suggest they stop seeing each other for awhile, in the hope that she would refuse and agree to do things his way. But, if she didn't, then maybe a separation would be for the best.

Tom hurriedly drove to his apartment and changed from his uniform into a pair of slacks and cotton shirt. Glancing in the mirror, a tired-looking, worry-lined face stared back. Coping with Bobbie's problems was beginning to take its toll.

Maybe it was time for him to go out and have a little fun. The closer he got to her house, the angrier he became. If she was drunk again, he was going to get drunk himself, maybe even pick up a girl. For over a year, he had no desire to make love to any other woman, but now the idea had a certain amount of appeal. There was still that unique magic when they made love, but at times she was so plastered by the time she came to his apartment she responded by rote. "This is going to stop," he resolved aloud.

As soon as he pulled up in front of the house, Debbie walked out to meet him. Her young face showed mature concern. For a moment he thought she might have been crying, something he couldn't remember ever seeing her do since he'd known her.

"Hi, Tom." She greeted him with a hug as had become their custom. She was a beautiful young lady, and Tom would have been proud to be able to call her his daughter.

"What gives, babe?" he asked kindly.

"Mom's still in bed, but I don't think she's sleeping right now. I let Hank go over to his friend's, so he wouldn't be around making a lot of noise. Now that you're here, if it's okay with you, I'm going over to Patty's and see if she can do something. I think you and Mom might want to talk in private."

There was some latent message. *What in the hell is going on?* Her manner was very subdued, almost gloomy.

"Sure, it's okay with me, but I still don't understand. What's happening? You look like you just lost your last friend. Why are you so upset?"

Debbie stood quietly, her head lowered to hide just a hint of a tear. Slowly raising her eyes to meet his, she announced softly, "Mom got a letter from Dad yesterday." She held his gaze for a moment, shrugged slightly and walked away.

"Oh, shit!" Tom rushed into the house, heading immediately to Bobbie's bedroom. She wasn't in bed, but he could hear the water running in the shower. Well, at least she's up. He stiffened, his eyes drawn to a single sheet of folded paper on the nightstand. Apprehensively, he picked it up and began to read the message carefully written in small, almost printed letters:

> "My darling Bobbie, First chance to write. Don't worry, I am fine. I miss you, Debbie and Hank very much. I love you with all my heart. Your love keeps me going. I don't know what I would do without you. Please write, we can now receive mail. Yours forever, Matt."

Tom held the letter for several minutes, reading and re-reading the precisely written words. "Shit," he repeated. His stomach tightened. Now he understood why Bobbie had gotten drunk. He could use a drink himself. This would have to come when he was out of town. How she must have suffered last night. When she needed him most, he hadn't been there to help her.

He looked up at that moment to see Bobbie standing in the bathroom door, a towel around her hair, silently watching him. He'd been so engrossed in the letter, he didn't hear her come out of the bathroom. She didn't look particularly refreshed by her shower. Her eyes were red and her face was puffy.

"Oh, my darling." He started around the bed, wanting to take her in his arms and comfort her, soothe away her pain.

Instead of welcoming his embrace, she put out her hand to stop him. "No, Tom, no more. I can't take it. I can't do this to Matt. You must go, and I don't want you to come back. Please, this is very difficult, but it's the only way I can live with myself." She was speaking rapidly, but with determination. When he started to protest, she pleaded, "Tom, please. I'm not very strong where you're concerned. And if you take me in your arms, I might give in—for now. But believe me, this is the only way. I am Matt's wife. He loves me and he is counting on me. I just wasn't cut out to be an unfaithful wife, and I think you can see from that letter that I can't possibly divorce him while he's over there."

He listened as the words came out like bullets, wounding deep. All his previous anger was gone, and he was overcome with pain and grief, and a feeling of utter helplessness. Even if it might be possible to change her mind in the future, it would be futile now. He edged reluctantly toward the door. "Bobbie, Hank's across the street and Debbie went over to Patty's. Are you sure you're going to be all right?" What he really wanted to know was if she was going to drink herself into oblivion.

Her reply was quick. "Yes, I'll be okay," and as if sensing his unstated concern, "and don't worry, I'm not going to drink any more."

"Bobbie, this doesn't change the way I feel about you. I still love you, and I still want to marry you. I'm going to leave now, if that's what you really want, but if you need me for anything at all, you call me. Will you do that?"

"Tom, thank you. Thank you for caring about me. But I hope I won't need to call you for anything."

Her decision seemed definite and final. Was this really the end for them? His voice was choked as he whispered, "Take care, I love you."

He turned and walked quickly to his car. Tears blurred his vision as he drove away. Tom Finley, old Love 'em and Leave 'em Tom Finley, was bawling like a baby over a woman!

CHAPTER 17

San Diego, August 1968.

Bobbie, sick at the expression on Tom's face, watched unhappily as he turned and dejectedly walked away. She could barely control a shiver. Lying across the bed, she picked up the letter and re-read it for the hundredth time, kicking off another round of tears. She couldn't leave Matt now, she simply could not write and tell him she loved someone else, not after what he had written in his letter. She would have to wait until he got home. And what then? What would people think of a woman who would discard her husband after what he had gone through? Was it possible she might never be free? She felt trapped, like a wild animal in a cage.

How was she going to get by without Tom? The emptiness, the loss she felt as he walked out the door was real and very painful. He had awakened a fire in her that she hadn't suspected existed. Just remembering it momentarily staggered her.

She had been so tempted to call him back, to tell him not to go, to never leave her, to run into the sanctuary of his warm arms. If only she could shed the shackles of her guilt, go on as they had been, satisfying her need for Tom, her burning passion. If only Matt had been killed, she would be free to marry Tom.

Her hand flew to her mouth as the realization of what she had just been thinking rocked her with the force of a tidal wave. "Oh, my

God! I don't believe I had such a wicked thought. I'm sorry, I'm sorry. Please forgive me, I didn't mean it," she sobbed.

****

Tom dressed in his swimming trunks and walked down to the swimming pool at the other end of the complex, taking along a novel he had been intending to read for some time. Finding an unoccupied lounge chair, he tried to focus his attention on the book, but the letters blurred together, his mind several blocks away, on Bobbie and the letter from Matt. A shadow fell over his book. He looked up to discover the cause of the shadow—a shapely yet vaguely familiar female figure.

"Well, hello, stranger," she smiled warmly. "I think this is the first time I've seen you at the pool since you moved in."

"Oh, hello Miss . . . Malone, isn't it?"

Even her dark brown eyes were smiling.

"You're right. I haven't used it much, but I'm going to correct that starting right now. I didn't realize the scenery was so nice." He let his eyes roam pointedly from her bare feet with painted nails to the tip of her freckled nose. It was quite a different image than he carried of the resident manager as a fairly plain Jane with her hair piled high on her head, glasses and a boxy business suit.

She tilted her head, elevated an eyebrow and smiled. "You kind of improve it yourself." She had a dimple in her cheeks when she smiled.

Motioning to the unoccupied seat nearby. "Why don't you join me?" Then a bit more solemnly, he added, "I could use a little conversation today."

"I'd love to. Can I get you a drink? We have a bar set up over at the club house."

"Hey, that sounds good, but let me treat you," he offered.

"Forget it," she flipped her hand. "It's free for the hired help—and that's me." She turned to leave. "What'll you have?"

"How about a lot of scotch and a little water?"

"Going to drown your sorrows?" She gave him an amused look.

"Am I that transparent?" Tom was surprised.

"Oh, not really. Just a hunch. Don't go 'way."

She disappeared into a small club room at the far end of the pool area, leaving Tom alone again with his thoughts. Maggie Malone was something of a surprise. There was more to her than met the eye, obviously. But what met the eye, in that revealing bathing suit, was pretty nice, too. Smooth tanned flesh tautly stretched over well-defined, well-proportioned muscles; not an ounce of flab that he could see, and he could see most of it. With her long, thick dark hair pulled back in a pony tail, she looked like a bubbly teen-ager, albeit a well-developed one.

Maggie came gliding back, radiating a sensualness about which she seemed totally unaware. She was taller than he remembered, perhaps 5'8" or 5'9", quite a contrast from Bobbie. For a fleeting second his heart tugged. He greeted Maggie, downed the drink in a single gulp, raised the glass and asked, "How about having dinner with me tonight?"

"I'd love to," she agreed eagerly. "I thought you'd never ask."

CHAPTER 18

<u>Zoo Camp, North Vietnam, Fall 1968.</u>

The fall of 1968 brought some exciting news. Matt and his cellmates established communication with the Garage, a cellblock full of prisoners located completely across the camp from the Stable. For days, they took turns standing on each other's shoulders, waiting and watching, until the conditions, at last, were favorable. When enough leaves had fallen off the trees, they finally made contact. This breakthrough brought a whole new group of men into the communication network, men who previously had been almost unreachable. It was a doubly important link since communication with the Garage, interfacing as it did with the Annex, made it easier for the men in the Zoo to transmit and receive messages to and from the more junior officers housed in the Annex. This was a definite victory, since the V, in their campaign to ignore the military chain of command, concentrated their propaganda efforts on these more junior officers. With this improved communication route, the camp SRO's directives could be passed quicker to the younger men.

For Matt, it was particularly rewarding. One of the prisoners in the Garage was Roy Roberts. Over the next few days, Roy, using a flash code, described his meeting with Bobbie when the ship first got back in the summer of 1966.

"She is stronger than I would have thought. Kat and I got together with her and the children a couple of times. Debbie's a big help. Hank's a handfull, of course, but they were really doing well under the circumstances."

"God, that's great news." He relayed Roy's message to his cell-mates. "You know, this is the first news I've received about Bobbie since I was shot down. I wonder if she's received my letter yet? I would have given anything to have seen her face when it arrived. After all this time, it must have been a shock."

When he and Lee were alone, Matt sheepishly confided, "I'm really glad I sent that letter to Bobbie. I'm glad I told her how much I love her. I just wish she knew how much. It has taken prison and this forced separation for me to realize what my family really means to me. Maybe it's just the possibility that I might never see them again, but whatever the reason, these past couple of years have been very revealing. I see things from a different perspective now. You know, Lee, I actually feel guilty when I think about how poorly I treated Bobbie sometimes, how little attention I paid to *her* needs and desires. She must have thought I was pretty damn inconsiderate and selfish, yet she never complained."

He shook his head, bit his lip and rubbed his forehead. "No, she wouldn't. She always did everything to try to make me happy and comfortable. I'm not much of a religious man, but I pray that some-day I will get the opportunity to let her know how I truly feel." He let his fingers move down his face, resting his still-shaking head in his hands. "Christ. I never realized how much she meant to me. I just always took her for granted. I took her love and gave her so very little in return."

Lee patted Matt's slumping shoulders. "Matt, you're blowing this all out of proportion. I know you pretty well after all this time together. You couldn't have been as bad a husband as you're making yourself out to be."

Matt stared at the ceiling. "I hate to think of her trying to raise the children alone, with no family close by to provide any assis-tance. Hank needs a man around as a role model and for discipline. I just wish there were someone, but she really has no one she can turn to."

"She'll manage, Matt. So will my wife, and John's. They are stronger than we give them credit for. They just let us think they're the weak ones, that they need us. It's an act. You'll see, she'll do fine."

Matt's head continued to move back and forth like the pendulum of a grandfather's clock. "But there are so many things I always did. I have a real hard time seeing how she can handle everything without some help. I don't think her dependence was an act."

****

<u>Christmas 1968, North Vietnam.</u>

Shortly before Christmas, Lee was removed from the cell. It wasn't unusual and no one thought much about it until the afternoon meal was brought, and Lee wasn't back.

Matt joked, "I sure hate to see good food go to waste. Wonder when Lee will be back?"

"If he ain't back by the time the guard comes in, they'll just take it away. I'll arm wrestle you for it." John put one arm on his knee and turned to Matt, grinning.

Lee still wasn't back by the time they lay down for the night. Matt frowned. "Where the hell do you think he could be?"

"Don't know." John was not quite as cocky as usual, an indication that he too was worried.

When they awoke the next morning, Lee's slab was still empty.

"Do you suppose he got in trouble for something?" Matt asked apprensively, trying to come up with a reasonable explanation.

Bill scratched his head. "I guess they could have moved him, but you'd think he'd have at least been allowed to say goodbye and get his extra clothes."

As the day wore on, messages flew about the cellblock like spitballs. Lee wasn't in any other cell. No one had heard of him being placed in a different building.

Their anxious questions to the guard were answered with the standard blank stare and a pig-like grunt.

More than a week passed without a word.

"Dammit, he can't just disappear without a trace." Matt complained in frustration.

John patted Matt's back, "He'll turn up."

Matt recognized that John was trying hard not to show the degree of his misgiving. They were all trying to cheer up each other, unsuccessfully.

Then, as quickly as he had been taken, Lee was returned, looking haggard and weak but showing no visible signs of physical torture.

"Where in the hell have you been? John demanded, catching Lee as his knees started to buckle.

Matt and Bill jumped to the other side of Lee to help hold him up. "We've been worried sick."

Lee, with the help of his friends, sprawled out on his slab, drank some offered water, and told his story.

"When I arrived at the Head Shed, the Rat handed me a piece of paper. He told me I had a package, but I had to sign for it. I read the form. Across the top were the words, 'Independence, Freedom and Happiness.' Below was the statement, 'In accordance with the lenient and humane treatment of the Democratic Republic of Vietnam, I have been permitted to receive this package from my loved one.' I knew that receipt would be used for propaganda, and in accordance with the directive requiring resistance before providing propaganda material, I refused to sign it."

His three cellmates nodded their heads in agreement.

"Immediately, I was thrown in isolation. The Rat ordered me to stand while holding my hands over my head until I was ready to sign. Matt, you remember that little maneuver. I've been in that damn Coop however long I've been gone, except for three times. I was so limp I couldn't stand, so they let me sleep for a few hours on the dirt floor."

He seemed ready to doze off. Then he continued, "Finally, I just decided what the hell. This is ridiculous. Besides, I wanted the damn package, so I signed."

Lee rolled over on his side, facing the wall. "Wake me up when they bring it, but right now I've got to sleep." He no more than finished the sentence, and he was out.

When the package was delivered a couple of days later, John cautioned, "Check it out. There might be some message."

"Here, Matt, you check the gum and candy wrappers—and don't eat all the damn candy." Lee tossed the goodies.

"John, check those vitamin bottles." Lee handled John several vials.

John immediately dumped the contents of one on his slab, examined the inside of the bottle, the insides of the labels on all the jars, and meticulously started refilling each bottle, one pill at a time.

Lee rolled his eyes, laughed, removed the rest of the contents and handled the box to Bill. "Here, pry apart the carton, might be messages in the glue joints, and see if you can remove the label, might be something on the back." Lee set to examining the rest of the contents.

Matt unwrapped each candy bar, and carefully pried apart the paper, checked each bar for holes or inserted messages, then shrugged, "I can't find anything." He broke off a large chunk of a Hershey bar and stuffed it in his mouth. "Hmmm." He licked his lips and then his fingers.

"Share, asshole," John scolded as he grabbed the remainder of the bar.

Matt glanced toward Lee, raised his eyebrows, licked his lips again, and grinned.

"Go ahead and pass them out." Lee directed.

"Look at this." John finished refilling the pill bottles and walked over to Lee. He reached down and picked up a box and waved it excitedly. "Real toothpaste, but only two toothbrushes. I guess we'll have to arm wrestle for who gets one of these."

Lee grabbed them back. "I'll share the toothpaste, and I'll give you my new Vietnamese toothbrush when they hand them out, but these I keep. Write your own wives and ask them to send toothbrushes. But, here, I'll share all the candy." He divided the candy and handed it out. "Matt, you're one piece shy, you'll have to take half of one from John."

John held his firmly to his chest, "You'll play hell getting any of mine."

But, later that evening, as he opened the last of the three bars, he handled half of it to Matt. "I just can't stand to see a grown man cry."

Matt crammed the half bar into his mouth before John could change his mind, smacking his lips loudly.

A few weeks later, the Camp SRO circulated a message, "It's

okay to accept the packages and sign the receipt. The U.S. government has probably gone to a lot of trouble persuading the Vietnamese to let these packages through. Be sure to check for messages."

Lee banged his forehead with the butt of his hand and snorted, "Now they tell us."

<u>Zoo Camp, March 1969.</u>

In early March, Matt was summoned to the Head Shed.

"You have a package."

"Great! Where do I sign?"

He signed the receipt and carried the battered corrugated cardboard box back to the cell. Here was his first contact from Bobbie in almost three years. He lovingly ran his finger across the return address, printed in her small neat hand. She was still at the same address. Good. He breathed deeply, summoning a memory of life before that fateful day.

"Open the damn thing," John demanded, "and pass out the goodies. I'm hungry."

Snapping back to reality, Matt divided up the contents and they carefully examined each item.

Lee was the first to finish. "Well, damn, there's no message in this stuff."

John threw up his hands, "Well, if there's a message in these, your wife is better at hiding than we are at finding."

Bill also reported no luck.

"Okay, the only thing left is the box." Matt started carefully tearing apart the glue joints. "Each of you grab a side, and let's check out the ridges."

When the box lay in shredded pieces on the floor, Matt inhaled deeply. He had really hoped there would be some message. "She was probably instructed what she could and could not send. More than likely, the Navy has told our families not to try to include personal messages, since it might jeopardize the delivery of all the packages." *Could that really be the reason?*

During the guards' quiet time, Lee received a tapped message from the men next door. "We got twenty-four cookies, going to eat three a day each."

He laughed as he repeated the message then he replied "We too received twenty-four cookies; ate twenty-four cookies today. Don't want to share with the rats."

Shortly after the afternoon meal, while Bill and John were still out of the cell, Matt   shared his gnawing suspicions with Lee. "Gotta make you wonder. Almost three years and not one word from her. If boxes are getting through, why no mail? At least I wasn't allowed to write, except for that one time for propaganda purposes. What do you suppose her excuse is?"

Before Lee could respond, Matt grimaced, grabbed his side, and hunched over.

Lee bent down and touched Matt's arm. "What's the matter, Matt? Did those candy bars and cookies finally get to you?"

Just then John and Bill returned from their dishwashing chores, and formed a concerned circle around Matt.

Matt winced as he straightened up. "I can't figure out what in the hell is going on. I've been having some pretty rough pains in my side, and I can feel this growth of some kind, right here." He pointed to a spot on his right side. "If I weren't sure it had been removed when I was a teenager, I would think I had appendicitis."

After almost three years of never receiving enough to eat, Matt had dropped from his usual 180 to about 125 pounds.

Lee examined where Matt indicated and frowned "Yeah, I can see something, and this area is swollen. You better see the camp doc."

"I did. He doesn't have the slightest idea what it could be. And the medicine he gave me doesn't help when the pain gets bad."

"Why haven't you said something?" Lee sounded offended.

"Well, I've talked with the camp doc, and he's excused me from the work detail for a few days. I didn't say anything before because there's not a hell of a lot you guys can do, and I doubt you want to hear me complain all the time. I can put up with the pain, it's just not knowing what's causing it that's frustrating. Does a tumor grow this fast?"

"Jesus, Matt, I don't know. Let's watch it for awhile. If it doesn't get any better, you better ask to see another doctor."

"A lot of good that's going to do." Matt snorted and tossed his head. "The only way I'm going to get any decent medical attention is if we get the hell out of here and go home, and that's not happening very fast."

"Let's speed it up," chirped John. "I've been checking things out, and I think we can get out. That's a false ceiling above us. I can crawl up there and get over to any of the other cells, and there's an opening to the roof down a couple of cells."

Matt, Lee and Bill looked at each other with raised eyebrows and open mouths.

"How in the hell did you figure all this out." Lee asked.

"I climb up there at night. I can pull myself up by leaning my bed against the wall and standing on it. I anchor the lower edge against your slab."

Matt stiffened. "You'll get all of us in trouble if they catch you."

John shrugged nonchalantly. "I haven't been caught yet. Hell, you guys didn't even know what I've been doing. What'll they do if they catch us—throw us in prison?" He laughed sarcastically, ignoring the testiness in Matt's voice. "Forget that stuff—what say we blow this joint? Look, I've already stored some rations and I swiped an extra shirt."

Matt's voice was louder than he intended. "Jesus Christ, John. We can't make it. So what if we get out of the compound. Where are we going to go from there? How do you think we can travel from here to the coast? We'd be caught before a day was up, just like those guys from Dirty Bird a year or so ago. It's too risky. We'd never make it. I'll take my chances on the government bailing us out—as slow as that seems."

Lee concurred. "We don't know enough about what's between here and the coast—or how we'd find Americans if we could get there."

Bill rubbed his chin. "Well, I think we ought to give it a little more thought. We certainly couldn't do it without more planning, but if we pool our knowledge of the area from our recollection of our aerial surveillance films, we might come up with something."

John clapped his hands together. "Well, at least one of you isn't a wimp."

He and Bill spent hours over the next weeks plotting a course to the sea, storing clandestine supplies and extra clothing.

Matt and Lee continued to protest. "I tell you, if they find that stuff up there, you're going to get us all killed."

One night, Lee, Bill and Matt were awakened by John's laughter. "Shhhh. What in the hell are you doing now? What is so damn funny that you gotta risk bringing a guard in here?" Lee admonished.

John ignored the rebuke. "I was just crawling around up there in the loft and I was over Commander Mason's cell. I could hear him stirring down below, so I called, 'Hey down there.' I heard some noises, but he didn't say anything, so I called again, 'Mike, above you.' He just about shit his drawers." John giggled again. "He said he heard his name being called from above all he could think of was that God was speaking to him."

"Dammit to hell, John, that isn't funny. Cut out taking unnecessary risks. This isn't a game, and the V won't be laughing. You know as well as we do what the punishment could be if you get caught, and it won't just be you." Matt was quickly losing his patience with John's dangerous antics.

"Oh, give me a break. I gotta do something to break the monotony of this place." John replied testily.

Much to Matt and Lee's consternation, John and Bill continued to make plans for "The Great Escape," as they dubbed it. Most of their plans were in place, the attic was filled with their covert treasures.

Finally, in early May, John announced, "We're about as ready as we can get. We're going out on the next dark night. Last chance. Are you sure you don't want to come with us?"

"John, please, reconsider." Matt was exasperated. "This is not a rational act. You're not thinking about the consequences. Have you thought about what the V will do to you if you're caught, or to us if you're not? You won't make it, but you'll probably get all of us killed." As the senior officer, his job was to try to keep his men alive. He was going to lose his entire command if John and Bill persisted.

But John was as flip as usual. "Just tell 'em you didn't know about it." He seemed intoxicated with his dream of escape.

Matt turned to Bill. "Try to talk some sense into him."

Bill stood quietly in the cell, looking undecidedly from Matt to John.

John pleaded with Bill. "Don't crap out on me now. We've got a plan, we've got the food, we've got extra clothes. With the rations we get here, we'll never be any stronger physically, so it's now or never. Bill, we can make it. I didn't start this with the intention of failing."

Matt shook his head. Talking to John was like talking to a head-strong teenager. He just wasn't facing reality. "John, you won't make it. Hanoi's too far inland. A six-foot-two gringo isn't exactly going to blend in with the scenery. But even if you succeeded, is it really worth what it's going to cost the rest of us—me and Lee, the guys next door, probably everyone in the whole damn cellblock?"

John was adamant. "I'd rather die than rot in this hellhole for the rest of my miserable life."

Lee joined in. "We'll get out. The government won't leave us here forever. I know they're working on a plan, even as we speak. This is not where I'd rather be, if I had a choice of here or home, but I'd rather be alive here than dead anywhere else. Give it up. Matt's right. You'll get us all killed."

Bill wavered, "Maybe we ought to rethink this."

"Oh, shit! You're a bunch of yellowbellies," John spat angrily.

Matt was at the end of his rope. He had to try to get through to John how insane his plan was. "Look, I don't like to do this, but you're not leaving me much choice. As your SRO, I'm ordering you not to go over the wall. I know I can't stop you, but if you do, it will be against a direct order, and if I live to tell about it, and you do, I'll bring you up on charges when we get home."

John spread his legs and placed his hands on his hips. "Fuck you."

"Damn it, John, I'm trying to keep us alive. Sleep on it. Just please think what will happen here to a lot of other people." Matt looked from John to Bill to Lee, shook his head, pursed his lips and crawled onto his slab, too wired to fall asleep. The air was thick enough to slice.

The next morning, the chill covered the room like early winter frost. To occupy his time and avoid the visual daggers coming his way, Matt took up the communication watch, gluing himself to the wall, his cup pressed tight. When he received the message, he went white. Turning to the others, who were trying hard to avoid getting in each other's way, a difficult task in the small cell, he spoke slowly. "Two men from the Annex over the wall."

Bill and Lee exchanged surprised glances; John sat on the slab and covered his face with both hands. "Sonofabitch," he moaned. "Well, looks like they beat us to it." He closed his eyes, bowed his head and raised one clenched fist. "God, I hope they make it."

Matt thought about what was going to happen. "What about that stuff in the attic? We've got to do something about it. All hell is going to break loose. They'll check everything. We can eat the food. But can we get the extra clothing out?"

"I'll get it," John said downheartedly as he climbed up in the ceiling and handed down the food. They ate it all, until they were about to puke. Bill did.

"What about the clothes?" Matt was still concerned.

"Even if they find it, they'll never know who put it up there or when. Besides, I don't think they'll look up there. The whole area is covered with wire mesh, and I've tied it back together; they won't think to look," John explained.

No one could come up with a better solution, so with some trepidation they left the clothing in the attic.

Within days, stories of torture started to circulate. They grew progressively more gruesome as the days wore on, building by building, coming ever closer. It was just a matter of time. The men in the Stable jumped nervously every time a guard approached.

After about a month, one of the senior officers from the Annex was thrown into the Stable. His eardrums had been broken, he had an infection in both arms from the strap treatment, and part of a bone protruded where his shoulder had been dislocated. Both of his arms hung at his side, useless. Despite his condition, he had not received any medical attention.

To the alarmed questions of his cellmates, Major Brooks described a campaign of terror unlike anything the Americans had experienced since their initial imprisonment.

"The V started with the men in the cell where the escape originated. They were severely beaten, and finally were forced to admit that communication existed between the Annex and the Zoo.

"Then they took all the senior officers to the Head Shed. We were whipped and beaten to the point that after several days, we said just about anything the V wanted us to. Eventually, the V got to the Camp SRO, and by the time they finished with him, he admitted he had organized and ordered the whole thing. The truth was that he hadn't even known it was going to take place. None of us did. The guys hadn't breathed a word to anyone about what they were planning."

"What about the guys who escaped? Did they make it?" John's face was sallow.

"They were recaptured the next morning. They went out about midnight through the roof and stayed out of sight until they came to a place where they could drop over the wall. They were discovered missing at about 0700 the next morning, the idiots left a piece of clothing snagged to the barbed wire where they went over the fence. It took the V only a couple of hours to track them down and bring them back. Neither one appeared to have been injured. I was in a room with one of them, Lieutenant Raker, for a couple of days. He said he and Ralston shook hands as they were led to separate rooms for interrogation—and no one has seen Ralston since. I'm pretty sure they killed him."

The injured officer then warned, "Get ready. The V aren't through yet. They are determined to destroy our entire communication system."

The very next day, the interrogations began.

The Rat was all business. "Have you been communicating with other criminals in other buildings?" His question was directed to all four, who were lined up against the wall.

"No," they replied in unison.

The Rat screamed. "You lie! We have learned of your communication methods. We know you have been violating camp regulations."

He looked upward. Matt, John, Lee and Bill inhaled sharply, their eyes wide in fearful expectation. The wire mesh that hid the entrance to the attic was right above the hole in the outer wall. It seemed like the Rat was looking right at it. They waited for the ax to fall, each stoically steeling himself for the torture that would follow.

The Rat ordered a guard to climb up to look out the hole. His head brushed against the wire. The men were barely breathing, staring straight ahead, afraid to look up, to watch. The guard peeked through the hole for what seemed like several minutes, craning his neck to get a view from several different angles. Then he jumped down, shook his head and said something to the building officer.

The Rat threw his hands in the air and motioned for the guards to lift him up. His cap brushed against the mesh. Another sharp intake of air. He removed the hat and threw it down to the guards, and stared out the hole, scowling down at the nervous men, then staring out the hole some more.

Grunting and snorting, he climbed down. His face was flushed. Flailing and stomping, he confronted the men, shouting, "I know you have been communicating. I don't know how, but we will find out." He stormed out.

The men exchanged disbelieving glances, too flabbergasted to speak. John was the first to find his voice. "Matt, come over here and give me a lift. I want to see what's going on."

John took one look and announced incredulously. "Jesus! What shit house luck. The leaves have completely obscured the line of vision between us and the Garage. Hell, I was just communicating with them last week."

That night, and for several nights following, the guards burst into the cell at various hours, checking if they could see a light from the other buildings. After each raid, Matt lifted John up to investigate.

"The light's barely visible through the leaves," John proclaimed. "It's certainly insufficient for communication. I can't believe they aren't smart enough to figure out that when the leaves are gone, it's an entirely different story."

"And I can't believe none of them spotted your mesh handiwork." Lee added, exhaling loudly and wiping his brow.

Gradually, the Vietnamese began to realize that the effectiveness of their questioning methods was forcing people to confess to things that were not true. Eventually they decided that the earlier stories must have been the correct version, and they finally halted the witch hunt. But not before they had completely wrecked the communication system. Every hole was plugged, every window was blocked, and hanging mats were installed between the cell-blocks.

On July 27th, there was another big move. Bill was the first to go. A few days later, the guard ordered the others to roll up their blankets.

Matt, John and Lee were relocated to a larger cell in a different building, nicknamed the Pool Hall, and acquired another cellmate, Lieutenant Commander Michael Hastings, a Vigilante backseater who had been shot down in March of 1966. A group of "new guys," as the new shootdowns were called, were in the cell next door. It soon became clear the new men didn't know how to communicate.

One day Matt noticed John feverishly working. "What are you doing?"

John held up the lead-based toothpaste tube and a single piece of toilet paper. "I'm writing the tap code and some other instructions for the group next door."

Matt tensed at the thought of another of John's hair-brained schemes. "You know what will happen if they catch you. If the guard comes around, you better eat that or stick it up your ass." He was smiling, but his manner was not as genial.

"Yeah, yeah, I know, but we've got to make contact."

Just as John finished his handiwork, they heard a guard opening the door next door; they would be next.

"John, here comes the guard. Get rid of that note—now!" Matt watched as John quickly dropped his shorts and stuffed the paper between his cheeks.

After a cursory examination of the room, the guard left.

"Whew," Lee exclaimed. "So how do you think you can get that message to those men?"

John explained his plan.

"God, that's risky. They'll torture the hell out of us if we're caught," Matt warned.

"We've got to take the risk." John was the rebellious type who chafed at discipline. Risk was almost a right of passage, his personal battle to show up his captors. "They're going to get a crappy message," he joked as he extracted the note, now tinged with brown spots.

His cellmates laughed, in spite of their concerns.

As in the past, they were the designated dishwashers for their building. The next day, after agreeing communication was worth the risk, they put John's plan into action.

Matt and Mike picked up an armload of dishes, then walked quickly around the corner of the building to the wash station. The guard followed them, as they hoped. Mike hung back just a little. Lee stationed himself so he could see Mike's signal, prepared to create a diversion by sticking his finger down his throat and vomiting if the guard tried to return. In a flash, John opened the flap and tossed the rolled-up, brown stained note through the hole. "Hey guys. Heads up," he whispered. Just as quickly, he shut the flap, picked up the dishes and strolled around the corner to join the others.

Later in the day, they received the first clumsy attempt at communicating, using the tap code. The beam on John's face almost lit up the cell and lasted into the night.

****

Zoo Camp, October 1969.

On Halloween day, as Matt was gathering dishes from the back side of the building, a scruffy-looking dog snuck up and nipped at his leg. He thought the dog was just being playful, or that it wanted something to eat. Matt caught the attention of the guard and by motions asked if it was okay to feed it the scraps.

The guard nodded his head affirmatively, and turned his attention back to smoking his thin brown cigarette. Matt dumped the uneaten food on the ground and watched as the dog devoured it. When he turned away and bent down to pick up another stack of dishes, he felt a stabbing pain in the heel of his right foot.

"Oh, shit!" Matt kicked at the retreating mongrel. Pointing to his bleeding foot, he yelled to the turnkey, "I need some iodine. That damn dog just bit me."

The guard threw down his cigarette, hesitated then trotted off at a less than enthusiastic pace, but returned shortly with the medic. After a perfunctory examination, the attendant handed Matt a bottle of iodine and left. Wincing, Matt poured the stinging medicine directly into the teeth marks.

Later that evening, they heard a dog bark, followed by what sounded like Vietnamese obscenities.

The following day, Sweet Pea, the new block commander, came to the cell. "What did you do yesterday, Tilt?" he asked in his broken staccato English.

"I didn't do a damn thing." Matt denied vehemently.

"No, no. no." Sweet Pea corrected, "What happened with the dog?"

"Oh," Matt sighed, relieved that he was not in trouble. "I was bitten by one of your damn scrawny camp dogs," he admitted.

"Very well," the interrogator advised. "Now we will have to rescue you from your disease."

Matt jerked around in alarm. "What do you mean, rescue me? From what disease?" he asked, edgily.

"The mad-dog disease."

"How do you know it was mad? What happened to the dog?"

"He bit a guard and was killed and burned."

Matt looked for guidance to his cellmates. Mike wiped his hand across his mouth and rolled his eyes and heavenward. Lee pursed his lips and shook his head. John shrugged.

"Can you give me a little time to think about it?"

"Do not wait long. Must start treatment soon," Sweet Pea cautioned as he left.

"How can they be sure the dog had rabies? They didn't perform any tests." Matt's consternation showed plainly in his eyes.

Silence hung heavy. Finally Mike ventured, "Yeah, but, you

can't be sure it didn't either. You must admit it acted pretty damn strange, biting you without the slightest provocation, even after you gave it food."

"That's true, but I don't have much faith in the Vietnamese rabies vaccine. The cure could be worse than the disease. I've heard horror stories even in the States of the side effects caused by rabies shots, not to mention the pain. What would you do? Come on, guys, I need some help here," Matt begged.

Lee cocked his head and sucked in the air around his gritted teeth. "What else can you do?"

John spoke with a straight face, "If you get rabies, you die. If you get the shots, fifty percent chance you'll die from the rabies, fifty percent chance you'll die from the shots. With odds like that, choice seems simple."

Matt was not cheered by John's attempt to lighten the mood. "Thank's a lot for *that* good news." But John was right.

With considerable misgivings, he summoned Sweet Pea. "Okay I'll take the vaccine."

The camp doctor, nicknamed Dr. Zorba, explained the procedure through an interpreter. "We will administer one shot each day in a circle around the navel. Take eighteen days."

The doc hauled out the large, weapon-sized needle. Matt recoiled in alarm, sending the doctor and Sweet Pea into a fit of laughter. Warily, Matt drew a deep breath, cocked his head to one side, grimaced and pulled away the clothing to expose his mid-section. The medic tried to stick the needle into Matt's muscular stomach. It failed to penetrate the skin, emitting a twanging sound as it bent from the pressure, slipping off his belly.

The next attempt was more successful.

After several days, Lee asked, "How's it going?"

Matt made a face. "The first few shots were less painful than I expected, but—." He pulled aside his shirt, displaying a red, swollen area around the navel.

"Ow," groaned Lee. "That looks sore."

"Yeah, it hurts like hell now. I guess my body can't absorb the vaccine like it did in the beginning."

Matt was waiting in the clinic for his final daily shot when Sweet

Pea found him.

"I have a letter for you, Tilt."

Matt tried to steady his shaking hands as he accepted the simple folded sheet. At last, a letter from Bobbie. He started to read. "Dear son . . . ."

He shook off the temporary disappointment.

"Can I keep it?" he asked after several minutes. "It's from my mother."

"No, I am sorry. You must give it back after you have finished." He seemed genuinely apologetic.

Matt read and re-read the letter, and reluctantly handed it back when the medic called him in for his shot.

In the weeks Matt was undergoing the rabies treatment, the V started to relax security measures they had instituted after the escape attempt. One day they came into the cell and opened the window they had previously bricked up. A few days later, they came in and knocked out one interior wall separating Cell 3 and the adjacent one, giving the prisoners a room twice its original size.

John was the first to comment. "Have you noticed the improvement in our treatment lately?"

Lee and Matt both agreed.

"Well, I've been trying to figure out what happened to cause it. There's got to be a reason. There's always a reason. Best I can figure, things started getting better about two months ago. What happened shortly before that—like about the third of September?"

After a thoughtful pause, Matt exclaimed, "You're right. Things started to improve less than a month after dear old Uncle Ho was laid to rest in his beloved rubber-tire sandals."

The next day, a new roommate arrived.

"Name's Daniel Herrington, Lieutenant Commander, USN, but my few friends call me 'Dirty Dan.'" The others soon understood why.

A few days after arriving, Dan received a card from his wife. Thumping the envelope on the bunk, he complained, "Can you believe this shit? Today is my fifteenth wedding anniversary. I've been in this stinkin' hellhole two years and that stupid broad sends me a card, no letter, no chow, just a fuckin' card."

"How about that. Fifteen years of wedded bliss," John teased.

"Oh, shit no. Not on your life. More like fifteen goddamn years of hand-to-hand combat. She's probably so busy getting laid every night, this was all she had time for."

"Hell, Dan," Matt countered, "I'd settle for a card. I've been here three and a half years, and all I've received are two boxes of rations. Not even a shitty note. I know some letters aren't getting through, but I can't help thinking maybe there's some reason Bobbie doesn't want to write, some bad news she doesn't want to tell me." He no longer felt compelled to hide his misgivings.

"Well, look at it this way, Matt. As the old saying goes, 'no news is good news.' At least you're getting packages, and you haven't received a 'Dear John' letter like some of the guys," Lee encouraged.

"I know, but almost four years is a long time for a woman to be without a man, particularly when she has children to raise. A lot of things can happen in that length of time. I think if something like that has happened, Bobbie just wouldn't want to tell me."

"Matt, don't anticipate problems. Have a little more faith in your wife," Mike urged.

"Oh, you're probably right. She's not the type to go out to look for another man, but if she did, I don't think I would want to know about it. When I get home, I don't intend to dig too deep about what she did while I was gone. If she volunteers any information, if she admits to having had an affair, then I'll just have to deal with it." The thought was unsettling.

Dan joined the discussion. "Oh, shit, Matt. I'd bet my left ball she's out fuckin' around. So what. Didn't you screw around on her when you were on cruises? If you weren't locked up in this joint, would you do without sex for that long?"

"Maybe not," Matt admitted sheepishly, "but I'd like to think my wife would."

· Dan bantered, "Hell, even that little Chink that carries the water looks good to me about now."

Lee laughed. "Dan, you're outrageous. Look, Matt, does it really make that much difference if Bobbie slept with some guy while you were gone?"

Matt didn't answer, but the thought of his wife in the arms of another man sent shivers through his body. He wanted to change the subject.

"Well, I guess there's one bit of good news. The shots were either okay, or the damn dog wasn't rabid."

CHAPTER 19

<u>San Diego, late Fall 1968.</u>

Not yet six, Hank was already strong-willed, defiant and disobe-
dient. Each time Bobbie attempted to be firm, she ended up caving
in, or she failed to follow through with some threatened punishment.
So many times she wanted to pick up the phone and call Tom.
Hank listened to him, minded him without question. Tom would
know how to handle him. Twice she went so far as to dial his number, but hung up each time before the phone was answered.

Many times, as she lay in bed alone, an aching would start, triggering a raging internal battle. One part of her said, "Call him." It
would mean Hank would have a man around, a man who could give
him guidance and discipline. That alone almost justified their illicit
romance.

But, each time she wavered, Debbie's strong religious ties held
her back. Debbie would never approve of her mother living with
another man while still married to her father, and she certainly
wouldn't condone Bobbie getting a divorce now. Perhaps under
normal circumstances a divorce might have been acceptable, but
with Matt locked away in a prison camp in Vietnam, it was out of
the question.

Still, her fear of Debbie's reaction could not stifle Bobbie's inner
battle. She needed Tom so much, and not just for Hank. One night
she awoke from a dream. She had been in Tom's arms; he was holding her close and kissing her. She moaned from the moisture-induc-
ing sensation in her groin. At that moment her desire for him was

stronger than her fears. She dialed his number. It was nearly 11 o'clock. If he were in town, he should be home. The phone rang three times. A woman's voice answered. Stung with humiliation and pain, she immediately dropped the receiver like it was a snake that had just bit her. He certainly hadn't waited very long before he had another woman living with him. Feeling that her heart had been rubbed raw, she dissolved into a breathless bout of tears. Even with the help of a strong nightcap, she didn't sleep much the rest of the night.

****

Tom returned to his exercise program with a vengeance, jogging along Mission Beach every morning for about an hour, covering several miles with his ground-eating stride. A couple of times a week, Maggie joined him. The trace of a bulge disappeared, and he was soon back in his lean, mean form. Exercise, Maggie, and his busy work schedule helped keep his mind off Bobbie.

Maggie turned into a real friend, sensing his need for female company, yet recognizing his desire not to become deeply involved. She provided companionship without asking for more. After a few weeks, he felt comfortable enough to discuss with her his relationship with Bobbie. She listened quietly as he bared his soul.

If Maggie resented his preoccupation with another woman, she never let it show. When, after a couple months of just being together, dining together, talking together, jogging together, he invited her to share his bed, she accepted. It was pleasurable, but it lacked the magic he felt with Bobbie. Sex with any other woman, he realized, was never going to be totally successful until and unless he got Bobbie out of his system. What a difference love makes. He simply couldn't imagine going back to the non-committed dating he used to enjoy.

Tom and Maggie settled into a comfortable, undemanding relationship, satisfying their mutual needs when both felt the urge. He suspected that she, too, might be recovering from a broken romance, but she never mentioned it and he never asked. He knew if she felt like discussing it, she would initiate the subject, and if not, he would let it alone.

Tom often fought the urge to call Bobbie. How was she doing? How were the kids? Was there a chance she might have changed her mind? With effort, he held back. It had to be done her way. She was right—she simply couldn't handle their relationship. If ever she was going to, it would have to be because she admitted she needed him, or wanted him enough to overcome her guilty conscience. And the first contact had to come from her. So he controlled his longing, pounding his frustrations into the sandy beaches.

In mid-December Tom returned from a flight around noon, and stopped by the personnel office. Marcia was in the office alone. "Larry around?" he asked. "Thought he might be available for lunch."

She looked up and smiled her toothpaste-ad smile. "Sorry, big guy, but he's already left for the day."

"Bummer." He turned to walk out, but Marcia stopped him. "Hey, are you doing anything special this afternoon?"

"No, I don't have any specific plans." Then he leaned over her desk, a devilish smile creeping across his face. "What's on your mind? Wanna' go play around on your old man?"

He had been at WCA several weeks when he first learned she had an "old man." He would generally make some suggestive comment to which she always had an equally flip response. It became a game of one-upmanship. One day, he walked into her office, leaned over her desk and asked in a voice loud enough to be heard by others nearby, "Well, Marcie, we gonna make out today?"

She dipped her head and gave him a "shame-on-you" smile, then motioned with her eyes and a nod of her head toward a large, formidable-looking man sitting across the room, who was rising to his full height of 6'6". Tom went momentarily numb when the menacing 250-pound plus titan approached him, wearing a surly look.

Marcia appeared anxious. "As usual, Finley, your timing is bad. My husband here absolutely refuses to allow me to play around when he's in town." Tom drew back in obvious discomfort as she pointed to the man who practically filled the room, and who, in a couple of monster steps, was now within striking distance.

Just as the stranger reached him, Marcia giggled, "Mr. Finley, I don't think you know my husband, Miles Miller."

Suddenly it registered. "Miles Miller!" he exclaimed, "with the Chargers?" She'd just nailed him good, and she'd have to pay, somehow. Tom cautiously extended his hand to the huge frame looming before him.

His bravado restored, he turned slowly to Marcia. "Jesus Christ! You didn't tell me you were married, let alone to this bone crusher."

He turned back to Miles, "It's a real pleasure to meet you." I hope you don't mind my flirting with your wife—all in fun I assure you."

For a moment Miles eyed Tom sternly, then broke into a hearty laugh and shook Tom's hand. "Yeah, I know. Marcie's told me all about you."

Miles later sent him tickets for a couple of Chargers games. Tom wanted to invite Debbie, an avid Charger fan, but he just couldn't bring himself to make the call, so he and Maggie went to the games.

Marcie's comeback pulled him back to the present. "Sure, if you're ready to face the consequences when Miles finds out. Frankly, I never thought you'd look good in a body cast. It would cover up too much of your appeal."

"So what else do you have in mind?" He raised his eyebrows a couple of times in Groucho Marx fashion, and folded his arms across his chest.

She explained her problem. "Well, I need to do some Christmas shopping, and my car is in the shop. They were supposed to have it finished by noon today, but they just called and said it wouldn't be ready until tomorrow. Miles is out of town with the team, so I'd like to bum a ride over to Fashion Valley. Larry gave me the afternoon off."

"Sure thing. And if you promise not to attack me, you can come into my den of iniquity while I change clothes. I'll even go shopping with you. I haven't done any shopping either. Not that I have very many people on my list," he added, suddenly somber.

Marcia tossed the pen and pad in her desk drawer, walked around to the front of the desk and patted Tom's shoulder. "Why don't we stop by Smuggler's Inn first. I'll buy you a drink or lunch or something for your trouble." She winked. "It's also very dark and private."

He laughed, his somber mood pushed aside. "Sounds like my kind of place."

After stopping by Tom's apartment, where he changed out of his uniform, they parked at the east end of Fashion Valley and walked the short distance to the restaurant. After a short wait, they were led to a booth at the back of the large dining room. They ordered drinks. As Marcia made casual conversation, Tom had the uneasy feeling that someone was watching them. Glancing up and looking around the dimly-lit room, he stared in disbelief.

Marcie noted the expression on his suddenly chalk-white face. "Tom. Is something wrong? You look like you just saw a ghost."

He stroked his chin nervously. "Well, it's . . . just that I . . . just spotted a—um—friend." He motioned with his head toward the other table. Marcie's eyes followed Tom's, stopping at a small woman trying very hard to appear not to be looking at them.

Marcia nodded. "Aha. Your secret love surfaces at last."

Tom gazed fixedly at the woman.

"Tom, oh, Tom." Marcia reached across the table and touched his hand. "Why don't you introduce us, so she'll at least know that we aren't an item."

He reluctantly tore his eyes away from Bobbie. "Oh, Jesus, Marcie, I don't know. I haven't seen her in almost four months—at her insistence. And besides, dammit, she isn't due any explanation about my activities anyway. She's the one who sent me away." But the pounding of his heart was no different from four months ago. It struck like a jackhammer against the walls of his chest.

Marcia patted his hand, "Go say something to her. I can feel the electricity between you two clear over here."

He smiled ruefully, and sighed. Slowly he stood up. With a reassuring look and an encouraging nod from Marcia, he walked over to the table where Bobbie was intently studying the menu.

"Hello, Bobbie." He tried to swallow the lump that was rising in his throat.

She looked up and feigned surprise. "Well, hello, Tom. Imagine running into you." She looked quickly at her red-haired companion, smiled nervously, then lowered her eyes.

"Yes, amazing, isn't it?" He continued to stare at her, searching it for a sign of—what?

Self-consciously, she looked up again and pointed toward the other lady, "Oh, I'm sorry. This is my friend, Sandy Marshall." Then she turned toward Sandy, "This is Tom Finley . . . an old friend."

Tom accepted the offered hand. "I'm pleased to meet you, Sandy." Though he spoke to Sandy, he scarcely took his eyes off Bobbie. What should he say? "Have you had lunch yet?" he asked both women. It was fairly obvious they had not.

"No," Bobbie replied.

"Then, why don't you both join us? We haven't eaten yet either. Marcie and I were just about to grab a quick bite before doing some Christmas shopping." He offered a hand to each of the ladies to help them out of the booth. Sandy stood and moved into the aisle, as if she assumed they were accepting the offer.

Bobbie remained seated. "Oh, no, we wouldn't want to intrude."

He took her firmly by the arm. "You won't be intruding." Then, in a gentler tone, he added, "Please come."

She hesitated. His fingers pressed into her arm, and his eyes pleaded silently. She slowly stood up.

Trying hard to control his jitters, Tom escorted them across the room to the booth where Marcia waited, smiling. As they approached, he caught the look of hostility Bobbie directed at Marcia.

Before he could make introductions, Marcia stood, moved out in the aisle, and extended her hand to Bobbie, "Hi," she said gaily, "I'm Marcia Miller. I'm so pleased you could join us." She moved aside and motioned for them to sit. "Please sit down."

When Sandy slid into one side of the booth, Marcia quickly took the seat beside her, leaving him with no alternative but to sit next to Bobbie.

For awhile, the conversation was forced and uncomfortable. At the first opportunity, but without appearing too obvious, Marcia changed the mood by a casual reference to her husband.

He heard Bobbie utter an almost unnoticeable sigh, and her shoulders relaxed.

The mention of football brought an excited response from Sandy. "Oh, I love football. I go every chance I get. Let me see, Miles Miller, um . . . isn't he all pro guard?"

"Yes." Marcia's eyes widened. "I'm impressed you know your football so well."

"In my previous life, I wanted to be a sports reporter. But, I'm the one who's impressed. I've seen his picture. Damn, he's a gorgeous hunk. You have my utmost envy."

After several more minutes of small talk, Marcia stood up. "Sandy, would you like to join me in the ladies' room?"

Sandy appeared a bit surprised, smiled, and looked quizzically at Bobbie, who was intently studying the design of a stained-glass window. Tom stood up.

"Excuse us. We'll be right back." Marcia winked at Tom.

He could feel Bobbie stiffen as his leg accidentally rubbed against her. She moved slightly away.

"Your friend is quite a football fan, isn't she?" He tried to keep the conversation light. "How did you meet her?"

"She's the office manager where I work." Her voice was very low.

"Oh, you've gone back to work? What are you doing?"

"I'm working as a secretary for a real-estate developer." She started to loosen up just a little as she talked about her job. "The office is just down in the Valley, not far from the house. It gives me something to do now that the kids are both in school full time."

Without thinking, he grabbed her hands, "Oh, Bobbie, I'm glad. It sounds like you're doing great."

She pulled her hands back, and intertwined her fingers, idly circling one thumb over the other. "Sandy has become a good friend. She has a big house east of here, up in the hills, with a pool. She's invited me and the kids out several times. It's really beautiful."

"So what brings you all out today?" He sipped his drink, and continued to watch her. Her nervousness made her appear all the more vulnerable, all the more appealing. God, he wanted to take her in his arms and hold her, and protect her.

Bobbie placed her elbow on the table, and leaned her head against the butt of her hand, running her fingers through her hair, and faced him squarely for the first time.

Control yourself, Finley.

"I realized I hadn't even started my Christmas shopping, so I asked for the day off. Sandy also had the day off, and offered to make it a day out. She said she needed to pick up a few things too."

"Hey, guys," Marcia called as they neared the table, "Sandy and I are going to cut out if you two don't mind. She's agreed to give me a ride home. I thought this would give you two a chance to catch up on old times."

Tom caught the latent message. "Please don't be angry with me, Tom, but I just need to pick up a couple of things. Also, I thought I'd show Sandy Miles' 'I love me' room."

Bless you, Marcie. He smiled and nodded his acceptance.

Bobbie's face registered alarm, but before she could object, Tom said reassuringly, "Look, I don't mind at all. I'll be happy to take Bobbie shopping and then home, or wherever she wants to go. I'd like to say hello to the kids anyway. I haven't seen them in some time." He added peevishly, "And since my shopping partner is deserting me, I have nothing better to do."

They all waited for Bobbie's response. She stopped twirling her finger over the top of her glass, looked up and smiled tentatively at Sandy and Marcia. Her voice was soft, almost inaudible. "Fine. If Tom's sure it's no trouble."

Marcia started edging toward the entrance. Tom stood up and walked toward the door with them. "Go on, girls, enjoy yourselves. I've got the check. And, Marcie, don't spend all of Miles' money in one place." To Marcia, "See you next week," and more quietly, he added, "and thanks."

She smiled knowingly. "Good luck."

Tom returned to the booth and scooted in next to Bobbie. He caught her eye and she quickly looked down, folding her hands primly in her lap. He reached over and put one hand on top of hers. "It's so good to see you. You're looking great, as usual. How are the kids?"

She turned her head ever so slightly toward him. "They're fine," she said quietly, removing one hand to stir her coffee. "Debbie's singing in the Glee Club at school and the church choir." She gazed at his hand now resting on her thigh, but didn't attempt to remove it.

He was growing weary of small talk. Slowly, he slipped his arm around her shoulders. "Bobbie, I've missed you terribly." He could feel her shoulders sag.

Her voice was very low. "I've missed you, too."

"Come on, let's get the hell out of here." He motioned for the check.

He drove straight to his apartment. As soon as they were inside, he pulled her rigid form into his arms. She put her arms around him and returned his embrace.

"Oh, sugar, I missed you so much." His voice was tender.

She rested her head on his chest and murmured something he couldn't catch. She offered no resistance as he led her toward the bedroom, nor did she try to stop him when he slowly began to undress her, smoothing her hair with his hand, gently following her cheekbone to her mouth, and testing the softness of her lips with his thumb. Still caressing her, he removed his own clothes and tossed them on a chair, then lay down beside her tense nude body. He moved deliberately and cautiously, careful not to force her. He stroked her breasts, and ran his fingers across her stomach. "Honey, I've been miserable without you. I must have started to call you twenty times. But each time I chickened out. I wanted you to be the one to call."

"I've started to call you several times, too," she admitted. "In fact, once I even let it ring. I was going to ask you to come over, but some woman answered." Her tone was suddenly much stronger and accusatory.

He remembered once Maggie commented that she had answered his phone while he was in the shower, but there was no one on the other end. She even joked that it was one of his girl friends checking up on him. "Maybe you dialed a wrong number," he offered disingenuously.

"I doubt it," she whispered, then moaned slightly from the pleasure of his touch.

His hands began exploring her body tenderly. He kissed her lips, her ears, her neck, his hands stroked her breasts, her waist, her womanhood, until she once again yielded to his seduction and erupted into a wild, frantic outburst, a climax that sent shudders through her body again and again.

Supporting his weight on one elbow, he stroked her face with his free hand, "Oh, darling, don't send me away again. I love you. I want to be with you. It can't be wrong, Bobbie, it can't."

He could feel her shiver. She sounded defeated. "Tom, I need you too much to keep you away anymore. I want us to be together, as much as we can."

She starting shaking her head. "Oh, Lord, if Debbie figures it out and turns on me, I don't know what I'll do, but I have to risk it. I can't go on without you. I know that now. I have never been so miserable as I was these past few months without you."

He hesitated, debating what he should say. "Debbie isn't going to turn on you, no matter what you do. She loves you, she wants to protect you. She'll back you in whatever decision you make. I think you'd be surprised if you'd just level with her; she understands more than you give her credit for."

Tom could see she didn't believe him, and was about to argue, so he moved on, "What about Matt? Will you write him and ask for a divorce, so we can get married now?"

"No. I can't. I must wait for Matt to return. You'll just have to go along with me on this. I can't send him the letter you want me to send. In fact, I haven't even been able to write him at all, for fear he'll read between the lines. You may be absolutely right. I've gone over and over this in my mind, trying to discover some magical solution. It might be better to do it your way - with a letter now. Since I'm a coward where Matt is concerned, I don't really want to confront him. Sending a letter could certainly be easier. And when he comes back and I have to face him, I will probably wish a hundred times over that I had sent a letter. But there is just something, I can't explain it, even to myself, but something that holds me back. I can't write that letter, Tom, I just can't. Please don't even ask me to."

"I think you're totally wrong," he said, not even trying to hide his disappointment. "You're just going to cause worse problems for everyone this way. If you wait to tell Matt when he gets back, it's going to be one hell of a mess. But for the time being, I'd rather have a part of you than nothing at all. I don't like sneaking around, I've already told you that. But . . . ." His voice trailed off. Her guilt was an insurmountable problem. But for the moment they were back together. He didn't want to risk losing her again. Why couldn't he have fallen in love with someone uncomplicated, like Maggie?

CHAPTER 20

<u>North Vietnam, 1970 - 1972.</u>

"Guess what the latest news is." Matt's voice was filled with sarcasm after spending several hours receiving and relaying tapped messages from the senior officers. "The Gooks are offering to let some of the 'most cooperative' PWs go home. The brass thinks it's just an effort to influence U. S. public opinion and the peace talks in Paris. The V expect the released prisoners to go home and tell everyone what 'lenient and humane treatment' we're receiving."

"Lenient and humane, my ass!" John snorted. "Who'd be so stupid as to say that?"

"The Gooks are starting to dangle the carrot to obtain their propaganda material instead of being quite as brutal as before. In exchange for cooperation, for 'showing good attitude,' some prisoners have been given fruit, candy, cigarettes, and other items we haven't seen before. They've been rewarded with extra rations of food and clothing and other special privileges."

"Who in the hell has been getting that kind of treatment?" John demanded, his voice rising.

Matt shook his head. "I don't know the names, specifically, but I think some of the more senior officers do, and they've been trying to stop it."

"So what the fuck are we supposed to do?" Dan asked.

Matt repeated the order. "The SRO's directive is we all go together—or no one goes. As fighting military men, we will return as a unit—with honor, or not at all."

"Yeah, that's the way it has to be," Lee agreed.

A few days later, the news reached the Pool Hall. "Three PWs disobeying orders, going to be repatriated. They've been informed they will be brought up on charges when the rest of us get home."

"Sonsabitches! I'd like to kick their asses," Dan stormed.

"Traitors," raged John.

"They're finished," Mike said quietly. "They'll get a dishonorable discharge, sure as hell, maybe prison."

"They damn well better," Matt agreed. "As much as I'd like to go home, some things like honor and duty take priority over our personal desires. I simply can't fathom how a career military officer who has gone through what we've all had to suffer, could betray his fellow officers and his country in this manner."

A couple of days later another message was circulated. Matt told the others, "Captain Dalton, the Navy SRO here at the Zoo, wants the word circulated that he is ordering one PW to go home."

"What!" John exclaimed loudly, then quickly covered his mouth. Outbursts could bring a guard and retribution.

"Shh," Matt ordered. "Gimme a minute to explain. It's Seaman Gifford he's ordering back."

"I've heard Gifford's name. Isn't he the guy who fell off his ship?" asked Mike.

"Yeah, that's the one," Matt replied.

"Christ! How'd he end up here?" Dan asked.

"Well, I understand he was picked up in late '66, clinging, half-frozen, to a buoy in the Gulf of Haiphong. The V were certain they had intercepted a master U.S. spy intent on blowing up their harbor. They refused to believe that he had simply fallen overboard from his destroyer."

"How in the hell did he fall off his ship?" Dan chuckled.

Matt repeated the story that had made the rounds. "What I heard was that he was walking along a catwalk taking a smoke late one evening during maneuvers. The ship rolled unexpectedly in rough seas; Tim lost his balance, grabbed but missed the railing, and toppled overboard."

"Jesus!" Lee exclaimed, "that's one of the reasons I joined the Air Force. Those ships remind me of little bobbing buoys in a great big black inkwell."

The four Navy pilots laughed, then Matt continued. "Luckily, his momentum carried him far enough away from the ship that he wasn't sucked under and cut into little pieces by the ship's screw. I guess he dog-paddled and floated for much of the night until his cries for help were heard around dawn by a Vietnamese fisherman.

"He was turned over to the Vietnamese Army, and from there taken to Hanoi, where he was introduced to a dose of the Green Room treatment. From what I gather, the V were convinced he was the toughest spy they had ever encountered. His story never varied even with their persuasive methods.

"They finally concluded he was probably the unluckiest sono-fabitch in the United States Navy."

Mike shook his head, "That's incredible."

"According to Dalton, Tim has no business being here in the first place. He didn't assume the risk of ending up as a prisoner of war like the rest of us."

"So what's he supposed to do if they send him back?" Mike probed.

"He'll have instructions to blow the whistle on what's happening over here, contradict the misinformation that is going to be spread by those three turncoats, and—he's going to take out the names of everyone anyone has known to be in the system."

"How is he going to smuggle out that information?" Dan queried, with the hint of a sneer.

"Major Darrock has roomed with Tim for a long time, and he says he has a good memory. He's going to teach him how to memorize the names of all the guys in here. It will provide a better accounting than Washington currently has."

"And how is this Major Darrock supposed to know everyone who's here? Hell, I've been here since late 1966 and I don't know many names," Dan countered.

"He doesn't." Matt paused as he looked around at his cellmates, "but collectively, we do. Every man who has the name of anyone they've seen in the prison system should pass it to Howie—Major Darrock—name, rank and service."

John's eyes lit up. Another "gotcha" against the V. "Hey, we're a good source. As the dishwashing crew, we know the names of lots of prisoners. Come on, let's put our heads together."

For the next several days, Matt or one of his cellmates passed the information on over one hundred men they had encountered in the prison system.

A few weeks later, Seaman Tim Gifford, armed with the names of over 250 prisoners, went home. So did three "deserters."

****

In September 1970, a guard came to the cell, gave the hand over hand motion to roll up blankets, and pointed to Matt and Dan.

The men exchanged concerned and questioning glances. There had been no previous hint of a move. Matt and Dan, quietly under the watchful eye of the guard, started gathering up their meager belongings.

After making a circular motion with his finger in the air, a gesture they knew to mean "get the lead out," the guard withdrew.

"Well, it looks like they're breaking up that old gang of mine," Matt said lightly, but his words sounded wooden, even to himself.

"Hey, I may get my own squadron yet," John grinned half-heartedly.

"Wonder if you're just being moved to a different building?" Mike asked hopefully.

"I don't think so, " Matt said dully. "I heard a truck out in the yard. I have a hunch we're out of here."

The guard returned, motioning for Dan and Matt to follow.

The men shook hands, and gave encouraging pats on the back to each other. Lee, hardly able to hide his unhappiness, wrapped his arms around Matt, fighting back a sniffle. "Buddy, look after yourself, and as they say in Jolly Old England, 'Keep your pecker up.'"

Matt attempted a feeble smile. "If I don't see you sooner, I'll see you—in six months—when we get out of here."

Mike patted Matt's back. "Take care, my friend."

John pulled Matt into his arms. "Take care," he admonished. Gone was his ever-present devilish grin.

"You, too." Matt lowered his head as he walked out of his cell, away from his friends.

Matt and Dan were loaded into a truck with several other prisoners. The guards issued the usual warning about no communication between prisoners. Many of the men blinked greetings, one tapped on Matt's knee, wondering what was going on. They made eye contact, and Matt raised his eyebrows and shrugged. Primarily, they all rode in silence. Matt looked at the emaciated crew, noting the lost look on each face. They probably were all going through the same emotions—normally powerful men used to being in control, now held in the grip of powerlessness and uncertainty.

Matt slumped against the rail of the truck, his eyes closed, thinking back over the past four years. What would he have done without Lee or John or Mike. They were like brothers. He felt closer to any of them than he ever felt with his own brother. It was going to be difficult without them. Would they ever see each other again? Why were they being separated after all this time? And, where in the hell was he being taken?

At the end of an hour's bumpy ride, they were released in the dirt courtyard of a prison southwest of Hanoi. The name they quickly assigned to their new prison was Camp Faith. The outer three-sided concrete wall was about eight feet high and covered with broken glass and barbed wire decor, with a sentry post at the outer corners. Over the fence, they could see the lush green forest a few hundred yards off in the distance. Matt counted four doors and several windows in the long cinderblock building. The shutters covering the barred windows were all open, a welcome sign. At one end of the courtyard appeared to be the bathing and dishwashing facilities.

Dan and Matt were directed to the first cell at the far end, away from the bathing area. "Hey, this is an improvement," Matt commented dryly as they inspected the interior. Eight bunks, four on each side, were stacked one above the other, and a small table and bench seat against the back wall. The concrete floor was clean.

"Yeah. No shit." Dan agreed. "When was the last time you were in a cell with even one window, let alone two, and open yet?"

"Well, it may not be a touch of heaven, but it's a step up from the floor of hell." Matt sat on one of the bunks.

They placed their things on two of the front bunks. As additional trucks arrived and were unloaded, more prisoners filtered in. Matt couldn't believe his eyes. "My God, Roy. How in the hell are you?" "Good to see you, too, pal." Roy tossed his possessions on the bunk next to Matt, and after giving Matt a hug, asked, "Say, have you run across Craig Hansen yet?"

Matt rubbed his chin. "Craig. I'll be damned. I didn't know he got bagged. No, I haven't seen or heard his name in the system."

"Yeah, he was shot down early in my last cruise, about four months before I was, which was in July 1967."

Matt continued to rub the stubble on his chin, shaking his head.

While the other prisoners were getting settled, Roy and Matt sat on one of the wooden slabs, talking quietly. The guards remained outside.

"Tell me what you can about Bobbie, and the kids, and what happened in San Diego and the rest of the world after I intercepted that ground fire." Matt grinned.

"Is that what got you? I was never sure if it was that or the MiG."

"Yeah, I think so. I was able to avoid the MiG fire. More about that later. Tell me about my wife and kids."

"What have you heard from Bobbie?" Roy asked.

"Not a word. And I'm getting a little concerned. If she's writing at all, it would seem that one or two or her letters would get through, that they wouldn't *all* get lost."

"Well, like I said at the Zoo, she was certainly holding up well when I last saw her." Roy went on to describe his first meeting with Bobbie, and the subsequent meetings before the ship pulled out again. "I'm sure there's some explanation."

"Oh, yeah, I'm sure there is," Matt muttered. But what was it he wondered uneasily.

****

In October, the cellblock commander called Matt to his office. "You have a letter." He handed Matt the pink, faintly sweet-smelling envelope.

Matt's hands shook as he recognized the handwriting. For several moments he just gazed at the envelope, swallowing nervously. After all this time, he was almost afraid to open it. Maybe it was a "Dear John." He looked up to see the block commander watching him curiously.

Gulping hard to purge the lump in his throat, he gingerly opened the envelope and carefully removed his one-page treasure.

> "My dearest Matt, We are all fine. I am working as a secretary. I enjoy it and it helps make the time without you pass faster. Debbie is a senior in High School, and sings with the Glee Club. Hank is growing so big, and he looks just like you. We had to put Ludwig to sleep. He was so old, when he got sick, there was nothing we could do to save him. Please take care of yourself. We are praying that you will be able to come home soon. With all our love."

Matt breathed heavily, licked his dry lips and closed his damp eyes. After reading the letter a second time, he started to feel euphoric. He gently folded it and started to put it in his pocket.

"You have to return the letter."

"Oh. Then may I keep it just a little longer?"

The officer nodded.

Matt re-read every word until he knew it by heart. Then he read it again, more attentive to the form of the letter. Could there be a hidden message? He mentally noted each capital letter, the first letter of each line, the first word of each sentence. He could find nothing that looked like a code. When the officer held out his hand, Matt reluctantly handed the letter back.

He sought out Roy as soon as he returned to the cell to share his exciting news. "Roy, it was a letter from Bobbie. I finally got a letter from Bobbie. She says everything's fine."

Roy smiled. "I'm glad, but I was sure that would be the case."

"Well, to be honest, I was starting to wonder. It's been almost four and one-half years since my last letter from her, the one I received on the ship a few days before I was shot down.

"Imagine, Debbie—a senior."

Then, abruptly, Matt scowled. "Roy, do you realize in a few months my daughter is going to graduate from high school, one of the most important events in her life, and I won't be around to see it. I've missed seeing her grow up. She was just a little girl, barely a teenager, when they saw me off that day at Miramar, the day we flew out to join the ship. Now she's almost grown. I've missed her first date. Who taught her to drive? Now she's about to graduate. Next she'll be getting married, and I'm missing it all!" An involuntary shiver started in his shoulders and swept downward. He breathed deeply two or three times to relax. He couldn't. He wanted to go home.

"Why can't this stupid war be over? Why do we have to pay such a high price for our government's involvement in this senseless war?"

"Matt, this sort of talk isn't doing any good."

"I know. That's what's so damn frustrating." But Matt could not shake his bitterness, or the persistent pain in his side that suddenly reared its ugly head, and once again doubled him over.

****

In late November, the men in Camp Faith were awakened by loud noises.

Matt jumped up and rushed to the window. "What in the hell do you suppose that was? It sounded like SAMs."

Roy, too, was up at the sound of firing. "I could swear I heard airplanes and helicopters."

"Hey, look. That looks like flak—over there." Matt pointed toward the southern sky. "Maybe it's some sort of raid. Maybe they're trying to rescue some of us."

"Could be. Too bad it's whoever's over there and not us," Roy conjectured as they continued to look toward the sound and lights.

After about a half hour, Matt shrugged his shoulders and crawled back into his bunk. "Whatever it was, it's over—and, dammit to hell, we're still here. I'm going to sleep." But he didn't, not for a long time.

The immediate upshot of the disturbance, commencing the next morning, was increased security, more guards and a renewed fear of violence.

"What do you suppose that was last night?" Roy wondered.

"I don't know, but there's going to be a massacre if it looks like the U.S. is attempting a rescue. I've never seen the V with so much firepower. Some of them even carry gas grenades and hand grenades," one of the cellmates opined.

"Yeah, at the first sign of danger, those SOBs are going to start hosin' away," predicted Dirty Dan. "Have you noticed, whenever any U.S. aircraft approaches, one of those AK47-toting guards is stationed at every door?"

"I'm not sure there even has to be a raid," Roy added. "Most of the guards are pretty damn excitable and they're not what you would call 'well trained.' If they get provoked, what's to stop them from just blowing one or more of us away?"

Dan agreed, "I can tell you, I don't like having them pointing weapons at me. They're unprofessional, impetuous, mental pygmies. Hell, it might even be an accident. They haven't a clue how to care for those weapons, but whoever's in front of that gun will be just as dead."

The men in the cellblock discussed the situation and tapped on the water pipes to the prisoners in another building. Their concerns were universally shared.

For three days, the men speculated on what had happened and what was going to happen. Had it been a rescue attempt? Most thought so. Had anyone been rescued? Would there be another attempt? What would they do if suddenly a helicopter landed in the courtyard? They speculated on how many would make it out. They plotted and planned where to be, what each one was to do. Every sound induced a reaction—listen, check the windows, check the doors. Then, as suddenly as it started, the anticipation was over. After less than two months at Camp Faith, the entire prison population was loaded into trucks and driven back in the middle of the night to Hoa Loa, the big prison in Hanoi. They were placed in one large room, all fifty-seven of them.

With so many in one cell, it was difficult for the V to enforce the no communicating rules, so the guards, for the most part, did little to prevent quiet conversations.

Matt and Roy leaned up against one wall, talking quietly. "That shooting the other night," Roy conjectured, "I bet you were right. It was some kind of raid, so the Vietnamese decided to move us all back together."

Matt nodded. "That's probably what the U.S. was trying to accomplish. With all of us back in one general location, that leaves the outlying areas clear to bomb at will. Speaking of new location, how do you like our new cage?" He made a sweeping gesture with his hand.

"Well, it's quite a change from the past couple years, but it is kind of crowded. I heard some of the guys talking; someone has figured it out to a gnat's eyebrow. Each man has about twenty-two inches of space if we all lie down to sleep at the same time."

"I'll take the congestion any day. It beats the hell out of solitary. I still find myself whispering, out of habit."

"Yeah, me too." Roy agreed, looking around the room at the small clusters of men talking in hushed tones. "But I still don't think we could get away with being too rowdy. Say, speaking of changes, now that the V is allowing us to do a few activities, have you joined in anything? Some of the guys are talking about forming a choir. I might try that."

Matt laughed. "I can't carry a note in a basket. But I have sat in on the bridge game a couple of times. Some of those guys are really good, and I've never played much. I keep looking around for some new guy—they keep talking about this fellow, Goren."

Roy laughed, "You idiot."

"I'm also sitting in on a Spanish class once in a while. Franco's family spoke Spanish at home, so he's a good teacher. It absolutely amazes me, the talent some of these guys have. Makes me feel rather inadequate."

"I know what you mean. Swenson is doing "The Caine Mutiny" one chapter a night. He can recite the lines almost verbatim, some even with proper accents. I don't think he's missed anything."

"All I can say is, this sure beats the past few years."

For awhile life was almost tolerable. Then, shortly after Christmas, following a surprise inspection of packages which revealed all the prohibited items the prisoners had been imaginatively concealing, tensions increased. All packages were opened, many items removed, and it became clear that some mail was being intercepted. The communication network went into overtime.

In February 1971, Matt heard some interesting news, and quickly sought out Roy. "Hey, did you hear the news?"

"About what?"

"One of the men in the cellblock just got a package from his wife. Under the label of a jar of peanut butter was a message the V didn't find. It said 'No POWs in Son Tay on 21 Nov.' So, we were right, it was some sort of a raid to try to rescue us."

The problem with the mail continued. After several weeks, the SRO circulated an order throughout the system. As a form of protest over the V's interference with the mail and packages, they were to stop writing letters.

By March, all letter writing came to a halt.

The senior officers from all the cellblocks were summoned to the block commanders's office. "We know that you have stopped writing as a sign of rebellion. This must stop at once. You must instruct the other criminals to write letters. If you refuse, you will be punished. Will you obey?"

"We cannot make the men write letters if they don't want to," the SRO insisted.

The block commander was irate. "We have been very lenient. We have allowed you many freedoms. If you do not obey, your privileges will be forfeited."

Again, the communication system spread the word. "Keep it up. We've got their attention."

The block commander summoned the senior officers a second time. "Criminals, you will bow to the guards. We have assigned more guards to your spaces to enforce our rules. From now on, criminals are forbidden to communicate with other criminals. If you fail to obey, you will be punished severely."

On urging from the SRO, the prisoners still refused to write.

Within a few days, word was received that six of the highest-ranking officers had been placed in irons. Several others had been thrown in solitary confinement.

"Looks like the V are retaliating," Matt whispered when the guards were out of sight.

A few days later, the building officer came into the cellblock and announced additional repercussions. "Communication will not be permitted. Violators will be dealt with quickly and harshly. You may no longer hold your group meetings. You have taken advantage of our good nature, and you will be punished."

A collective groan went up from the cell.

"Silence," the building officer stormed.

Within two days of receiving the new directive, one of the senior officers in the cellblock was dragged out of the cell for communicating.

As soon as the guards disappeared, Roy found Matt hunkered against a wall. "I guess the V meant business," he said.

Matt stood up and exhaled. "Yeah, and I'm not sure we're picking the right fight."

Roy looked at him, questioningly, but a guard returned before he could speak.

The SRO issued another directive: "Resist as long as you can, then write unacceptable letters. Say that you have been sick, that your health is poor; that our treatment over here is bad; that you are not receiving any mail. Write that the V does not give us our packages, or that they remove things from our packages. Say that we are not permitted to go to church. Whenever a letter is written that cannot be sent, it is submitted to higher authority along with the recommendations of the block commander. This way, maybe some of our complaints, the very things we've been trying to talk to them about, will filter up to those higher in command. It's worth a shot."

Gradually, mail deliveries resumed. Packages were less disturbed. Within a few weeks, communication, though not officially permitted, did not meet with any consistent punishment.

Then they received another directive. "The SRO thinks we're making progress. The V are starting to relent. His staff thinks now is the time to press. We're to send one officer to go with representatives from the other cellblocks to inform the Camp Commander that we are going on a hunger strike if they refuse to allow our demands."

"What demands?" Roy asked.

Matt reported what he had heard. "The return of the men previously thrown in irons, warmer clothing, to be able to hold church services and conduct language and training classes again. Most of all, recognition as prisoners of war and recognition of the military chain of command."

"You don't sound very enthusiastic," Dan said. "Sounds like reasonable requests. Don't you agree with this approach?"

Matt expressed his misgivings. "I don't think they'll do it."

"Well," Roy shrugged his shoulders, "All they can do is say no."

Matt shook his head. "Unfortunately that's not all they can do," he warned, remembering the mistreatment and torture of earlier years.

The response of the Vietnamese, who had been making a concerted effort to build the prisoners back up physically, bore out Matt's concerns. They simply said, "Okay, no eat—no drink."

The guards came into the rooms and dumped all the water.

"And you will not be allowed to take baths."

Within two days, word came down, "We can't survive without water. We'll have to agree to eat."

But the V now had the upper hand and knew it. The camp commander announced, "Before you will be provided food or water, you must agree to make coal balls."

"Well, so much for our glorious experiment. We're still their prisoners, and they aren't about to let us forget it," Matt noted wearily.

"Yeah, but we've got to keep pushing, particularly to be treated as prisoners, not criminals," Roy insisted.

"You're right. A lot of this bullshit is about saving face— theirs—ours—whoever," Matt remarked bitterly. "I'll bet the peace talk negotiators have to go through the same shit. How do you lose without looking like you've lost; how do you downplay a win so the other side saves face? Who's got the ball, whose court is it in? Hell, at this rate we'll be here another five years," Matt ignored the comforting pats on the back by his friend, found an empty wall space and staked it out.

Roy walked over and touched Matt on the shoulders.

"Dammit, Roy, I want to go home. I want to be with my family," Matt grumbled.

"I know. Me too." For once Roy sounded almost as depressed as Matt felt.

Matt turned and slammed one fist into the wall. *Ouch, Dumbshit!* Then he snorted, "That'll really show 'em." He rubbed his bruised knuckles.

Within hours, the SRO sent a message to the Camp Commander which ended the confrontation. "The Geneva Convention provides that officers may be required to do manual labor only when there are insufficient enlisted prisoners of war. Since we are all officers, we have determined it will be permissible to make coal balls."

"Good save," quipped Dan.

Gradually, as 1971 came to an end, the V started giving in to some of the POW's other demands. Church services were once again allowed, and some of the men formed another choir. Little by little, pencils and writing materials were returned, and the men resumed the educational classes. Many of the senior officers who had been placed in isolation in a different camp were returned. Once again, the men were permitted to exercise. A special meal was provided at Christmas 1971.

As a military unit, the men were about as well organized as they could be. Their communication network was functioning well. Matt briefed his group.

"The Camp SRO and his staff have come up with a policy to deal with just about any exigency. No one is to meet with any of those delegations that come over here without submitting to torture first. You are to resist all attempts to be used for any propaganda. The brass is relatively certain that in the event of a Son Tay-type raid, the guards are under strict orders to start shooting, so they have devised a plan intended to minimize the number of casualties in the few minutes it will take an attacking force to gain control."

He went over each man's specific assignments. "Now, memorize where you're to be and what you're to do. We must be prepared."

The bombing of North Vietnam resumed in April 1972. In the middle of May, a guard entered Cellblock 1 and ordered, "Pack your gear, your clothing, dishes and water containers, everything. Because of the bombing, you must be moved for your own safety."

Among the prisoners in Cellblock 1 were a couple of Thais and some South Vietnamese officers. One reported, "Better get ready for a long trip. I overheard the guards talking. We are being sent to a prison far up in the hills of central North Vietnam near the border with China."

After thirty tedious and tiring hours, they arrived at their new camp. Matt's truck was one of the first to enter the compound, and he counted as the other eleven trucks unloaded. Fifteen to twenty men emerged from each truck, so by his calculations there were more than two hundred prisoners here.

As soon as they were released into the large center courtyard, Matt started looking for old friends. Roy and Dan had both been in separate trucks. He didn't see them. He spied Lee about the same time Lee saw him, and they almost ran to each other and embraced.

They were still together, talking, when the cells were assigned and they once again wound up as cellmates.

A few weeks after they arrived, the first mail was delivered. In it was a letter for Matt.

"Hey, Lee, I just received a letter from Bobbie."

"Great. So her mail is getting through now?"

"Well, sort of. This is only my third letter in six years, but, it's got some pretty good news."

"Well, are you going to share it?"

"In 1970, I heard from one of the new shoot downs that I was up for promotion. I didn't know if I could get away just straight out asking about it, so I wrote this double entendre letter to Bobbie. I asked 'How is our garden growing? Have you planted the silver leaf oak in the front yard?' Since we don't have a garden, I hoped she would recognize the silver oak leaf as the insignia for commander.

"Look. She says, 'We planted the silver leaf oak tree.' How about that? I've been promoted to Commander in absentia."

"Oh, Christ! Now you'll be impossible to live with." Lee complained teasingly. "You already outdated me in rank, now you'll outrank me too. Congratulations, *Sir*." He gave an irreverent single finger salute.

Each day, since there was no reading material, a camp official read the news of the day over the camp radio. In October 1972, the announcement caused quite a stir.

"An agreement has been reached between the United States and North Vietnam." A cheer resounded through the camp as repatriation fever spread faster than a wild fire in dry timber.

But a few days later, the collective temperature abruptly cooled. "The agreement between the United States and North Vietnam is off. The United States has refused to negotiate in good faith." The immediate response was various expletives, followed by near silence. Gloom, as thick as a heavy fog, once again settled over the camp.

Matt and Lee discussed the developments.

"The Thais overheard the guards talking. There had been a lull, a cessation in the bombing, while the negotiators were attempting to hammer out the accord, but now that the plan has been scrapped, they say the bombings are resuming," Lee reported.

"Yeah, I heard those B-52s are really doing a number. At least the elections at home didn't cause a halt in the bombings, as the North Vietnamese had counted on," Matt observed.

"If the U.S. keeps that up, this war will be over before you know it. This will be our last Christmas in prison. I predict we will be home in less than six months."

"Your and your damn six months. But, you know what, this time, I think you may be right. I sure as hell hope so." For the first time since staring down the barrel of that militiaman's gun—six and a half years ago, Matt felt hopeful.

CHAPTER 21

<u>San Diego, Early 1973.</u>

In mid-January 1973, Bobbie received a call from the Navy. "Mrs. Tillet, we are happy to inform you that an agreement has been reached with North Vietnam for the release of the POWs. Your husband should be coming home very soon, perhaps within a month. There are just a few remaining formalities to be worked out. We'll keep you informed."

She was stunned after he hung up. What was she going to do now? How could she possibly face Matt? What could she say?

She and Tom had settled into a more or less comfortable arrangement. He was never really satisfied with the necessary deception, but he quit complaining after a while. He probably just gave up on ever changing her mind. He just didn't understand that the charade was necessary. The children wouldn't understand how much she needed Tom. They would think she had deserted their father.

Even though Tom was a regular visitor on weekends, often doing things with them, particularly with Hank, Bobbie never let on that her frequent evenings out were in any way connected with him. She fabricated excuses for being out at night, leaving Sandy's telephone number as a contact.

Sandy had been a godsend. Shortly after she and Tom resumed their affair, Bobbie felt the need to confide in someone, someone with whom she could unburden her soul. She trusted Sandy to keep her secret. Of course, it also helped that Sandy wasn't acquainted with anyone in the Navy. Granted, she hadn't been overly enthusiastic with Bobbie's plan, but had agreed, somewhat reluctantly, to contact Bobbie at Tom's should she receive word of any problem at home. Fortunately, no problem ever arose, so her adulterous trysts had been successfully concealed.

Now, she was facing the moment of truth. Matt was coming home. She should be elated, but all she felt was fear. Her world was about to crumble. Tom would absolutely insist on telling Matt the truth as soon as he returned.

How would the children react when she announced just as soon as their father got home that she wanted a divorce? All her years of carefully hiding the affair would be down the drain. Debbie was sure to put two and two together. Her plan to delay telling Matt until he came home had a lethal flaw—one she had overlooked until now.

Somehow she must convince Tom to give her some extra time with Matt, enough time so that it wouldn't look as if she were just waiting for his release to get a divorce. It must be made to appear that, after all this time apart, they just weren't compatible anymore. It was probably true, anyway.

That meant just one thing—she was going to have to live with Matt again, pretend to have a marriage—for at least a short period of time. Then, after a while, she could say it just wasn't going to work out. Maybe she would be so changed that Matt wouldn't even want to stay married, or, maybe he would be.

As Bobbie struggled with the problem over the next several days, she formulated a plan. It would require Tom's cooperation, and that would probably be the most difficult part. If she could win his approval, she wouldn't have to admit anything to Matt; he could go on believing she had waited like a loyal wife, and the truth would never have to come out about her and Tom—not to Matt, not to the children, not to her friends, not to her parents, and not to the other POW families. There were bound to be some divorces after the men got back. It was deceptively simple. She and Matt would just be among the unfortunate ones who couldn't make the adjustment. No one would be to blame. Their marriage would just be another casualty of the war. Divorce. Now that it was about to happen, it sounded so scary. Her folks would be so disappointed. They didn't approve of divorce, and they liked Matt. She sighed. At this point, it was the only alternative. There was no undoing; no unringing the bell. She must move forward, but cautiously.

The more she thought about it, the more she liked this vision of the future. It was so much nobler and it would be less painful for everyone concerned. Matt would be hurt worse if he found out the truth: that she had been in love with someone else nearly the whole time he was gone. Actually, she would be doing him a favor by concealing her disloyalty.

But how to convince Tom? If he knew Matt was coming home, he would start making plans for their future, for her divorce, for their marriage. That was all he had been waiting for all these years. She had to admit that he had been as much of a father to both Debbie and Hank these past five and a half years as Matt had been before his capture. He had devoted so much time to doing things with them, taking them to ball games, fishing, to the beach, camping at Rosarita Beach in Baja. With a fleeting sense of regret, she wished Tom could have been their step-dad, instead of just "a friend of Dad's" who was lending a helping hand.

Bobbie didn't mention the news to Tom or the children. This way, they wouldn't get their hopes up for nothing in case something happened and the whole thing fell through, as it could certainly still do. It also gave her more time to formulate her plan; fine tune the details.

She had just about worked out her argument for Tom. The setting had to be perfect. She would fix a cozy dinner for two in his apartment, complete with candles and wine. Then when the mood was right, she would break the news and try to win him over.

The phone on her desk rang, shattering her meditation.

Tom's voice was excited. "Bobbie, I just heard on the news that they've reached an agreement with North Vietnam to release the prisoners. Haven't you heard anything from the Navy?" The last part sounded more like an accusation than a question.

She slumped back into her chair. Her spirits, soaring a moment before in anticipation of executing her carefully formulated plan, plummeted. How in the hell was she going to explain not having told him?

Tom pressed. "Bobbie, did you hear me? I said Matt is coming home. Hasn't anyone told you? I can't imagine that they'd make a public announcement without first giving the wives the word."

Bobbie stammered, stalling to think of a plausible excuse. "Oh, Tom, is it really on the news?" She hoped she sounded thrilled. "It's just, well, you caught me by surprise. I haven't seen or heard any news since I came to work this morning."

"Well, have you or haven't you been told anything by the Navy?" Tom's voice conveyed obvious irritation.

"Sugar, I was going to call you later today to suggest that I come over tonight. I was planning to fix a nice dinner and break the news; I wanted to surprise you. I was contacted a couple of days ago. They said they thought things were being worked out, and that the men might be released soon. Actually, I had the feeling from what they said that it wouldn't happen this quickly, but they did say it might be announced publicly before they got back in touch with me personally. If it's on the news now, that means everything has been worked out. I can hardly believe it. Why don't I come over tonight so we can work out our plans." Bobbie was pleased with how quickly she recovered. The story sounded credible, even to her.

Tom was silent for several seconds. "All right," he agreed, "that sounds great. We've got lots of plans to make now. Finally!" He sounded satisfied.

"Yes, we certainly do." At least she did. "I'll be over around seven. Why don't you pick up a couple of steaks, salad fixings and baking potatoes. Oh, and your favorite wine. This is definitely a special time to celebrate." She tried to sound bubbly.

"This calls for champagne." She could hear the enthusiasm in his voice.

She breathed a sigh of relief as she hung up the phone. Through some quick thinking on her feet she had gotten out of one problem, but the bigger one still lay ahead. She would have to use all her wits to convince Tom to go along with her plan for Matt's return.

The problem with Tom temporarily solved, she now needed to find Hank and Debbie to tell them before they, too, heard the news on the radio.

She approached her boss's desk. "Mr. Peterson, would you mind if I left a little early?"

He looked up. "Not at all. I hope it isn't bad news," he added anxiously. He had always treated her as someone special because of her husband's situation.

"Oh, no, Mr. Peterson," she smiled pleasantly. "On the contrary, I just received a call confirming that the POWs are being released soon."

Mr. Peterson jumped up from his chair with a wide grin. "Oh, my dear, I can't say how thrilled I am for you." He placed his arm around her shoulder, giving her a big bear hug. "Of course you can take whatever time off you need. I'm sure you're anxious to share this exciting news with your children.

"Oh, Mr. Peterson, thank you. You're right, I want to find the children and celebrate with them tonight."

Debbie's car was in the driveway when Bobbie drove up. Good. She was at least in the neighborhood. Bobbie ran up the sidewalk to the front door. It was open; Debbie was home. Bobbie hoped she had not heard the news.

Debbie looked up from the dining room table where she had been doing homework. "Hi, Mom. Aren't you home early?"

"Sort of," Bobbie replied vaguely. "Have you seen Hank yet?"

"No, I don't think he's been home since he got out of school, because things were all locked up when I got here a few minutes ago." Debbie resumed her homework.

Bobbie walked past her daughter to the telephone on the kitchen cabinet which separated the kitchen and dining room. "Have you heard any news on the radio or TV today?" She dialed the Postens.

"Unh-unh." Debbie shook her head.

Mrs. Posten promised to send Hank home right away. Bobbie poured a Coke for herself and one for Debbie, sat on the bar stool by the cabinet and lit a cigarette, contemplating how to break the news.

"Mom, what are you doing home so early?" Debbie sipped her Coke. "And why do you want Hank to come home? Frankly, I could use another hour or so of peace and quiet.

"Just wait 'til Hank gets here and I'll tell you both," Bobbie replied, trying to sound mysterious.

Debbie shrugged and went back to writing.

It was fun anticipating their happiness. She smiled. Then her smile slowly turned into a frown as she considered how they would react when she had to tell them about the divorce. She took a long drag off her cigarette.

Just then, Hank burst through the front door. "Gee, Mom, why'd you want me to come home? We were right in the middle of a game." He flung his schoolbooks and jacket onto the living room chair.

Bobbie ignored his snit. "Well, it just so happens I have news I thought was worth more than your precious game," she said. She had their attention now.

"Well, what is it?" Hank was still grouchy.

"If either of you had turned on a radio you would know, but I'm glad you didn't. I wanted to be the one to tell you. Your father is coming home."

Debbie dropped the pencil she had been twiddling between her fingers. A spontaneous blink, a slight quiver to her lower lip, then the mask descended. Bobbie felt a stab in her heart as she watched her daughter who had become so adept at hiding her emotions. She was doing so now with no effort whatsoever. A stranger would never guess that she had just learned some very joyful news, not unless they had been watching very closely. She sat stoically in the chair, her gaze riveted somewhere beyond the sliding patio door.

Hank, on the other hand, after a few seconds of silence jumped high into the air, letting out a tremendous whoop. "When? How do you know?" he demanded.

Bobbie modified the facts slightly to fit with the story she told Tom. "I hadn't said anything earlier because I didn't want to get your hopes up needlessly, but it looks like it is almost certain now."

Hank continued to jump up and down, shouting, "Oh, this is great. I gotta go tell the guys." Without waiting for his mother's permission, he grabbed his jacket, yelling as he ran down the sidewalk, "My dad's coming home! My dad's coming home!" to anyone who cared to listen.

After the door slammed shut behind Hank's exuberance, Debbie spoke for the first time since Bobbie's announcement. "That's really good news, Mom. Have you told anyone else?"

Was she referring to Tom? Bobbie brushed off the idea. "Now, who would I tell before you two," she asked, sounding nonchalant.

"Oh, no one in particular. I assumed you had to tell your boss something in order to get off early." Her voice betrayed nothing. "How did you hear it was on the news, anyway? Do you listen to the radio at work?"

Was there a hint of suspicion or sarcasm in Debbie's voice? "Oh, a friend heard it and called. You know news like this is going to travel fast, and everyone wants to be the first with the congratulations." She didn't think it was necessary to mention the name of "the friend."

Debbie's gaze penetrated deep, but after a lengthy pause, she seemed to accept this explanation. "That's great," she responded, picking up her books and heading toward her room.

Bobbie finished her cigarette and turned her thoughts to Tom. She had to win his approval.

When Debbie returned, she kicked off her plan. "Honey, tonight's my bowling night. I don't want to miss it since all the gals will be eager to hear the news. Can you fix something for Hank if I go ahead and leave a little early?"

"Sure, no problem." Then, unexpectedly, "Do you know when Dad will be coming home?" This was the first apparent sign of interest.

"No, not really, but the Navy official who called said it could be within a month or less. I'm sure we'll be contacted again real soon with all the details." Poor Debbie, was she afraid to feel any emotion? Something still could happen and it could all fall through. Was she bracing herself against that possibility, or was there something else? Observing the tightly controlled body of her daughter, Bobbie was more convinced that she must delay any confrontation with Matt. The children must be allowed to have their reunion with their father in a calm, family atmosphere. Someone needed to reach Debbie, and it was possible Matt could do it. After all, she seemed to have "shut down" emotionally only after he had been shot down. That would be good ammunition to use to make her case with Tom. He might be more agreeable to waiting if he were convinced it would be best for the children. That was the argument she would use tonight.

Tom was still in the shower when she arrived, but, as usual, he had left the patio door open. She went into the kitchen. Sure enough, there were all the things she needed, and a bottle of champagne on ice. Just then, Tom came out of the bathroom, wrapped only in a towel. His face appeared younger, happier. Before she could dodge out of the way, he caught her in a tight embrace, squeezing her firmly against his damp body.

When he finally released her, she drew a long breath. "Whew! That was quite a greeting."

"Just the beginning," he winked as he patted her bottom.

Turning around, she tried to resume cooking, but he nuzzled her neck from behind, tickling her ear with his tongue.

"How about getting dressed and pouring us some of that champagne while I finish the salad?" she scolded, trying to avoid his advances.

"Yes, ma'am, I'll get right on it," he saluted in mock obedience.

Tom was in excellent spirits, better than she had seen in a long time. There was no point upsetting him or causing a big disagreement right now. There would be plenty of time to face the issue after Matt returned. She was sure she could think of a way later to gain the time she needed to put her program in action.

CHAPTER 22

<u>January - February 1973, North Vietnam.</u>

When Matt and Lee first arrived at the new prison in 1972, the V started building a bakery. Observing the progress, Lee had jokingly prophesied, "You know, this war is about over. That bakery is going to be completed just about the time we get to go home."

In January 1973, the bakery was finished. On the day the first shipment of flour arrived, the guards started jerking out the radio speakers, the last thing they did before abandoning a camp.

"What did I tell you?" Lee gloated.

"This may be the first time in six and a half years that you've been right," Matt conceded.

All the prisoners were assembled in the courtyard with their gear to be loaded into the trucks. Twenty-six miserable hours later, considerably better time than on the trip up, the trucks drove into the familiar arched gate leading into Hoa Loa prison in downtown Hanoi.

"Welcome back to the Hanoi Hilton," Lee commented sarcastically. Matt scoffed, "Home, sweet home—but hopefully not for long."

They were led to Cellblock 7, a large cell similar to the one they had been in when they were brought back from Camp Faith. As soon as they entered the cell, John Billings, Mike Hastings, Craig Hansen and a couple of other men rushed over to greet them.

They all exchanged bear-hugs with the men from the other camp. "God it's great to see you guys again."

"You too." Matt echoed.

John introduced the tall, chisel-faced man. "Matt, Lee, Jim Holiman, another A-4 driver." They all shook hands.

Roy turned to Craig. "Man, is it good to see you. We've been trying for months to find out what happened to you."

Craig started to give a quick rundown of the small outlying prisons where he had been held since his capture, but before he could finish, John interrupted, his excitement uncontrollable.

"Man, it's really been a show. After that first wave of B-52s came over the city, all the guards who used to stand around harassing the prisoners were gone—like nowhere to be found!" John's devilish grin was very much in evidence.

"We heard about the big bombers," Matt said, "but the Rat told us that sixty of them had been shot down."

John snorted. "That's bullshit. As best we can tell, only thirteen were shot down, and we believe all of the crews got out safely."

Mike continued with the update. "You guys were the only group sent out of Hanoi. Where have you been?"

"We were taken to a high-security prison up near the China border, reportedly built in the early days of the war. We called it 'Dogpatch.' I think we were the first prisoners; it didn't appear to have been used before. It didn't have any electricity, and if you can believe it, they didn't have any matches, either. So we had to keep a kerosene lamp or a candle burning all the time." Matt grinned.

Lee added, "It was a well thought out design though—heavily bolted doors, windows with locked screens and few common walls. The entire courtyard was surrounded by high eighteen-inch-thick walls. Each cellblock had eight individual cells, its own wash area, and a tank of water."

Matt jumped back in. "Oh, the crapper was really uptown too. Instead of honey buckets, most of the cellblocks were equipped with two-trackers. We called them the Hanoi Jane Urinals."

"Wow, such luxury." John said. "I hope you pissed on one for me."

"How far was it?" Jim asked.

"It took about thirty wretched hours to get up there. We took a bunch of barely passable side roads. We were never allowed out of the trucks, not even to relieve ourselves. We each had one hand manacled, so you can imagine what fun it was to pass the honey bucket! Do you have any idea how much you itch after thirty hours when you've got shitty piss splashed all over you?" Matt wrinkled his nose.

The others grimaced, then laughed.

Matt continued, "Lee and I saw each other as soon as we arrived and ended up in the same cellblock. Roy and Dan were there, but in different cellblocks, so we didn't see much of them. Coming back was a little quicker, but not much better. We weren't camouflaged, as we had been going, but they tried to keep the canvas flaps closed. The smell of gasoline fumes from the drums in the back with us caused a lot of the guys to puke, and between the vomit and the gasoline smell, it was a fairly ratty experience."

Lee added, "It really wasn't too bad, as prison life goes, but we did lose one guy though. Shortly after we got there, a lot of us came down with a high fever and nausea. The V did what they could, which of course, isn't much, because they obviously didn't know what caused it. They took our temperatures three times a day, then stood around shaking their heads, looking perplexed. Whatever it was seemed to run its course after about ten days, and most of us recovered. But, there was one guy, a young Marine Captain, who was so ill, they brought him back to Hanoi. The camp commander told us a few days later that he died."

"So tell us how things are going here," Matt urged.

"Since you left, there have really been some changes! The V seem to know it's all over but the shouting, so they've really changed their tune. We're finally allowed to help run the camp. They are working through the senior officers, and we have a lot more freedom," John explained.

"Apparently the camp commander finally realized we would follow orders better if they came through our officers. They still keep the Camp SRO in a separate cell, but he and his staff meet with our guys just about every day. I think the camp CO feared he would lose control once we learned that the war was over, but by working with five of our senior officers, both the V's programs and ours seem to be operating pretty well."

Mike added, "We're getting medical treatment when we need it. It's still primitive, but it's there. We're getting adequate food, if you can call this garbage 'food.' We've even been receiving milk and bread every day."

****

On 29 January, all the prisoners were called to the courtyard. John, Craig, Mike, Lee, Matt, Jim and Roy stood together.

John spied a partially concealed camera in a second-floor window of one of the administration buildings. "Something big's up. There's a camera crew up in that window. They're looking for more propaganda."

Others saw the camera too.

"I want to address you on a matter of greatest importance," stated the camp commander, speaking through an interpreter. "The United States and the Democratic Republic of Vietnam have signed an agreement. This agreement calls for the repatriation of all prisoners of war. In addition, the agreement requires that the prisoners be notified of the contents of the agreement within five days. This agreement was signed on twenty-seven January. The Democratic Republic of Vietnam is showing its good will and good intentions with respect to this repatriation agreement by notifying you early."

He stopped, waiting and watching for the reaction of the men. No one said a word, no display of any outward emotion. The prisoners stood silently, at rigid military attention, eyes straight ahead, as the camp CO continued to read the text of the agreement. When he had finished, guards distributed copies of the agreement to each prisoner.

The camp commander seemed puzzled. "I don't understand. Aren't you happy?"

Almost in unison the men turned their backs on the camera, denying the V any propaganda value. A few raised extended middle fingers as they started walking away.

Once back inside their cells, out of the sight of the Vietnamese, out of view of the cameras, it was a different story. Even with years of practice at submerging their emotions, no one even tried to hide his excitement while reading the agreement.

When they finished, John poked Matt and pointed. "See that microwave tower just outside the wall?"

"Yeah."

"The V turned the lights out on that tower in early '71 when the U.S. was bombing the hell out of things. They haven't been turned on since. Lots of guys say that when those lights come back on, it will mean we are really going home. What you want to bet they turn them on tonight?"

That evening, as darkness approached, the entire prison population watched anxiously over the prison walls. Suddenly, the lights on the tower lit up like fireworks, followed by a spontaneous cheer. Things were definitely looking brighter.

The next morning, Lee and Matt were sitting in their cell excitedly discussing their release and what they would do when they got home. A roar of laughter rose from the courtyard. John came running in, holding his side.

"What'd we miss?" Lee asked.

"The V just ran their flag up the flagpole for the first time since the bombing started."

"What's so funny about that?"

"What is it that the V does best?"

"Screw up?"

"You got it! They hung the flag upside down."

****

On the first of February, the senior officers were finally freed from their individual cages and allowed into the camp with the rest of the prisoners.

John, who throughout almost six years of imprisonment never lost his fondness for practical jokes, particularly against the V, wasted no time putting it to use to welcome back one of the SROs. Life had been too restricted; he was dying to create some chaos.

While the others watched from a discreet distance, John sidled up to Captain Dalton, the senior Navy officer, and whispered confidentially, "Captain, we've got a real problem."

Captain Dalton was a profoundly religious man as well as a very proper Naval Officer. If the men in his command had a problem, it was his problem. He was ready and willing to assist whenever he could. "What is it, John," he asked soberly.

"Come over here, Captain. I don't want anyone else to hear." John stealthily moved to a private corner so as to hinder observation, leading the anxious officer with him. Surreptitiously turning his head from side to side, he leaned closer to the Captain and whispered, "Sir, there's a queer among us."

The Captain looked alarmed at John's revelation. Expressing his dismay in a voice full of concern, "Oh, John, are you sure? Do you know who it is?"

Quickly kissing his own fingers John pressed them against the startled officer's cheek, and in a falsetto voice, said, "Me!" and with an effeminate wave of his wrist, hastily darted away, snickering.

Matt and Lee just shook their heads, trying hard not to laugh at the look on Captain Dalton's face. It had turned from concern to disbelief; then he chuckled as he realized he had been had.

"Billings, you suffer from some sort of psychological disorder. I'm going to reflect it on your fitness report," Captain Dalton yelled.

A few days later, the V started making new cell assignments. Mike was placed in a cell with his front seater, Lee and Matt were placed in a cell just down the hall, John and Craig were taken to another, and Roy and Jim to yet another, Lee, ever watchful for hopeful signs, ventured, "I think I know what these moves mean. The guys in the first cell are the oldest shootdowns, the guys in the next cell are next in order. They're assigning us cells by shootdown date."

Matt thought about who was in the various cells. "You're right!" he admitted. "We're probably in the first group then, one of the special advantages of getting bagged early." For the first time in almost seven years, Matt allowed himself to believe it—they were going home! His long-held concerns about what he might find there were temporarily forgotten.

The first group, plus the sick and wounded, were issued their position numbers and their going-home clothes. Matt, Mike and Lee were in that group. John, Roy, Craig and Jim missed the cut.

"It won't be long," Matt said reassuringly, as they all met and discussed what was happening.

Lee tried to joke. "See what getting early reservations does for you?"

They all laughed nervously. John tried to ease the concern. "Hell, we've all been here a year or so less than you guys. I'll trade another couple weeks for that extra year any day."

At the back of every mind was the concern that something could still go wrong, could interrupt the process, or stop it midstream.

Back in their cell, Matt examined the bag—underclothes, blue shirt, grey cotton twill trousers, zipper-type jacket, and a pair of shoes. "This is the first pair of shoes I've had since the day I was shot down, unless you want to count the rubber-tire sandals I lost in the Hanoi March."

Lee chastened, "Who are you to complain? I didn't even get the rubber-tire sandals. You've always enjoyed the privileges of rank."

"Yeah, asshole, some privileges," Matt countered.

Each day brought changes, numbers were jockeyed to make room for the sick, and in one case, for a man whose mother was dying. Matt and Lee were comfortably high on the list - they were going to be in the first group.

Finally, on 12 February, 1973, the guard directed them to put on their new clothes.

"All right!" they yelled in unison, jumping up and hugging one another as soon as the guard was out of earshot.

"It's true, buddy, it's really happening. We're going home!" Lee exclaimed excitedly.

Matt observed, "Yeah, your six-month prediction is finally coming true. California, here I come." He tossed the pajama-type garments he had lived in for almost seven years into the corner. "I'll never wear pajamas again."

When instructed, they lined up with the other men in single file in exact shootdown order, Matt a few numbers in front of Lee, Mike a few in front of both of them. Then, in crisp military fashion, they marched through the courtyard, between rows of their solemn-faced buddies awaiting their turn, toward the buses that would carry them to freedom. Matt gave a high sign as he passed Roy and John. They smiled, nodded and John gave a barely noticeable thumbs up.

As he passed through the heavy wooden and metal gate at the entrance to the prison, Matt was handed his going-away present, a little black bag containing two packages of Vietnamese cigarettes, a box of matches—the first he had received during his entire confinement—a toothbrush, toothpaste and a new bar of lye soap.

Quietly, almost somberly, they moved toward the waiting buses. The first bus filled and pulled away, disappearing from view as it turned the corner. Matt and Lee boarded the second bus, and as soon as it was full, it too pulled away from Hoa Loa prison.

"Well, how do you like the limousine service provided by the Hanoi Hilton?" Lee asked.

"It's going in the right direction!"

On the bus, an occasional hushed conversation could be heard, but mostly the men were quiet as they viewed the devastation of what had been Hanoi unfolding before their eyes. The evening before, the Camp Commander had forecast, "Tomorrow, you will see what Nixon has done to our country."

The bus drove down dusty streets lined with Vietnamese. Occasionally Matt saw a raised clenched fist, but most just went about their business, watching curiously, their demeanor a raw contrast to what he witnessed during the Hanoi March in 1966.

Lee commented, "You know, I can't help but feel a little sorry for these people. Most of them are simple, hard-working peasants. They don't deserve what their government has done to them." Through the broken window of the bus, Matt and Lee observed Vietnamese workers, many carrying heavy shoulder poles, walking barefoot along the dirty, bomb-pocked streets. Some had lost limbs; others were in need of medical attention.

"Yeah, I know what you mean," Matt agreed, "but don't forget most of them took part in this war, in one way or another. Even the women, children and old folks manned the guns, fired the missiles, and carried the grenades, oftentimes into the midst of our unsuspecting servicemen."

"I know, but you gotta remember they were defending their homeland, doing what their government told them to do. Just as we were doing what our government asked of us. Wouldn't you expect our families to join the battle if the war were waged on our soil? Can you really blame them?" Lee argued.

"Ask me again in a few years," Matt said flatly.

Lee tilted his head and looked at Matt obliquely.

"No, you're right." Matt conceded, then rubbed his mouth and chin. "I suppose I can't blame them. War is waged by governments, not the people."

As they negotiated through narrow residential streets, Lee pointed to meager homes, shared with pigs and chickens. "Those are the lucky ones, they have something to eat."

Matt shook his head as the scenes of poverty and misery rolled past the bus window. He commented, "Somewhere, a long time ago, I heard a description of a Communist society. It went something like, 'A whole, big group of people sharing a whole lot of nothing.' It sure looks like that's an accurate definition."

Their bus pulled up in front of a building that resembled a church. Matt looked at the bench-type pews similar to those in the small country churches back in Nebraska. "Isn't this supposed to be the airport?"

"I thought so, but I don't see any planes."

"I don't see the first bus either."

A twinge of fear shot through Matt. Had they been deceived into thinking they were being transferred to one place only to be taken out to some remote area to be killed? Could this have been the V's greatest hoax?

The sound of a large airplane's engines lessened his apprehension, and an announcement by a Vietnamese official eliminated it. "The first airplane is almost full. It will be necessary for you to wait for the second plane. We will be moving to the other side of the airfield very shortly."

Each man was given a sack lunch and a bottle of warm beer.

They heard a large airplane taking off. Matt nudged Lee and gave a thumbs up. "That's one!"

After what seemed like an eternity, but was in reality only a few minutes later, they were transported to the other side of the field. A gleaming C141 was just landing.

"That is the most beautiful airplane I have ever seen, even if it isn't a fighter," Matt proclaimed.

Like the streets and buildings of Hanoi, Gia Lam airport evidenced the havoc wrecked by the U.S. bombers. Every window of the buildings not totally destroyed had been shattered by the concussion from the bombs.

As ordered, the men lined up behind an imaginary boundary. On one side were uniformed Vietnamese officials and the prisoners. On the other side were several U.S. military officers in good old U.S. military uniforms, and that beautiful plane to freedom.

At the word from one of the Vietnamese officials, the men started forward, marching smartly and proudly to the point of demarcation where they passed from Vietnamese control and were welcomed by their U.S. escorts. Matt, his heart beating wildly, saluted, shook hands, saluted again, and was led through a maze of people and flashing cameras toward the C141. It was 1230 when he boarded, Lee close behind. Ten minutes later, the plane carrying Lieutenant Commander Mike Hastings, Commander Matthew Allen Tillet and Lieutenant Colonel Lee Wilson on the first leg of their long journey home, taxied down the runway. The huge bird shuddered as it struggled to become airborne.

Even after they were in the air, it was difficult for Matt to relax. He told his escort, "The Vietnamese could still shoot the plane out of the sky. I'm not going to feel really free until we're out of Vietnam."

Just then the pilot announced, "Feet wet! We have just cleared North Vietnamese airspace." A swollen dam broke. Years of restraint disintegrated. A resounding cheer erupted from the newly repatriated POWs as they scrambled over seats and crowded into the aisles, slapping backs, shaking hands, and hugging each other.

The Air Force nurses, doubling as stewardesses, served cold American beer and mixed drinks during the flight to Clark Air Force Base in the Philippines. At 1630 on 12 February, 1973, their Freedom Express touched down.

"Pinch me just to make sure I'm not dreaming. I've never been so happy to have an ex in front of my designation—EX POW sounds good!" Mike and Matt wrapped their arms around Lee. Matt reminisced, "Old buddy, I'm really going to miss you. We may not see each other for awhile. Let's stay in touch. When I get down to Florida, I'll look you up."

Lee just patted Matt's shoulder, his eyes wet. They all shook hands.

"Commander Tillet?" A tall young man saluted Matt. "I'm Lieutenant George Edwards, your debriefing officer. I'll show you to your room in the base hospital, Sir. Over the next couple of days, I'll try to bring you up to date on the past seven years. I know you probably want to freshen up and change clothes, so I'll give you some time to get settled, and then when you feel like it, we'll begin."

Matt examined one of the two beds in his hospital room. Antiseptic clean. He sat on the edge of the bed, then lay his head back on the fluffy pillow, and closed his eyes. When he opened them at the sound of steps, he was astonished to see Lee walking over to the other bed.

"Can you believe it? All that time in prison together, and here we are - roommates again!"

"Oh," Lee quipped. "Nothing to it. I made reservations - six months ago!"

They both laughed heartily. God, it was good to laugh out loud without fear of drastic repercussions or torture, Matt thought. He rose from the bed. "The first thing I want is a long, hot shower and a shave."

A few minutes later, he called to Lee. "Have you figured out how to use this new-fangled shaver that's in the Red Cross kit?"

Lee examined the injection-blade shaver. "Hell no. I can't get the blade in." After several minutes the two of them, working together, mastered the new technology, and shaved for dinner.

While they were getting settled, Matt noticed a white-coated man standing outside their room.

"What in the hell do you think you're doing?" Matt stepped into the hallway and asked, annoyed.

"Oh, I'm just hanging around in case there is anything I can do to help."

"Bullshit! You're a shrink, aren't you?"

"Yes," the man admitted. "We're here to observe the behavior of the former POWs."

"Get lost! We're not specimens under your goddamn micro-scope," Matt stormed.

"No problem," the man smiled politely and walked away.

Matt returned to the room. "Dammit, I'm tired of never having any privacy. I couldn't do much about it in Vietnam, but I don't think we have to put up with it here. I don't intend to be treated like a bug."

Lee smiled. "You tell em, Tiger. . . . Why don't you just shut the door?"

Matt grinned sheepishly. "Yeah, I suppose that would work. Why didn't I think of that?"

That evening the repatriated prisoners trooped down to the hospital cafeteria, anticipating their first taste of "real" American food.

"Where's the steaks?" several asked.

"Hey, I want pork chops!" shouted another.

The doctor in charge of the hospital explained, "We think it would be best to let you gradually get used to American food."

Almost to a man, the ex-prisoners protested vocally and loudly.

One of the senior officers spoke for the group. "Anyone who could eat the slop we've been served in prison and survive can certainly handle good old standard military chow."

Several doctors who were in the dining hall conferred. The head of the hospital spoke. "We understand your wishes. We'll take the matter under consideration."

After the bland evening meal, each man was allowed to call anyone they wanted anywhere in the world. Colonel Nelson, the most senior ex-prisoner of war, made the first call. "Mr. President, on behalf of all the ex-Prisoners of War, I want to express our heartfelt gratitude for your efforts in gaining our freedom."

There was a pause.

"Is there anything else we need? Well, Mr. President, since you ask, there is one thing that would certainly help. We'd like some good old American chow, you know—stuff like ham and eggs, meat and potatoes."

Another long pause. "Yes, Mr. President, I'll certainly call you if we need anything else. Oh, now that you mention it, there is one more thing. Could you include some ice cream?"

Matt's first call was to San Diego. He inhaled deeply several times while listening to the crackling phone lines and impatiently waiting for a voice to answer. After several rings, Matt immediately recognized the voice of his wife.

"Bobbie." His voice was trembling.

"Matt? Matt, is that really you? Where are you? How are you?"

"Yes, honey, it's me. I'm fine. We're at Clark Air Force Base in the PI. How are you? How are the children? Are they there?" His heart was still racing, but gradually the trembling disappeared from his voice. Bobbie assured him everyone was fine. Debbie and Hank both sounded so grown up. Debbie reminded him that she was going to be twenty-one this year. And Hank couldn't stop asking questions. Finally Bobbie had to take the phone away from him.

"I'm sorry, Matt. Hank is so anxious to see you. When will you get to come home?" she asked.

"I think in a couple of days. I suppose after they run some medical tests to make sure we aren't being used for germ warfare, we should be flying on home. I think they'll be flying me directly to Miramar, so you all wait right there." Like Hank, Matt had many questions, but he realized there would be time for answers later, after he got home and could hold all of them in his arms.

"We'll be at Miramar to meet you," she assured him.

"I love you," Matt whispered, remembering his promise to himself.

There was a slight pause. "We love you too. Hurry home."

That night, for the first time in six years, eight months and twelve days, Matt lay down between clean, crisp white sheets pulled tightly over a comfortable mattress. He tossed and turned. He could tell Lee was doing the same.

"Lee, I'm exhausted, but I'm too excited to sleep. How about you?" Matt whispered.

"Me too. But, Matt, remember, you don't have to whisper anymore." Lee chuckled.

They spent most of the night anticipating their homecomings, how their families would look, how much they would have changed, and speculating on what kind of duty assignments they might expect.

The next morning, after a near sleepless night, Matt and Lee dressed in their new uniforms, and went to breakfast.

They looked at the selections on the breakfast buffet, which included just about anything anyone wanted to eat.

"Apparently the President of the United States pulls a little weight," Lee joked.

As Matt walked toward a table, he passed by the dessert section and started counting. "He must pull a *lot* of weight. There are sixteen flavors of ice cream over there."

CHAPTER 23

San Diego, February 14, 1973.

An elaborate reception awaited the Southern California ex-POWs when their plane landed at Miramar Naval Air Station in San Diego.

Captain Stoddard, the senior officer aboard the flight, was the first to deplane. To the whirring and humming of the television and movie cameras, the hundreds of gathered officials and assembled families of the returnees, he made a short, simple and emotionally charged speech, after which he hobbled to the waiting arms of his wife and four sons.

Watching restlessly from the window of the aircraft, Matt felt an uncontrollable pulsating flutter in his neck. He couldn't remember ever feeling so excited. At last, it was his turn to deplane. He emerged into the cool, damp air, searching the crowd for a glimpse of Bobbie, Debbie or Hank. The officer beside him tapped his shoulder; that was his cue. Matt swallowed hard, straightened his new uniform and hat and smartly saluted as he reached the familiar tarmac below. Home at last! More than a few times over the past seven years he doubted that he would ever see this day.

Words alone could not sufficiently describe his joy and exultation; he would have liked to kiss the ground, throw his hat high into the air and yell like a cheerleader at an Army-Navy football game. But that would have been inappropriate. So, like those who preceded him, he stood tall and erect in proper military bearing, suppressing his emotions, as he had been so well trained to do these past seven years, while dutifully saluting, smiling and shaking the hand of each of the dignitaries until he reached the end of the line.

Looking down the red-carpeted aisle that extended from the plane to the roped-off area of cars, he spotted his family and sucked in his breath. He had been warned to expect a big change, but he just wasn't prepared for the beautiful young lady his daughter had become, and was that Hank? Hank, a tot clinging to his mother's hand when Matt left, was almost grown, already taller than his mother, and his hair was longer than hers too. Yet Matt would have recognized him anywhere. It was almost like looking into a mirror thirty years ago.

Hank's smile lit up his whole face. When Matt waved, Hank broke free of Bobbie's grip, and bounded the several yards toward Matt, literally vaulting the final few feet into Matt's open arms.

****

Bobbie recognized Matt the moment he appeared at the top of the stairs, and waited anxiously as he made his way through the line of well-wishers. *Surprising how much he looks the same. True, his hair is grayer, he's thinner, gaunter, and certainly he looks a little older, but still the same stalwart Matt.*

Somehow she had expected more changes. Actually, she hadn't known what to expect. Maybe she secretly hoped there would be some obvious changes, something everyone would notice, something that might warrant her rejection of him. But as she watched him hug Hank, saw his familiar crooked grin, she felt a twinge deep inside. Their eyes met, not *all* her feelings for him had disappeared. Odd. She felt an urge to rush into his arms, but at the same time hesitant to move forward, fearful that her secret would be revealed, some neon sign would flash, "I wasn't true to you." She was also aware that their every move was being filmed, and she didn't want Tom to see an overly enthusiastic reunion on tonight's six o'clock news.

When Matt and Hank, arm in arm, headed their way, Bobbie and Debbie walked quickly toward them. As they grew closer, Bobbie picked up the pace and upon reaching Matt, easily slipped into his eager embrace.

Ignoring the cameras recording every move, Matt pulled Bobbie into his arms and kissed her long and fervently. "Oh, honey, it's so good to be back," he murmured between kisses.

"It's good to have you home," she whispered. No matter what happened in the future, it *was* good that he was back.

With one arm still around Bobbie, Matt pulled Debbie close.

"Welcome home, Dad." She gave him a warm hug and kissed his cheek.

Hank threw his arms around the backs of his mother and sister, and they all stood huddled together while the cameras clicked on. Matt made no attempt to hide his tears. This day had been a long time coming.

Another family approached the carpeted area, anxious to see and greet their returning hero. Bobbie's Casualty Assistance Officer politely suggested, "Sir, perhaps you might prefer to go on out to the car where you will have more privacy."

Matt nodded. Keeping one arm wrapped firmly around Bobbie and squeezing her shoulder frequently, he placed his other arm around Hank, while Debbie walked on the other side of Bobbie.

As they neared the rows of waiting black limousines with their darkened windows, Hank was tossing questions a mile a minute. "How was the flight, Dad? What were you doing in the PI? How long did it take for you to fly home? Did they hurt you in prison? Gosh, it's great to have you home!"

Matt laughed and answered each question as best he could, only to be hit by another bombardment as soon as he had finished.

The roomy interior of the big black limo had two plush sofa-like seats facing each other. Lieutenant Commander Nelson shut the door and discreetly moved away from the car.

At last, for a few minutes at least, Matt had his family all to himself. He took Bobbie in his arms and once more kissed her ardently. He felt her stiffen.

"Welcome home, Matt," she laughed nervously, seemingly embarrassed at the intimacy of his embrace in front of the children.

Debbie echoed her mother, "Yes, Dad, we're really glad to have you home." She reached across the aisle and clutched his free hand, squeezing it reassuringly.

Bobbie straightened up and moved slightly away. "When the welcoming ceremony is over, we are to go in a caravan to Balboa Hospital. You will be staying there for a couple of days, but I understand that visiting rules will be very relaxed. You will probably be able to come home in two or three days at the most." She paused and nervously wrung her hands.

****

Debbie was uncomfortable as she watched her parents. She felt sorry for her father, for what she imagined he had been through in prison, and for what he would have to face when her mother asked him for a divorce, as she would no doubt do soon. Tom had been far more patient than most men would have been. Debbie didn't delude herself that they weren't sleeping together, but she had never been able to fault them for it. She wished her mother had done as Tom wanted: gotten a divorce a long time ago and married him. The unhappiness and disappointment that was going to result now was going to be far greater. Also, it would have been nice to have been able to treat Tom as a father when she was growing up. She cared for him very much. He had always been there for her. More important, he could have been a more positive influence with Hank; not that he didn't do what he could, but discipline was not one of her mother's strong suits, and Hank needed the daily attention of a firmer hand.

Now, as she watched her father, saw his tears of joy and sensed the excitement he felt at being back with what he thought was his devoted wife, it was all she could do not to cry. He was going to be so hurt when he learned the truth. As much as she ached for him, she didn't envy the ordeal her mother was facing: When and how to tell this loving and expectant husband the heartbreaking news. If only her mother had trusted her, shared the burden of her "secret" love affair, maybe she could have helped, or could help even now. Instead, her mother always gave those transparent, made-up excuses to get out of the house to be with Tom. It was almost offensive that she would think Debbie so naive and gullible.

It had always been perfectly understandable, right from the start, how her mother and Tom had fallen in love. They were, to Debbie's way of thinking, better suited temperamentally than her mother and father. The most important thing was that her mother needed a man, someone to love her all the time. Many of the Navy wives could handle the long separation, the loneliness, but not her mother. Debbie was just grateful that someone as honorable as Tom had been there. A lesser man could have really taken advantage of Bobbie. Debbie had always felt a closeness to Tom, perhaps because he had never tried to lie to her or deceive her about his feelings for her mother.

From the very first word that her father had been shot down, and later when it was confirmed that he was a prisoner, Debbie recognized that her mother was going to need help if she were to survive the ordeal. By now she could automatically numb her inner turmoil and disguise her panic with an apathetic, impassive exterior. It had become second nature. Practicing her art, she tuned back in to the present.

****

Matt watched Bobbie carefully as she spoke. Something was amiss. What message was she trying to convey? Why was she so nervous? Why was she so distant? Was she somehow complaining that his release and homecoming had happened too quickly to suit her? For him, the past few days had just dragged by, the longest since his early days of torture when his pain had made each day an endless nightmare. Why would she have wanted their reunion to be further delayed? Unless there was something she needed to prepare for. Was he just imagining things? He hoped so.

While they waited for the ceremonies to end and the drive to Balboa Hospital to begin, they visited. Or rather, Hank and Matt did. Matt tried several times to include Bobbie and Debbie, but at each lull in the conversation, Hank jumped back in with another stream of questions. "What was it like in prison?" he questioned.

Before Matt could respond, Bobbie scolded him sharply, "Your father doesn't want to have to think about that right now."

"Oh, that's okay," Matt assured them, "it doesn't bother me to talk about my prison experiences." But the conversation was ended, with Hank falling sullenly quiet. Matt tried to smooth things over, "Son, we'll have lots of time. I'll tell you whatever you want to know—later."

Matt used the ensuing period of silence to study his wife closely. She had changed. Her usually bright, shiny eyes had lost much of their sparkle. She couldn't hide the crow's feet around her eyes, even with the unusually heavy makeup. Her once trim, tiny figure had some noticeable bulges and sags.

Matt recalled his conversations with LCDR Edwards, his debriefing officer at Clark. During those 72 hours, George tried to bring Matt up to date on almost seven years of change. "Many things," he warned, "are going to be different from when you left. Tastes and styles have changed. Women's dresses are shorter. The mini-skirt, which stops above the knees, is quite popular. And you won't believe the hairstyles, because I can't." It had been hard for Matt to envision what George was describing, but now he understood. Bobbie, he observed with a twinge of disappointment, was embracing the new styles. Her dress stopped above her knees, and her graying hair was plopped high up on her head. It looked just like what George had described—a cone-shaped beehive.

It was quite a contrast from the picture he still carried in his mind, even after seven years, of Bobbie on the windswept ramp at Miramar, holding Hank in her arms, waving goodbye as Matt waited his turn to take off and fly out to join the ship. Her soft short blonde hair was so pretty; so nice to run his fingers through. She looked so young and fresh then. He definitely didn't like these new fashions, but maybe in time he would adjust or grow accustomed to them. He was always slow to adapt to new ideas and drastic changes. In keeping with promises made to himself in prison, he vowed not to express his disappointment to Bobbie, at least not directly. Perhaps he could figure out a more subtle way to encourage her to wear her hair the way she used to.

Since entering the car, Matt kept his arm tightly draped around Bobbie's shoulder, squeezing her against him every few minutes, just to make sure this was all real. Her warm body smelled of a delicate perfume. It was going to be so wonderful to hold her nude form against his tonight, to make love again. *God, I hope it works.*

Matt, like Hank, was full of questions. He tried to fill the conspicuous silence on Bobbie's part by asking about what had been happening to friends and acquaintances while he was gone. Her answers were short and sometimes evasive, not conversational and informative as he wanted. Perhaps the families had been advised to treat the returnees with kid gloves. He would have to set the pace, break down the barriers if they were going to get back on an even keel.

"What happened to Hugh and Laura?" he asked, referring to the couple of old friends that Bobbie had told him were divorced. "I thought they were the perfect couple."

Bobbie seemed unwilling to elaborate on the bad news. "As I said, they got a divorce."

"Yeah, I know you said that, but what happened?" He pushed for more details.

Bobbie squirmed uncomfortably. "He found someone else—his secretary," she admitted reluctantly.

"Well, I'll be damned," Matt exclaimed. "I thought they would have survived hell and high water together. Too bad—they were a nice couple. Where are they now?"

Clearly Bobbie didn't want to pursue this line of conversation. "He was transferred back East with his company. I heard he took his secretary with him and they've since gotten married. Laura and the two boys are still here in town. She had to sell the house though, and she and the children live in a dingy little apartment in a rundown section of town. I don't think she did very well financially, for some reason, at least not to hear her tell it. I thought with community property laws in California she was entitled to half, but somehow he got around it."

Matt shook his head over the news, surprised that Bobbie even knew what kind of property laws California had. Perhaps when you have a close friend who goes through a divorce you learn about those things. Or did she have another reason to have inquired?

Then he asked about his cousin, Martin, and his wife, Amelia. They had all gone to school together. Matt and Martin lived on adjacent farms and spent many summers baling hay and shucking corn, and many winters chopping firewood down by the creek. They also walked to grade school together. After Matt graduated and left for the Navy, he heard that Martin and Amelia, both in Matt's class in school, had gotten married. When he left for Vietnam in late '65, they were living up near Los Angeles.

Again Bobbie hesitated and seemed unwilling to continue. Her reticence annoyed him. "Dammit, Bobbie, quit treating me like a baby. It isn't necessary to protect me from bad news or the real world. I'm not going to fall apart. You're acting as though you have to shield me from the truth if it's something I'm not going to like, or if it's bad news. You don't. I'm just trying to catch up on what's happened to our friends over the past seven years. If it's good— terrific. If it's not so good—that's too bad. But please, just give it to me straight. Just think of this as your husband coming home after a long cruise. Remember how we used to spend hours catching up on all the news." Matt recalled how, after one cruise, they stayed awake until three in the morning while she, between lovemaking, filled him in on a scandalous affair.

Bobbie turned and faced him for the first time. "But, Matt, you haven't just gotten back from a long cruise; it has been an eternity. You left in a whole other lifetime. I can't even remember in some cases whether people I know are our friends or just mine. But you're right, I do feel uncomfortable discussing other people's broken marriages before we've even had an opportunity to get acquainted again. About Martin and Amelia, if you must know, they're divorced too; have been now for five years, and I understand they're having a hell of a time with one of their children who's using drugs. Martin works down here in San Diego now and Amelia still lives up near L.A. If I'm not mistaken Martin just got remarried, or is about to get married, to some gal he met down here." Her eyes were flashing anger.

Obviously, discussing their divorced friends was a sore point, which Matt vowed to avoid for now. He spoke directly to Debbie. It would have to be safer ground. She had been so quiet since they got in the car. "Debbie, tell me, what has been happening with you? Do you have any special boyfriends, or are you spending all your time studying?"

"Well, sir," she began much too formally, "I'm in my second year of college. I get pretty good grades; in fact, I made the dean's list last semester. I'm taking a lot of science courses. I think I want to be a nurse."

"A nurse, you say? Well, that sounds good. And boyfriends?" he reiterated the part she had ignored. "You must have a lot of suitors, or else the guys around here need glasses."

"Oh, Dad," she blushed. "No, there's no one special."

"Well, good. I was afraid you might be close to marriage by now, and I wouldn't have a chance to check him out," he joked. Then, changing the subject, he asked, "Where are you going to school? San Diego State?"

"No, sir, I'm going to a junior college for the first two years. I prefer the smaller school environment, and it's cheaper. I'll have to transfer to State this fall, to get my bachelor's degree."

"How do you get to school?"

"I bought a car, a good used Datsun," Debbie explained. "For graduation and Christmas last year Mom and Gramma and Grampa Simms gave me money, and with what I had earned the previous two summers, I was able to pay cash for a 1968 model. It's not anything fancy, but it gets me around. Mom bought my insurance to begin with, but I've been working part-time since I graduated, so I make enough to keep it running." Matt witnessed the first glimpse of what might be classified as enthusiasm from his daughter.

"Well, honey, that's terrific," he beamed. "I'm very pleased to hear what a good money manager you've become." He added jokingly, "I hope you've been using that talent to help your mother. As I recall, she wasn't the best at balancing checkbooks." Bobbie threw him a feigned hurt look, and then laughed a little. Debbie just smiled and nodded in agreement.

As Debbie brought Matt up to date on her activities over the past few years, Bobbie tried to relax. Matt's nearness made her extremely nervous. She was torn between an overwhelming desire to melt into his embrace and her need to maintain a chilly distance. She was surprised at how physically attractive he seemed, more than she had remembered. His arms, when he pulled her close, were still strong and powerful. But if she encouraged him or built up his hopes, it would be all the more difficult to make the break, to satisfactorily explain why she wanted a divorce without divulging her past indiscretions. She must try to delay intimacy as long as possible, or risk sacrificing any chance to gain Tom's cooperation. But why was she so flustered and shaky? If all she wanted was to wait a decent interval before getting her divorce, why did her heart flutter at Matt's touch? She was bewildered; she hadn't thought her emotional ties to Matt were so durable. It was a complication she had not counted on.

Bobbie's demeanor did not escape Matt. As he and Debbie talked, he saw his wife relax, her inexplicable reserve beginning to thaw. Still, she sat stiffly next to him, instead of nestling into his arms as she always had when he returned from a cruise. They were more like two near-strangers on their first formal date. Matt sensed her reticence and removed his arm from around her, making no further attempt to caress or embrace her. He was disappointed that she didn't grab his hand and hold it as she used to do, or place her hand on his leg and squeeze his inner thigh. Apparently it was going to take a little time to get reacquainted. Only Hank seemed unabashedly overjoyed at Matt's return. This reunion was not turning out exactly the way he had envisioned it, but he was too happy to be home to give it more than a passing thought. Given a few days, he was sure everything would be like old times.

Lieutenant Commander Nelson knocked politely before opening the door. "The ceremonies have concluded, Sir. We're ready to leave."

The string of cars proceeded slowly, away from the flight line toward the center of the base, out the main gate, and then south on Highway 163. Thanks to the flashing-light siren-blaring escort of the California Highway Patrol, the trip to Balboa Hospital took only a few minutes.

As quickly as the men had checked into their rooms, they congregated in the lounge area, toasting their return with champagne that had been carefully concealed and smuggled in by a few enterprising wives.

For the first few hours, privacy was impossible. Those who tried soon gave up in defeat and joined the boisterous party. It was well after midnight before any measure of quiet was restored and the exhausted ex-prisoners of war were able to retire to their respective rooms.

Many of the men disappeared with radiant wives behind closed doors. A few had no one. Back in his room, Matt waited for some signal from Bobbie. The chauffeured limousine could take Debbie and Hank home and return tomorrow morning to pick up Bobbie. That's what he hoped would happen. But how should he proceed? Bobbie wasn't acting at all like the warm, affectionate wife who couldn't wait to get him in bed, the Bobbie he remembered from those early cruises. The old Bobbie would have suggested they get started on that third baby she wanted—immediately. But the new Bobbie was making preparations to leave.

"Honey, you look absolutely beat. I'm going to go home tonight and let you get a good night's sleep," she announced.

"I'm not *that* tired, if you want to stay," he whispered, pulling her close.

Self-consciously, she glanced at Debbie and Hank waiting by the door. "I'll see you tomorrow. You get some rest now."

Her message, while sounding solicitous, was clear: she didn't want to spend the night with him. Hurt and confused, he mustered a half-hearted smile and kissed them goodnight, then watched from his window as they climbed into the car and it sped away, disappearing into the darkness.

CHAPTER 24

San Diego, February - March 1973.

While waiting for Bobbie to pick him up after his three-day hospital stay, Matt mulled over his long-delayed and eagerly-awaited homecoming, and her less than ecstatic reception. He compared it to some the other men had received. She had declined to stay with him any night. Some of the wives had been there every night, and most of the days as well. She came for "visits," brought the children and left quickly. They "visited" very little, Hank doing most of the talking. That old concern he felt in prison before he received a letter crept back over him. *You better brace yourself for some unpleasant news, my friend.*

Bobbie pulled up in front of the hospital in the Buick he had purchased before he left on his first cruise. Opening the passenger door, he commented, "You go ahead and drive. I think I better do a little practicing off the main streets first."

As they passed through the familiar neighborhood, Matt noted that things hadn't changed that much, except the trees; they were larger. It was encouraging; maybe it wouldn't be that different at home, once things got back to normal.

"I'm glad you're driving. There's a lot more traffic than when I left."

He noticed how tightly Bobbie gripped the steering wheel, and how stiff her responses were to his general, try-not-to-say-anything-controversial questions.

"When did you stop lightening your hair? I never realized it was quite so dark."

"This is my natural color. I got tired of bleaching it."

"Oh. I always thought the lighter color was natural. It must be quite a bit longer, too. How long have you been wearing it up like that? I always thought it was so pretty, loose around your face like you used to wear it."

"That's not the style anymore," she retorted curtly. She kept her eyes glued to the road.

Something was definitely wrong; Bobbie was too edgy, too defensive. Perhaps here in the car with no one else around was a good time to get it out in the open. "Bobbie, is something wrong? You don't seem very excited to have me home, not like I had expected, and certainly not like I had hoped. Is there anything you should be telling me?"

Matt braced himself for bad news. Already, four of his buddies, including John and Jim Holliman, had been greeted with requests for divorce. Could her less than enthusiastic welcome portend a similar fate for him? Well, he had prepared himself for something unpleasant as best he could while he was in prison. He just hoped he could handle it. If there were someone else, she could spare him the details. But, of course, a lot depended on what Bobbie wanted. If she were in love with another man and wanted a divorce, there was probably nothing he could do. Just the thought caused a dull aching pain inside. His stomach tightened involuntarily, and he felt suddenly cold. He wanted his family back, he wanted them all to be together again. He had dreamed of it for far too many lonely, pain-filled nights to give up easily.

Maybe she had an affair and it was over, but her conscience was bothering her, and she would have to admit it to clear the air, before things could get back to normal. The idea of Bobbie making love to another man brought a deep feeling of rage, a different kind of pain accompanied by an urge to strike out at someone. He was no longer chilled.

Intellectually, he had done everything possible to prepare himself for this. He could still understand, given the time and circumstances, how it could have happened, but facing it squarely, on an emotional level, was going to be a lot more difficult that he had anticipated. *I mustn't let her think I blame her,* he kept repeating to himself as he waited to hear what she would say, certain it wasn't going to be good.

Bobbie kept her eyes riveted to the road. "No, Matt, there isn't any one particular thing I should tell you. It's just that, well, after seven years, I feel like we're almost strangers instead of husband and wife. I don't feel comfortable with you. What I'm saying is, please give me time, don't make a lot of sexual demands just yet, don't rush things. It will take some time to get reacquainted." She chanced a quick glance at Matt. He was staring straight ahead, his jaw set firmly in that old familiar, determined way, his fists clenched tightly at his side. She felt a flicker of remorse; it was going to be painful to have to hurt him. She already had done so with just those few truthful words, and there would have to be more, some less truthful. But they would have to come slowly, over the next few months so as not to give away her secret.

She didn't want to be hated or denounced like one man's wife who told her husband on the trip to Balboa hospital that she was in love with someone else and was going to get a divorce. The wives' grapevine was abuzz that first night. No, when they split up, she wanted people to think that they tried to work it out, but it was just one of those things. There would be plenty of other divorces once the thrill of the reunion wore off. All she had to do was postpone the inevitable for a little while. That meant she would have to string Matt along for a few months. For the time being Matt was a hero; there was a spotlight on everything either one of them did. Right now there must be three to four hundred people at the house, waiting to welcome Matt home. She would just have to wait until things calmed down.

Why couldn't Sandy understand? When she arrived early this morning to help prepare for the onslaught of people they expected for Matt's arrival, Bobbie had taken her aside, to explain her plan and gain her support, should it be needed.

"I've got to figure out a way to delay asking Matt for a divorce."

Sandy looked surprised. "Why? I thought you were just waiting for him to get back, so you could get your divorce and marry Tom."

"I don't want to tell him about Tom. I just want it to seem that we couldn't work things out after all this time."

"Bobbie, that's unfair. Tom's waited for six years. How much longer do you think he'll wait? And, if you're going to divorce Matt, don't string *him* along. That's cruel."

Bobbie had been adamant. "No! It's better my way. What's a few more months after this many years for Tom? And Matt won't be hurt nearly as bad if he thinks we just couldn't get along, than if he thinks I wasn't faithful. That would injure his pride. When you get to know him, you'll see that he's a very proud man. You'll agree with me, I know you will."

"No." Sandy shook her head emphatically. "No. The proper thing for you to do is be very honest with Matt right now, forget worrying about what anyone else thinks, just do what is right. If you try to drag this out, everyone's going to suffer. Don't ask me to be a part of this scheme, I won't. I think it's a terrible idea, and I'm disappointed in you." Sandy was resolute.

Bobbie still hadn't summoned the courage to discuss her plan with Tom. It was strange that he had said so little about it when she stopped by his apartment after leaving Matt in the hospital that first night. They had a couple of drinks and made love, but Tom only asked how Matt was and how long he would be in the hospital. Now with Matt home, it was going to be very difficult to see Tom, to talk to him or to be with him. Perhaps that was good, because that would help delay the moment of confrontation that much longer. She had no idea how long Matt would be home before he had to report to some new duty assignment, but she guessed it would be at least a month or so, and apparently there was the possibility of him going back into the hospital for some surgery.

Gingerly she reached over to Matt, who had remained silent for several minutes. She touched his arm. He sat very still, a grim, unhappy look on his face. "Matt, I'm sorry. I didn't mean to hurt you. Maybe I'm all screwed up, but it's very difficult after all this time to just continue as if nothing has happened. You've been gone over *seven* years. That's a long time. I've changed—I had to. I'm sure you've changed. I've tried to raise the children as best I could. It wasn't always easy alone, and I never quit hoping you'd return soon. But now, well, I think we need to take it slow and easy in getting back together." She paused, seeking the right words. "I'm your wife, and I want to be your wife again. I'm just asking you to be patient, and give me a little time to adjust to being married again. A couple of days is hardly enough time after seven years to make that adjustment." She had to stall him. He might sense her lack of responsiveness, and perhaps figure out why. He was already sounding suspicious. Plus, it would also be easier to gain Tom's cooperation if she weren't sleeping with Matt.

Matt remained silent. She looked at him pleadingly. "Matt, please say something. Tell me you understand, at least just a little."

Slowly Matt turned his head to face her. There was sadness in his eyes, but they looked piercingly into hers. "Okay, Bobbie. I won't press you. For seven years the thing that kept me going, even in my darkest times, was thinking how great it would be to get back home and hold you in my arms. That dream helped me retain my sanity, just knowing that you were here, waiting for me. No, I won't say I understand, because I don't. I expected you would feel the same way, I had even hoped you would stay with me in the hospital that first night, the way many of the other wives did, but it was quite obvious you weren't interested. So I put off the operation on my stomach for awhile just so I could get home to be alone with my wife. But if that's what you want, okay, we'll wait until we are better acquainted." There was sarcasm in his last sentence. Then he added, "But I have a hunch there is still something, one very important thing that you are neglecting to tell me."

Before she could deny his accusation, they arrived home, and were immediately surrounded by hundreds of friends and neighbors, as well as members of the press. The house was bedecked with a hand-painted "Welcome Home Matt" sign, its colors running in the drizzling rain. As soon as he stepped out of the car, Matt was besieged by well wishers. Some he recognized on sight, others only after they introduced themselves, and others he simply did not remember. After about an hour, he noticed Bobbie, laughing, go into the house. He still could not get free. The television cameras whirred and flashes exploded right and left as Matt shook hand after hand after hand, and received hugs and kisses from friends and total strangers alike. Many showed him POW bracelets with his name and shootdown date.

One elderly lady who lived down the street explained, "I've been wearing this for five years, praying for your safe return. Now that you're back, I'd like you to have it." She had tears in her eyes as she slipped the metal bracelet off her arm and clamped it around Matt's wrist.

All the attention was staggering. He would have liked nothing better than to go into the house, shut the door and be alone with his family, such as it was at the moment, but he could not ignore these people who seemed to care so much.

Slowly, the crowd started to disperse, with comments like, "Let the poor guy get some rest," and "They'd probably like to be left alone." They were right, but when he finally walked into the front room of his often-dreamed-about home, he found it full of people. The table was filled with food of every description.

Hank was waiting by the door, and wrapped his arms around his dad.

"Hi ya, fella," Matt hugged his son.

A beaming Hank introduced his friends. "Dad, this is Alan Posten. He lives just up the street." Then, he pointed to the others, who stood open-mouthed, staring up at Matt. "This is Larry, this is Eddie, this is Skip." Matt smiled and shook hands with each of the lads, who stepped forward only after being pushed by Hank. Hank's eyes glistened with unmistakable pride as he announced exuberantly, "This is my dad."

His son's enthusiastic welcome warmed him. Why didn't all the family react this way?

Debbie, three clean-cut young men, and a pert-nosed girl with a beehive hairdo similar to Bobbie's, stepped forward as Hank and his chums, who had clearly found their voices, boisterously made their way to Hank's bedroom.

Debbie, demure and respectful, introduced Matt to her friends. "We all sing in the church choir, Dad," she explained. "We have practice this evening, so we're going to have to leave in a little while, but everyone wanted to meet you." Debbie's friends were all quite respectful and proper.

After introductions all around, Debbie kissed him lightly on the cheek. "Have to go, Dad. See you later." Looking around the room, she shook her head and patted his arm. "Don't overdo it. Just tell these people to go home if you get too tired."

Matt was perplexed. On the one hand, she showed genuine concern, on the other, she acted as if he had never been gone; everything was very matter-of-fact, very casual, almost as though he had just gotten home from a long day at the office. He sensed a reserve, like she couldn't risk getting close to him. It wasn't anything he could put his finger on, but it certainly wasn't what he had expected. He witnessed the reception given other returning fathers by their teenage daughters, and his had not been the same. Why? What had changed while he was gone? Why weren't things going like he had expected?

Matt had little time to dwell on his daughter's behavior as another group of people approached. He shook hands and tried to connect names and faces.

Bobbie caught his attention. When he made his way to her side, she was standing beside an attractive redhead Matt did not know, but he had noticed her before, watching him, studying him with an intensity that he found a little unsettling. Maybe she was another shrink. "Honey, I want you to meet my best friend, Sandy Marshall. This lady has just been my lifesaver," Bobbie explained, "always around to lend a hand when I needed help or someone to talk to."

Matt smiled. "I'm very pleased to meet you, ma'am. Thank you for being such a help to Bobbie while I was gone." Her hand shake was firm, her eye contact direct.

"Hey, we need more coffee," someone called, and Bobbie excused herself.

"I'm very happy to finally meet you too, Matt." Sandy's smile was warm and friendly. "I almost feel like I know you already, I've heard so much about you from Bobbie."

"How did you two meet?" he asked.

"We worked together. I was the marketing director at the construction office where she came to work as a secretary when Hank started school. We were the only two females, so we banded together for self-protection. I quit a couple years later and started my own real estate sales office—so if you want to buy a house," she dipped her head and smiled, her large brown eyes inviting, "see me."

"Well, I really thank you for being her friend." He was glad she wasn't a shrink, but why did he feel like he was under her microscope?

"I'd like to be your friend, too. It's probably going to be—shall we say—a little crazy for awhile; it can't help but be under the circumstances. If you find yourself in need of someone to talk to, or if you two just need to get away from the crowds for a little privacy, call me. I have a big house out toward the college area, and I want you to feel free to use it if you need to. I can't guess what's going to happen, but it's yours whenever you need it for whatever reason."

Matt studied her carefully. She seemed to be sincere, but why would he want to use her house? What did she think was going to happen? *What in the hell is going on?*

"That's very kind, but I wouldn't want to impose on your hospitality."

Sandy shook her head slightly and looked him squarely in the eye causing him to momentarily look away. "When you get to know me better, you'll know I don't offer anything I don't mean. If I would consider it an imposition, I simply wouldn't offer. It isn't a big deal. All I'm saying is, if things get hectic, or if you need to get away, my home is available." She gave him another measuring look, and sort of shrugged.

"Excuse me, I'll go help to give Bobbie a break. She's been at it since five this morning."

Matt watched as Sandy retreated, her auburn hair glistening as she passed through the sun shining through the patio door and disappeared into the kitchen. *Attractive lady,* he noted, still puzzled over her offer. She was not the type he would have expected Bobbie to make friends with—too self-assured, too independent. Perhaps she had provided the strong shoulder that Bobbie needed. Maybe that was the bond. His musings were interrupted as another friend from the past walked over and extended his hand.

As Sandy had predicted, privacy was a scarce commodity during the first week home. By the following weekend, Matt and Bobbie were frazzled.

Sandy noticed the signs and renewed her offer. "You two look like you really need to get away. How about coming over to my house? The pool is heated and the Jacuzzi is the best answer I know for a tired body or mind."

Matt started to protest.

Sandy quickly interrupted. "Look, Matt, I've got three unused bedrooms with baths. So before you reject the idea, let me assure you, again, it is *not* an imposition. Now tell me honestly, have you guys had a chance to sleep in until nine o'clock any morning this past week?"

They both shook their heads.

"Eight? Seven? Six? I bet not. And I know that you don't get to bed until after midnight. Please. You need to get away. You need some time for yourselves, and my house is a hell of a lot better than a motel - and more private. No one will know you're there. I'll stay here. Debbie and I can take care of all emergencies. Matt, if this place could survive for seven years without you, it'll survive another weekend, but I'm not sure you guys will without some rest."

Matt waited to see what Bobbie's response would be. He certainly wouldn't mind finding a little privacy. He'd prefer to stay in his own home, but Sandy was probably right, if this past week was any indication, it wouldn't be found here.

Bobbie considered Sandy's offer. She knew from Sandy's continued admonitions to tell Matt the truth, that Sandy was hoping her home would provide the proper setting. But Bobbie had no intention of doing that. If they accepted, it would mean that she would have to be intimate with Matt, but given her new plan, that was going to be necessary anyway. Otherwise, he would continue to be very suspicious, and she needed to put his mind at ease.

Bobbie was the first to speak, "Well, what do you think, honey? It would be rather nice to get away from the crowds, wouldn't it?"

Matt glanced from Bobbie to Sandy; both women were waiting for his answer.

He shrugged slightly. "Well, I guess that's okay, if that's what you want."

Sandy smiled. "Great. Pack a few things. I was hoping you'd accept. There's booze in the bar, beer in the fridge, and I laid in some easy-fixing food—bacon, eggs, a couple of steaks, potatoes. You'll be able to find things. Oh, and I put out robes for both of you for the pool. There's also swimsuits, but you really don't have to use them. I rarely do—no one can see you unless they're sitting up on a hill with high-powered binoculars. Here's the keys."

As they loaded a couple of bags into the Buick, Sandy added, "I want you to make yourselves at home—and don't worry about answering the phone, my answering service will pick up after the second ring. Just enjoy."

Sandy's house was at the top of a hill overlooking the valley below with a view extending to the ocean.

"How in the hell," Matt wondered aloud to Bobbie as they stood by the pool and looked down on the city lights twinkling like distant stars, "can she afford a place like this? This is really something. I thought you two used to work together."

Bobbie was more relaxed than she had been since Matt returned, and she leaned cozily against his shoulder, watching the dancing lights. "Well, she never talks about her past much, but I think she inherited some money from a relative several years ago. She bought this right after her divorce. Her ex may have had money too, I really don't know. She just doesn't talk about it. But from what I can tell, she has been making very good money since she went into real estate a few years ago. The place is probably worth ten times what she paid for it. It is lovely, isn't it?"

Matt, encouraged by Bobbie's snugly manner, slid his arm around her shoulder and gave her a squeeze. "Yeah, it's very nice. Maybe someday we can have something like this. Would you like that?"

Bobbie glanced up and smiled, and responded dreamily, "Um-hmm." Their eyes locked. Slowly, Matt turned her body. He lifted her face, pulled her close and kissed her passionately on the lips. She kissed him back.

Matt fixed drinks from the well stocked bar, and turned on the Jacuzzi. While they waited for the water to heat, they had more drinks. As they relaxed in the hot bubbly spa, the combination of several stiff drinks and the hot water took its toll. Matt wasn't used to drinking.

They headed unsteadily inside. For Matt, the beautifully decorated bedroom was a blur. He removed his wet swimsuit, and stumbled into bed beside Bobbie, who had managed to change into a nightgown.

Bobbie was alert enough to know what was happening. If her plan were to work, she would have to sleep with Matt and act like his wife. She might as well start now. She lay quite still, waiting for his expected advances. Perhaps it was the liquor, but the idea of making love with him wasn't as unappealing as she anticipated. In fact, she encouraged him.

In spite of the spinning room, Matt was somewhat sobered by Bobbie's caresses. For the past week, they had shared a bed, nothing more - she as far on her side as the double bed would allow, creating a gulf between them as wide as the Sea of Cortez. "Cold" would not adequately have described her behavior. Not only did she not want intimacy, she seemed not to even want physical contact, pretending to be asleep if he tried to caress her.

Now she was touching him, stroking his thigh and pressing her body close. It was the moment he had dreamed of for over seven years. He wanted to respond. He tried to respond. His body would not cooperate—he could not get an erection. It just wouldn't come up.

Matt passed out, whispering apologies. Bobbie, sobered, lay frustrated beside her husband. She couldn't believe what had just happened. Matt was impotent, and she had wanted him; really wanted him to make love to her. She wasn't pretending. His touch, his shy glances, his firm body stirred her. How could this be? She was in love with another man—wasn't she?

Matt awoke early the next morning with a terrific headache and a vague memory of what had happened. He attempted to slide out of bed without disturbing his sleeping wife, but she awakened when he started to turn over.

"Honey, I'm sorry about last night. I don't know what happened. Maybe, hopefully, it was just the booze."

"Shh, shh, shh," she whispered, moving closer to his warm body, so that they were touching. She started rubbing his chest and hips, and Matt could feel his desire rising. As they kissed and caressed, his problem of the night before was forgotten, and he made love to his wife like he had dreamed of doing so many times.

It was all over very quickly, but Matt was elated. They were husband and wife again. Life was beautiful. Jokingly, but with an honest sigh of relief, he bantered, "Well, how about that? It still works."

"Yes," she murmured contentedly, "and quite well too."

Matt lay in the bed long after Bobbie got up. *Apparently, she isn't going to need any more time to get acquainted.* He savored the thought contentedly.

Slowly, over the next few days, the daily stream of visitors to their house dwindled to just a few. Now, more often than not, it was old friends who came by to welcome Matt. Occasionally, a stranger who had worn a bracelet would stop, leaving the bracelet for him, and the mail brought more bracelets.

"I can't believe the number of letters," he remarked to Bobbie. "Have you read them? I had no idea people could care so much." He looked solemnly at one stack. "I have to admit some of them bring tears to my eyes. Here's one, 'My son went into the Army the day you were shot down. He was killed two years later, so I prayed every day that you would come home safely. Having you to look after has kept me from going crazy.'"

Matt swallowed, his eyes downcast. "How do I respond to someone like that? She lost a son, but she prayed for me. . . I don't understand."

Bobbie examined the three shoeboxes full of bracelets, picking up a couple and rubbing her finger across the name inscribed. "Well, I guess a lot of people were praying for you." She then pointed to the large stack of letters, neatly paper clipped in groups. "Have you answered *all* these letters?"

Matt ruffled through a few loose ones on the top of the stack, pausing to read a line or two. "Oh, sure. It's the least I can do."

He picked up a pen and took one of the letters off the stack. Bobbie watched him read it feeling a tug on her heart strings. He was such an honorable man. What was she doing? No, what had she done?

Except for the occasional press interview or requests to appear at or speak to various civic groups, life in the Tillet house began to return to normal that first month. Ford Motor Company had made available any Ford product for one year's use to each of the returning POWs. Matt selected a white LTD, and the dealership had it ready for him in one day.

Bobbie drove him out to La Mesa to pick it up. "You going to be okay driving?" she asked.

"Yeah. I've been practicing and I feel comfortable. I *still* can't believe the increase in traffic, though."

"Want me to wait and follow you home?" she asked as he opened the passenger door.

"No. Thanks. I might as well solo." He laughed. "Besides, it'll take an hour or so to complete all the paperwork. No need for you to wait for that." He leaned over and kissed her cheek. "Oh, I'm going to run a couple of errands—gotta go by the hospital and a couple more places, so don't be worried if I'm gone two or three hours."

Bobbie nodded. "Okay, I think I'll do a little shopping while you're gone, then." She smiled and waved as she drove away and headed toward Tom's apartment. Her mind was racing faster than her speeding car as she dashed down the interstate.

Hank just couldn't find enough time to do all the things he wanted to do with his dad. "Dad, come go to the beach with Alan and me this weekend. You haven't seen me surf yet."

"Okay. Let's check with your mom and Debbie. Maybe we can all go."

Debbie sounded genuinely disappointed. "Gee, I'm sorry, Dad. I have to go to the library to study for mid-terms. I really wish I could though."

Bobbie also had plans. "You guys go enjoy yourselves. I have some things to do around here, and a little shopping."

Matt jogged along the beach, then spread out the grass mat on the sand and sat watching Hank display his surfing expertise. "Son, I'm impressed. That really looks difficult, and you make it look easy, but isn't the water awfully cold when you fall in?"

"Yeah, sort of. I'd like to get a wetsuit, but Mom has been too busy."

"Well, I've been trying to figure what to get you for a late Christmas present. Can we go find one now?"

"Now? . . . Sure."

It was late afternoon when they returned with a new wetsuit and a new knee board. Bobbie wasn't home. When she returned about an hour later, she was all smiles. "I'm sorry to be late," she apologized. "I was looking at the new summer clothes, and I guess I got carried away."

"Want me to carry in any packages?" Matt asked.

"Oh, no. Sorry. I didn't get to the grocery store." She seemed flustered. "I told you . . . I got lost looking at clothes."

In mid-March, Matt developed a persistent high fever and called Dr. Howser.

"I want you to check into the hospital so we can run some more tests."

Bobbie dropped him off about 8 p.m. At ten o'clock, he called her to say good night—and to hear her voice. He didn't like sleeping alone anymore. The phone rang and rang, but there was no answer. That was odd. She should have had plenty of time to get home. He flicked on the T.V. and watched the news, then called again. Still no answer. Maybe she'd gone over to Sandy's. He dialed Sandy's number. A sleepy-sounding Sandy answered on the third ring.

"Hi, Sandy, this is Matt. Is Bobbie there with you?"

"Matt?" Sandy asked uncertainly.

"I'm sorry if I woke you. I thought Bobbie might have gone over to your house."

"No, Bobbie isn't here. I haven't seen her. She isn't at home?"

"No," he said, "and I've been trying for the last hour, but there's no answer. Debbie's out of town and Hank's spending the night at a friend's. She left here around eight. I'm a little worried. I can't imagine why she isn't home by this hour unless something happened."

"Look, I wouldn't worry. Bobbie's a big girl. She's been taking care of herself for quite awhile now. I'm sure she's all right.

Probably she stopped somewhere to visit friends and lost track of time. Look, you get your rest. I'll locate her, I know a couple of places she might be. I'll tell her to call you first thing in the morning."

Matt hesitated. "Well, maybe if you find her right away, she could call now." He would sleep better if he heard her voice and knew she was okay.

"Don't let her think you're checking on her."

"Oh, I didn't mean it that way—I wasn't checking on her. I just wanted to tell her good night, but when she didn't answer, I became concerned." He paused, suddenly disturbed by her comment. "Why would you think I was checking on her?"

"Oh, damn it, she's not being fair to you, and you ought to know it by now. You deserve better treatment."

Matt stiffened. "Sandy, what are you talking about?" he demanded, hoping it wasn't what he feared.

"I'm so sorry. I shouldn't have said anything. I didn't mean to blurt it out like that."

"Well, you did. So now please explain what you meant." He found himself trembling uncontrollably.

"I really didn't want to be the one to tell you this. It's not my place."

"Tell me what?" he asked grimly.

"I ought to keep my nose out, but I care for you—right now a lot more than I care for Bobbie—and I guess, since I've let the cat out of the bag, I don't have much choice. Besides, you deserve to know the truth." She paused.

"I'm waiting," Matt said icily.

"She's probably at her boyfriend's where she goes every time you're not around."

Her words, like a knife, plunged into his heart.

"Matt, are you there?"

He controlled his voice with difficulty. "Yes, I'm here. Would you care to expand a little on what you just said?"

"I'm very sorry to be the one to break the news to you, although it was going to come out sooner or later. Her boyfriend wants to get married, and he's not going to wait forever. But, look, I don't want to say any more over the phone. If you'll just act like nothing has happened, don't even mention trying to call her, when you get out of the hospital, I'll tell you the whole story. Will you do that?"

Again there was a long silence. Finally, he asked flatly, "Do you know the other man?"

"Yes, I've met him. He's a WCA pilot. I'll give you names and dates, but not now. When you get home, make up an excuse to get out of the house and come over here. But, you're not going to like what I'm going to tell you," Sandy warned.

"I already don't like it," he said stonily, hung up the phone and pulled the sheet over him. A chill was causing his entire body to shake.

After two days of tests, Dr. Howser came in to discuss his choices. "Your fever was caused by an intestinal infection. You've probably got a lot of those pesky little critters running around inside. We've given you some antibiotics, and you can pick up a prescription on your way out. That will take care of that. But I'm still not certain what's causing your persistent pain, and I definitely want to do that exploratory surgery. If you can hack it, I'd prefer to put it off until August or so. I have to go on a summer cruise and I don't get back until late July. Besides, a few more months of good diet and exercise will put you in better shape."

"Okay," Matt agreed. "Can we make a firm date, so I'll know what to do about finding myself a job?"

Dr. Howser checked his calendar. "How about the first week in August?"

Matt called Sandy. "I'm ready to be released from the hospital. Would you pick me up?" He waited, heard a sigh and more silence.

"Okay," she said finally.

He climbed into the passenger side of her Mercedes.

Did they give you a clean bill of health?" She tried to hide her nervousness with casual chatter.

"Not entirely. They're going to operate in August," he replied. "Now what's this about Bobbie and another man?"

"Let's go to my house. I bet you haven't had any lunch. I'll fix you a sandwich, and I've got some cold beer in the fridge, and then I'll tell you all I know." She glanced at him and quickly back to the freeway, driving to her house without further conversation.

As soon as they went inside, she handed him a cold beer. "Sit down and drink your beer. I'll fix some sandwiches."

He stopped her. "Thanks, I'm not hungry right now. The beer's plenty. Just tell me what you've been trying to put off."

She grabbed a beer for herself, sat down in the stuffed chair across from him and fumbled with the pop top.

"Come on, Sandy," he coaxed, but his voice was firm.

As gently as she could, she told him of Bobbie's long-standing affair and how she had come to know about it and the part she played in it. "You have to realize that you have been gone for a long time. It was very difficult for Bobbie trying to raise the children. Hank was more than Bobbie could handle alone. He needed a man's guidance." She took a sip from her beer, studied his face for any outward signs. There were none.

"Tom has always been there to provide the discipline and male companionship. He has been very good to Bobbie and the kids. Frankly, I don't know how they would have made it without him."

"Remind me to thank him when I meet him," Matt snapped bitterly.

"Look," she said softly, "I understand how you feel, but I'm just trying to explain that they were always very discreet, so the children never knew what was going on. They have always considered Tom just a friend who was trying to help."

As she related some of the activities the other man had engaged in with the children, Matt started to understand Debbie's behavior. She had figured out what was happening, and now she was fighting a battle of loyalties, to the man who had been like a father for the past six years, and to him. That would account for her coolness and reserve. Matt was now the intruder, coming back and interrupting a perfectly happy relationship.

More than likely Hank didn't know anything, never suspected any special relationship between his mother and the other man—hence his zealous welcome at his father's return. Matt did think it a little strange, however, in all their conversations, and all the things they had done together, many of them the same things the other man used to do, that Hank had not once mentioned Mom's friend.

Perhaps he was just old enough to realize it might cause a problem.

Matt felt a cold, numb hollowness inside as Sandy finished her story. "You said you knew his name. What's the rest of it? Good old Tom who?" His voice dripped contempt.

She rubbed her forehead, and closed her eyes. With a sigh, she replied, "Tom Finley. He's a WCA . . . ."

Matt sucked in his breath and jumped up, knocking over his half-full beer as he did so. Raw blistering anger consumed him. "Tom Finley!" he yelled in disbelief. "That goddamn sonofabitch!"

"What is it? Do you know him?" she asked, astonished.

"Know him? Know him?" he shouted. "You're goddamn right I know him. He was my roommate on the cruise when I was shot down." I slept in the same damn room with that bastard for six months—and he's been sleeping with my wife ever since." He was trembling.

While Sandy sat in stunned silence, Matt thundered on. "I could kill that sonofabitch and get away with it! No one would blame me."

She jumped up and grabbed him by the arm. "Matt! Matt!" she pleaded, "please calm down, relax, don't say things like that. You're scaring me. You don't mean what you're saying."

Matt pounded his fist into his open hand. His jaw muscles bulged. "That goddamn SOB couldn't wait to get horizontal with my wife. I'll kill him!"

"No! No, Matt." Sandy was crying now. "No, you've got to get control of yourself. You mustn't do anything foolish."

As he started to stalk away, she made a desperate grab for his arm. He flung it loose, sending her sprawling on the floor. In an instant, he was at her side, lifting her in his arms.

"Oh, Sandy, I'm so sorry. I didn't mean to hurt you. I just lost control for a moment. I'm so sorry. Are you hurt?" Gently he placed her on the sofa, concern and repentance replacing the anger in his eyes.

"It's okay. I'm fine, really I am. I know how upset you must be." She grabbed his hands and held them tightly. "Matt, let them alone. Don't do anything foolish that you'll regret. If she's dumb enough to want a divorce, there are any number of women who would be thrilled to have a man like you."

"I want to talk to him," he announced quietly. "Can you get him over to the house? I want to talk with him and Bobbie together."

She hesitated. "What are you planning to do? I won't help you unless you promise there won't be any violence. I mean it." She had regained her composure and was firm.

He laughed mirthlessly. "No, Sandy, I'm not going to touch either one of them. I just want to hear their intentions, his and hers, face to face."

"Well," she assessed him carefully. "I'll see what I can do." She frowned. "But I'm not promising anything."

"That's fair enough." He took hold of her arm. "Sandy, I'm really sorry. Are you sure you're okay?" His face displayed his concern.

"I'm fine. Come on. I'll take you . . . home."

When Sandy dropped Matt off at the house, Bobbie's car was in the driveway. "Do you want me to come in, to explain how you got home?"

"No, thanks. I can handle it." He smiled, an unmistakable mischievous twinkle in his eye, all traces of his earlier outburst gone.

She quickly drove away. *Oh, shit. Why did I open my mouth?*

"Hi, I'm home," Matt called out as he entered the unlocked front door.

Bobbie came down the hall, "What are you doing here?" she asked in surprise. "How did you get home?"

"The answer to your first question is, I live here," he answered lightly, "and to your second, Sandy brought me home."

"Sandy?" It was an unmistakable question.

"Yeah. I tried to call you, but didn't get an answer, so I called to see if you were over there. Since you weren't and I was ready to leave, she offered to pick me up. She's a rather interesting lady." Matt almost laughed to himself. Every single word was true—almost.

Bobbie was puzzled by Matt's behavior. He seemed to be enjoying a private joke. But, thank goodness, he hadn't bothered to ask where she'd been, so she didn't have to make up some excuse. Actually, she'd gone yesterday evening to Tom's apartment to try to gain his support for the delay program she was still working on. As the days had turned into weeks after Matt's return, Tom had grown more insistent on telling Matt and starting the divorce.

"Maybe it isn't even too late to start our own family," he had suggested when they first went to bed last night, sounding both hopeful and discouraged at the same time. But, as she laid out her plan, he became angrier than she could remember ever seeing him.

At first, he absolutely insisted they confront Matt together. "Bobbie, this has gone on long enough. You've got to tell Matt—*now*. I'll go with you. You don't have to face him alone. But there is simply no reason not to get this over with. I think you have to admit I've been patient. But Matt's been home over a month, and it doesn't look like you've made any attempt to tell him the truth."

She pleaded, "If you'll just give me a little time, I'll be able to get a divorce without Matt or the children ever knowing about us. No one will have to be hurt. No one will have to be blamed. With just a little more time, I can tell Matt that it just isn't going to work. There have been several separations since the men came back. We will just be one more."

Tom punctuated his argument with broad hand gestures. "You can't hide the truth forever. If we get married soon after your divorce, Matt and the others will put two and two together. Come on, let's go see him, get this over with. It isn't the end of the world. Lots of people have gone through divorces and survived. You and Matt will too."

"Tom, please," Bobbie begged. "Please, just give me one more month. Just thirty more days."

Finally, he had compromised. "I'll give you one more week, not a month. One week will allow time for Matt to get out of the hospital, so you can have some private time. One week, Bobbie, no more. You can tell him in your own way, or we can go together, whichever you want, but within seven days, Matt must be told." His voice left no doubt the subject wasn't open to discussion or further compromise.

Even a month was not anywhere near long enough, she knew, but she had to accept his terms—or nothing—at least for the moment. When she left him this morning, he was still very disturbed, and she wasn't absolutely sure he wouldn't do something to mess things up, despite his one-week concession.

One thing was becoming absolutely clear. She did not want Matt to know about Tom Finley. She had never thought of Matt as being a skillful lover, but with a little encouragement from her, he was becoming almost as good in bed as Tom. Oh, he lacked some of Tom's finesse and technique, but it didn't seem to detract from her sexual satisfaction with him. Sleeping with both of them was actually very exciting. A few years ago, she never would have imagined it possible to be in love with two men at the same time. And she now realized she did love them both, for different reasons and in different ways. It was clear one of them was going to be hurt, but which one? Matt was so dependable, steady, reliable, predictable, all the qualities she thought she resented. Now she realized just how sexy, how attractive he appeared to other women—including Sandy, she was sure. Bobbie had noticed the open envy at functions they had attended. But, if she was going to work things out with Matt, she had to keep him from finding out about Tom. But how? Could she tell Tom it was over between them? Could she end it? Would that be the right decision? She didn't know which voice was her heart, and which was her head.

That night Bobbie and Matt made love. There was something different about him. He was acting very strange and mysterious, but Bobbie found it stimulating. Even his manner of making love, fierce and almost violent, was more exciting than ever. She went to sleep a very satisfied woman. Matt finally fell asleep next to her, exhausted and thoroughly spent, both physically and mentally.

CHAPTER 25

<u>San Diego, March 1973.</u>

Sandy was up very early the next morning, hoping to get to Tom's apartment before he left, if he wasn't already away flying, but almost wishing he wouldn't be there. She was fairly confident Tom would agree to go with her; he had been urging Bobbie to confront Matt ever since he was released. Although this day was bound to come, she wished she had not played a part in it, now - or during the past five years. She was still totally bewildered by why Bobbie had insisted on waiting until Matt got home, and *then* not telling him right away, as she assumed had always been the plan.

Tom answered the door in his jogging suit, looking sweaty. To his puzzled look, Sandy spoke quickly. "I need to talk to you. May I come in?"

Tom stepped aside. She wasted no time explaining why she was there. She could almost hear the wheels turning in his head.

Finally, he spoke, "Matt knows about us? And he knows the other man is me?" His question contained a hint of accusation.

"That's right, Tom, he knows. I told him." She rushed on before he could comment. "I know that sounds terrible, and I'd like to explain."

"No shit!" He cocked his head. "This should be interesting."

"I really didn't mean to blurt it out like I did, but he sounded so concerned when Bobbie wasn't home by eleven at night, and I was just so angry at her for being so deceitful. I've been begging her to have this meeting. I even threatened to say something, but, honestly, I didn't intend to. But when he apologized for doubting her, I just . . ." she grimaced. "I just got carried away, I guess."

Tom continued to look at her, a bemused look on his face. She went on, "I know it wasn't my place, but I don't approve of the way Bobbie's been treating him—or you. You both deserve a decision, one way or the other. Right now she's just enjoying the best of both worlds, and she seems to want it to continue indefinitely. Frankly, I'm not sure how she can rationalize sleeping with two men at the same time."

"What!"

She knew at once from the astonished look on Tom's face that Bobbie had not been truthful with him either. She covered her face momentarily with her hands. "Oh, shit, Tom. Another oops! I've done it again. I just keep digging it deeper, don't I? I really didn't know you didn't know."

If Tom had been wavering before, he wasn't any longer. "When are we supposed to meet?" he demanded angrily.

"Anytime after nine. The kids will have left for school by then."

"I'll get dressed." He left her standing in his living room. She was getting used to steely-eyed looks from iron-jawed, grim-faced men. It was really rather amazing how similar Tom and Matt were. Similar in so many ways, yet obviously very different in others. Either one of them was too good for Bobbie, but as things stood now, she realized enviously, Bobbie could probably have her pick. Sandy knew, having been single for almost fifteen years, that the supply of desirable men in her age bracket was pretty damn limited. Bobbie had two of the best in that small select group wrapped around her little finger. It didn't make sense.

Tom reappeared, showered, shaved and looking not so much the worse for wear. "Okay." He walked past her brusquely and opened the door, "Let's go keep our date."

They pulled up in front of the Tillet house at ten past nine. Tom had remained stone-faced throughout the drive, barricaded behind his impenetrable composure.

Matt responded immediately to their knock. The two former roommates stared uneasily at each other for several seconds, like two boxers sizing up the other in the middle of the ring.

Sandy was the first to speak. "Good morning, Matt." After an awkward pause, she continued, "Look, why don't I wait in the car or come back later? I'm sure you all would like to meet in private." Matt opened the screen. Still eyeing Tom warily, he addressed Sandy, "No, that isn't necessary. Come in, please," and then added reluctantly, "Tom." He stepped aside and gestured for them to enter, calling in a louder voice, "Bobbie, we have company." He motioned toward the couch. "Please have a seat."

Sandy sat down, mesmerized, her eyes glued to the men's faces. Each one reminded her of a battened-down building in a coastal town awaiting the approaching category-4 hurricane. Each was boarded up as best he could be, but some of the siding was about to be ripped off.

As if suddenly remembering his manners, Matt offered, "Would either of you care for coffee? I just made a fresh pot."

Sandy shook her head and Tom muttered a quiet, "No, thanks, not right now."

Matt shrugged. Tom had just opened his mouth to initiate the discussion when Bobbie walked into the room.

"Did you say we have company," she asked. "Who is . . . ." She stopped in mid-sentence, her eyes grew wide in disbelief and shock; her mouth dropped open. Lifting her hand to her mouth and staggering backwards, she cried, "Oh, no!"

In total control, Matt asked cynically, "I believe you know my ex-roommate, Tom Finley, don't you?"

Bobbie continued to shake her head back and forth and stare, dumbfounded. Then, glaring at Tom, she shrieked, "How could you? How could you do this to me?" She began to cry uncontrollably. Grabbing the car keys from the coffee table, she rushed blindly toward the door. Quick as lightning, Matt stepped in her way.

"Let me go!" she screamed, "Let me go!"

Matt wrestled the keys out of her hand and stuck them in his pocket. Bobbie was on him like a tiger, kicking, biting, scratching and clawing, all the while screaming, "Let me go!" Tom made no attempt to interfere, but stood immobile beside Sandy, who was watching in bewilderment. Matt pinned Bobbie's arms behind her.

Sobbing loudly, she sank to the floor at Matt's feet, moaning, "Oh, no! Oh, no!" Tears and makeup streaked down her face.

Almost gently Matt reached down and lifted her to her feet. "Come on, Bobbie," he said indulgently, "come and sit down. We've all got a problem. Let's discuss it like adults."

Sandy could not believe her ears or eyes. Yesterday she had feared Matt would murder Tom; today he was in complete control, treating Bobbie like a naughty child. His hostility toward her, no doubt very deep, was invisible, unascertainable from his actions.

Bobbie lay on the couch where Matt had placed her, curled up in a fetal position. Without a word, Matt turned and walked into the kitchen, returning with a cup of coffee in each hand. "As I recall, Tom, you drink your coffee black with sugar," he said, placing a cup in Tom's hand, setting the other on the table next to Sandy. He returned a second time with two more cups, then drew up a chair and sat down, facing the trio.

Bobbie continued to cower on the couch.

Matt's voice was crisp and controlled. "Well, Tom, I'd like to know what your intentions are toward my wife."

Tom spread his arms in an appeasing gesture. "Matt, first I'd like to say that no one ever wanted to hurt you."

"Skip the bullshit," Matt interrupted. "I'd just like to know your plans—now, from this moment forward."

Tom shrugged resignedly, looking at Bobbie. She was still sobbing, curled in a ball, covering her head with her arms. "What can I say? I love her. I want to marry her. I've wanted to marry her and make a home for the children for the past six years, but she wouldn't consider sending you a 'Dear John' letter while you were in prison. I thought it would have been better for all of us, and I haven't changed my mind." He shook his head as he looked at Bobbie. "I still want to marry her if that's what she wants. Matt, I want to tell you, even if you don't believe me, I'm sorry for the way . . . ."

Again Matt cut him off. "Look, just don't give me any of your shit about being sorry, or not wanting to hurt anyone. I know how you operate with women. Remember, I lived with you. It must have really been a feather in your cap to score with a married woman whose husband wasn't around to protect his interest, and no doubt it was an even bigger plum because she was my wife. You knew I didn't approve of the way you screwed around with every split tail you met. It must have given you a lot of satisfaction to know you were banging my wife." He drew out the last words.

"Matt, I can't blame you for feeling this way," Tom said, "but it wasn't like that at all. I deserved everything you thought of me back in those days, but I fell in love with Bobbie without wanting to, and without being able to help myself. Oh, sure, I should have walked away before it got out of hand, but I didn't, and I'm not sure I could have. I'm sure I'll never be able to explain it to your satisfaction, though, and I'd probably be feeling the same way if I were in your shoes."

Tom realized Matt was in no mood to accept explanations, and his attempts to justify or explain what happened would only exacerbate the situation. He was acutely conscious of the emotion Matt was trying so hard to control. Given a little more provocation, there might be violence. Tom searched for a way to defuse the explosive atmosphere. He could handle Matt in a man-to-man fight since Matt was still in a weakened condition from his years in prison, but that wouldn't do anyone any good, least of all Bobbie. He went on, hoping to end this unpleasant confrontation and make a strategic withdrawal as quickly as possible, "What do *you* want to do now, Matt?"

Matt glared at Tom for a few seconds, then looked over at the still whimpering Bobbie. "What I'd like to do is beat the shit out of you—and maybe whup her ass—but it wouldn't accomplish a damn thing." Walking over to Bobbie, he grabbed her roughly by the arm and pulled her almost to her feet. "Quit whining like a baby! You're part of this discussion, so let's hear what you have to say." His manner was anything but gentle now.

Bobbie stood despondently in front of them, her face distorted from crying, averting her eyes from both Tom or Matt. Then she looked at Sandy and yelled, "You bitch, get out of my house! You're the one who set all this up. Get out of my house! You just couldn't wait to jump in bed with my husband, could you? Could you?" She took an ominous step toward Sandy, who jumped up and backed away.

Tom grabbed Bobbie. "Come on, Bobbie, cool down! Matt

found out about us on his own; I decided it was better to get it all out in the open. No one's to blame for this mess but us. So just straighten up and let's discuss it sensibly."

Bobbie turned on him, kicking and screaming. "*You* decided! *You* decided! *You* agreed to wait until I could find a way to tell Matt, my own way. Get out! Get away from me! I never want to see you again! And take that bitch with you!"

Tom touched his face, and felt warm blood on his hand as he rubbed it across his cheek. Shoving Bobbie roughly onto the sofa, he headed toward the door. "Come on, Sandy, let's get out of here before someone gets hurt."

Sandy followed quickly, stopping to pat Matt gently on the arm. "Things will work out, Matt," she said encouragingly. "Things will work out. Just give me a call if you need a place to stay." She left without so much as a look in Bobbie's direction. How had she ever been friends with this woman?

Sandy was glad she was driving. Tom sat next to her, livid with anger. "Tom, I'm so sorry. I don't know what to say, except that I wish I hadn't had anything to do with this."

He didn't answer until they reached his apartment then he faced her. "Sandy, this isn't your doing, not at all. You were used, just like . . ." he paused, "some others I know. I'm sorry you had to witness it; it was pretty awkward. But, thanks for the ride."

"You going to be okay?"

"Yeah, I'll be fine — but I'm not so sure *they* will." He motioned with his head up the hill toward the Tillet house. With a fleeting, rueful smile, he shut the car door firmly and disappeared inside his apartment.

Sandy sat silently in the car for several minutes. "Aw shit," she said aloud. *This must be my week for aw shits.* This whole thing was so ludicrous she wanted to burst out laughing—or scream. With a deep sigh, she drove home.

Inside the house, Matt turned forlornly toward Bobbie. She sat quietly where Tom had pushed her, fiddling nervously with her fingernails. Matt picked up an overturned coffee cup, carried it into the kitchen, and returned with paper towels. Carrying the remaining dishes into the kitchen, he busied himself washing them.

Bobbie slunk into the dining room and mounted a bar stool at the kitchen counter. Twisting her wedding ring, she spoke quietly. "Matt, I can't even begin to apologize; there just aren't any words to say how sorry I am. I have hated myself ever since this started. I wanted to tell you when you got back, and beg your forgiveness, but I just didn't have the courage. I knew you would hate me, and I didn't think I could stand that. Now I suppose you hate me anyway."

He leaned against the sink, shoulders drooping. For several moments, he stared out the kitchen window.

Her stomach tightened at the look on his face.

"No Bobbie, I don't hate you. I'm just very disappointed that you weren't honest. Tom was right about one thing, it would have been better if you had told me in your first letter, instead of constructing a glass palace of lies. I would have preferred that to clinging to the expectation of returning to my *loving wife*."

Bobbie turned away from his withering accusatory unforgiving eyes. After an uncomfortable pause, she forced herself to ask, "Okay, so what now?"

Even if he didn't divorce her, he would never trust her again, and she wasn't sure she could live with him, knowing that. But Tom might not even want her any more. Just yesterday everything had been going so well. She was on the verge of salvaging her marriage, but now nothing was the same.

"Well, I guess I better find another place to stay for awhile till we sort this out."

"Yes, I suppose that would be best. But where will you go?" she asked, remembering Sandy's parting words.

"I can get a room at the BOQ. What are you going to tell Debbie and Hank?"

Resentment surged through him. *All because of her shabby damn affair!* He turned quickly and fled, before he said the hateful things he was thinking.

CHAPTER 26

<u>San Diego, March 1973.</u>

Bobbie sat silently on the stool for several minutes, impaled by the look of contempt Matt had flung at her.

Her body shook as she recalled the fiasco—her part in it and her reaction to it. She had behaved inexcusably. *God, how can I face any of them again?* A blush of shame spread over her face.

Looking back, she had to admit that Tom had been right, as even Matt had attested. She should have done whatever was necessary to get a divorce and marry Tom. It would have made so many things so much easier. Anything that would have avoided the disastrous meeting between Tom and Matt.

As Matt left, she had been tempted to throw herself at his feet and beg his forgiveness, beg him to stay with her. But he would have laughed at her. And that look. As though he couldn't stand to be in her presence. That look would haunt her forever. Never had she been the object of such scorn or contempt.

And what about Tom? He had been so angry at her when he left. How was she going to make things right with him? How badly did she want to? She thought about his electric touch, his arms around her, his warm lips on hers—all those magical feelings that once set her on fire. Their memory now left her inexplicably cold.

Was it possible her marriage could somehow survive this morning's debacle? If so, it would be because of Hank. He was her one drawing card, her ace in the hole if she wanted to try to win Matt back. But, should she try? Could she live with his knowledge of what she had done? Could she face his disappointment and mistrust every day? She knew him well enough to know he would never truly forgive her, never really forget. Things just never would be the same. She had guaranteed this outcome the moment she traded her loneliness and fidelity for the exciting, but inexcusable, liaison with Tom. Matt was not the type to understand or forgive such an indiscretion. No, Matt was gone forever. He would never want her again, never trust her again, nor ever love her again.

She had better concentrate on salvaging her relationship with Tom. Maybe after the pain of losing Matt eased, she and Tom could be happy again. She had been happy with him before, when Matt wasn't around. And Matt sure as hell wasn't going to be around anymore. If she had been using Matt's imprisonment as an excuse not to marry Tom, she didn't have that excuse anymore. So, was she ready to carry forward their long-postponed plan—divorce Matt and marry Tom? What would Tom do now if he found out or even suspected that she might have chosen Matt over him? He seemed so confident of her love for him. Until a few weeks ago, she would have agreed. How was he going to react now that he knew she had been sleeping with Matt? Tom must never suspect the depth of her inner conflict since Matt returned, or that in the final analysis Tom was second choice. She would have sold her soul to the devil if it could have saved her marriage to Matt, but she had already made that sale six years ago. So now all her efforts would have to go to salvaging what was left between her and Tom.

She roused herself from the stool, downed the last of the cold coffee, bathed and changed into a brightly colored dress and drove to Tom's apartment. His car was in its space. Her pulse quickened as she rang the bell.

After Sandy dropped him off, Tom simply wanted to think, to digest the morning's events. The best place for that was the beach. When he returned to his apartment, he lathered himself and stood for a long time beneath the pulsating needles of water, settling his nerves and cooling his anger. He had just finished his shower when he heard the doorbell. He slipped into a pair of jeans and opened the door. It was Bobbie.

Except for a raised eyebrow, Tom showed no other reaction. He leaned against the door, his fingers draped over the top. She wished he would say something, or do something, that would make it easier, but he just stood there, shirtless and damp, giving no clue what was going on behind his deep blue eyes. How to begin? With no way to test the water, she waded in. "I made quite an ass of myself, didn't I?"

That admission caught Tom off guard. He had been prepared to stay angry with her, to counter her arguments; he hadn't expected this forthright approach—it was so atypical of Bobbie. Without really intending to, he grinned. "Yes, I'd have to say you did." He stepped aside and nodded for her to enter.

"So what happened after I left?" That question had been spinning like a Kansas twister through his mind all morning. "Where's Matt?" He hadn't thought things would be resolved between them so quickly, one way or another, and he hadn't expected any contact from Bobbie for a much longer time.

She sat, uninvited, on the arm of his big leather chair, and replied simply, "He left. He's going to get a room at the BOQ."

Tom turned abruptly. This was an unexpected development. Then he frowned. "What about the kids?"

"They are still at school and don't know anything yet. Hank is not going to like it; he has been so excited having his father back. I'm not sure about Debbie; she has been rather cool toward him. I haven't the vaguest idea how I'm going to explain it to them."

Now was the time for truth. "You aren't going to have to explain anything to Debbie. She knows about us. She's known all along."

Bobbie's eyes widened and she shook her head. "What are you saying? We've always been very careful."

Tom told her of his and Debbie's conversation. "I probably should have told you years ago."

Her reaction was not what he expected. She exhaled deeply. "Well, that's one less person I'll have to put on a false front for."

"What would you have done if you'd known the truth before?" he asked.

She studied the ceiling. "I don't know; I honestly don't know. I was so sure we'd been so clever in keeping our affair secret, that we had been so 'discreet.' I also thought she would totally disapprove. It kind of shatters my smugness."

Tom's anger began to fade. The revelation that she had been sleeping with Matt while letting him think otherwise still stung, but he realized that it would have been next to impossible for her not to have done so without admitting her affair. After all, she still was Matt's wife. But now that their relationship was out in the open, maybe things were working out for the best. Who knew how long Bobbie would have procrastinated otherwise? This morning's confrontation, unfortunate and disagreeable as it had been, had not come a moment too soon.

Bobbie massaged her eyelids. "What happens now? I suppose there will be a nasty divorce and everything will have to come out. Everyone will know about us."

Tom slapped his forehead with his open palm. "Bobbie, you're the only one who's ever wanted to keep our love a secret! I didn't like it from the start, I haven't liked it for the past six years, and I don't like your attitude now. I would have been proud to take you by the hand and introduce you to my friends and co-workers. I would have been honored to have been able to treat your children as my own. I didn't and I still don't give a damn about what Matt's friends know or think. What difference should that make to us? No doubt his closest friends will know—from him. Most of the others won't care, and those who do won't matter to us. They're not part of our lives. When we're married we won't have any contact with that group of people. What they think of us will have no effect on our lives. Nor would it have had for the past six years, if you could have just been honest about the whole thing from the beginning."

The level of his voice increased. "I just wish to hell you'd quit being so damned concerned about other people's opinions." Tom was growing angrier by the minute. All his accumulated submerged distaste for their clandestine affair started to rise like a hot air balloon. He strode into the bedroom, grabbed a shirt, and returned.

Bobbie shook her head. "Well, even if I didn't care about what other people think, I care about my son, and I'm scared to death about what he's going to think—and do." She started to pace. "I might have been wrong about how Debbie would react—apparently

I was—but it's different with Hank. He's crazy about his father; he worships him. I've got to give him time to adjust to his Dad not living at home, and he's not going to take too kindly to it."

Tom threw his hands in the air. "You haven't listened to a damn word I've said. What I've been talking about is honesty." He moved directly in front of her, his nose only a few inches from hers. "What's wrong with just telling the kid the truth—you do know what the word means, don't you?"

She blinked and turned away from his fierce stare.

He continued, a little calmer. "Of course it'll take a while for him to adjust, but he'll accept it sooner or later. Lots of kids have had to face the fact that their parents were getting divorced, and quite often they don't like it at all." He put both hands on her shoulders, forcing her to face him. "It's something you can't keeping hiding—like you tried to do with our relationship. When Matt doesn't come home tonight, Hank's going to ask some hard questions, and lady, you better be prepared to give him the right answers."

He dropped his hands and walked away. "He'll forgive you much easier for the past than he will for the future if you try to deceive him. I swear, I can't figure you out. You just come up with one excuse after another, and the sad truth is we'd all be better off if you'd been honest from the start. But it's never too late." He knew he was being hurtful, but it didn't matter. Right now, she either had to face reality or Matt could have her. He'd had enough of her to last him a lifetime.

Bobbie's eye blazed. "Look, I didn't come here for a lecture on morals from you. I don't think you qualify. I'll handle my son the way I see fit. I had hoped after that disaster this morning you would be able to understand how much better it would have been to have waited, to have given me enough time to make a gradual break with Matt." She put her hands on her hips defiantly.

"But no! You and that tramp had to come busting in, ruining everything. You just couldn't wait and let me handle it my way— not even after you said you would. I don't even know why I came here. I should have known you wouldn't understand, wouldn't help me. I just don't see what it would have mattered so damn much—

after six years—to have waited another month or so. Well, I can tell you one thing. I'm not going to go home and tell Hank that I just kicked his father out so my lover and I could be together. No, I'm not about to do that, and I'll thank you not to interfere!"

Tom's shoulders slumped and he grimaced. Bobbie was still finding ways to delay the time when they could be together. Would she ever be free to marry him? Suddenly, he had a disturbing thought. Did it still matter? Today, he had been exposed to a side of her he'd never seen before and he undeniably didn't like it.

"Bobbie," he said, taking her firmly by the hand and leading her toward the door, "I have a flight later today. I want to be in shape to make it. You go on home and work out *your* problems—if you can. You've got to make some decisions. I can't make them for you. Matt can't make them for you. You're on your own on this one, kiddo." He opened the door and gently pushed her outside.

Enraged, Bobbie jumped in her car. "Bastard," she stormed. She drove straight home, fixed a strong drink and downed it. She fixed a second drink, grabbed her cigarettes and lighter, and plopped down in her favorite chair. Her focus slowly changed from her anger at Tom to the events of this morning. When she saw Sandy and Tom, she had wanted to die. In that one fleeting moment, it hit her with meteoric impact: she had lost her chance to work things out with Matt.

She took a drag off her cigarette, and pulled out the leg rest on the chair. Curious. Why should the thought of losing Matt have governed her actions? She had been ready to throw him away before. Yet the more she thought about it, the better she understood why her strongest emotion at that moment of truth was utter despair. Matt would see through her web of deceit. Too late, she realized how much she did not want to lose him.

Staring blankly at the silent TV, she stuck a polished fingernail in her mouth and started chewing, removing it only to take another sip of her drink. How she felt this morning—for that matter, how she felt now—was difficult to understand, or explain, even to herself. She ground out her cigarette in the ashtray and dropped her head in her hands. She had not felt this much loss even when she was told that Matt had been shot down. If only Tom Finley had never come into her life!

She prepared another drink, walked down the hall and into her bedroom. Sitting the drink on the nightstand, she sprawled out sideways across the bed—the bed where Matt had made love to her last night. She buried her head in a pillow, still strong with the scent of his aftershave.

When Tom returned from his overnight trip, the first thing he did, was to make a phone call.

"Mission Bay Estates, Miss Malone speaking," said the voice on the line.

"Hi, Maggie, this is Tom Finley. How would you like to have dinner with me tonight, and maybe take in a movie?"

He could hear the brightening in Maggie's voice. "Sure, I'd love to."

CHAPTER 27

San Diego, May - October 1973.

"Dad, why don't you stay at home with us anymore?" Hank asked for the umpteenth time. It was Sunday evening and the question was always the same.

Matt turned his head away. "I can't, son. Not for awhile, anyway."

"Why? I don't understand. Why can't you come back home? Why are you living at the BOQ?" Hank persisted.

Matt patted his son's arm. "I can't explain it to you, Hank, because I don't really understand myself. It just has to be this way. Your mother and I need a little time to work out some problems."

"Then I want to stay with you." Hank's face was contorted, on the verge of tears. Matt watched his eleven-year-old son struggling to behave like a man. He was raised to believe strong men didn't cry. Crap! Maybe crying would do him some good too; he sure as hell felt like it about now.

"You can't right now, son. Maybe later on, but not now." Matt could feel a spasm starting in the pit of his stomach.

"But, Dad . . . ."

The spasm worked its way higher. Matt started the car and cut him short. "No buts, Hank. I just can't live at home, and you can't live with me as long as I'm at the Q. That's all. It's not something I want to talk about, so let's drop the subject, okay?"

Hank fell silent for the remainder of the trip home. The burning sensation in Matt's stomach grew stronger.

When they arrived at the house a few minutes later, Bobbie greeted them at the door. A sullen Hank rushed past her and headed toward his bedroom. She watched him momentarily, then turned to Matt with an apologetic smile. "Would you like to join us for dinner? The children would love to have you stay."

He didn't trust her sincerity, but presented in this manner, there was no way to reject the invitation without giving the children the impression he didn't want to be with them. "If it's no trouble, I guess I could stay." He noticed her hair was down and loose, the way he liked it.

During dinner, he commented, "Your hair certainly looks nice that way."

She reddened slightly, and lowered her eyes to her food.

Debbie agreed. "I like it better that way, too, Mom. I think it makes you look younger," she added with a mischievous grin.

"Okay, you two, no ganging up." Bobbie looked sternly from one to the other, pretending to be pained.

Hank, who had been quiet most of the evening, joined in. "Yeah, me too."

Bobbie stepped out on the patio to have a cigarette while Debbie and Hank did the dishes. Matt helped clear off the table and then joined her, watching quietly as she took a long drag and blew out the smoke.

She saw him watching and shrugged. "I've tried to quit. I just can't seem to do it."

Matt shook his head. "I wasn't being critical."

"I just know how you feel about it." She made eye contact, then turned away, looking at the stars.

After the kids went to bed, Matt brought two cups of coffee into the living room. He handed one to Bobbie, and sat next to her on the couch. "Do you want a divorce?" he asked.

Her head jerked up in surprise. It was several seconds before she answered. "I . . . I . . . don't know." She sat the cup down and dropped her head. "No, that's not true. I don't really want a divorce. It would make Hank so unhappy. But I'm not sure there's any alternative. I don't see how it could possibly work out for us." She glanced at him. "Would you ever be able to forgive me?"

Matt sighed. He had asked himself that question a thousand times, and he still didn't know the answer. He kept his head bent low. "I don't know. I think if you had admitted it when I first came home, and told me it was over, I could have accepted it. Seven years *is* a long time. Things happen."

He glanced at her. Her shoulders sagged, and she wrung her hands. She looked so sad. He was almost tempted to take her in his arms. Instead he took a deep breath, and continued. "I'm not interested in sharing my wife with my old roommate. You have to choose between us. You can't continue to date him and be married to me."

She shook her head. "This has nothing to do with Tom—not anymore." She pushed her hair back. "I think he may be seeing someone else, anyway. I just need more time to try to figure out if things could work out for us. Seven years *is* a long time. I'm not trying to excuse what I did, it was wrong, but . . . ." She tilted her head. "You have a memory like an elephant. I'm afraid you'd be suspicious of everything I did. I'd always be walking on eggshells. As much as I would like for us to get back together, I'm so afraid it wouldn't work."

Matt sat stiffly, saying nothing, his head bent, staring at the floor.

"What about you? Do you think we could make it?" she asked softly.

Matt raised his eyes, focusing on the wall. "I don't know." He shook his head as he spoke. "I know that I don't want to lose my family, and I'm willing to make a lot of allowances, but I don't think it's up to me . . . ." He finished his coffee. "I don't think you're being totally honest, and I think it *does* have something to do with Tom."

He stood up. "I'm going to go now. You think about it. Do you want to be married to me, or do you still want to shack up with him?" He headed toward the door. His anger was kicking in; the very thought of them together chafed already raw nerves. "I'll pick Hank up next Friday evening."

****

Shortly after returning from the Governor's party for the California ex-POWs, which he had attended with three other soon-to-be-divorced POWs, Matt received another invitation. The return address on the envelope, in raised gold letters, said, "The White House," and was addressed to Cdr. and Mrs. Matthew Tillet, USN, c/o Balboa Hospital. The invitation bearing the Presidential seal said,

> *"The President and Mrs. Nixon*
> *request the pleasure of the company of*
> *Commander and Mrs. Tillet*
> *dinner on Thursday evening, May 24, 1973,*
> *at 7:00 o'clock.   Black Tie."*

Matt went downstairs to the Q's small bar, looking for company. His BOQ room reminded him too much of solitary confinement in prison. He saw one of his BOQ ex-POW neighbors, Steve Nelson, alone at a table in the rear, having a beer. Matt hadn't known Steve in prison, but found they had a lot in common when they met at the Q. Steve's wife had been more emphatic in her rejection. She didn't even bother to show up at Miramar. Matt waved, and Steve motioned for him to come over.

"Did you get that impressive invitation?" Matt asked.

"Yeah, but I don't know who to take," Steve acknowledged. "I'm pretty sure my wife won't go, and how do you take one of two teenage daughters? I'm trying to find out if they'll allow me to bring both of the girls. How about you?"

"Dammit, Steve, I want my family back. I want what I had before that last cruise. But, when I permit myself to think about her and Tom, it makes me crazy. I'm afraid to stay around her, afraid I'll do something I'll regret." The waiter brought Matt's beer. He paused, paid for it, and took a sip.

"I know." Steve nodded. "I'd like to beat the shit out of Patty and that jerk she's living with."

Matt shivered, his mind flooded by an unwanted tide of remembrances. "In prison I had a dream—a dream of having my family all together. Hank needs a father, a full-time father, not a weekend companion."

Steve nodded. "My son's already out on his own. He doesn't say much. I've only been able to get together with him two or three times. Both the girls treat me like I'm the intruder. They stick by their mother like glue. My whole life is as shattered as my damn arm and leg." He raised his right arm that was a good two inches shorter than the other, displaying his useless right hand, with its rigid claw-like fingers.

Matt shook his head but said nothing. He knew Steve did not like to talk about the injuries that had almost killed him when he was shot down and were never treated by the Vietnamese, leaving him with one useless arm and a constantly oozing leg wound from the embedded shrapnel.

They both sipped their beer. Finally Matt banged down his empty glass. "I don't know about you, but I've spent enough time alone to last a lifetime. I want my family back. I can't imagine starting over. I don't like the bachelor life. Dating in my forties was not in my game plan, but then neither is living alone." Matt motioned for the waiter and ordered two more beers.

Steve swallowed and leaned forward. "Matt, would it work? After what she's done, even if you got back together now, would it just be delaying the inevitable? I've been thinking about that long and hard, and I'm not sure I could go back. Not that I have any choice anymore, since Patty filed for divorce this week. I was served yesterday."

They sat in silence until the waiter left.

"Sorry about Patty," Matt said. "I guess you sort of figured that was coming?"

Steve nodded silently, his sad eyes saying volumes.

"Will it work?" Matt continued. "I don't know, but I'm willing to try. I don't even want to think about the alternative. Fancy parties don't mean very much when you're by yourself. I learned that at Governor Reagan's party. No offense, you guys were good company, but I'd have liked to share it with someone I could cuddle up with. I'm thinking about inviting Bobbie to Washington. What is that saying—'Better the devil you know than the one you don't?'"

"How do you plan to try to put Humpty Dumpty back together?"

Matt thought for several moments. "Perhaps the trip to Washington will provide the glue. If I can get Bobbie away from San Diego, just the two of us—away from the memories, away from Tom's influence, away from the familiar surroundings. If I get her all to myself, surrounded by the glamour and excitement of an evening at the White House, maybe she'll come to her senses."

Steve sat back and absorbed the plan. "And what if she says no?" he asked quietly.

"At least I'll have tried. But we can't go on in this state of limbo. I don't like uncertainty. I didn't like not being in control of my life for seven years. I like it even less since we've gotten home."

Steve stood up. "I wish you luck. I think I'll call it a day."

"Me too."

On Sunday, when Matt again dropped off a tearful Hank, he stayed a while to talk with Bobbie. As long as the conversation wasn't about anything personal, they got along fairly well. When the subject turned to travel, Matt thought that was a good opening.

"Bobbie, we have an invitation from the President to a black-tie dinner party at the White House on the twenty-fourth of this month. There will be lots of celebrities. It should be a lot of fun. If we could get away by ourselves. . . . Well, what I mean is, would you like to go with me?"

He caught the surprised look before she flinched and turned away. It was several moments before she replied. "Are you sure you want me to go?" Her tone suggested she didn't believe him.

He tried not to appear too eager, "Sure, I'd like for you to go with me. I think you'd enjoy it. And maybe it would do us good to spend some time together."

Again Bobbie hesitated. "Well, it certainly does sound like fun, and getting to meet the President, but . . . ." More hesitation. "Okay—if you really want me to."

Matt clasped his hands together. "Great. I'll send you the itinerary so you'll know what clothes you'll need. Buy yourself a new gown. I'll be in touch later this week."

From the kitchen barstool, Bobbie watched the lights of his car pull away from the curb. Stunned and confused, she poured herself a stiff drink, walked into the den and turned on the late news.

Why had he asked her to go? Was there the slightest chance he might want to get back together? Was that really what she still wanted? She replayed in her mind the arguments for and against it, until the drink relaxed her enough, and she fell asleep in the chair.

Matt took Hank home early on Sunday evening the week before they were to leave. He wanted to confirm the arrangements for the White House and see if Bobbie also wanted to go to the huge welcome-home celebration sponsored by Ross Perot to be held a couple of weeks later in Dallas. Both of these events would provide excellent opportunities to spend time alone with her. And if things went as he hoped, he might suggest they get back together. He wasn't naive enough to think there wouldn't still be problems, but he wanted to give it a try.

Debbie was alone at home studying for finals.

"You know when your mother will be home?" he inquired as he approached the table.

Debbie looked up from her mound of papers. "No, Dad, sorry. She didn't say where she was going or when she would be back."

"Would you ask her to give me a call tonight if possible, or tomorrow morning early? I need to give her information on the Washington trip."

"Sure." She smiled.

"Wish we could all go." Matt patted her shoulders. "Maybe we can all take a trip later, like we . . . ." He stopped as he saw Debbie's smile slowly start to fade.

She looked down at her papers. "That would be nice."

Matt sensed his daughter's emotional upheaval. They rarely spent much time together, she was always so involved with her school. Maybe this would be a good opportunity to visit.

"Would you like to go grab a bite to eat? Hank and I haven't eaten dinner yet, we just snacked all afternoon."

Debbie kept her head bowed. "I'd really like to, Dad, but I can't. I've got to study for my chemistry test." Her voice was very soft. She picked up a pencil and tapped absently.

Just then Hank hung up the phone and popped into the dining room. "Hey, Dad, I'm not hungry either. Alan wants me to come over and see his new surfboard. Is that okay with you?"

Matt shrugged. "Okay. Run along. I'll see you in a few days." He turned to Debbie. "Please don't forget to have your mom call me tonight or in the morning."

"Okay." She looked up, their eyes locked for a moment before she glanced away, bending over the papers and starting to write. "Goodnight, Dad." It was barely a whisper.

Matt drove slowly back to the Q, his thoughts on his daughter. Had those been tears in her eyes? She tried so hard not to show it, but he had just seen a glimmer of how hard this separation was on her. Another reason he and Bobbie needed to work things out.

The harsh ringing of the phone woke Matt from a troubled sleep. The bedside clock read five to seven. He answered and heard Bobbie's voice. "Matt, I can't go with you to Washington. It just wouldn't work out." Before he could protest, the phone went dead.

Matt sank back onto the bed, numb. He remained that way for several minutes, feeling a hollowness in the pit of his stomach, like he had been kicked by one of those old mules on the farm. Only his eyes moved, taking in the dismal-drab government-issue furniture that mirrored his mood.

It was only two days before they were to leave. Why had she waited so damn long? Now it was too late to make arrangements to take Debbie or his sister, or anyone else for that matter, since the White House needed several days to issue the necessary clearances. He could think of any number of people who would have been thrilled for a chance to meet the President and the celebrities.

He swung his legs onto the floor and sat on the side of the bed, massaging his face with both hands. He felt raw pain, like in prison when they ripped open an old wound. "Dammit." He spat out the word. "Damn you, Bobbie. Damn you, Tom Finley."

Sitting next to Mrs. Nixon at the White House helped improve Matt's spirits.

Matt was wondering around the White House after the impressive dinner when Mike Hastings found him. At the same time, Lee walked over. "How in the hell is it going," Lee asked as they greeted each other.

Mike smiled, "Well, it's going pretty damn good for me. I've been dating Rachel, my nurse when we were at Balboa, and we're getting married the end of next month."

"Congratulations!" Matt and Lee said in unison.

"Matt," Mike continued, "I'd like you to be my Best Man."

Matt beamed. "I'm honored. Give me a call when we get back to San Diego. Oh—I'm staying at the BOQ." He pulled a piece of paper out of his pocket, and wrote down the number and handed it to Mike.

"What happened?" Lee asked, frowning.

"It appears there was some truth to my concerns about not getting those letters."

Mike shook his head, and patted Matt on the shoulder. "There's Rachel. I better get over there. Matt, I'll give you a call next week—and I'm sorry to hear about Bobbie."

"Me too," Lee said sadly.

"So, tell me what's been happening with you?" Matt said.

"We're still in Florida. I made Lieutenant Colonel and I'm expecting orders soon." Then, spotting his family, he invited, "Come on over and meet my wife and girls." He motioned toward a group of several people touring the White House.

After introductions, Lee decided to join his family on the tour. "Let's get together in the morning for breakfast. I'll give you a call when we're up and around."

Flying back to San Diego, Matt thought about his friends. Lee was a lucky son of a gun; Bridgette was as charming as Lee had described her in prison, and all three of his daughters were bright, intelligent and attractive—and very attentive to their dad. Matt couldn't help feeling a little envious.

After her last-minute refusal to go to Washington, Matt wasn't about to give Bobbie an opportunity to stick it to him again, so on the following Friday, he and his three soon-to-be-divorced BOQ buddies, Jim Holliman, Steve Nelson and Doug Donnelly, traveled solo to Dallas.

No sooner had they settled in their rooms, when one of Jim's commercial-pilot friends called to invite them to a party.

"There's going to be some Dallas Cowboy cheerleaders, a bunch of airline stewardesses and a lot of booze. Would any of you gentlemen be interested in attending?"

No arm twisting was required; they practically stumbled over one another as they raced to the door.

"Ya'all want to come on over to our apartment complex tomorrow?" drawled the young lady who had been designated or had designated herself as Matt's unofficial hostess for the evening, making sure his glass was never empty and he was never left alone. "It's a big old place with tennis courts, pool, gym, sauna and Jacuzzi. A lot of stews live there; and there's always something going on most Saturday afternoons," she told Jim and Matt as they were preparing to leave.

They exchanged glances. Jim made a face. Matt interpreted it to mean "try and stop me."

"You've talked us into it," he laughed.

Saturday found Matt, Steve, Doug and Jim swimming, lounging around the pool, drinking ice-cold beers, playing shuffleboard, ping pong and visiting with the girls—lots of girls, lots of pretty girls, lots of scantily clad girls—while trying to keep cool in the muggy, stormy Dallas weather.

Matt completed several laps in the Olympic-size pool and was resting at one end when several girls he had not met the night before joined the group. Matt had never seen so many tall, long-legged, long-haired, slim-waisted, big-bosomed beautiful women in one place in his life. The airlines must have had a mold, to have been able to turn them out so uniformly.

A slender, attractive brunette with long, bouncy hair sat down next to him at the edge of the pool, cautiously dipping her toes into the water.

"Hi, I'm Amy Carson," she said pleasantly. "I'm just here for an overnight. We heard about the party when we landed and decided to crash. Having a good time?"

"Hi, Amy Carson. I'm Matt Tillet. I'm pleased to meet you, and yes, I'm having a very nice time."

She extended her hand, laughing. "Glad to meet you, Matt Tillet. Are you one of the POWs?"

"Afraid so. And you? Where are you from?"

"South Carolina." That accounted for her accent. "But I live with my roommate, Julie, in an apartment complex kind of like this right outside of Chicago. What about you?"

"San Diego."

"That's my favorite route. I fly into San Diego every second or third month, whenever I'm senior enough to get the flight."

"You're senior enough to bid for the good routes? How long have you been with the airlines?" he asked in a disbelieving voice.

"Seven years."

"I didn't think you looked old enough for that," he confessed.

"Thank you. But, believe me, I'm definitely old enough." She sprawled out on a towel beside him.

"Perhaps we could have dinner the next time you're in my area." Sardonically, he thought to himself, *I just asked a lady for a date. See—that wasn't so hard.* Maybe he could get the hang of this dating game more easily than he had anticipated.

"I'd love to."

Just then they were joined by another tall, slim woman with long light-brown hair. Matt decided the hair was the way to differentiate them. Amy introduced her co-worker, Julie Fairbanks. "Julie and I try to fly together every chance we get. She's my roommate."

At that moment, Jim hoisted his dripping muscular form out of the pool and joined them. After introductions all around, they staked out an umbrella-shaded table and spent the rest of the afternoon together. It was late afternoon when Jim reluctantly reminded Matt of the evening activities. "I think we better get ready to go, or we'll miss the party." Then turning to Julie, "You gals aren't by chance hostesses for this party tonight, are you?"

Julie and Amy shook their heads. "No, and we have a very early flight back to Chicago in the morning. We better let you get going."

"Not before we know how to get in touch." Jim stood up, looking around.

Julie found a pencil and paper in her bag. "Looking for this?" she asked, grinning, as she wrote their address and phone number and handed it to Jim.

Jim fingered the paper. "Didn't you say you can bid for the San Diego run? Why don't you try to get it next month, and give us a call when you're coming out?"

Julie and Amy exchanged glances. "We'll give it a try."

"Promise?"

"Promise," Julie assured him.

Matt turned to Amy. "We'll look forward to hearing from you. Jim, did you give them your phone number?"

Julie located another scrap of paper and wrote down Jim's and Matt's phone numbers.

"I like her," Jim commented as they rushed back to the hotel. "I want to see her again."

Matt laughed. "Yeah, I kind of got that message."

After they picked up their hostesses for the evening, they headed to the Convention Center for an old-fashioned Texas barbecue. Then buses transported the group to the Cotton Bowl. The biggest non-athletic crowd ever, estimated at 60,000, gave a standing ovation, lasting more than three minutes, as the 450 uniformed former POWs marched smartly into the stadium.

Bob Hope headlined the entertainment, as he had at the White House. "I have a message from the President for you. He said to return the silverware you took last week."

****

Matt had just arrived at his BOQ room after the return flight from Dallas when he heard a knock. When he opened the door, a uniformed Marshall asked, "Commander Matthew Tillet?"

"That's right. What can I do for you, Officer?"

"I have some papers for you, Commander Tillet." The officer placed an official looking document in Matt's hands. "You have been served, sir."

Reading the paper, Matt felt like a cat must feel just after it has been declawed and neutered. Bobbie had filed for divorce while he was gone.

He wadded up the papers and threw them across the room. "Well, so much for getting back together."

Bobbie's refusal to go with him and her unexpected decision to file for divorce had something to do with Tom, despite her denials.

That was the only thing that made sense. Matt had almost convinced himself he could accept what was past, but he wasn't willing to writhe in some hangman's noose of uncertainty while she still carried on her disgusting little affair. Feeling very battered, bruised and betrayed, and more than a little disappointed, he was determined to find out once and for all.

On the night he knew she usually went out, he stationed himself around the corner where he could observe the house without being seen. She left about nine. He tailed her directly to an apartment at the far end of a complex near Mission Beach. When the door opened in response to her knock, Tom opened the door.

Matt parked in a dark stall where he had a view of her car and waited. *Now I'm reduced to a goddamn sneak*, he thought bitterly. The minutes and hours dragged on. His fingers stiffened with tension from clutching the steering wheel. By midnight, he had all the proof he needed. Leaning back against the headrest, he closed his burning eyes and stretched his aching shoulders.

Several times during the next few weeks, Matt tried to discuss a settlement. "Bobbie, what do you want?"

"I don't know, Matt. You should talk to my lawyer."

"This doesn't have to deteriorate into a big pissing contest where only the lawyers come out with anything, does it? Can't we discuss it sensibly between just you and me? Why do you want to involve the lawyers?"

"I don't want to argue with you, Matt, and I don't want to discuss the settlement with you. I never could win an argument with you. My lawyer advised me to tell you to call him. I think it would be best if you did."

"Is this really what you want?"

"I don't think there's any other way." She turned and walked out of the room.

Reluctantly Matt resigned himself to the inevitable, and, after discussing his options with Steve and Jim, contacted Steve's attorney.

"I won't contest the divorce, but I'll be damned if she's going to take me to the cleaners."

In August, Matt re-entered Balboa Hospital for his long-delayed operation. A few minutes after he completed check-in and was shown to his room, the phone rang.

"Commander Tillet, the BOQ has transferred a call to you here," the operator announced. "Long-distance from Chicago."

"Thanks. Go ahead and put it through."

"Matt, this is Amy Carson. Do you remember me from Dallas?"

"Of course I do, Amy. How nice to hear from you." They hadn't seen any more of either Amy or Julie in Dallas after that one afternoon, and he had pretty much forgotten them, bogged down as he was in his divorce negotiations.

"Julie and I were able to get the flight to San Diego this month. We're coming in this evening at five thirty. We'll be staying at the Inn at Shelter Island, should be over there by six. I know it's quite short notice, but we'd love to take you and Jim up on that dinner invitation, that is if you're still interested."

"Amy, I'm really sorry. I'm at Balboa Hospital for some exploratory surgery, they're doing some tests and blood work tomorrow. But I'll sure try to get hold of Jim, though, and let him know where you'll be."

"Oh, I hope it's nothing serious." She sounded genuinely concerned. *Well, at least someone cares.*

"No, I don't think so." Then as an afterthought, "I hope you'll give me a raincheck for the next time you come in."

"Of course." Amy's voice was cheery. "I'll try to give you more notice, too, and good luck on the operation."

Matt called Jim. "Say, do you remember those two gals, those stews from Chicago we met in Dallas?"

Without a pause, Jim responded, "You mean Julie and Amy? You bet I do. Why?"

"I just got a call from Amy. They're flying out here this evening. Want to take them to dinner?"

"I wouldn't miss it. Where will I find them?"

The next evening, Jim bounded into the hospital, obviously excited. "You know, Matt, Amy's really a nice gal. You ought to make it a point to see her the next time she comes out, if you're up to it." But, as Matt soon learned, Jim's interest was Julie. "I don't want to be alone anymore. Six years of dreaming about coming home to a warm, loving wife is a long time to have it just tossed back in your face on the ride to the hospital. The idea still appeals to me—particularly the part about the warm, loving wife. In a way, I feel too old to start over, to have another family, but on the other hand, I've been robbed of my first family. I'm not going to get to spend much time with the boys. Betsy and her new husband-to-be will be moving to northern California next month, and, of course, she'll take Eric and Bob with her. Jim Junior's ready to start college, but he'll probably go up north too. So where does that leave me? Alone—again."

Jim rattled on, revealing surprising plans. "Julie and I walked and talked for a couple of hours last night after we dropped off Amy. She's really a terrific girl. We hit it off great. The only problem is that she's only twenty-six, and she wants a family of her own—kids, the whole nine yards."

Matt's jaw dropped, and he blinked. "You mean you and Julie have already talked about getting married? But, this was only the second time you've seen the girl. Isn't this just a little too soon?"

"Yeah, I know. I know how it sounds. But, hey, look. I haven't been married for years. Oh, true, I didn't know it, but my wife had just been waiting for me to get back so she could be free to marry the man she's been living with for the past three or four years. I barely got a welcome-home kiss. I got more love from Julie last night than I received from my wife after being gone for six years. Why should I waste any more time?"

"Don't get me wrong, but, well . . . you just met this girl. I wouldn't want to see you jump off the deep end unless you were sure she was the right one. There are a lot of women who might be interested just because they think all the returning POWs have a lot of money." He laughed sarcastically, then continued. "Now I'm not suggesting that Julie might be like that; I just want you to be sure you don't make a mistake while you're on the rebound, so to speak."

Jim was practically bouncing with confidence. "Yeah, well, that's what I intend to find out. They'll be back out here at least once a week, and sometimes twice, for the rest of this month. We're going to spend that time getting acquainted. But don't be surprised, buddy, if you're asked to play best man very soon. I think I've found what I want. Wish you could do the same." He turned solemn. "By the way, how're things going with Bobbie?"

Matt became quiet. "Well, I guess a pretty good indication is that she hasn't even come by to see me while I've been in here. She's got a lawyer, and I went to see Steve's lawyer, so now I've got a lawyer, but nothings been decided yet. The biggest obstacle seems to be the property settlement. Whoever said it's a man's world has never been through a divorce."

Jim nodded in grim understanding.

"Sometimes, when I go over there to see Hank, she hints that she wants us to get back together, but I think she's just trying to weasel a better settlement out of me, because the next time I turn around, she's back in the sack with the SOB she's been hanging around with. Did you know him when he was in the Navy?"

"No, but you hotshot fighter pukes don't mix much with us mere mortal bomber pilots under normal conditions." Jim laughed as he stood and slapped Matt on the shoulder. "Hey, pal, gotta run. Hang in there. As your English roomie used to say, 'Keep your pecker up.'" At the door, he turned. "Oh, by the way, give me a call when they let you out of this place, and I'll pick you up. I don't imagine you'll be driving for awhile. I just found an apartment. You're welcome to stay with me if you'd like."

"Thanks," Matt said gratefully.

After Jim left, Matt lay in the bed reflecting. How in the hell could he be thinking about marriage after essentially one date? But he seemed more excited than Matt could remember since they found themselves both living in the BOQ.

If Matt stayed in the Navy, there would be sea duty. He wasn't about to give another woman a chance to screw around on him while he was gone—not ever again. But—to each his own. He'd be happy for Jim if that was what he wanted, and hope for the best.

When Matt woke up the next afternoon, Dr. Howser stopped in to see him. "You should be as good as new in a few weeks."

"Fine—but what was the problem?"

"You had an appendectomy several years ago, didn't you?"

"Yeah, I think it was right after I joined the Navy," Matt replied.

"Well, lesions formed near the scar tissue, and they were growing out like fingers, strangling your intestines. We've removed all of them, but that incision is going to require several weeks to heal."

Matt pointed to the dressing covering a cut from above his navel to just above his peter. "Did you have to make it so damn long?"

"Don't worry, Matt, it heals from side to side, not end to end," Dr. Howser laughed.

"Shit." Matt made a wry face and grinned, it hurt to laugh.

A few days later, Matt's communicator roommate from the Zoo showed up to take him home. "I told Jim I'd come get you," he explained. "I got this neat apartment right on Mission Beach. You can run on the beach and bicycle to your heart's content," he promised. "Jim's place is up near State College, and there isn't even a track close enough to do you any good. Besides, I just bought a beautiful ski boat, and as soon as you're able, we'll do some waterskiing on Mission Bay."

Matt tried to refuse. "I don't want to put you out like this. I mean, you and Liz. . . ."

John's wife had shown him to a separate bedroom his first night home, and he hadn't wasted any time or tears. He'd quickly met Elizabeth, a WCA hostess, and they were already living together. He had taken her to Washington, but since he was still technically married to someone else, the White House would not clear her to attend the official functions. John, as stubborn and irreverent as ever, said, "To hell with them," and in their formal attire, John and Liz had painted Washington D.C. red—alone.

He'd also taken Liz to Dallas. John was clearly out to make up for his lost six years, and he wasn't about to explain or apologize to anyone for the way he was doing it.

Now, noting Matt's hesitancy, he interrupted, "Come on, pal. Stay with us. Don't even think you'd be intruding, for Christ's sake. You shouldn't be alone at a time like this, and besides, Liz is a good cook. It'll be better than the Navy chow you'll get at the Q, and you know Jim can't boil water." Then he confided, "You'll love Liz, like I do. We just got back from a fabulous week in Acapulco—a pre-honeymoon you might call it. As soon as my divorce is final, we'll be getting married, so don't go all moral on me, okay?"

Now it was Matt's turn to scoff. "Oh, come on. You know me better than that. I'm damn glad you have found someone, and you know it. Okay—I'll come, but just for a few days." In their many years together in Vietnam, Matt had come to understand John, and he knew a lot of his audaciousness was on the surface only, camouflaging a sensitive nature. Had he refused, John would have been hurt.

Over the next several weeks, Matt gradually worked up to an aggressive exercise program. His first step was to ride John's new 10-speed bike. Then, as he grew stronger, he started jogging, short distances at first, and later several miles each day. Then he added sit ups and push ups. As his strength returned, he felt he had worn out his welcome.

"John, I'm really grateful to you and Liz for letting me stay here, but I know what happens to house guests after too long, so before you start calling me Charlie Tuna, I'm going to get out of your hair. I feel better than I have in years, and I owe it all to you and Miss Liz. You're a lucky SOB to have found her."

"You're right, and thank you. But you don't have to go yet. You're as good a house guest as you were cellmate."

Matt smiled. "If I hadn't wasted so much time trying to reconcile with Bobbie I might have already found someone like you and Jim have done." But he knew better.

October 1973, was memorable in two respects. Jim and Julie were married, and Matt and Bobbie were divorced, after finally reaching a mutually acceptable property settlement. Now Matt was really alone—again. It felt like he was back in prison, a prison of despair.

CHAPTER 28

<u>San Diego, November 1973.</u>

"I've bid for the San Diego run in November. That means an overnight trip every six days. Here's my schedule." Amy handed Matt a sheet of paper.

She had flown in several times since Matt got out of the hospital. They had been Best Man and Maid of Honor at Jim and Julie's wedding.

She was, as Jim had correctly assessed, a nice girl. Matt found himself looking forward to her visits. He was lonely. Her affection and attention filled a tremendous void, and helped combat the misery he felt from Bobbie's rejection. But, there was one small problem. She made it quite clear early in their relationship that she wouldn't go to bed with him. Amy, to Matt's dismay, was what might be called, in these more liberal modern times, an old-fashioned girl. She was saving herself for marriage. Matt had gone without sex for over seven years if you counted his last cruise and prison, and, except for a brief hiatus when he was living at home with Bobbie, another nine months. Once again, he was celibate, and not by choice. It didn't help matters that he found Amy attractive and desirable, or that she was extremely loving—up to a point. For Matt, life without sex had been easier in prison. There hadn't been any inducements.

During her visit in mid-November, after a day at the beach and a nice dinner, they returned to his BOQ room. He longed to hold her in his arms, take her to bed and make love. As always, gently but firmly, she turned him down, leaving him frustrated and sexually charged.

"I can't be the kind of girlfriend you want. Call me old-fashioned, call me a prude, whatever, but I'm not going to bed with you unless we're married."

Amy was certainly attractive, he always enjoyed himself when he was with her, and she certainly felt good when she was in his arms. But—marriage?

"Are you saying you want to get married?" he asked hesitantly.

"Sure I want to get married. I'm twenty-eight years old. My biological clock is ticking. I want a family. But don't panic, I'm not trying to rush you. I don't think you're ready to discuss marriage. Maybe in a few months, but I don't want a husband who's on the rebound. You still refer to Bobbie as your wife; you still think of yourself as married."

"Well, technically I am married until sometime in April, but that doesn't have to stop me from thinking about someone else, maybe even loving someone else," he said defensively.

She looked at him skeptically. "What do you think about starting another family? I'm seven years older than your daughter. I want children. If you married me, you could have children the same age as your grandchildren. Are you prepared to go through all that again?"

He had been giving these hard questions a lot of thought, ever since Jim told him that he and Julie were going to start a family as soon as possible. Having children still in high school when he was in his sixties didn't hold much appeal. "Hmm . . . ." He scratched his head and grinned, then changed the subject. "Are you still coming out for my birthday the end of the month?"

She shook her head and gave him a wry smile. "If you still want me to. Jim and Julie have already made all the plans."

A few nights later, Matt lamented his situation with Steve in the Q Bar. "Amy's a nice girl, and she'll make some lucky man a good wife someday, but starting over—with babies, diapers, two o'clock feedings—it's not for me. I wasn't that thrilled with it the first couple of times around; it definitely doesn't sound more appealing now at my age. I'd like kids to be about five when they're born."

Steve chuckled.

"But, dammit, Steve, I am so sick of being alone. All I could think about when we were in prison was coming home, and, what do they call it, 'living happily ever after.' Boy is that ever storybook fiction."

"I know, pal. I'm in the same boat. You've at least had Amy to date. I haven't found anyone I wanted to see a second time, and just dating a gal to get laid isn't all it's cracked up to be. Never thought I'd say that, used to think it was great. So, do you have any other prospects?"

"Well, paying for sex never interested me, but then I was never quite that needy. Variety may be the spice for some guys, but I prefer a blander diet. Bobbie was my first steady girlfriend, and there hasn't been anyone else. I'm not sure I'd know how to act with casual dates. But," he paused, reflecting, "now that you mention it, maybe I do know someone. She's a good looking woman, more my age."

"Wow. If you're not interested, give me the number," Steve joked.

"I've had a lot on my mind, but you're right, I'll call her tomorrow. I want to start looking at real estate. That'll be my excuse for calling her."

"You thinking about buying a house?" Steve asked, interested.

"No, I'm *going* to buy a house, I'm *thinking* about sex," Matt answered drolly.

Steve laughed. "You nut. You sound horny."

"Oh, shit, I didn't know it made a noise."

Steve stood. "See you later." He was still chuckling as he walked away.

Matt didn't wait until the next day. It was still early when he returned to his room. He dialed Sandy's number. Without hesitation, she accepted his dinner invitation for the next evening.

It had been a long, long time since Matt had come calling on a lady. He hoped flowers were still considered appropriate. He was feeling apprehensive as he drove to Sandy's house, and just a bit guilty. While he considered himself basically an honest man, his present intentions were something less than honorable. That bothered him, but not quite enough to turn around.

Sandy, aglow in a soft green pantsuit which accentuated her figure and complemented her flowing auburn hair, greeted him warmly. "You don't know how pleased I am that you called. I have often wondered how things were going for you." Her voice was husky and warm.

When she saw the flowers, she smiled broadly. "Please come in. Let me get a vase for these."

From the entry, he could look through the open living room windows and see the lights of the city. It was quite spectacular.

"I'd forgotten what a gorgeous view you have," he said, walking toward the back wall of glass.

"Thank you." She joined him at the window. "It really is nice up here, particularly when it's warm enough to be outside."

"Yeah, I remember," he said, recalling the weekend he had spent with Bobbie, the first time they had made love. He felt a momentary hollowness.

Sandy stood close, the smell of her perfume drifting toward him. "How about something to drink before we leave? I know you drink beer, and I have some nice and cold, or would you prefer a mixed drink?" She touched his arm ever so slightly, bringing him back to the present with an electrifying jolt.

Matt stared straight ahead, reluctant to look her in the face. The warmth of her touch radiated through him; her nearness was more disturbing than he anticipated. She was a desirable woman, more so than he remembered. He felt a tightening in his groin. "A beer would be fine."

She returned shortly with a cold beer and some cheese and crackers, and nodded toward the family room. "Let's go in there. I still have a little fire left in the fireplace, and the view is better. You can see the Coronado Bridge."

The hardwood floor in the family room was covered with a rich Oriental rug. A pool table sat in the center of the room, behind the white plush couch across from the huge stone fireplace, which was still glowing brightly. The three outer walls were floor-to-ceiling windows.

At Sandy's direction, Matt sank into the sofa. She placed the hors d'oeuvres on the glass coffee table, treating him to a view of smoothly swelling breasts barely concealed by the green silk. With a graceful motion, she turned and walked over to the bar along the inside wall. He admired the way she carried herself—straight, proud and confident. He felt a definite awareness of his maleness.

Returning with a tall iced drink, she sat down next to him, just near enough that her frilly blouse brushed against his shoulder. She faced him. "Tell me, what have you been doing lately? Have you been back to the hospital yet?"

Matt updated her on the past few months, including the fact that he and Bobbie were divorced.

Sandy stared at the floor and sipped her drink as he spoke. "I'm sorry, Matt. I've never been particularly happy with my part in that. I've never been able to decide if I blurted that out completely by accident, or whether . . . well, you know . . . whether I had a deeper motive. I've tried to rationalize that the truth would have come out sooner or later and that it was best, but then I see all the pain and unhappiness, and I just wish, for once, I could have kept my mouth shut. That, by the way, is not exactly my strong point—keeping my mouth shut, I mean."

Matt laughed at her candor, then turned somber. "Well, I guess it was for the best. I suspected something was going on almost from the beginning. There were just too many signs, but I ignored them because I didn't want it to be true. Who knows how long she would have kept pretending, if you hadn't said something."

She took his hand in both of hers. "You're being generous, and I thank you. But, without my interference, you two might have worked things out. I can't forget that. And, maybe, just maybe, I had ulterior motives. What would you think of me if I said I kind of hoped to be around to pick up the pieces?"

Stunned, he tried to decide whether her effect on him physically or her honesty was most startling. "I'd say I'm not used to women being so honest, and I'm a little surprised. You certainly never acted like you were interested."

"Maybe you ignored those signs, too." She raised one eyebrow. "But I think Bobbie definitely saw them. Don't you remember her accusations that . . . that morning?"

"No. I guess my attention was rather narrowly focused." He tried to laugh.

"So—why *did* you call after all this time?"

Matt fumbled for the right words. "I've been intending to call sooner, but . . . I don't know . . . actually . . ."

"It's all right, Matt. You don't have to explain. I didn't mean to put you on the spot. I'm just glad you decided to call now." She leaned over and kissed his cheek.

He felt an urge to kiss her. Hesitantly, he put his arm around her shoulder and gently pulled her toward him. She didn't resist. Sliding closer to him so that their bodies touched, she lifted her face to receive his kiss.

Matt felt the familiar tightening in his groin. Flustered, he stood, taking her arm to assist her. "We better get going or we'll miss our reservations."

Sandy stood, facing him, very close. She slipped her arms around his neck and pressed her body close to his. Her kiss was deep, passionate, probing.

"To hell with the reservations," he whispered gruffly, as he folded her in his arms.

The next morning Matt woke up in Sandy's satin-sheeted king-size bed. He sat up, alone, naked and startled, uncertain where he was. He saw his clothes crumpled in a heap on the floor. As he reached for his shorts, he remembered.

Sandy entered carrying a tray. "Good morning, sunshine," she said brightly, setting the tray on the table beside the bed. The plate contained ham, eggs, coffee, juice and a single candle stuck in a muffin. "Last night you mentioned that today is your birthday, so I decided to fix you a birthday breakfast. I bet you haven't had breakfast in bed in years."

She was wearing a flowing black negligee that revealed her ample breasts. His eyes paused there momentarily, wanting to explore that exquisite valley.

She followed his gaze, then looked at him and smiled, amused.

Flustered, he coughed. "You didn't need to do that. I'm really sorry. I didn't mean to fall asleep and stay the night."

She sat on the bed beside him. "You don't have to apologize to me," she chuckled. "You didn't talk me into anything. You know that, don't you? I've dreamed about a night like this since that first day in February when you walked into Bobbie's living room. Of course, at that time, I thought Bobbie was going to be asking for a divorce, and you would be needing someone to—shall we say—fill the void. I don't care what your reasons were for coming up here last night. I'm glad you did, and don't feel guilty if you were just looking for a little sex. In case you didn't notice, I was more than happy to oblige. You may not believe this, but women like sex too, or at least I do. I've been single a long, long time, and there isn't much out there in our age bracket. You, my friend, are quite a guy, in bed or out."

Matt nuzzled her neck and started unfastening the buttons on her lacy gown. "And you are quite a lady," he said admiringly as he slid the robe away. Caressing her nipples, he teased, "I bet you didn't know I'm a bird watcher."

She looked surprised. "A what?"

"A bird watcher, and I've just spotted a white-breasted mattress thrasher."

She wrinkled her nose and chuckled.

"You're right about one thing, though," he said, straight-faced, "I haven't had breakfast in bed in a long time."

Her laugh was muffled as he covered her mouth with his own and crushed her, once more, against his naked chest.

About noon, Matt prepared to leave.

"You're welcome to stay," Sandy invited. "We could do something special for your birthday."

"We already have," he said playfully. He was tempted, not having felt this good in a long time, but then he thought of Amy and the birthday dinner planned by Jim and Julie. "Thank you very much, but I've already made plans. May I call you later?"

"I'd like that."

When Matt returned to his room the light on the telephone was blinking. He called the Q operator. He'd had one call from Hank, and another from Debbie. Both wished him a happy birthday. There was no answer when he called the house, so he decided to go for a swim. He wasn't due at Jim and Julie's until evening. While he swam, his thoughts were on Sandy. How had he failed to notice her before? She was witty, brutally frank, a whiz at pool and damn sexy—not a bad combination.

His exercise complete, he returned to his room to dress for the evening. Just as he stepped out of the shower, the phone rang. "Happy birthday." It was Bobbie, sounding as if she might have had just a bit too much to drink.

"Thank you," Matt replied coolly.

"I thought," she continued with a slight slur, "since it was your birthday, we might have dinner together tonight. Besides, there's something I'd like to talk to you about."

This was the first time since they had become embroiled in the divorce negotiations that she had initiated a request to get together. There had been a time, not very long ago, when he would have dropped everything in the hope of a reconciliation. But she had disappointed him too many times.

"I'm sorry, Bobbie, but I already have plans for tonight," he said, offering no explanation, since what he did was none of her business anymore.

There was a slight pause on the other end. "Oh . . . okay . . . some other time. Happy birthday." He heard the click as she abruptly hung up.

Amy was supposed to fly out for his birthday party. It wasn't her regular trip, so she had to catch a hop.

Jim greeted him at the door with a beer. "Hey, buddy, good to see you. Happy birthday."

Matt looked around. The table was set for four; balloons and streamers covered the room, and in the center of the living room was a huge colorfully decorated cardboard birthday cake. "You guys shouldn't have gone to so much trouble."

Julie chastised, "Oh, come on. It was fun. We're just waiting for Amy. She should be here anytime."

Matt nodded and turned to Jim. "Hey, how's school going?"

Jim motioned for Matt to sit on the couch, then withdrew a chair from under the table, turned it backwards and sat down. "Not too bad, but the students—they are so *young*. They make me feel like an old man." He puckered his face.

Matt grinned. "Yeah. Maybe it's because we are getting older. I'm having a hard time accepting the fact that I'm forty-one years old today." He made a face. "So, what are you taking?"

"Going for my master's in business management."

They finished their second beers and Julie took the glasses into the kitchen. Jim excused himself. They reappeared to the out-of-tune strains of "Happy Birthday." Julie carried a birthday cake, covered with several lit candles.

Matt stood, feeling sheepish. He'd never mastered being comfortable when he was the center of attention. Just as the song ended, the top of the cardboard cake popped off and a laughing, sparkling Amy jumped out of the cake and into Matt's arms. Laughter erupted from the three of them at the startled look on his face.

After dinner, Matt and Amy prepared to leave.

"Hey, we may not see you two again before the end of the year," Jim said. " Why don't we plan something for New Year's Eve?"

Amy looked at Matt. "Fine with me. I have a three-day break. I can fly out the day before."

Matt hesitated. "Well, sure, okay. That sounds like a good idea. Where should we go?"

Julie volunteered. "I have time to make some calls and check out what's available. I'll call you with the details."

They said good night to Jim and Julie, and returned to Matt's BOQ room. For his birthday, Amy spent the night in his room—in his twin bed, in his arms, warm and cuddly, but still definitely off limits.

He dropped her off at the airport the next morning.

"I'll call you as soon as I know my schedule for New Year's." She gave him a loving but hardly passionate kiss. "Happy birthday, Matt."

The following Saturday, Matt started house hunting. He spent the day checking out areas where he might want to live. Returning to his room that evening he found a note from Steve pinned to his door.

"Oh, shit." Matt looked at his watch. It was six o'clock. He'd forgotten the birthday party for one of the POWs that started at eight, but he could still make it.

"Whose your date tonight?" Steve asked when Matt called.

"Dammit, Steve," Matt groaned, "I couldn't ask anyone this late. I'll just go by myself."

Steve pressed. "Come on. I've finally met a real nice girl and she thinks we're going with another couple. Surely you know someone who wouldn't mind a late invitation. Don't tell me a stud like you can't find a date."

Matt sighed. "Okay, give me a few minutes. I'll make a phone call and call you back."

"Sandy, this is Matt. Do you have any plans for this evening?" he asked tentatively.

After a slight pause, she replied, "Well, only if you call curling up on the couch for an evening of heavy TV 'plans'. In that case, I have a fairly exciting evening planned, complete with popcorn."

"Look," he said apologetically, "I know it's awfully late to be asking, but would you like to go to a birthday party with me tonight?" He expected she would beg off; her hair wasn't fixed, or she didn't have anything to wear.

Instead her voice was full of excitement, "Oh, I'd love to. What time, and what do I wear?"

It was early in the morning before Matt and Sandy left the party. They rode in silence, her head snuggled against his shoulder.

"I really appreciate you going with me on such short notice," he said as he pulled into the circle drive in front of her house and slipped his arm around her shoulder. She once again pressed close to him.

"I had a lovely time, Matt. Your friends are delightful. I think Steve and Jennifer kind of like each other."

He pressed her shoulder and was quiet for a moment. "I'm ready to look at houses. You have any to show me?"

"Sure."

For several minutes they embraced in the car, Matt uncertain how to proceed.

"It's awfully late for you to have to drive back to the BOQ tonight," she whispered softly. "Would you like to stay here?"

CHAPTER 29

<u>San Diego, December '73 - January '74.</u>

In mid-December, stuffed with junk food and worn out from two days of non-stop rides at the free weekend provided by Disneyland for the returned POWs and their families, Matt and Hank headed back to San Diego late Sunday evening. As they neared the house, Hank again raised the familiar question, "Dad, are you ever going to live with us again?"

Matt simply didn't know what to say anymore. He and Bobbie were divorced, just waiting for some legal six-month period to expire. He took his frustration out on Hank. "Son, please stop nagging me about that. I've told you several times, I just can't live at home right now. You'll have to talk to your mother if you want a better answer."

Hank dropped his eyes, turned his head toward the side window, and became silent.

Matt studied his son out of the corner of his eye. It was hard to realize the boy was just thirteen years old—he was already taller than Bobbie and Debbie, a little on the skinny side, but muscular. He was going to be a handsome young man when he grew up, taller and better looking, by far, than his old dad. But thinking back to his days on the farm, Matt realized there was no comparison between his and Hank's level of maturity at the same age. It was probably the changing times; kids weren't required to grow up as fast anymore. And without a father to teach him, Hank's emotional maturity seemed stunted. He was still a "little boy" in many ways, despite his size—a little boy who wanted his mom and dad together and just couldn't quite grasp the complexities of husband and wife relationships. Neither could he for that matter, Matt acknowledged sadly.

He felt a surge of bitterness at the damage being visited upon his son as a result of his last "extended duty"; bitterness at the government that took so long to get him out of prison, anger at himself for putting his family in that situation, and fury at Bobbie—for not being able to provide the discipline Hank so sorely needed, and for not being the faithful wife he had expected. She knew he loved her, how could she have done this to them? Tom was no better; he should have seen how vulnerable she was; yet he didn't have the decency to walk away. *If only I'd remembered that damn flak site. My one second of inattention has resulted in an awful lot of pain.*

As they neared Bobbie's house, Matt tried to lighten the mood. "You better bone up on your Monopoly game or I'll beat the pants off you at Christmas."

Hank shrugged his shoulders and continued to watch the passing scenery. When they pulled up to the driveway, he slid out of the front seat before Matt turned off the engine. "Thanks, Dad. I had fun at Disneyland. I'll see you Christmas."

Matt leaned against the steering wheel for several minutes after Hank disappeared into the house. Then, heaving a long sigh, he slowly drove away. This is not what he had envisioned while he was in prison dreaming of coming home. That dream, like so many others, had turned into just another nightmare. And he couldn't see any light at the end of this tunnel—no six months and it will all be okay. Resolving their problems held less chance of success than those early Paris peace talks.

At Bobbie's invitation, Matt arrived at the house early Christmas morning. She made no reference to her call on his birthday, but her attitude was a bit reserved. Debbie, on the other hand, was warmer and more attentive than she'd been since he came home. The wall that she had erected seemed to be coming down—brick by brick. Not that she was effusive—that wasn't her nature—but it felt comfortable, and that was great progress. Hank's peevish attitude had disappeared.

After dinner, Matt, Hank and Debbie played Monopoly on the

living room floor. Between games, when Debbie went into the kitchen to refill their Coke glasses, and Hank went to the bathroom, Matt sadly surveyed his old kingdom. It would be nice to have the family all together this way all the time. He would have been willing to make a lot of allowances to have that. His face must have mirrored his thoughts, because when he looked up, Bobbie was leaning against the door frame staring at him. As their eyes met, she diverted her gaze and hastily left the room. Did he see tears?

After Hank won the third game, Debbie stood up. "You guys go ahead, it's late and I'm tired."

"You're right," Matt said. "I didn't realize how late it was getting. It's time I hit the road, too."

Hank grabbed his hand. "Dad, you don't have to leave tonight, do you?"

Matt put his arm around his son's shoulders. "I'm afraid I do."

"Why don't you live with us anymore?" Hank persisted. "I don't want you to go. Please, Dad, please stay here, or take me with you. I want to live with you."

He squeezed Hank's arm. "You know I want to be with you, and we will be. Your mom and I are trying to work things out. We just need more time. But, we'll do lots of things together, just like we have been. Maybe we can go fishing later this week."

He gritted his teeth, but gave up trying to explain the inexplicable. "It's your bedtime. You go on to bed, and I'll call you tomorrow." He kissed his son and watched as Hank walked dejectedly toward the bedroom, his head bent, his shoulders stooped like an old man's. *Dammit! Dammit! Dammit!*

Debbie, who had observed the exchange, stared contemplatively at Hank's disappearing figure. For a moment she appeared to want to say something, then apparently changed her mind and walked over to Matt. "Goodnight, Dad." She gave him a peck on the cheek and a reassuring hug. "It was really good to have you home for Christmas." As she left, she pointedly avoided her mother who was returning to the living room.

Watching Debbie disappear down the hall, Matt turned to Bobbie, glaring. "Dammit, if you don't tell those kids about the divorce, I will—and I'll tell them why! Why in the hell can't you be honest, for just once in your life?" He spat out the words.

Bobbie answered meekly. "Matt, I don't know what to say. Hank loves you so much. I'm afraid he'll hate me. He'll think it's all my fault you went away."

Matt looked at her with contempt. "Well, whose fault do *you* think it is? Because of your filthy affair, I've lost my family. Hank's miserable because he's got a part-time father, and Debbie's so uptight and mixed up because of her loyalty to you she doesn't know where to turn. Only you and your friggin' lover go on your merry ways." He was having difficulty controlling his growing rage. "I mean it, dammit, you level with those kids, or you aren't going to like what they hear from me!" He gave a scornful snort, turned on his heel and stalked out of the house. He would never allow himself to strike a woman, but it was surely tempting.

As soon as he returned to his austere BOQ room, he called Sandy. "Merry Christmas. Would you like to come over and go for a swim or play some tennis tomorrow? We'll have the place pretty much to ourselves, it's like a ghost town around here. Then maybe we can grab a bite later."

"Sure, sounds like fun."

Returning to his room as it started to get dark, sweaty from some hard-fought games of tennis, Matt flipped on the television just in time to catch an advertisement for a New Year's Eve party.

"Oh, that reminds me," Sandy remarked, "I received a couple of tickets from a client to a New Year's Eve party at Mr. A's. Would you like to go?"

Matt paused uncomfortably. "I'd love to, but I made plans several weeks ago with my friend, Jim. He's already booked reservations."

"Oh. Okay. I know it's late, but I just got them the day before Christmas, and thought I'd take a chance."

Matt caught the flicker of disappointment, but she smiled. He motioned toward the bathroom, "Go ahead and shower first. I'll run down to the bar and bring us a couple of drinks."

Slipping out of her swimming suit, she rubbed his bare chest and ran her finger under the waistband of his swim trunks. "I have a better idea," she coaxed.

Later, Matt dressed and went downstairs to the little BOQ bar. Just as Sandy finished her shower, the phone rang. She hesitated, then decided to answer it. "Commander Tillet's room."

"This is Amy Carson calling from Hawaii. Is Matt in?"

"I'm sorry, he's down the hall."

"Could you get him please, I'm calling long distance." The voice sounded irritated and demanding.

No, actually, I'm standing here in his room with no clothes on, and the Navy would frown if a naked lady went parading through these hallowed halls, Sandy wanted to say. Instead, her reply was cool. "Just a minute."

She put the phone down and was trying to wiggle her still-damp body into her pants when Matt walked back into the room. She handed him the phone and disappeared into the bathroom.

When the conversation ended, she emerged from the bathroom, now fully dressed. "I'm sorry, Matt, I didn't mean to pry. I thought it might be a call you wouldn't want to miss." She paused, then continued icily, "I guess it was a call you didn't want to miss, at that."

"Look, I want to explain about Amy."

Her voice was frosty. "You don't owe me an explanation about your personal life."

"No, please, let me explain. I met Amy in Dallas when Bobbie wouldn't go with me. My friend, Jim, married her roommate in October, as soon as his divorce was final. When she and Julie were flying out here, we would double date. Several weeks ago, we made plans to get together for New Year's Eve. But she's just a friend. I swear to you, I've never slept with her."

"Matt, you don't have to explain," she repeated.

"But I want to. I want you to understand. She and I are just friends. She was nice to me when I was feeling pretty low, and I feel indebted to her. Since Jim and Julie got married, I've only had dinner with her a few times when she has the San Diego flight. But that's as far as it goes." He moved toward her.

She stiffened noticeably and stepped away. "It's okay, Matt. Who you date is your business. You've never promised me an exclusive arrangement. So, let's just drop it, okay?" She turned away, but not before he caught the steel-like glint in her eyes.

He tried again. "Let's go get something to eat, and we can talk about this."

"I'm not very hungry right now. I think I'll go on home. I have quite a bit of work to catch up on." She picked up her overnight bag and left, shutting the door very securely behind her.

Matt downed both of the drinks, and lay back on the bed. This dating business wasn't all it was cracked up to be. Unhappily, he reflected on the past ten and a half months. His life seemed to be in limbo. He could hardly wait to get back to work, get back to flying, back to an environment where he had some control; he sure as hell didn't seem to have any in his personal affairs.

Things weren't exactly turning out as he had expected. When they learned they were going to be released, he and Lee spent a lot of time speculating about what would happen when they got home. He'd figured he'd have a few weeks of leave; that he'd take the family on a really great vacation—maybe two to make up for the lost time—and then he'd get back to work. Except for a few speaking engagements with some of the other POWs, he'd been fairly useless to the Navy and a complete failure in his personal relationships. Fortunately, the former was about to change. He'd been cleared to return to flying status. After several phone calls with his detailer, he'd found a squadron job at Miramar starting right after the first of the year.

The next morning, Matt reflected on the turn of events. He'd hoped to spend most of the weekend with Sandy, playing some more tennis, maybe doing a little swimming or having a picnic at the beach. But it didn't appear that was going to happen. He hated the idle time. At home there was always something to do—mow the yard, trim the hedge, wash the car, fix a leak. To take up the slack, he decided to take a long jog, wash his car and call Hank. He changed into his running gear.

****

At his birthday party, Amy had said she would fly in a day or two early, but after that last phone call, he wasn't surprised she hadn't.

It was New Year's Eve afternoon before he heard from her. "I just arrived. I had a late flight last night, filled in for another stew who had an emergency." It was clear from the tone of her voice she had not brought the sunshine from Hawaii; more like she had brought a few icicles from a Chicago blizzard. "I'm going to take a nap, so I'll be able to stay awake until midnight," she continued in the same dull monotone. "What time are we supposed to meet Jim and Julie?"

"They're coming over here about seven-thirty," he said.

"Okay, can you pick me up between seven and seven-fifteen?"

"Sure." What else could he say?

"I'll see you then." The connection went dead.

The four of them celebrated New Year's Eve at the Hotel del Coronado. Or rather, Jim and Julie celebrated. Amy didn't have much to say, pleading a headache.

As soon as Jim and Julie dropped them at the BOQ parking lot, Amy headed toward his car. "I'm sorry, Matt, I really have to go back. I have to catch an early morning flight back to Chicago."

Matt considered trying to explain about Sandy, but decided against it. What was there to say? *Since you won't go to bed with me, I found someone who will.* She was miffed and an explanation wouldn't help, certainly not the only truthful one he could give, and he couldn't think of a lie that would work either.

At her hotel, he parked in a darkened waiting area. "Do you know when you'll be back out here?" He slid toward her and draped his arm around her cold shoulder.

"No, I have the Hawaii flight again in January." She gave him a lukewarm goodnight kiss. "I'll call you if I get San Diego in February. Goodnight. Happy New Year." She opened the car door. "You don't need to get out."

****

Since coming home, Matt had been assigned to the hospital. Right after the first of the year he was report to his first "real" assignment—as Executive Officer of a training squadron at Miramar. In October, he would fleet up to Commanding Officer.

He was excited to think about having his own squadron, a real squadron, not the prison-cell variety, but it meant lots of work. He had to re-qualify to fly and getting back into full swing of the operational Navy required he carry home a briefcase full of papers every night.

Having plenty of work was fortunate, however, since his love life had gone to hell in a handbasket. Both Sandy and Amy were upset with him. Instead of two girlfriends just a short time ago, he appeared to have none again. He was quickly learning that if he feasted on the pleasures of life, he was likely to get indigestion.

For the first couple of weeks, Matt was buried in paperwork during the week and spent the first two weekends with Hank.

But the next weekend Hank begged off. "Dad, if you don't mind, I'd like to go to the beach with Alan and the guys. The surf's up, and there's supposed to be some great waves."

"Okay, pal. Have a good time, but be careful. I can use this weekend to do a little house hunting. I'll call you about next weekend."

"House hunting?" Hank gave him a startled look.

"Well, I . . . I need something bigger than the BOQ . . . so you'll have a room of your own," he explained.

"Oh, okay. See you next weekend."

Matt exhaled slowly as he hung up the phone. He'd just had a good opening to tell Hank the truth. Why had he chickened out?

Matt valued Sandy's judgment on real estate matters. It was obvious from her success in the business that she knew what she was doing. She'd promised to help him find a place. And, though he didn't like to admit it, he missed her—missed her sense of humor, her cheerfulness and in general, her companionship.

Just what little time they had been together, it was clear that dating her was going to be somewhat akin to riding a roller coaster, with exciting highs that took his breath away, only to slam him firmly back into his seat of reality. In a little more than a month, he had learned that among her other chameleonic attributes, she had a volatile temper. When she got angry, usually a storm erupted, but like a Kansas tornado, it rarely touched down, was over quickly, and the sun was usually shining the next day. But she sure as hell didn't accept him as lord and master.

She'd already walked out of one party when he left her alone while he visited with old friends. He'd been gone about an hour, maybe a little more, but he left her with Steve and Jennifer, it wasn't like she was really alone. But, when he returned to the table, it was empty. He waited, thinking she'd gone to the little girls room, or to get a drink. Finally, when Steve and Jennifer returned from the dance floor, they said she fumed something about him not acting very much like an officer and a gentleman and she was going home.

He couldn't believe it. How dare she walk out on him and embarrass him in front of his friends. He drove straight to her house; he was going to make it clear if they were going to continue seeing each other, that was unacceptable behavior.

When she answered the bell, and before he could get in a word edgewise, she exploded. "Go home, and don't bother to call me again if that is how you're going to treat me. No wonder Bobbie looked for someone else. I can't believe someone who seems as nice as you can be that rude and inconsiderate."

He tried to interrupt, "But, I . . . ."

She didn't even hear him, and barely took a breath. Good thing there were no real close neighbors, because the level of her voice would have surely woken them. "I sat there for over an hour— alone. I didn't know anyone but Steve and Jennifer, and they were wrapped up in each other. I don't suppose it even occurred to you that I might have been interested in what you were discussing, had you had the courtesy to come get me. And, it obviously never occurred to you that we were at a dance. You can pay Steve back— he bought me a couple of drinks. In the future, if I want to be alone at a party, I'll go by myself, and you can go screw yourself!" She slammed the door and shut off the light, leaving him standing red faced in the darkness.

Driving home, his swallowed his anger. Well, that wasn't exactly true—it had been shoved down his throat. While his behavior might be perceived as a bit "lacking," Bobbie would never have said a word. He might have make a few adjustments.

It had been three weeks. Hopefully the latest storm clouds had blown over by now, as they had a few days after the dance. He didn't like being in the dog house; he wanted things back as they had been before. He dialed her number. "Hi, this is Matt. How are you?"

"Fine."

Too little to discern her mood. He waited for more. There wasn't anything.

"Say, you said to give you a call when I wanted to go look at houses. I'm ready. Do you still have anything to show me?"

"Sure. Do you want to go today or tomorrow? I'll need to set up appointments."

"Today if you can, and perhaps tomorrow, too. Is that too much?"

"Oh, I think I can arrange it. Give me an hour or so. Shall I pick you up at the BOQ?" She sounded all business.

"Why don't I drive on out to your house?"

"Suit yourself."

Sandy met him at the door, looking very professional in her camel-colored slacks and matching jacket. As soon as he stepped inside the house, he pulled her into his arms. She didn't resist, but she didn't press close to him or kiss him back either. *O . . . kay, old buddy. All is not forgotten or forgiven.*

He pulled her closer. "I missed you." He gave her a long, lingering kiss, and could feel her body relax.

She lowered her head, eyeing him suspiciously over the rim of her glasses. "I bet this is how you treat all your real-estate agents," she said, her lips curling into a half-smile.

Whew. He'd weathered another storm.

Matt was determined to come to a decision on a house this weekend. He was anxious to get out of the BOQ and into something he could call his own. He and Bobbie had talked about buying the house they were renting before his last cruise but the opportunity had never presented itself after he returned. Now, with little else to call his own, a home was very important—something tangible, something that gave him a sense of stability. He needed that.

By the end of the weekend, he had narrowed his choices down to two. One was a small three-bedroom townhouse in a new development in an older area of town, about ten minutes from the base. Matt liked the price, financing and location. It was less than five minutes from his old house. Hank would be able to ride his bike over. The other was a nearly new, four-bedroom single-family home, with a pool, large family room and entertainment area. It was in one of the newer subdivisions only five minutes from the base, but on the other side from Hank.

Over dinner, Sandy explained why she favored the bigger house. "The owners are very anxious to sell, they've been transferred and they've already purchased another home. His company will make up whatever they lose on this house, so it can be bought well below market value. It would be a terrific investment, not only because of its current price, but also because you can expect a lot better appreciation in single-family residences than townhouses."

"But it's just me. What do I need with a house that big, and with a pool to look after? That's the beauty of the smaller one. When I go to sea, which I'll probably have to do in a couple years, I can just close it up, and all the outside maintenance is taken care of by the homeowners' association."

"Maybe that's okay for right now, but what about in the future, in a few months or a year from now? Wouldn't you like to provide a home for Hank? You've said so enough times."

"Sure, but the other place is big enough for both of us. If I go to sea, he'll have to stay with his mother, anyway."

"Do you plan for it to always be just you and Hank? Don't you think maybe in the future you'd like to get married?"

Matt flinched. There was that "M" word, and not too subtle either. In fact, as he was quickly learning, not very much about Sandy was subtle. It was pretty easy to know where you stood. If she was mad, you knew it; if she was happy, you knew it. And, he surmised, if she wanted to get married, you were going to know about that too. This was the first time she had actually mentioned marriage, but it was fairly clear from her actions and reactions of the past few weeks that she expected their relationship to be an exclusive one. At this point, it was probably safe to assume she wanted it to be a permanent one, as well.

How would she react if he said he wasn't interested? Actually, that wasn't entirely true. It would be nice to have her to come home to, to be able to hold her warm body every night, instead of just now and then. But it was too soon for him. Jim and John may have found "love at first sight" but he wasn't wired that way. He was a cautious man, he liked to deliberate, to consider his options carefully. His quick decision to buy this house was actually out of character, but it this case, he'd already made up his mind that he was buying, he just needed to figure out which one. He hadn't at all made up his mind that he wanted to get married again. The pain from the first go-round was still too raw.

"Look, you're a nice gal, and I care for you very much, but I'm not interested in marriage right now, and maybe not for a long time. If I stay in the Navy, which I plan to do, there's always a chance I'll have to go to sea. That means going on six, eight, even ten-month cruises. I don't intend to get married and leave a wife alone again. I hope you can understand, but . . . well . . . that's how I feel."

"I wasn't proposing," she corrected frostily. "I merely suggested you might want to consider the possibility. And, as I recall, I'm not your only candidate. But, I agree, the townhouse has numerous advantages for a dedicated single man."

Without another word, she wrote up the offer.

CHAPTER 30

San Diego - Spring 1974.

For several months after Matt moved out, Bobbie and Tom continued to see each other once or twice a week. At Bobbie's insistence, they met only at his apartment and still in secret, as before. He couldn't do anything with the children anymore, since Hank was often over at his dad's, or, as Bobbie so often warned, "he wouldn't understand why another man is coming around now that his dad is back. Remember, you were supposed to be Matt's friend. I certainly don't want Hank telling Matt his 'old buddy' is hanging around."

Bobbie was still walking a tightrope, refusing to admit to Hank that she and Matt were divorced. Instead she devised a story of sorts—that they needed "more time" to get reacquainted, and it was better if they lived apart until they worked out their problems. It astounded Tom that Hank bought it, and it was even more surprising that Matt didn't set the record straight. There could be only one reason that made sense: Matt still wanted to get back together.

Once Tom angrily accused Bobbie of wanting that too. Actually, he believed it was just her nature to procrastinate, but it might prod her into action. Yet even after she filed for divorce, she continued to feed Hank that ridiculous story.

More and more Tom turned to Maggie for companionship, for love, for understanding. As the weeks passed, she became more important with each encounter. She was warm, undemanding, and most of all, she had her head screwed on straight, which was more than he could say about Bobbie these days. Despite a couple of disappointing love affairs, the details of which she had shared with him during the past few months, Maggie had retained a good attitude toward life and love. With her, he was starting to feel the old stimulation he once thought possible only with Bobbie.

It was quite possible Bobbie would never marry him because of her cowardly inability to face the consequences of Hank's reaction. That realization, coupled with his growing fondness for Maggie, made it less imperative that Bobbie make up her mind. He wasn't sure he still cared. Should he—could he—just walk out? What would she do if he did? *Jesus, am I staying out of guilt?*

Bobbie recognized Tom's growing lack of interest. She had to make up her mind. She had given in to his ultimatum back in May to get a divorce "or else," because of her certainty that Matt would never forgive her. Every time they got together, Matt ended up angry and upset with her. How could he ever forgive her? She couldn't forgive herself. Had she gone to Washington, on that slim off-chance, that would have meant the end with Tom. She couldn't risk it.

Then, in late November, after an argument with Tom in which he accused her of still being in love with Matt and Matt in love with her, she had swallowed what little pride she had left and called Matt, using his birthday as an excuse. If Tom were right about Matt, as he was about her, then she was ready to get down on her knees and beg Matt to come home. It had taken more than a couple of drinks to bolster her courage, and then when she called, he had flatly rejected her. He had sounded so cold and disinterested. It left no doubt in her mind that if there ever had been a chance, it didn't exist any longer.

So she had drowned her sorrows and the next day crawled back to Tom, insisting she loved him. But every time she saw Matt and watched Hank's growing unhappiness, she wished Tom Finley had never come into her life.

But now, she knew she was skating on dangerously thin ice, and could lose him too if she didn't act, and quickly. She couldn't face a future without a man, and it was readily apparent that Matt had found someone else. Even Hank complained about how much time his dad spent with "that other woman." He had seemed fairly put out at his dad a few weeks before, and she had inquired why.

"He's busy with someone else this weekend, so we're not going to do anything," he had complained, pouting.

"Did he say what he was doing?" She knew she was prying, but her curiosity got the best of her. Matt had been spending almost every weekend with him, unless Hank had other plans.

"I don't know, he didn't say. I just know he has a date with your 'old friend.' He's *always* with her."

Clearly, Hank was referring to Sandy. Why couldn't it have been anyone but her?

On the positive side, however, Hank's complaints had finally provided her the opportunity to tell him about the divorce without having to reveal the real reason. "Honey, there's something I've been wanting to find the right time to tell you. Your father and I are getting a divorce."

"Why?" he shrieked. "So he could be with *her*?"

"No one is to blame. After more than seven years of being separated, we just couldn't work things out." She was fully aware that he was blaming Matt and, more importantly, Sandy. She could do more to dispel Hank's perception, but he probably wouldn't believe her anyway. For that matter, it was Sandy's fault, just in a different way than Hank imagined. At least Matt couldn't complain anymore that she hadn't told him.

A gnawing fear that Tom was seeing someone else had been nagging at her for several weeks. She could wait no longer. After one of their more enjoyable evenings, but which still failed to muster the same excitement as before, she made her move. "You don't feel that same old magic any more, do you? It's not like it used to be, I can tell."

Tom propped himself up on the pillow, watching her dress. There had been a time when he couldn't get enough of her, when her tiny nude body sent lustful stirrings through him even after they had just made love. Now, he watched dispassionately. She was right, but he hedged. "Bobbie, I have loved you for so long, you're like a habit. And maybe that's bad. But I get so tired of sneaking around."

He shook his head, a sad expression on his face.

"Do you still want to marry me?" She asked hesitantly, nervously shifting her feet.

Tom remained silent for a long time, troubled. He didn't know what to say; he really didn't know what he wanted anymore.

Finally, he responded. "Yes, Bobbie, if that's what you want. I'd sort of given up hope, you always seemed to have one more excuse waiting in the wings. I didn't think you wanted to marry me," he added with a rueful smile.

Bobbie could sense his reservations. *There's someone else. I know it.*

"I do love you, and I do want to marry you—the sooner the better."

For over six years he had hoped to hear those words. During those years, even a year ago, he would have felt like the luckiest man in the world if she had spoken them. Now, he felt very little emotion except surprise. He stared at her for a long time until her words finally sank in. She had just accepted his long-standing proposal.

Slowly, he rose from the bed, walked over to where she was standing, and gathered her close to his still-sweaty nude body. Pulling her back down on the bed, something like the old desire rekindled itself.

Hank was spending the night with Matt, so Bobbie stayed the entire night, uneasily wrapped in Tom's warm, strong arms. She slept very little, wishing things were different. But Matt was gone. Tom also spent a restless night, crying out once in his sleep. The name sounded like "Maggie."

****

Since reporting to the Squadron, Matt had little time during the week for anything other than work. He spent almost every evening trying to bridge the gulf of his inexperience. While he had sat in prison, he missed filling a lot of the little "blocks" of experience that normally prepared a jet jockey for squadron command. The Chief of Naval Personnel had directed selection boards to treat the returning POWs as if they had completed the blocks, but it was clear to Matt when he reported that he had a few gaps.

Learning his job was just one of his problems. Another was Hank, whose slouching insolence was becoming difficult to abide.

It was obvious something was different when he picked Hank up on Friday evening after having to beg off the week before for a squadron function.

"What's the matter, son? What've I done now? I'm sorry about last weekend, but . . . ."

"You and Mom are divorced," Hank blurted, his tone accusatory.

Matt heaved a sigh. *Finally.* "I'm sorry. We tried . . . ."

Again Hank interrupted. "Yeah, I can see how hard you tried," he sneered.

"Hank, you really don't understand . . . ."

"Oh, don't I? You think I'm just a kid, that I don't know anything. Well, I *understand* more than you think." His voice dripped with indignation.

"I'm not going to argue with you, but you really don't understand." Matt tried to be firm, but knew he was failing miserably. He'd wanted Bobbie to tell Hank about the divorce, but it obviously hadn't helped. Whatever she'd said, however she'd explained it, he was still the villain in Hank's eyes. Matt gritted his teeth. He had thought Hank's knowing about the divorce would solve things. "I wish you wouldn't blame me for this. I . . . ."

"Don't bother to make any excuses. I know what happened. You were planning this all along. *That's* why you were 'house hunting.'" Hank turned away.

It was clear he had tuned out anything else Matt might want to say. Hank wouldn't believe him now even if he told him the absolute truth. Matt drove in silence the rest of the way to the house.

Hank's hostile attitude failed to improve all day Saturday, and by early Sunday morning, Matt, exasperated and depressed, took him home. The rancor continued to varying degrees during the following weeks, to the point that spending a pleasant weekend together became almost impossible.

****

Tom and Bobbie planned their wedding. It was going to be a quiet ceremony at home with the children and a few close friends. She selected a date in early June, when Debbie would be out of school and could stay with Hank while Bobbie and Tom were on their honeymoon. That way, she wouldn't have to say anything to Matt in advance. She was still waiting for the right moment to tell Hank and Debbie, to present them with a final confirmation of her infidelity. Would Hank figure it out? Would he hate her as he now did Matt? Even her belated attempts to defend Matt hadn't eased Hank's rage.

Tom started volunteering to fill in whenever anyone wanted a sub, so they would owe him some flights later. He told only a few of his closest friends at work that he was getting married, but hadn't mustered the courage to say anything to Maggie yet. She must suspect something since he hadn't called her in three weeks.

One Thursday in May, Tom flew a plane up to San Francisco for some repair work. He finished sooner than expected, and was able to deadhead on the next WCA flight back to San Diego. Maggie occupied his thoughts. *I've got to tell her about the wedding. But, how? What do I say? That I love Bobbie? But do I? If so, why is Maggie the only one I've been thinking about?*

He wished so many things could have been different. Could he really go through with this wedding? The realization finally struck him: he had fallen in love with Maggie. But did she feel the same? He had to see her, talk to her, hold her in his arms one more time. But if she loved him too, could he walk away and marry Bobbie? Could Bobbie handle the rejection? What would she do? She had chosen him over Matt, divorced Matt, even though it was clear to Tom that Matt would have been willing to take her back, to overlook what had happened. Could he do that to her? She still needed him as much as before, maybe more. He grappled with his indecision all the way back, and as they neared San Diego, he still wasn't sure what he was going to do. He would make a final decision after he talked with Maggie.

It was a crystal clear, sunny day in the skies over San Diego. Visibility was almost unlimited. Captain Simpson set up for the steep glide path to the runway located near the water, just on the other side of the last ridge of hills. A modest residential area lay nestled below.

Michael Edwards, a 21-year old student pilot, was literally flying high as he maneuvered a Cessna 172 on his first solo ride. He had taken off just minutes before from a small private field in the southern part of San Diego. As he soared high above San Diego, he could look down and see Interstates 805 and 15 below as they ran up from Tijuana. He could just glimpse Interstate 8 off to the north that he knew continued from the beach out to the desert and on into Arizona.

The WCA 727 crew was busily engaged in the usual instrument checks in preparation for touchdown when approach control announced, "WCA-909, traffic in your area, one hundred eighty degrees, about one mile. Looks like a small plane."

The co-pilot searched the skies off to the south and southwest. He saw a small plane about five miles out, moving away. "There it is. It's clear. No problem." He relaxed and returned to the landing procedures.

In the high-winged plane, it was difficult to see directly above, and Michael Edwards was too excited and too inexperienced to be aware of the importance of dipping the wings occasionally to check above him. As a result, he never saw the huge WCA jet, not even when its undercarriage ripped the wings off his little Cessna, and sent it spiraling helplessly to a fiery grave in the residential streets below.

In the first-class cabin, Tom's conversation with one of the stewardesses was obliterated by the horrifying sound of metal scraping against metal.

WCA-909 bounced around violently, failing to respond to Captain Simpson's frantic attempts to keep it under control. He and the co-pilot struggled desperately to arrest the plane's sharp plunge right up to the moment it plowed through the middle-class neighborhood just past the 805 freeway and burst into flames, spewing fire and the bodies of 144 passengers and a crew of eight over a two-block radius.

Bobbie heard the news of the plane crash while she was still at work, where she had returned shortly after separating from Matt. It was nearly the only topic of conversation. She learned more of the gruesome details when she arrived home and watched the six o'clock news, startled to discover that it had been a WCA plane. How sad, Tom would know the crew; they might even have been friends. She wished she could call him and offer her condolences, but he had flown up to San Francisco earlier and wouldn't be back yet.

She went to bed and turned on the small set in the bedroom to watch the eleven o'clock news. Due to the complicated process of identifying bodies and notifying next of kin, the announcer said, only the names of a few of the crew and passengers were being released. The station started scrolling the names of the WCA employees first. Suddenly, Bobbie bolted upright and gasped, "Oh, my God!" Bile rose in her throat and she clasped her trembling hands over her mouth.

Among the list of WCA personnel who had perished was Thomas Eliot Finley. She collapsed on the bed, moaning, "Oh, Tom, Tom. What am I going to do?" A deep garbled sound escaped from her throat. Owing to her own determination to keep their relationship a secret until the last possible moment, not a single one of Tom's friends had known to call her, to spare her the horror of learning such news from a television announcement.

****

Matt had moved into his sparsely furnished townhouse in early April and spent all his free time the next several weeks trying to furnish it, to turn it into something that belonged to him, something he could be proud of. It was coming along nicely, and the results, with Sandy's helpful input, were turning out better than he expected. On the car radio coming home from work, he heard about the crash. They missed the six o'clock news because he and Sandy were out shopping for furniture until the stores closed.

As soon as they entered the house, he turned on the TV, anxious to learn if anyone he knew had been on that plane. A pilot in his squadron had recently resigned to fly with WCA. As the names of the WCA crew and employees were flashed on the screen, Matt stared, "Well, I'll be damned," he muttered half to himself and half to Sandy.

Sandy, catching the name at the same time, turned to Matt and cried out, "My God! Thomas Eliot Finley? Is that Bobbie's Tom?" Matt nodded his head. "Yes, the very same. I'll just be damned. You know, there was a time when I'd have liked to kill him myself. Now . . . ." His voice trailed off as he grimaced and shook his head sadly. "I wonder how Bobbie is going to handle this?" He had a sudden urge to call her and comfort her. She would need someone now.

Sandy stared, horrified, at the television screen. "Poor Tom. Oh, how sad."

****

Marcia Miller and Larry Chasteen were among the large contingent of WCA employees and naval officers at the memorial services for Tom.

After the program, Debbie spotted Matt and Sandy and another couple. "Mom, excuse me for a minute." She headed toward them.

Just as Debbie left, Marcia walked over to where Bobbie and Hank were standing. "Bobbie, I'm so sorry for your loss," Marcia said softly.

Bobbie caught Hank's startled look and smiled nervously. "Why don't you go say hello to your father, too?" she urged. "And ask Debbie to come back. I'm ready to leave." As he hesitated, she took Marcia's arm, turned and moved out of Hank's earshot. "Thank you. It was quite a shock to learn about it on the news."

"Oh, my God." Marcia's hand flew to her face. "Bobbie. I'm so sorry. I should have called you. It was so hectic, I just didn't think to call anyone except those on the list." She put her arm around Bobbie's shoulders. "I'm so very sorry."

Bobbie shook her head. "It's okay. It would have been a shock, no matter how the message was delivered." She patted the hand on her shoulder. "Anyway, not many people knew, so I'd just as soon leave it that way for now. I don't want to deal with well wishers."

A brief upturn of Marcia's brow was her only visible sign. "Okay. Well, I'm really sorry. He was a super guy." Marcia gave Bobbie one final comforting pat on the shoulder and walked away.

Bobbie felt the tears forming as she watched Matt hugging Hank and Debbie chatting with Sandy. She bit her lips and turned away.

Hank stiffly accepted Matt's hug, but made a point of ignoring Sandy. "Debbie, Mom's ready to go," he announced with a scowl. He turned and started walking away.

Matt grabbed Debbie's hand. "How's your mother?"

Debbie frowned ever so slightly. "She's okay I guess. Tom's death was a shock. It's so sad, but . . ." She shrugged, searching for but not finding the right words.

"I'll see you guys soon," Matt said.

Bobbie turned just in time to see Debbie and Hank coming her way. Out of the corner of her eye, she saw Marcia nearing Matt's group. As soon as the children were within earshot, she called, "Let's head to the car, I have a terrible headache."

Sandy saw Marcia approaching, smiled and raised her arm in a half-wave.

At that moment, Liz smiling broadly, waved. "My goodness, it's Marcia."

"You know her?" Sandy asked, surprised.

"She's my best friend; going to be my matron of honor when John and I get married next month. We used to work together, until just a few months ago. We were stews together, then I went to reservations and she went to work for Larry—the big boss," Liz explained, hugging Marcia when she reached them.

After embracing Liz, Marcia turned to Sandy.

"Marcia, how nice to see you again," Sandy said, shaking the offered hand. "Sorry it's under these circumstances."

Marcia shook her head. "I feel so bad for Bobbie. Tom hadn't listed her yet as someone to notify and she learned of his death on the TV. I should have called her. I just feel terrible."

John and Matt approached just in time to hear Marcia's comment.

Sandy and Matt exchanged startled glances. Sandy quickly recovered. "We saw it on the eleven o'clock news too." Then she changed the subject, "Is your husband with you today? I've wanted to meet him ever since you showed me his trophy room."

Marcia beamed. "No, as usual, he's out of town, but I'll make it a point to introduce you—soon."

"Oh, Marcia, I don't think you've met Commander Tillet. He and Tom were squadron mates when Tom was in the Navy." Sandy said.

She caught the wide-eyed look of surprise. *Oops. Bigmouth, you've let another cat out of the bag.* Quickly recovering, she continued, "Matt, this is Marcia Miller. She worked with Tom at WCA. Her husband is Miles Miller of the Chargers." Then, addressing Marcia, "Matt and John were roommates in Hanoi."

Matt and Marcia shook hands, Marcia also promptly regaining her composure. "It's so nice to meet you, Matt, and a very belated welcome home." Turning to the others, she apologized. "Liz, call me about the wedding plans. But I gotta run. I rode with Larry and he's ready to leave." She turned and smiled. "Matt, it was a real pleasure to meet you. I hope to see you again. Bye, Sandy."

John put his arms around Liz. "We have to go too. We're flying out to New Mexico, so I can introduce Mom to my bride-to-be." He pulled Liz close. "Matt, I'll call you when I get back. You're going to be my best man."

"Looking forward to it." They waved, and he turned to Sandy. "Shall we go, too?" He glanced over where Bobbie had been. She and the kids were gone.

"Now what do you suppose Marcia meant by that comment about Tom not listing Bobbie—yet?" he asked, as he opened the car door.

"I'll bet Tom and Bobbie were about to get married," Sandy speculated.

Matt paused, pursed his lips together and took a deep breath, but said nothing, shutting the door and walking around to the other side.

Sandy glanced at him as he got behind the wheel, and decided to change the subject. "Did you see that tall good-looking brunette over on the right side? I wonder who she was? She really seemed to be distraught."

"No idea." He seemed lost in thought on the rest of the drive home.

CHAPTER 31

<u>San Diego, Summer & Fall, 1974.</u>

After not hearing from Amy for several weeks, out of the blue she had called to let Matt know she would be flying into San Diego during May. With no reference to the New Year's Eve fiasco, she accepted his invitation to have dinner at his new house. She let him know each time she was going to be in town and they returned to casual dating—dinner or a movie. Once in a while, they made it a foursome with Jim and Julie, who were expecting, and ecstatic about it.

It was hard to understand what she wanted their relationship to be. She knew he was seeing someone when she wasn't there. She dropped just enough hints that he was sure she also dated others. Was that supposed to make him jealous? Their relationship—what it was, where it was going—was like the elephant at the party that no one talked about. He couldn't bring himself to openly broach the subject, and both seemed willing to let it proceed without clarification. He liked Amy a lot—as a friend; he liked to be with her. But marriage, particularly with babies, as she seemed to want, wasn't for him. But was he being fair to her? Did she really expect that eventually they'd get married or was he just a convenient San Diego escort?

Amy was flying into San Diego during the month of July, and Matt invited her to have dinner on Saturday night. To avoid a repeat of the January cold spell, he had never mentioned to Sandy that Amy was coming to town again occasionally, and to cover for his upcoming date, he called Sandy Friday evening and told a little white lie. "I'm going to take Hank out to dinner Saturday. I'll call you sometime Sunday, after I take him home."

She protested. "Your divorce is final now. You act like you don't want him to know you date anyone, as if that would be disloyal to his precious mother. Why can't we go out together, like a family?"

"You know how he acts around you. You know how he's been lately. I just want to try to spend a nice evening with my son, and I can't do it if you're there." He tried to sound annoyed.

There was a long pause. "Well, have a good time." He could hear the rancor in her voice. Another pause. "By the way, you shouldn't be so anal retentive about note-keeping. You left your date book open by the phone." This time her voice was as hard as a diamond drill bit. "Enjoy your date with Amy."

The line went dead.

Oh, shit! I've screwed up again.

While waiting for the ice to thaw, as he was sure it would—eventually—Matt decided to go visit his folks. He'd been back to Nebraska only once since returning home. He scheduled a cross-country training flight to Offutt and rented a car.

Spending the weekend in Holt in that old dilapidated farm house with its uneven, sloping floor, and seeing how difficult it was to take care of Mom, now totally bedridden with MS, renewed his desire to buy them a little house in town. Often, in prison, he'd promised himself that when he got home, if he got home and could figure out how to afford it, he was going to try to make his folks' life a little easier.

It still angered him that Dad had always drunk so much and pissed away everything they could have saved. But he softened as he watched his big burley father tenderly caring for his mother, changing her catheter and feeding her. It hadn't been easy for Dad either. But how in the hell could be help them? If only he had more time.

He waited until the next weekend to contact Sandy. First, he had a box of chocolates delivered to her office, then on Friday, he called.

"John and Liz are in town this weekend, and one of John's friends has a ski boat. Would you be interested in going skiing?" He made no mention of their last conversation.

She hesitated for a few moments, then accepted. She hadn't been skiing in ages, and it sounded like fun. No need depriving herself just to punish him.

John and Liz were skiing when they arrived. John's friend, Pete, drove the boat near the shore, allowing John and Liz to glide in. "Hey, Matt, give it a try," John called. Matt protested, "I don't know how. I'm just going to enjoy the beach and watch you guys."

John persisted. "Come on." He demonstrated how to get up, using two skis.

"Go on, Matt, you can do it," Sandy urged.

Several times Matt struggled to get up, spending more time in the water than on it. He was finally able to stay up for one entire turn around the bay.

"Okay," he said as he plopped down on the towel next to Sandy, "your turn."

John handed the skis to Sandy, while Pete idled the boat nearby. She discarded one of the skis, waded out into the water, slipped her right foot into the single ski and leaned back. "Hit it," she yelled.

Pete gunned the engine, and Sandy popped up like a cork. John turned to a surprised Matt. "Look at that! She's cutting a rooster tail that even the chicken himself would envy."

After several turns around the bay, she came in. "Come on, Liz. Come join me."

While Liz and Sandy skied together, jumping the wake, criss-crossing each other, and generally making it look easy, John and Matt sat on the beach, drinking a beer and watching.

"That's quite a gal you got yourself there," John teased.

Matt shook his head. "Every time we're together, I discover something else she can do. I didn't know she even knew how to ski, let alone like *that*. Do you know she's got a private pilot's license, too. At least I've got it over her there; she can't fly a jet—well at least I don't think so."

John laughed. "Sounds like you're a little intimidated."

"Hell no," Matt scoffed, "I'm a lot intimidated. I simply can't figure out how she and Bobbie ever became friends. I've never known two more different women. Bobbie had no interest in anything athletic, and this one can beat me in half the things we do. I swear, I'm going to have to take tennis lessons, she won three of five games the last time we played. That's just downright unacceptable."

John laughed and handed Matt another beer while the girls continued to ski. "Sounds serious."

"She wants a commitment I'm not ready to make, even though everyone else, it seems, thinks I should. The whole squadron's pushing for us to get married. Not a party goes by that at least one of the junior officers' wives doesn't say something, clearly indicating they would look very favorably on a wedding. I'm afraid they're going to be disappointed."

As the girls glided in toward the beach, John grabbed a ski and said over his shoulder, "You may want to re-think that. She's good for you."

October was approaching, and Matt was ready to assume command. The past several months had been difficult, but rewarding. He had learned to fly A-4s and enjoyed the role his squadron played as the adversary in air combat training for the fleet squadrons. It was every pilot's dream—to command his own squadron. It was finally coming true for him, a few years later than most of his peers, but those were the breaks. *Don't dwell. Don't focus on what might have been. Make the best of what is yet to come.* Still, a feeling somewhat akin to remorse shot through him.

He started working on the invitation list for his Change of Command. Right away, he recognized he had a problem. Should he invite Bobbie? Sandy? Amy? All of them? What if they all came? How would he handle the seating?

When she saw the invitation list while helping with some of the arrangements, Sandy commented drolly, "Well, how very nice. All of the women in your life to share your big day. Will we all be 'your date' or are you providing escorts?"

Matt shrugged. He didn't know.

The first acceptance was a telephone call from his sister, Bonnie. "Matt, I'm so thrilled. I've never been to California, and I can't think of a better excuse to come out. I want to see my big brother when he gets his well-deserved squadron. It'll be just me though; Ray can't get away."

Bobbie declined, but Debbie called to say she would bring Hank with her.

Amy called to accept. "I'm really looking forward to your Change of Command. I know you'll be busy that morning, so Jim and Julie will pick me up. Thank you for asking me."

As the acceptances poured in, Sandy seemed to enjoy watching him squirm. She was aware who was coming, but instead of being peeved, as he expected, she seemed to get some perverse pleasure out of his predicament. "Poor baby, got yourself in a bit of a pickle, huh?" She gave him a cheeky grin.

"No shit, Sherlock," he growled under his breath.

But her continued flippancy served its purpose, and slowly he began to laugh. It was a predicament of his own making. "You're as full of shit as a Christmas duck," he said with mock sternness as he rose from the chair, grabbed a pillow and tossed it at her. She dodged, grasped his arm, and in the scuffle that followed she ended up on the floor in his arms. He could work on his dilemma another time. One way to shut her up was to keep her mouth otherwise occupied. He did a masterful job, even if he said so himself.

The day before the ceremony, Matt had to resolve the problem. He had to give the junior officers who were acting as ushers a seating chart for the special guests. His children and Sis would be seated on the front row. That was all of his family that would be there, so he could fill up the rest of the row with others. He really hadn't asked either Amy or Sandy to be his "date." But he was sure both expected to be.

Sandy would be bringing Bonnie, so it would be awkward to separate them, but this meant seating Sandy in the first or second seat. Since Amy was coming with Jim and Julie, he seated them on the outside edge of the front row. No doubt there would be repercussions about that placement, but it was the best arrangement he could think of, and he could explain his reasoning later to Amy, if she objected. It would be a very busy day, and he'd have to be attending to *all* his guests, so maybe he could get away with treating neither of them as "dates," that is unless Amy was staying overnight.

At 1100 hours, with the gonging of the bell and the blowing of the boatswain's whistle, Rear Admiral A. S. "Smokey" Swanson, the speaker for the ceremony, arrived.

As the Honor Guard bearing the flags approached the reviewing stand down the center aisle, Matt glanced at his guests. As was customary, those attending for the outgoing CO were seated on one side of the aisle, and those for the incoming CO on the other. The right side was full of Commander Robinson's family: his wife, children, parents and his two brothers and their families. He had so many there, they took up two rows. Matt's guests were to the left as he looked out. Sandy was in the first seat, next to Bonnie, then Debbie and Hank. John and Liz were next, and then came Jim, Julie and finally Amy in the farthest outside chair.

Wistfully, he noted the few "family" on his side of the aisle. Of course Mom couldn't come, and Dad wouldn't fly, and wouldn't leave Mom alone in any event, even for a few days. He wished otherwise, but it couldn't be. Melvin and his wife certainly could have come with Bonnie, but he didn't even receive a reply from them. Matt mentally shrugged as he thought of the inexplicably strained relationship with his younger brother. And Bobbie. They'd gone through a lot together. Too bad, now that there were some rewards, they weren't able to share them.

He looked out at the crowd. He might have a small "family" contingent, but he was overwhelmed at the number of friends who were in the audience. He saw many familiar faces on both sides of the aisle, and no empty seats.

He noticed Amy peering curiously toward the center aisle, toward the flags and Sandy. At that moment, Sandy, her long auburn hair glistening in the San Diego sunshine, had her back to Amy, intently watching the advancing Color Guard.

Matt still didn't know if Amy had to fly out today. *It's going to be very interesting after the reception. How do I get myself in these messes? And how in hell do I handle two dates?* He dismissed the thought, concentrating instead on his own brief remarks to be given in a few minutes. He had almost memorized his speech, having practiced it so many times, but Sandy, at his request, had typed it for him using a large font in case his memory failed him.

The Admiral rose and walked to the podium. After acknowledging the outgoing CO's wife, children and extensive family, Admiral Swanson directed his remarks to Matt's family. "We're very happy to have with us Commander Tillet's son, Henry, his daughter, Debbie, and his sister who came out just for this day all the way from Nebraska, Mrs. Bonnie Layton." Then, with Sandy sitting where a wife would normally sit, he nodded toward her, gave her a friendly smile, and said, "And Sandy, it's very nice to have you with us, as always."

Oh, shit. Matt swallowed hard. It had never occurred to him that the Admiral would so "personalize" his address.

The reaction was immediate. From under his hat brim, lowered to cover his red face, Matt observed two or three open mouths, one noticeably belonged to Amy. If she had any doubts before about how much time he spent with Sandy when she wasn't around, she didn't after Admiral Swanson's welcoming remarks.

Sandy couldn't have scuttled her competition better if she had used a torpedo. Could she have put the Admiral up to it? No. He wouldn't put it past *her*, and the Admiral was a practical joker, but he wouldn't intentionally embarrass the incoming CO, even as a prank. But Matt no longer had to worry about how he was going to juggle two dates; the Admiral had solved that for him, probably permanently.

After the ceremony, Matt and Commander Robinson went to the head of the receiving line. Jim was the first one through the line.

"Congratulations, buddy, you really deserve this," he said. They shook hands and Jim patted him heartily on the shoulders.

Julie, almost eight months pregnant, gave him a hug. "This is as close as I can get," she teased, patting her large tummy. "We're so happy for you."

Next came Amy, her well-practiced airline stewardess smile firmly in place. "Congratulations, Matt."

"Will you be staying? Perhaps we can get together later," Matt asked, holding her hand, but holding little hope for a positive response.

"Sorry. I'm flying out this afternoon. I knew you would be . . .

busy . . . but thanks for including me in your big day." She extracted her hand from his. "We have to go now."

"Call me when you're in town," he urged. "I think we should talk."

She tilted her head and gave him a "you've got to be kidding" look, smiled her practiced smile, and left.

John and Liz came through next. "Well, pal, now you've really got your squadron. Congratulations. I'm still waiting, but I've got orders as XO of a squadron at China Lake. We're headed up there right now to check out housing, so can't stay, but couldn't miss your big day."

Over the past year, Sandy had attended many Navy functions. She often found herself sitting with the Admiral and his wife, while Matt was off tending to whatever Matt tended to at those things. She saw them and waved.

"Hi. Nice ceremony," Mrs. Swanson smiled, as Sandy joined them at one of the buffet tables.

"Yes," Sandy smiled, "it was." She turned to the admiral. "Sir, I think you may have been very instrumental in helping to eliminate some of my competition."

Both of them looked at her quizzically.

When she finished explaining, the Admiral's wife raised her hand to her face. "Oh, my God. How embarrassing that must have been for Matt." Then she added, "But deserved. The idea—inviting two dates."

The admiral shook his head. "That is terrible," he said. "If only I'd known, I'd have handled it differently. But, I've never seen Matt with anyone but you. I thought you guys were good as married."

"Thank you, Admiral." She couldn't help smiling, even though she felt bad for Amy. "You may have helped that along."

Just then Matt joined them. "Admiral, I wanted to thank you for being our speaker."

The Admiral harrumphed noticeably. "Well, as I understand from this young lady, there may be a problem."

Matt frowned and furrowed his brows.

"The Commander's failure to properly brief his senior officer on his 'extenuating circumstances' is going to be properly reflected in his next fitness report," the Admiral proclaimed sternly, then grinned.

Matt looked at Sandy, his face still mirroring concern and uncertainty. She crinkled her nose. Slowly it dawned on him. She'd told the Admiral. Now he was doubly embarrassed. He shook his head at Sandy, frowning, then clearing his throat, he turned to the Admiral. "Sir, I'd like you to meet my sister and my son and daughter."

Hank's behavior put a severe dent in an otherwise near-perfect day for Sandy. Anytime she came near, he gave her a look of pure hatred. Whenever he saw her approaching while he was standing by Matt, he deliberately turned and walked away. Even when Matt scolded him for his rudeness, he just stared sullenly.

Debbie, on the other hand, was gracious toward Sandy, and noticeably more attentive and affectionate toward Matt. No doubt Tom's tragic death had removed the biggest obstacle to the complete normalization of their relationship.

The crowd cleared out except for a few hardy stragglers. Matt gathered his little group together, "Let's go over to the house," he suggested.

Hank turned to Debbie. "Take me home first," he demanded pointedly.

Matt's shoulders slumped. "I wish you'd come to the house. Aunt Bonnie would like to spend some time with you and Debbie."

"No. I want to go home." He shot another dagger at Sandy.

Matt shut his eyes and breathed deeply, controlling his response. "Okay, if that's what you want. We'll pick you up about eight-thirty or nine in the morning. We going to show Aunt Bonnie the Zoo and Sea World. Couldn't let her miss that on her first trip to San Diego."

Hank's face assumed a pout. "I don't want to go. I've done that before." He turned and started to the door. "Debbie, can we go now?" He disappeared into the hallway.

Sandy spoke quietly to Matt. "You know, I'm not going to be able to go with you tomorrow either. I promised one of my salesmen that I would cover for him at an open house." She put her hand on Matt's shoulder. "Honey, I bet if you asked Hank again and told him it would be just you all, he'll probably change his mind and go. Why don't you ask him?"

Matt's lips formed a thin line. "No. Thanks for the offer of the 'unexpected appointment,' but if he doesn't want to go with *all* of us, he can stay home. I'm fed up with his inexcusable behavior." He turned on his heel and walked over to Debbie.

"Dad, I'm sorry. I'm not going to be able to go tomorrow either. The choir is going up to L.A. for a concert. I'll take Hank home and then come over to your house. I want to spend some time with Aunt Bonnie."

Matt, Sandy and Bonnie spent Saturday at the Zoo and Sunday at Sea World.

"Sis, I've got to go in today. It's my first day as skipper—wouldn't look good if I didn't show, but I'll try to get away around noon to take you to the airport," Matt explained as he prepared to leave on Monday morning.

Bonnie wrapped her arms around him. "Go enjoy yourself, big brother. I'm so proud of you. Sandy will be here soon, and she and I will get along just fine, don't worry about us. I just can't tell you how happy I am for you."

He placed his uniform hat on his head and started toward the door.

"You look so handsome." She breathed deep and smiled contentedly. "By the way," she teased, an impish smile on her face, "I like Sandy."

He grinned and nodded his head. "Yeah, I guess she's kind of likeable—in a strange sort of way."

Sandy arrived just after Matt had driven away.

"Come on upstairs and visit while I finish packing," Bonnie invited.

By noon, they hadn't heard from Matt. Bonnie was concerned. "How long does it take to get to the airport?"

Sandy thought it strange he hadn't called, but tried not to let on. "Oh, it's less than a half hour. But, if he doesn't show in the next few minutes, we probably better go ahead. Who knows, he's probably busy, and couldn't get away."

They were loading Bonnie's luggage into Sandy's car. "I think I hear the phone," Sandy said as she raced back inside.

She was pale when she came back to the car. "He lost two pilots in a mid-air collision this morning."

"Oh, my goodness," Bonnie gasped.

"I'll take you to the airport. He's going to be tied up until late tonight. One of the guys was married. He'll have to notify the wife."

CHAPTER 32

San Diego, Late 1974, Early 1975.

Dealing with Hank continued to be a challenge. Whenever Matt called, Hank made one excuse after another not to see him. Shortly before Christmas, Matt called again. Bobbie answered. "I heard about the mid-air. I'm sorry," she said, sounding genuinely sympathetic.

"Thanks. The one fella's wife has gone back to Florida, where her folks live. They didn't have any children. The other guy was single." He paused. "You doing okay . . . I mean . . . well . . . I haven't seen you since Tom's services. Are you getting along okay?"

There was a long pause. "I . . . ." He heard a sharp intake, then her voice sounded stronger. "I'm doing fine, really, but thank you for asking."

There was a moment of silence, then she continued. "I really wish you'd do something with Hank. I can't handle him. He doesn't mind a thing I say. I wish you'd talk to him."

Matt could feel a flush starting in his neck. His voice became sharp. "For Christ's sake, Bobbie. I haven't seen the kid since his outrageous display at my Change of Command. Every time I call he's going to the beach, or 'has other plans.' I was calling today to see if I was going to be able to get together with him and Debbie at Christmas. I'd like to have them come over at least part of the day."

A long silence. "Maybe it would work better if you came over here and spent the day with us. I know Hank doesn't like to be around Sandy."

"Oh, shit. Look, Bobbie, we aren't married anymore, and it's time he understood that—that you and I aren't going to get back together, that I'm not going to come back there to live, and that you and I are going to see other people. He does know about you and Tom by now, doesn't he?" It was a struggle, but he was trying to keep his voice at a decent level.

Another long pause. "I'll ask him if he'll spend Christmas with you, but I can't promise."

Matt sighed. "Look, I'll call you back in a couple of days. Check with Debbie. I'd like to have part of my family at least a few hours at Christmas, if that's not too damn much to ask."

"I'm usually home by five-thirty, so call after that." There was a long enough pause that Matt thought she had hung up, then he heard her exhale. "Matt . . . he'll come."

Matt sat on the stool by his kitchen bar and bowed his head. *Damn.* How did things go so unbelievably wrong? What in the hell could he do to change them?

Now he had to deal with Sandy. She wasn't going to like to be excluded, even for a part of Christmas Day, but he had to try to spend some pleasant time with Hank and Debbie, and that wouldn't happen if Sandy was there, unfair as it might be to her. As much as he'd like to delay the confrontation, waiting to get this handled wouldn't make it easier, and if she exploded, she'd have time to get over it by Christmas. Or not. Nothing he planned these days went the way he expected, so why should this be any different? He hoped she wouldn't stay mad long—he didn't want to be alone for the rest of the holidays.

He picked up the phone. "Hi, want to come over? I'm about to burn a burger on the grill. I could do two just as easy."

"Half hour." She sounded so chipper. That would change, he knew.

After dinner, Matt announced, "I've invited Debbie and Hank over for Christmas." He braced himself.

"Oh, that's great. I'll display my cooking prowess and fix a turkey dinner with all the trimmings." Her voice was excited.

Oh, shit. This is not going well. She didn't understand what I meant.

"Honey, I . . . I . . . well . . . Oh, well, what the hell," he muttered under his breath, but she heard. "Hank won't come if you're here." He couldn't look her in the eye, but he saw enough before he turned away.

"Oh." She swallowed, searched the ceiling for cobwebs or something, and swallowed again. "I see." She blinked rapidly, then took a deep breath, sitting very rigid, her hands clasped in her lap. A long uncomfortable silence. Finally, she looked at him with the intensity of a sniper with the target in her cross hairs. "You've been divorced for almost a year. Bobbie was about to marry her lover, and Hank still blames *me*." Her voice rose ever so slightly. "And you aren't doing one damn thing to tell him the truth?" He could tell it was a question by the inflection at the end, so why did it sound so much like a condemnation or accusation?

"Honey, please don't be angry," Matt pleaded. "It's just for the day . . . ."

She didn't let him finish. She rose from the couch and headed to the door. "I'm not angry," she said calmly. "Hurt a little. Disappointed is a better word. Matt, I've heard you and your friends talking, and I have a pretty good idea what you went through in prison. I think you're one of the strongest men I've ever known. You're one of the few men I really admire. That's important to me. That's one reason I hang in even when you act like it's useless. But, how can you be so strong and yet so damn weak at the same time—when it comes to dealing with Bobbie? She doesn't deserve whatever it is that's holding you back."

She threw one parting shot over her shoulder as she left. "Where in the hell did you leave your guts—check 'em at Clark?"

Well, at least she didn't slam the door. He waited, listening for the screeching tires. Nothing. Maybe that was a good sign—or maybe not. He almost preferred the explosion, it was more predictable, and might be over sooner.

He sat for a long time, the TV blaring in the background, but paying it no attention. Despite her harsh words, he couldn't be angry at Sandy. As usual, she called 'em as she saw 'em, and he hated to admit, she saw 'em pretty clearly. He was a bit of a wimp where

Bobbie was concerned, and he wasn't exactly sure why.

He called Bobbie again the day before Christmas. "You didn't answer my question the other day. Does Hank know about you and Tom? Does he think Sandy is the reason we got a divorce?"

Bobbie's voice was defensive. "It *was* Sandy's fault. If she'd just kept her mouth shut, I was ready to break it off with Tom, but I knew when you found out about us that it was too late. You'd never forgive me. If she'd just kept out of it . . . ."

"Dammit to hell, Bobbie, that's bullshit and you know it. You can't shift the blame for your actions. The truth was going to come out sooner or later. I already suspected something. If you'd just told me from the beginning, like when I asked you on the way home from the hospital in the car. It didn't take long for me to figure out there'd been someone else. But, if you'd said it was over, you were sorry—we could have gone on. It wouldn't have been without problems, but we could have worked it out. I even tried to get back together after I found out—but you wouldn't even go to Washington with me. You were the one who didn't give us a chance."

"That's not true! But I felt so guilty. I just knew you'd never forgive me." She was sobbing.

"Oh, quit bawling . . . ." He just couldn't conjure up any sympathy. "So, does . . . Hank . . . know . . . about . . . you . . . and . . . Tom?" He punctuated each word.

She sniffled. "I don't know what he thinks."

"Dammit, Bobbie. Can't you see what this is doing to the kid? Can't you just this once put your son first, and tell him the truth? How can I 'talk to him,' as you asked the other night, if he refuses to see me, if he hates me for something he thinks I've done?"

He heard more sobbing. "Oh, crap. This isn't getting us anywhere. Tell Debbie to come over as early as they are up and about." He slammed down the phone.

Sandy's words echoed in his ears. "Her lie is destroying your only chance for a real relationship with your son. You've got to tell Hank what has happened. It just isn't fair to either of you to continue like this. He's rejecting you because he feels *you've* rejected him, in favor of 'that horrible woman'—me. This is his way of getting back at you. Even though Bobbie has told him about the divorce, she obviously didn't explain the reason why, and he still blames me and you." It was pretty clear she was right. He'd dug himself one of those stupid Vietnamese fox holes, and it was filling with water. But how could he correct it now? Hank wouldn't believe him. He could fly supersonic jets; he could land those same jets on a bucking ship in the middle of a choppy ocean; he could train men to go into battle; and he had withstood as well as any of them the torture meted out by the Vietnamese. So, why couldn't he figure out how to deal with women and little boys? He'd just never thought about how complicated relationships could be.

Debbie and Hank arrived a little before noon on Christmas Day. "Wow. You look very Christmassy," Matt said as he admired his daughter's red and white outfit.

Just then Hank sauntered in, carrying a handful of packages. "Where'd you want these?" he snarled.

Matt turned to look at his son and winced. His mid-back-length stringy hair looked like it hadn't been shampooed in weeks. A good bet was that it hadn't been near a comb either. His jeans were ragged in the knees and along the bottoms, and his tee-shirt was dirty and torn.

Matt caught himself before he let out a gasp. He couldn't believe the change in only two months. He recovered sufficiently to speak. "Bring them over by the tree . . . here, let me help you."

"No need." Hank turned away as Matt approached, then dumped the wrapped boxes on the couch and floor.

Matt rubbed his hands together, completely unsure of what to do next. He started by putting on a cheerful face. "Well, how shall we handle this? Your old dad is trying his hand at cooking a turkey. It should be done about three. Shall we open presents before—or—I bought a Monopoly game. We could play a couple games first, then eat, and then open presents?"

Debbie went into the kitchen. "Dad, the turkey smells great."

"What you lookin for?" he asked as he heard her opening cabinet doors.

"I'm looking for glasses. Why don't I fix us a Coke, and we can play Monopoly first. Do you have any chips or pretzels?"

Matt showed her where the Cokes and glasses were, pulled a bag of chips out of the cupboard and broke open the game.

Hank had sprawled out on the couch and clicked on the television.

"Son, you shouldn't slouch like that, it's bad for your posture."

"Who cares," Hank sneered.

Matt bit his lip. "Come on. Let's see if I can beat you guys."

Debbie sat three Cokes and a bowl of chips on the table and started sorting the money.

"I don't want to play," Hank announced, picking up the TV remote.

Debbie saw the look on her father's face. "Come on, chump. Don't be a punk. It'll be fun. Besides, it my turn to win."

"No, I don't wanna—go ahead—I'll watch TV." He slumped more.

Matt inhaled sharply. He'd like to pop the kid alongside the chops, and kick his butt, but maybe Hank would snap out of it if he said nothing. Getting into a pissing contest with him on Christmas wasn't going to help their sputtering relationship.

Debbie grumbled something inaudible in Hank's direction, then turned to Matt. "Okay, Dad, let's see how good you are," she said cheerily.

After dinner, Debbie and Matt cleared the table and washed dishes. Hank immediately returned to his spot on the couch, blending in like a used throw pillow. They had been unable to draw him into any meaningful conversation. His responses were one or two syllable grunts, reminding Matt of the Vietnamese turnkeys.

"Okay, time for opening presents." Debbie put on a red hat trimmed with white fur and a white tassel. "I get to hand them out." Then she turned toward her brother. "Turn off the TV, jerk, and get your fanny over here." She laughed, but there was something in her tone that even Matt recognized meant business. He chided himself. He should be the one exercising discipline. He'd always been the disciplinarian in the family. What happened?

Hank reluctantly crawled over to the tree, but his etched-in-stone pout remained securely in place. Debbie handed him a box, which he proceeded to open as if it was doing someone else a favor. Matt waited. Hank stood up and held the wetsuit against his frame, measuring it for size. Slowly, a smile crept over his face. "Gee, Dad, thanks."

"There's another package out in the garage. It was too big to wrap. Go check to the right of the back door." Matt pointed.

Hank jumped up and ran through the enclosed patio to the garage. He was beaming as he carried a shiny surfboard back into the house.

"Wow. This is just what I've been wanting. How did you know?" He rushed over and hugged Matt.

"Well, I went to that shop where we went last year, and they told me what you'd been eyeing."

"That's great, Dad. Thanks."

We should have opened presents earlier, if that's what it took to change his behavior.

Too soon it was time for them to leave. "Son, when do I get to see you show off that new board?" he asked, hoping maybe the gift had "bought" him a better relationship.

"Maybe this weekend. Call me."

It was late Wednesday evening, and Matt hadn't taken any leave; he had to work Thursday and Friday. It was probably too late to ask Sandy to come over, but he sure could use her company. Today had been a bitch. Given her cool reserve since he told her of his plans, he wouldn't bet any serious money on it. With a prayer to the Sailors' Patron Saint of Hopeless Causes, he called. "Hi, I just wanted to wish you a Merry Christmas."

"Merry Christmas to you, too. Did you have a nice day with the children?" He could detect no anger, but her voice lacked its usual brightness.

"Well, let's say it was an interesting experience. I'll tell you about it when I see you. Honey, look, I'm sorry about . . . ."

"Forget it," she interrupted. "He's your son. You've gotta do what you've gotta do."

There was that tone again—dull, disappointed, dispirited. He'd prefer angry. With that he knew what to expect. "I've got some turkey left. Would you like to come over?" he ventured.

"When, tonight?" A sudden change in the tone and velocity

betrayed her controlled sound of disbelief. "You're out of your mind. Call me this weekend—if you don't have other plans." She hung up.

He could still hear the sarcasm in her voice, which could portray exactly how she was feeling better than anyone he knew. Or maybe it was just that she was less reserved about expressing how she felt than anyone he knew. Whatever—he knew where he stood; it wasn't going to be in *her* arms tonight. But, he was also confident it would thankfully all blow over in a day or two.

Hank's changed behavior resulting from his delight at his Christmas gifts lasted about a month. During that period Matt went to beach to watch him surf, and they went to a Chargers game. Matt's invitations to come over to the house or go out to dinner were rejected, and by mid-February Hank was back to displaying his former hostility, and usually was unavailable when Matt called.

After dinner one evening and a few too many drinks, Matt's frustration exploded as rage at Bobbie. He ranted to Sandy. "Why doesn't she make that kid get a haircut? Why doesn't she exercise more discipline? He is becoming a delinquent, and she does nothing."

"Why don't you?" she asked laconically.

"It's hard enough to do anything with him," he said defensively. " We spend so little time, I don't want to waste it all fussing at him about his hair or his dirty clothes or his grades, or his attitude."

"It isn't going to get any better until Hank knows the truth. You're not being fair to either one of you." She never varied from what she recommended.

"You may be right, but you don't understand. I don't know what Bobbie has said to him, but if I try to tell him the truth now, I don't think he'll believe me. And if he did, it would shatter his feelings for his mother. I can't do that. They got along—together—without me for several years, and I don't feel like coming back and coming between them. Right now, he's all she's got."

"This isn't about what Bobbie needs. She forfeited that. *Hank* needs a father, *Hank* needs at least one responsible *parent*. You show you care by exercising some discipline, teaching him right from wrong, proper behavior, proper dress and proper appearance, not by ignoring what he is becoming. He's laughing at your standards and throwing them in your face to get back at you. He wants you to be aware of his obnoxious behavior—anything, just so you'll have to notice him. He's furious at you for leaving. And since you have chosen to leave Bobbie on her exalted throne in his eyes, he's angry for another reason. You abandoned not only him, but his beloved mother as well."

Matt shook his head in protest, but Sandy continued stubbornly. "He was a good boy when you came home. Oh, he needed a firm hand now and then, but what kid doesn't?" Her demeanor softened. "Remember how excited he was the day you came home from the hospital? You were his hero, and he made no bones about it. He wanted the whole world to know."

Just as quickly, her face hardened. "Now he's turning into a real problem child. He needs help, he needs you. He needs you to be a father—not a bystander. You need to provide a home for him on a regular basis."

Stung by the irritating realization that he should have followed her advice months ago, Matt lashed out. "You'd use any ploy to get me to marry you, wouldn't you?"

Sandy rubbed her forehead and pushed some hair back. "Matt, you're a fool. I wasn't talking about us. I wasn't even *thinking* about us. I'm talking about your relationship with your son. I've heard you and your friends discuss the tap code and the various methods you used to communicate in prison. Hank's sending messages; he has a code too. Why don't you work as hard trying to crack *it*?"

"Yeah. And what makes you the expert? Just how many kids have you raised?" He was being hateful and he knew it, but he couldn't stop himself. He was mad at himself, but it was easier to take it out on her.

Sandy clenched her jaw and stood up. "I'm going home. If you don't want my opinion, don't ask for it. But think about this—when you stick your head up your ass, you lose four of your five senses."

CHAPTER 33

<u>Late 1975.</u>

The end of Matt's command was fast approaching. As soon as he received the word of his next set of orders, he called Sandy to share the news, even though he knew she wouldn't be thrilled. She wasn't in, so he left a message.

A few minutes later the phone rang in his office in the squadron spaces.

"Hey, Tilt. What you up to these days?" asked the male voice on the other end.

"John? Is that you? Where in the hell are you?"

"We're in town for just today. Liz and Marcia and some of her other WCA friends—about six of the gals—get together every year for a dinner to celebrate who the hell knows what." He laughed. "How about you and I grabbing a bite tonight?"

"Sure. Come on over to the house. I'll burn us a burger. See you there in a half hour."

John, looking tan, fit and trim was parked out front when Matt arrived.

"So, how's the duty up at China Lake?" Matt inquired as he unlocked the front door and they went inside.

"Not bad. Flying's good. There's a couple of decent ski slopes within a short drive, so we're taking up skiing. You and Sandy will have to come up this winter. We got base housing that's pretty nice, and Liz has fixed it up like a show place. . . ." He breathed deeply and smiled. "Matt, I'm a lucky sonofabitch. Liz is the best thing that ever happened to me." He paused, looking around Matt's town-house. "Hey, place looks great. I definitely see a woman's touch here. Looks like Sandy has been decorating her nest. Any marriage plans yet?"

"Shit! Not you too." Matt derided. "*Sandy* has plans. The squadron wives have plans. Even the Admiral has plans. I just don't know. I really don't know what I want. I don't know what to do with her, or what I'd do without her. One thing is certain, it ain't dull. But I can't convince myself I'm ready for marriage."

"Umm . . . well, it worked out okay for Jim and me. Say, have you seen Jim and Julie's little boy? He's a button. They really seem happy."

"Yeah, I know they do," Matt admitted, still surprised at their solid relationship given the short time they had known each other before getting married. "You did know that Mike and Rachel had a little boy, didn't you?"

"Yeah. We got the announcement, but I haven't seen him. Liz and I are even trying to have a baby. Figured I couldn't let another bomber puke outdo me." He laughed again, then turned somber. "But to tell the truth, it isn't looking too good. You know, Liz is already thirty-seven. Her biological clock doesn't seem to be coop-erating. We've put our name on an adoption list, just in case."

"How . . . umm . . . n-n-nice," Matt sputtered.

"Don't be sarcastic, asshole." John admonished. "I wasn't too thrilled at first, but I'm warming to the idea. I missed most of my three kids' childhood, and like Jim's, they don't seem to miss me now. I think now that I'm a little older, I could be a better father. I'm a damn sight better husband." He winked.

"Yeah, yeah. Quit bragging, Stud," Matt joshed, then continued, "No, I mean it. If that's what you guys want, that's great. Honest. I just don't know what I want. Sandy's hot for marriage, but I don't think she's hot for kids. That's a plus. John, it's a pisser. I don't want to be alone, but I don't want to risk leaving a wife again while I go to sea."

John frowned and popped another beer. "Got your orders?"

"Talked to my detailer today. Going to be the Executive Officer on a small carrier. It's based here in San Diego, but it's in the

Western Pacific right now."

"Well, congratulations. I know that's what you've wanted. Me—I'm not eager for sea duty if I can help it. Wanna snuggle every night with my baby." He grinned broadly.

Matt shook his head in mock censure, took out some hamburger, formed it into patties and lit the charcoal grill on the patio just off the dining room.

John followed Matt out to the patio. "Personally, I think Sandy's good for you. You can be pretty uptight about some things. She keeps you on your toes, and makes you laugh a little in spite of yourself. That can be a difficult assignment—I know from experience— you tend to see the half-empty glass all the time—and she does it well. That gal knows more jokes than a drunken sailor. She's a real pistol."

"One that needs a silencer," Matt chuckled as he turned the burgers. Then his face sobered. "I just don't want to make another mistake."

"Horse pucky. You can't compare Sandy with your ex. Besides, you're a man used to making split-second decisions—you couldn't fly a damn fighter jet if you didn't."

"Quit lecturing," Matt scolded. "You sound like her agent."

"Coward. You haven't changed much. You're still an insufferable hard ass, just like you were in prison," John argued.

Matt walked back into the kitchen, handing the plates and silverware to John. He was starting to feel just the slightest bit of irritation with John, as he often had in Vietnam. He tried to use a joke as a diplomatic exit. "Besides, if the Navy intended me to have a wife, they'd have issued me one."

John ignored Matt's attempt at levity. "You're a fuckin' uptight puritan. My only question is what in the hell does she see in you?"

Matt shrugged faintly and changed the subject. "Isn't it a hell of a note what's going on in Vietnam?"

John shook his head sadly. "I can't believe all we went through there was for nothing. The military could have won that war so easily. It really galls me to see this happening."

"The military brought the North to their knees in 1972—we *had* won the war," Matt corrected. "Why in the hell did the politicians give it away in less than three years. What was it all for anyway? Why were we over there—if it wasn't to free those people from tyranny? Now the South Vietnamese are going to be slaughtered."

John shook his head again. "And the Commies will just keep gobbling up those other little countries."

Matt nodded, "I think with Nixon's troubles here at home and all the anti-war shit that went on when we were gone, there just wasn't the political will to win."

"I'd sure hate to think we spent all that time over there, lost our families, and some of us—like Steve—lost a lot more—all for nothing," Matt grumbled as he took up the burgers.

"Me, too," John agreed.

"Speaking of prison, did you hear about Wilson?" Matt asked.

"No, what's up?"

"He's going back to England as deputy base commander of that base right outside of London—Alconbury, I think it's called. He'll be back in his old stomping grounds. He called from back East. Sounds like everything is going great with Bridgette and the girls."

"That's great. Hope he has an extra room for me and Liz when we go to England. Jim made Commander and is getting a new job too."

"I hadn't heard. What is it?"

"A training squadron at Beeville."

"Good. Oh, I saw Craig Hansen the other day at North Island at a Change of Command. He's getting a ship—can't remember the name—Tulsa, Waco, something like that. It's one of the support ships to a carrier group like the one I'll be on. Different carrier though."

They finished eating and Matt cleared the table.

"So, you ready to move on? Ready for that sea duty you've lusted after?"

Matt stared out the patio window for several seconds. Finally, he replied. "Well, I'm trying to keep competitive. I'd like to screen for command of a carrier or a base. But, I guess if I could, I'd stay on as squadron skipper indefinitely. It's the best job I've had in the Navy. We've had a good group of guys this year. Five of my junior officers are former POWs, younger guys that got shot down late in the war."

"How's Roy doing?" John asked as he followed Matt into the living room with a fresh can of beer.

"He's my XO, you know."

"Sure. Change of Command for two of my old roomies. Wouldn't want to miss that." John leaned back on the couch and laced his fingers behind his head.

"He and Kat are real troopers, except well . . . Kat has been sort of cool toward Sandy—polite but distant. I guess she thinks she would be disloyal to Bobbie if she were nice to Sandy. If only she knew!"

"Yeah, Liz got the same treatment from some of the 'old wives,' as she calls them. So what did Sandy do?"

"Nothing. Well, actually, she defended 'em. Said they all went through a lot together, and it's understandable they'd stick together. I guess since no one knows about Bobbie's affair, it's safe to assume some of them think Sandy broke up my marriage."

John held up a pack of cigarettes and nodded toward the patio. They walked outside.

"Well, she's being kind. Everyone knew about my wife's affair and how she dumped me that first night home, and some of them are still cool to Liz." John lit a cigarette and took a deep drag, looking around the patio. "Don't you even *own* an ashtray?"

Matt went back into the kitchen and found one. "Here." He set it on the small patio table. "I see you're still driving those nails. I thought Liz wanted you to quit."

"She does."

"In fact, I thought Liz said you *had* quit."

"Umm . . . well . . ." John shrugged. "I don't smoke in the house or in front of her, but I take the dog for a lot of walks. Just keep it between you and me, okay?"

Matt snorted. "Dumbshit. A non-smoker can tell when her lover is smoking."

John grinned. "Now who's lecturing?" He looked at his watch. "Jeez, look at the time. I've got to pick Liz up in twenty minutes. Tell Sandy we said hello and don't forget what I said. You're a fool if you let her get away."

After John left, Matt finished the dishes, the words echoing in his ear. He definitely didn't want to let her get away, but why couldn't things stay the way they were? Why was everyone pushing for marriage? They didn't need a piece of paper to do things together, to have fun together.

He finished the last of his beer, and leaned back on the couch. After about fifteen minutes, frustrated, he flicked on the TV. Analyzing relationships, particularly his own, was not his thing. He felt completely out of his element.

He was almost asleep when the phone rang. It was Sandy. "Hi, got your message. Sorry, I was having dinner with some business associates. What's up?"

"I'm going to be the XO of a small carrier."

"Well . . . ." There was that telltale pause while she tried to figure out how to respond honestly without sounding too negative, the way he knew she'd feel. "I guess you're pleased. You're getting your precious sea duty. What happens now?"

"I go back to Newport, Rhode Island for three month's XO-CO school. That'll be over before Christmas. Then I fly out to the PI right after the first of the year to join the ship for the end of this cruise and ride it home."

"Oh . . . well . . . congratulations." It sounded like she was going to choke on those words.

A couple of weeks before the trip, Sandy dropped by Matt's townhouse after work. "I just finished showing some property up the street, and thought I'd see if you were home." She walked over to where he was sitting and looked over his shoulder at the maps and tour guides covering the table.

"You know," he said, turning to face her, "I'm glad you stopped by. I was just thinking about you."

She raised an eyebrow. "That's nice. It's comforting to know you think about me sometimes when I'm not around." She leaned over and kissed him lightly on the cheek. "Sometimes I wonder."

"Oh, I think of you now and then, but don't let it go to your head." He rose from his chair and gave her a more appropriate welcome. "Actually, I was thinking about having someone go with me on the trip. Somehow you came to mind."

Well, it's about time, you jerk. She'd make him pay now for waiting so damn long and taking her for granted. She'd almost had to wire her mouth shut these past few weeks, as had been done when she wrecked a motorcycle and broke her jaw, to keep from asking why he hadn't invited her to go, but her pride wouldn't permit her to invite herself.

Although normally a spontaneous person, she knew the value of a poker face. Her grandfather had taught her to be a card shark before she was old enough to go to school. Right now she felt like she had drawn to an inside straight. "Oh, how so?"

"Would you like to drive back with me?" he asked. "If you could get away, that is." He waited for her expected enthusiastic acceptance.

She bit her lower lip, shaking her head ever so slightly. *Let him squirm.* She'd be damned if she was going to give him the satisfaction of knowing how much she wanted to go. "You'll be gone— what—two or three weeks?"

He watched her face. Normally, when she was excited, she didn't have to say a thing. But she wasn't displaying the exuberance he expected. It hadn't occurred to him that she wouldn't want to go. Maybe he should have said something sooner. "Yeah, two to three weeks. I have it all laid out. Look here." He pointed to his maps. "We could stop at a few sights along the way, then stop in Nebraska to visit my folks. I'd need to spend about a week there, but I could show you my old watering holes. Then, we could head up north and cross over into Canada." He followed the map with his finger. "Drive through this part of Canada, and then drop back across the border here at Niagara Falls." He finished tracing the trip. "You could fly back from Providence."

He looked at her expectantly. "Could you get away that long?"

"Well . . . if I'd had more notice, I might . . . um." She puckered her mouth as if considering a deep dilemma.

He couldn't believe she didn't want to go; he'd been counting on it. Just then, he detected the mischievous twinkle in her eyes. "You asshole. You've been putting me on."

"I love it when you kiss ass," she smirked.

He gathered her in his arms. "Don't give me any sexy ideas." He kissed her roughly. "Stay with me tonight." He stroked her cheekbone and rubbed the tip of her nose.

"I don't have any pajamas here."

"All the better," he retorted, leering.

Driving home the next morning, Sandy reviewed this latest somewhat surprising turn of events. Asking her to go, to meet his folks, maybe that was a good omen. After two years she could certainly use a little encouragement. It also meant she could help him realize one of his dreams, but she wanted it to be a surprise. She was glad she'd kept her mouth shut for a change and forced him to take the initiative. She made things too easy for him.

There were so many activities at the base the week before the Change of Command, plus all the details of the trip to be finalized, that Sandy spent almost every night at Matt's place. He was in the garage, organizing things for the trip, when the phone rang.

"Grab the phone, would you, honey?" he called.

She answered the phone, then stuck her head through the sliding patio door. "Matt. It's Bobbie. Something's wrong; she's crying."

In three quick strides he was by her side and grabbed the phone. "What's the matter?"

"You've got to take Hank. I can't handle him anymore," Bobbie sniffled. "We just had a terrible argument, and he wants to come live with you."

Matt heaved a sigh. "Bobbie, you know he can't live with me right now. I'm leaving this weekend."

"*I* know that, but try telling him that. I can't do anything with him anymore. I need your help. He doesn't listen to a thing I say, and he disobeys me all the time." She started weeping again. "Matt, will you talk to him? He says he hates me. He's right here and he wants to talk to you. Please, try to make him understand what happened," she pleaded.

"What's this all about?"

A still whimpering Bobbie replied, "Hank'll tell you."

Hank hurriedly made his plea. "Dad, I want to come live with you. I don't want to stay here anymore. Will you come get me, now?" He emphasized the last word in a raspy voice that told Matt he had been crying too.

"Son, why don't you want to stay with your mother? Besides, I'm just getting ready to leave town, you know that." *What in the hell had happened?* Just the week before Hank had blown him off.

"I'm not going to stay with her anymore because of what she did to you." He sounded defiant and determined.

"Hank, what are you talking about? What do you mean—what she did to me? Your mother didn't do anything to me."

"Yes, she did. She made you leave. It was her that wanted the divorce so she could be with her boyfriend. I always thought *you* were the one." Hank started sobbing.

Matt sat down on the bar stool, stunned. So the truth had finally come out. No wonder Bobbie was crying. All her months of procrastination and years of lying had finally earned her the wrath of her son.

"Son, there are many things you don't understand . . . ."

Hank interrupted. "She lied to me. She knew I thought it was all your fault, and she didn't say a thing to defend you, until tonight."

Matt caught the last comment. *What could she have said tonight that would have caused this, and why?* "Hank, she did it because she was afraid you'd act just like you're acting now if you knew the truth. She loves you very much, and she didn't want to risk your disapproval."

Hank was quiet for several moments, then asked in a calmer voice, " Can I come over and spend the night with you?"

"I don't think that would be a good idea. You and your mother have a lot of talking to do, and I think you should do it now. I want you to stay there and try to work things out. Friday morning is the Change of Command. You can come out to the base with me, and we'll spend the rest of the day together, just the two of us, if you'd like that. And if you still have questions after talking with your mom, we'll see if we can't get everything straightened out before I have to leave. Is that okay?"

A long moment of silence. Finally, "Yeah, I guess so." Matt could hear the disappointment in his voice.

"Fine." Matt was relieved. "I'll pick you up at eight Friday morning."

After he hung up, he related the conversation to Sandy. "What do you suppose he meant that Bobbie had lied to him—until tonight? With Tom getting killed, she shouldn't have had to explain anything," he mused, mystified.

"Well, whatever the reason, I'm glad Hank finally knows the truth. Now, maybe, you two can have the kind of relationship you've wanted. I still don't understand why you let her get away with this for two and a half years. Why, Matt? Why didn't *you* do something?"

Matt walked out to the patio, checked the grill and put the steaks on. "I don't know exactly. At first I didn't do anything because I guess I thought we might get back together—and the problem would disappear. By the time I accepted the fact that it wasn't going to happen, I expected Bobbie to explain it in a way that didn't make it appear it was anyone's 'fault.' I know now that wasn't particularly practical, but I didn't think it would do the children any good to smear their mother's reputation. I guess I always hoped that some-how, magically, they would understand, without my having to say or do anything. But, in retrospect, I probably should have insisted that we both sit down and explain things to them."

Matt paused, reflecting. "I think the reason she and Tom didn't get married was because of her continuing fear of how the children would react if they suspected they had been lovers while I was gone."

Sandy set the table as he talked.

"I don't think it would do any good to pick Hank up this late at night, do you?"

She shook her head, but he continued before she could respond. "I'd just have to dump him back over at her house first thing in the morning. I can't possibly take time off before Friday. I suppose we could delay leaving on the trip a day or two, but I don't think that would really solve anything. Damn! I wish I knew what happened to cause this now. For two years I've urged her to tell him. Why *now*?"

He carried the steaks in to the table. They ate in silence, Matt obviously deep in thought. While Sandy cleared the table, he sat on the kitchen barstool, drinking a beer. "You know, before I was shot down, I never really questioned my decision to stay in the Navy or to become a pilot. I liked what I was doing and I never expected to get shot down. I guess none of us did. Until it happened it didn't even seem like a possibility. But, at that point, there wasn't much I could do to alter the situation."

He started pacing, using the can like a conductor's baton to emphasize his point. "But I don't think Bobbie ever really liked the life of a military wife. She didn't like the separations, being alone so much or so long at a time. That was harder for her than most of the other squadron wives. And I guess I wasn't very supportive. I was concentrating on staying competitive; I always felt I had to work harder because I didn't go to the Academy, so I didn't have a lot of time to be concerned with how she was feeling. In prison, when it dawned on me that my family was more important than making the next promotion, and it finally registered that I probably hadn't been the best husband in the world, I decided I would offer to leave the Navy when I came home if that was what she wanted, but before we could discuss that . . . well . . . we never even got a chance to talk about it."

Sandy finished loading the dishwasher, walked into the living room and sat down on the couch. Matt sat beside her. "Now, I'm not sure what I should do. If I refuse these orders and insist on staying in San Diego, I can kiss all future advancement goodbye. I've worked hard to get where I am, and I really don't want to throw it all away. Besides, I don't know what I could do as a civilian. Not much demand for an over-the-hill pilot, and I'm not aware of many flying desk jobs."

Sandy patted his thigh.

"But this thing with Hank is really troubling," he continued. "He needs me, and if I leave, I may really fail him. It's just a hell of a time for this to happen. One good thing, if you can call it that, is that I won't be gone for a complete cruise. When I fly out to join the ship, it will be more than halfway through its deployment, so I'll be there a few weeks and ride it back to San Diego. Then we'll be in port for several months for an overhaul."

While Matt brooded, Sandy carried the empties to the trash can and brought him another cold beer. As soon as she sat back down, he picked up where he had left off, one drink bolder. "You know, I don't think, despite all Bobbie's efforts, she succeeded in hiding the truth from Debbie. Too many signs point to her knowing. My daughter's no dummy. But her loyalty was to her mother, regardless of how she felt. Once, shortly after I moved out of the house and was living at the BOQ, I asked Debbie out to lunch. I still wanted very much to get my family back together, and I hoped I might be able to enlist her support. I asked her what she thought was happening to our family. She just averted her eyes, said she didn't know, and changed the subject. After that I never brought up the separation again, but I felt betrayed, and I guess a little hurt. After all, she's my daughter too, and it wasn't my fault that things worked out as they did. All I wanted was an honest, open discussion. I wouldn't have cared if she had defended Bobbie's actions if that's the way she felt—I just wanted to be able to discuss it and explore possibilities. Honesty was the least I had expected from her, given her strong church ties, and I thought her behavior was very dishonest. But after a few months I saw a change. I think she finally got fed up with Bobbie's behavior."

Sandy thought she had the perfect solution. "Honey, now that Hank knows the truth, he shouldn't have any reason to resent me anymore. If we were married, you could get custody, and he could live with us—at least part of the time."

Matt's mood changed as quickly as the strike of a rattler. "When and *if* I'm ready to get married," he hissed, "I'll let you know. Until then, just quit bugging me!"

He regretted his outburst the minute the words were out of his mouth, but it was too late. He heard the swift intake of air and saw the equally swift dilation to her pupils. Her eyes filled with tears.

"Look, dammit, I'm not your ex-wife. I wasn't the one that let you down. I've done nothing but love you and try to comfort you and support you, yet I'm the one that's getting all the shit. It was Bobbie, not me, who screwed around on you while you were gone. I don't know what I would have done under the same circumstances—maybe the same thing—but I'll be damned if I'm going to be condemned for what she did."

She brushed away her tears, her mouth forming a thin straight line. "It's getting so that I can't even mention the word marriage without it setting you off. It 'bugs you.' I'm 'pushy.' Maybe I'm wasting my time." She paused, shaking her head. "You know what I think is really your problem? I think, heaven help you, that you're still hung up on your ex-wife. You'd have to be an idiot to still want her. Then, on the other hand, she *did* toss you aside for another man. She told me once, when she was trying to enlist my support for her little game, that you were a proud man. Well, maybe you've got to have her back to soothe your wounded pride, even if it's only so you can be the one who gets in the last toss."

She picked up her purse and searched for her keys. "I'm going home. I'll be at the Change of Command Friday. Beyond that, it's up to you. I'll not pack unless I hear from you."

She slammed the door.

Matt finished his beer and smashed the empty can in his hands. *Why do I do that?* Lately he seemed to be saying a lot of harsh things, things he didn't really mean—the words just came tumbling out before he even thought about them. *Damn.* Life used to be so much simpler before he was shot down—Bobbie always accepted his decisions unquestioningly. Was this a new behavior since coming home, or was it just that Sandy reacted so differently?

As soon as he got a break the next morning, he called Sandy. "I'm sorry," he began contritely, "I was upset about Hank and I had no right to take it out on you. Of course, I still want you to go with me; you know that trip wouldn't be any fun without you."

"Honey, I'm sorry too," she said. "I flew off the handle last night. I knew you were upset; I should have kept my mouth shut, but you know how hard that is for me." She could hear Matt chuckling. "You know I'm looking forward to this trip as much as you are. So, let's just forget what we said to each other last night, okay?"

Matt smiled to himself. "Why don't I give you a call when I get home after work and we'll grab a bite? In fact, why don't you bring your bags over. Are you packed?"

"Are you suggesting I move in with you?" she teased.

"Well . . . uh . . . let me give that one some thought," he stammered, amused. Damn broad, she never missed an opening. She had all the subtlety of a flamethrower. Apparently her mother never taught her the meaning of the word no. But, you had to give her an A for persistence. Actually, he had to admit it was sort of flattering; lesser women would have given up by now.

On the morning of the Change of Command, Debbie, who had acquired a nursing job in a little town outside San Francisco after completing nurses' training in the spring, called Matt just as he was leaving the house. "Dad, I'm really sorry, but I won't be able to make it. I just can't take time off yet."

Matt was disappointed, but he had expected it. After several minutes of friendly conversation, he indicated that he was running late and had to cut it short.

"Dad." There was a moment of silence. "I . . . well, I just want you to know that I'm proud you're my father." He could hear the catch in her voice.

"Thank you, honey. I'm very pleased to hear that and I'm glad you're my daughter."

"Bye, I love you."

As far as Matt knew, his daughter had not shed a tear since he'd been home, but he'd swear she was crying when she hung up the phone. Not even her presence at the Change of Command could have touched him deeper.

Bobbie came out to the car when he arrived to pick up Hank. "He's almost ready. I'm sorry, but I won't be able to go to your Change of Command. I just can't afford to take the time off. Maybe we could have a drink later, when you bring him home . . . or tomorrow. I really need to talk to you," she said, plaintively.

They were going to be late if Hank didn't hurry up. "I'm sorry, but I'm leaving early in the morning." Then he saw the sad look in her eyes and his tone softened. She looked so pathetic that he almost wanted to hold her, to comfort her, even after all that had transpired.

"Look, I don't know what happened or how Hank found out, but I told you many times there was going to be hell to pay if you didn't tell him the truth. I'm sorry," he said, shaking his head, "I really am, that it came out now, just when I have to be away. I wish I could be here—to help Hank," he added pointedly, recalling Sandy's accusation. "But I can't and you're just going to have to work it out as best you can."

She bit her lower lip and nodded in mute understanding.

"How in the devil did he find out, anyway? I thought you had covered all your tracks." He was unable to mask the sarcasm.

Tears sprang to her eyes. "Matt, please don't hate me so. If there were any way I could change what's happened to us, make right all I did wrong, I'd do it."

He was slightly annoyed with her tears and her tardy repentance, and angry with himself for his physical feelings. Why hadn't she expressed those sentiments before—before Tom died—when they could have made a difference? "So," he asked, an edge in his voice, "like I said, how'd he find out?"

She lowered her eyes and muttered quietly, "I told him."

Matt looked at her in disbelief. "You what?" he asked incredulously.

"I told him," she repeated softly. "He was so angry with you, I just couldn't take it any more. He said he wasn't going to go to your Change of Command, that you didn't care anything about us, so why should he care about you. I've done enough to hurt you without destroying your son's love for you. I just couldn't do it any more, watching him day after day getting unhappier and unhappier because he thought you didn't love him. My love just wasn't enough. So I told him. I told him it wasn't you, but me, who had wanted the divorce, and I told him why. I said it was because I was in love with someone else, but even that wasn't entirely true. It was just that I had destroyed any chance for you to love me." She looked like the life had drained out of her.

He hesitated, then cupped her chin and lifted her tear-stained face so that their eyes met. "I'm sorry too, Bobbie. I wish things could have been different." Then he added gently, "but they're not, and I'm afraid it's too late to change a lot of things now."

Just then Hank appeared at the front door and joined them. Except for his long hair, which was tied neatly in a pony tail, he looked fresh and clean and even wore a pair of dress slacks instead of his usual threadbare jeans.

Matt dropped his hand from her chin. Bobbie put two fingers to her lips and lovingly touched them to his cheek. "Have a safe trip," she whispered, and turned quickly.

He looked from his son to the disappearing form of his ex-wife, and mourned silently. *Life's a bitch.*

At the ceremony, Matt once again viewed the guests from the podium. Hank sat next to Sandy, the only "family" on his side of the aisle. He'd put John, Liz and Marcia on the front row. Jim and Julie were already in Texas, and although he had invited Amy, he had received, as expected, a simple note of congratulations, along with her apology for being unable to attend. Except for a Christmas card last December, he had not heard from her since last year's Change of Command. It still bothered him the way things ended for them.

Bonnie too had declined. "We'll celebrate when you get here," she bubbled. "By the way, is Sandy coming?"

"Yeah, I asked her to come with me. It's a long trip alone," he explained.

"Good. She's going to make you a good wife."

Matt shook his head. Jesus. Everyone had him married, now even Sis. "Yeah, I know, and I've been tempted to tell her that several times," he joked, "but I've wisely kept my mouth shut."

"You sure you don't want us to have a shower while you're here?" Bonnie teased.

"Don't you even mention the word marriage while I'm there," he warned. "And certainly not to her."

Sandy, sitting next to Hank, debated how to approach him. When he sat down, he had actually smiled, so she waded in. "How's school going?"

He continued to stare at the reviewing stand, but answered quietly, "Fine."

"What are you now—a freshman?"

"No, I'm a sophomore. I'll be fifteen next month." This time he turned to face her. She would have liked to take him in her arms. This poor child has suffered so much emotional turmoil in his short life. But she clasped her hands in her lap.

"Gee, that's hard to believe. I understand from your dad that you're quite a surfer."

His eyes brightened and he grinned. "Yeah, I'm getting pretty good. I'd like to go to Hawaii some day and ride those big ones."

"That sounds like fun. Maybe you'll get to." Her mind was plotting.

"I hope so."

He seemed inclined to say more, but the ceremony started. Sandy smiled inwardly. What a change in the young man's attitude.

After the reception, as the three of them neared the car, Matt turned to Hank. "Well, son, how would you like to spend the rest of the day?"

Glancing from Sandy to Matt, Hank shrugged. "Why don't you just drop me off at home. I'm sure you've got lots of last-minute things to do to get ready for your trip. The guys should be out of school by the time we get home, so we'll go to the beach."

Sandy and Matt stared at each other. He seemed to have totally accepted their plans to go away together. Then, without a trace of the hostility of the previous year, he started chattering like the enthusiastic boy Matt remembered from his first few months at home.

"Hey, Dad," he chirped, "Maybe when you're here in January you'll have time to watch me surf. I think you'll be surprised. I can even teach you—it's a lot of fun."

"You tried to teach me before, remember. It was a disaster. However, I promise to watch you before I fly out to join the ship." Then he added, as his plan of more than nine years before renewed itself, "Would you like to come out to Hawaii and ride the ship back with me if they have a Tiger cruise? Think you could miss a week's school?"

"Yeah!" Hank said excitedly.

Sandy recalled their earlier conversation. "Hey, maybe you'll be able to ride those big waves when you're over there."

"That would be super. Dad, do you think I could?" His voice was animated.

Matt looked questioningly at Sandy, who raised her hands, palms up and shrugged. "He just told me today that's what he wanted to do. Sounds like perfect timing to me."

Matt put his arm around his son. "I'll work on that." Then he pulled lightly on Hank's ponytail. "By the way, how about getting a hair cut?"

Hank laughed. "Yeah, I guess it does look kind of ratty. But, Dad, honest, I can't get one like yours—the guys would laugh me off the beach."

Matt rumpled his son's shaggy mane. "You could get six inches sheared off and still look like a hippie." Matt wrapped his arms around his son, and for the first time in a long time, Hank really hugged him back.

Holt, Nebraska, October 1974.

As soon as they arrived in Matt's hometown, Sandy put her plan into action. Many times over the past year Matt had lamented about his folks' living situation and repeated his long-held desire to buy a house in town for them. "My cousin has a lot, just a block from Main Street, that he would sell me for a reasonable price. But, I don't know a thing about building a house."

The second day there, after having breakfast with his folks, she borrowed his car under the pretext of wanting to do a little shopping.

She stopped at the real estate office. None of the available listings was acceptable. Next she drove by where she thought the vacant lot should be. It was perfect. Her next stop was the builder's office. Building a house from scratch wouldn't work—they couldn't finish it before freezing weather stopped construction.

The contractor had another suggestion. "We handle pre-fab homes. They're actually very good quality. We could get the basement dug before the freeze, and you could have a pre-fab home up and ready for painting in about forty, forty-five days."

Sandy checked out several plans, and selected the one that seemed the most appropriate—two bedrooms, one bath with single attached garage. The best part was the living room-kitchen arrangement; it was an open plan. Mrs. Tillet's bed would go next to the big picture window in the living room, and she would still be able to visit with anyone in the kitchen or dining room area. After pricing it out, Sandy stopped at the bank. The bank president, she knew, had gone to school with Matt. It didn't matter, Matt was such a hero in that little town, they would have just about given him the key to the bank. A few thousand dollar loan on a house was a piece of cake. For around $35,000 he could have his folks in a new house by Christmas.

That night, when they were alone, she unveiled her plan. Matt laughed at her. "We couldn't possibly get this done in a week," he protested.

"Yes, you can! It's all ready to go. All you have to do is call your cousin and buy the lot."

"You're a hopeless optimist," he declared, still unconvinced.

"No. I think you normally get the results you expect to get. If you expect to fail, you will. I don't put a lot of effort in that direction. Now, do you want to get your folks that home or not?"

By the time they left, a week later, Matt had purchased the lot, obtained a loan, and signed a contract with the builder, who promised, "Matt, you can move your folks in by Christmas."

At Matt's insistence, Sandy flew back at Christmas to meet him in Nebraska. Bonnie and Ray had painted the new house inside and out and had the carpet and flooring installed before Matt arrived, and it was almost ready. Matt and Sandy bought a stove and refrigerator, and they moved his Mom and Dad into their new home on Christmas eve.

Matt shook his head in disbelief as they decorated a small tree. That night, he held Sandy in his arms, extra close. One of his prison dreams had become a reality, and he knew it wouldn't have happened without her.

CHAPTER 34

<u>1976.</u>

On his first morning back in San Diego, Matt called Hank. "Hey, we just got back late last night. Could we go to the beach today? I saw on the news that the surf's up, and I've only got this weekend before I have to head out to the Western Pacific."

"You really want to go?" Hank asked, sounding as if he didn't quite believe Matt.

"Let's do it. I'll pick you up in an hour," Matt said.

"Super! Hey, you gonna try surfing?"

"Thanks, but no thanks. Once is enough," Matt said, laughing, recalling the first disastrous attempt. "I'd break my neck, and I can't afford to do that right now." He could hear Hank's laughter on the other end.

"I'll be quite content to sit in the sand and watch you," Matt assured him.

"Okay. See ya in an hour." Hank was still laughing as he hung up.

Matt turned to Sandy. "Want to go to the beach? Hank's going to demonstrate his prowess."

"Thanks, but you guys go ahead. I need to check on some listings. Could you drop me off at the airport? I left my car in long-term parking."

Hank came bounding down the driveway as soon as Matt pulled up. They fit the surfboard into the back, and he jumped in.

"Hank, I think you've grown another couple inches since I saw you last," Sandy said. She also noticed, but didn't comment on the fact that his hair was shorter and shiny clean.

Hank smiled, no hint of the former resentment. "Yeah, probably. Mom calls it my growing spurt."

"I also note you are turning into quite a hunk," she complimented him, after noting the rippling muscles and firm tone of his body.

He reddened, and smiled broadly.

"Matt, your son is going to be better looking than you. You better talk to him about self-defense—from the girls that I bet are all over him."

Hank turned redder than before, and grinned sheepishly.

"Oops. I think it's too late," she added.

"Here we are," Matt announced as they reached the airport.

Sandy got out of the front seat, and Hank got out of the back. She held out her arms, and he gave her a hug. "Hank, you take care. In case I don't see you again until your dad gets back, you have my phone number. If you need anything, just call."

"Thank you, ma'am." He smiled again and crawled into the front seat.

As he started to drive away, Matt called out the window, "We should be back around six. I'll give you a call."

That night, Matt was more animated than she could remember in a long time. The day with his son had been good therapy.

"You should have seen him," he exclaimed excitedly. "He's really good."

"Did he get you to try it again?" she asked, smiling mischievously.

"No way! I just barely stuck my foot in the water—it was cold. But we did stop by one of the surf shops and I got him another wet suit. Makes shopping for him pretty easy. He'd already outgrown the one I bought last year."

She watched him carefully as he talked about his son, pleased. It was about time they had a real father-son relationship. Now it could happen.

She rubbed a finger across his forehead. "You got a little red."

"If the ship has a Tiger cruise," Matt continued as if he had not heard her, "I'll leave you some money and send you the details. Will you arrange to get the tickets for him?"

"Sure. But are you going to clear this with Bobbie?"

He grimaced. "Oh . . . yeah . . . I guess I better."

"And, don't forget. If you're in Hawaii, even a day or two, Hank wants to ride the big waves. You've got to make sure that happens. It's his dream."

"Okay. I'll check it out. I'm sure some of the sailors will know where to go."

Matt heaved a big sigh of satisfaction. "When the ship gets back, we're going to spend a lot of time with him. I've got a lot of lost time to make up for, and I've just discovered that my son is a pretty neat kid."

One word stood out to Sandy. "I'm glad you put it that way—*we're* going to . . . . It sounds like you're thinking in terms of *us* long range." She looked at him teasingly.

"Don't go there," he admonished.

Still fighting it, you chicken. She smiled. "One day we'll go *there* together. I'm betting on it."

He pulled her close. "I'm leaving for a long cruise. You gonna jaw all night, woman, or give me a proper send off?"

"Bon voyage, baby," she whispered, snuggling into his arms.

Matt's first letter to Sandy announced his promotion to captain. "This may affect my orders. They may not want one captain working for another, the CO of this ship is a captain too. On the other hand, I have a lot to learn, so I certainly don't mind. But if they do want to cut me new orders, I'll probably have to go to the Pentagon. Twenty-five years in the Navy, and I've never been stationed at the paper palace back there."

Sandy was not surprised at the tone of his letters. His goal had been to forge ahead with his Navy career, to continue the climb as long as she'd known him, particularly after things fell apart with Bobbie. She wouldn't object to being a Navy wife, and she was sure she could handle all that went with it—a lot better than Bobbie had.

A couple of letters later, Matt expressed a new theme. "I've asked my detailer to find me a job in San Diego. I've been doing a lot of thinking on this cruise, and I have decided I want to spend the rest of my time in the Navy in San Diego, or get out. It's time I put Hank first. My chances of making admiral are pretty slim anyway. I just missed filling too many of those 'blocks' in the seven years I was gone. I've decided to concentrate on being a father."

Wow, she thought. What a turnaround. Staying in San Diego would suit her just fine, as a Navy wife or the wife of a retired officer—just as his wife. That decision boded well for that to happen. She could just feel it. He had to be away from her to realize how much he needed her. He'd been fighting admitting he loved her for a long time, but he was losing ground.

A few days later, Sandy received another letter. "The ship is going to sponsor a Tiger Cruise this year. I've already written Hank about it and given him the dates. It's a few years late, but maybe we'll get to do it yet. Please call him to see that he's still coming, and if he says yes, I'd really appreciate it if you would make all the arrangements from that end. Don't tell him, but I've checked with some of the sailors. I know where the big waves are. Looks like there'll be time to do it—a couple of days at least."

She could sense his excitement just from the tone of the letter.

****

The ship was making preparations to leave Subic Bay in the Philippines in front of an incoming typhoon. Matt was alone in his office wrapping up the mountain of paperwork created because some sailors had gotten in trouble with the civilian authorities. He'd been trying to arrange one young offender's release. If he were left behind to face the local authorities, he would have to make his way back to the ship at his own expense, and then face disciplinary action there too.

Matt called "Enter," to the knock on his outer door. The captain and the ship's chaplain solemnly walked in.

****

The shrill ringing of the phone by her bed woke Sandy. She glanced at the clock. *Crap. This better not be a wrong number or one of those prank calls.* Her new dog sleepily lifted its head from the foot of the bed.

"Sandy, this is Matt," the voice on the line said.

"Honey! How great to hear from you," she said enthusiastically, suddenly wide awake. It wasn't like Matt to call at four o'clock in the morning without some good reason. Maybe he'd decided to invite her to meet him in Hawaii when the ship returned. She'd been hinting in her letters she would like to come.

He'd been silent for a long time. "Matt, are you there? I can't hear you."

"Yes, I'm here." His voice was flat.

"Matt, what's wrong?"

"Hank's dead."

Sandy gasped. "What did you say?" His voice was so low, maybe she had misunderstood.

"Hank's dead. I just received the Red Cross message a little while ago. There's a typhoon headed this way and the ship is pulling out to sea to get out of the way, so I don't have much time."

She was too stunned to think clearly. How could Hank be dead? "Darling, is there anything I can do before you get here?"

"I'm not coming back. The airport at Manila is already shut down, so I can't catch a plane. The ship will be en route before I could get back. Hank's dead; there is nothing I can do for him now, anyway—except bury him. I'll take some leave and spend some time with Debbie when we get back. I don't think I'd be much use to anyone right now. I need some time to sort things out."

"Oh, Matt, I can't tell you how sorry I am." She started to sob. "What can I do to help?"

"Look," he said heavily, "you might go over to Bobbie's and see if you can help with the funeral arrangements. I want to take care of everything financially. I'm sure Bobbie's not in any condition to handle things, and that just leaves Debbie. I hate for her to have to do it alone. If Bobbie refuses to let you help, then just let it go. If she doesn't object, then perhaps you and Debbie can make the arrangements. I really hate to put you in this position, but with this storm, even if I tried to come home, I probably couldn't get there before the funeral. I don't know when they'll resume flights."

She breathed deeply and wiped her eyes. "Of course. I'll go over first thing this morning and do whatever I can. Darling, what happened? Can you tell me, or do you not want to talk about it?"

Matt sounded sadder than she had ever heard. "All the message said was that there was a surfing accident—he was knocked unconscious and drowned before help got to him. I think it happened late yesterday afternoon, your time."

"Honey, I'm so very, very sorry." She heard a sharp intake of air on the other end. Matt was crying too.

After a barely audible "thanks," she heard the phone go dead. She dropped her head in her hands and wept, pulling the small terrier into her arms and rocking. Suddenly she grabbed the paperback novel she had been reading the night before and hurled it across the room.

She got up and fixed a pot of coffee, then returned to bed. Ratman, the name the previous owners had given to the rat terrier as a puppy, curled up in the crook of her arm. She had agreed to take him initially as a favor to her clients, an elderly couple who was selling their house and moving into an apartment that didn't allow pets. It was a lucky move. He had been the best companion she could have asked for in those long nights without Matt.

Her thoughts turned to the house down in the valley. For the first time since the scene in Bobbie's living room, Sandy could feel sympathy for her. She'd done some stupid things, she'd handled things badly, she'd hurt a lot of people, including herself probably most of all. But now Bobbie, who needed someone more than just about anyone Sandy knew, was alone. Tom was gone, and now the main reason for Bobbie's deception was gone.

At nine o'clock, Sandy knocked on Bobbie's door. A teary-eyed Debbie opened it and accepted Sandy's hug. Bobbie was slumped in her favorite chair, the one with the twisted frame, smoking a cigarette, her chin resting on her chest, her shoulders hunched forward. She barely opened her swollen eyes when Debbie announced Sandy's arrival, mumbled an "okay," and raised one hand to her mouth as another round of sobs wracked her body. Debbie closed the door to the den, and motioned for Sandy to sit in the living room.

"Honey, your dad asked if I would come over and help you," Sandy stated, a little uncertainly.

"I know. He called this morning." Debbie was still the same in-charge person Sandy had known her to be when Matt was in prison.

"Is that okay with you?" Sandy asked hesitantly.

"Sure. Poor Dad. He only had a few minutes, I guess they were holding the ship for him to finish his phone calls so they could get out of the way of that big storm over there. I think this really knocked him for a loop. Mom told me the last time I talked with her by phone how excited Hank was about getting to go on the Tiger cruise." Debbie dropped her eyes, fighting off tears.

"Your dad was too. I've never seen him so excited, in fact." Sandy wiped a tear. "I'm just so glad they were able to get back together before this happened."

Debbie looked out the window, sniffling.

Well, they had to do it. "Where's Hank?" Sandy asked reluctantly.

"At the funeral home. Mom laid out some clothes. I guess we ought to take them over and make the arrangements." Debbie grabbed a Kleenex and wiped her nose.

"Honey, is this going to be okay with your mom?" Sandy asked, still concerned about what Bobbie might do.

"I think Mom realized—and accepted—some time ago that what happened with her and dad was her doing. I don't think she blames you. And, I want you to know—I don't. I'm just glad you've been there for him. He really needed someone when he came home—the way things were—just like Mom needed Tom when Dad was in prison. I know Mom loved Dad, and I think she wanted to get back with him, even before Tom's death, but she just couldn't. Dad's not a real forgiving guy, and she was afraid he'd never forgive he. He probably wouldn't have, not entirely."

Sandy was shocked at the depth of Debbie's understanding—and acceptance—of the situation.

After a pause, Debbie continued, "I appreciate your coming over; I appreciate your help. Mom can't function at this moment. Mrs. Posner is out back. She is going to stay with her while we're gone."

With Debbie's help, Sandy handled the funeral and burial arrangements for Matt's fifteen-year old son. At Debbie's request, she sat with her and Bobbie in the family area.

****

The ship returned to the 32nd Street pier a couple months after Hank was buried. Sandy could do little but watch and offer comfort as Matt tried to purge himself of a memory too painful to remember. Fortunately, supervising the overhaul was quite time-consuming. He didn't need idle time to think. He left early in the morning to beat the traffic and usually returned home late in the evening, burying his pain in his work.

When they had first started dating, he would often jerk and moan or cry out in the night, no doubt nightmares of the torture he'd suffered in prison. Over time, they'd declined. Now she could only watch helplessly as those demons returned. Often she would touch his clammy skin, try to wake him from the really bad ones or wrap her arms around him, trying to shut them out.

Except to go out to the grave, he said very little about Hank, yet it was obvious he was never far from Matt's mind, memories silently welling up like blood from an open wound.

One Saturday they went to the beach. Sandy packed a picnic lunch and filled a cooler with beer and sodas. Late in the afternoon they strolled along the water's edge, watching the sun fading below the horizon.

"Over there is where Hank tried to teach me to surf," he said quietly, pointing. He stopped walking and looked down at the sand between his toes.

Sandy squeezed his hand.

"He was good," Matt murmured.

"I know." Again, she squeezed his hand.

They walked further in silence, right at the edge of the water, allowing the incoming tide to cover their feet and ankles, then walked on the hard-packed sand when the tide went out.

Suddenly Matt stopped and stared off in the distance.

"This is about where it happened." He looked forlornly at the incoming waves, only a couple of feet high, took a few steps further into the water, and let the sea splash against his ankles and occasionally up to his knees. For several minutes he just stood there, looking out over the horizon, as if Hank might suddenly appear on his surfboard.

CHAPTER 35

San Diego 1977.

Thick dark clouds shrouded the carrier in the morning mist like a
ghost ship of olden days. It slid majestically under the Coronado
Bridge, slipping between and under the steel girders and beams so
closely it appeared to almost touch them. Sandy shivered in the
biting breeze as she waited dockside for the carrier to pull into the
32nd Street pier. It was the end of Matt's second cruise. She felt a
chill like an icy wind off a glacier, but not just from the morning
dampness. She pulled the light jacket around her for warmth, and
walked over to stand amidst other family members. Visiting helped
pass the slow-moving time, and the air around the bodies seemed
warmer.

The ship moved at a snail's pace toward the dock after it first
became visible in the San Diego Bay. After eight months, a jet boat
would seem slow, and right now time seemed to be standing still.
Even when the carrier drew close enough for the families to wave at
the sailors, the crew still had to go through the endless tasks of dock-
ing and tying up. Sandy spotted Matt up on the deck and waved.
Somehow in the sea of family and friends, he saw her too, smiled
briefly and waved back, then continued talking into the walkie-
talkie.

She was, pursuant to his instructions, among the first small group
to board as soon as the gang plank was in place. He was waiting as
she stepped onto the ship and gave her a quick hug. "Let's go down
to my quarters and get out of this crowd." He wasn't prone to public

displays of affection, particularly in this setting, and certainly not under the watchful eyes of his crew.

Sandy followed him below. Once inside the privacy of his quarters, she snuggled into his arms. "I've really missed you," she whispered. "Welcome home."

"I missed you, too." He surrounded her face with his hands and she felt the warm hard touch of his kiss, sending another kind of shiver through her. She pushed closer, not wanting the embrace to end. But after a few minutes he dropped his arms and moved slightly away, clearing his throat.

"My orders came through. I'm going to be the XO at Miramar."

"Matt, that's wonderful." She sat on the edge of his bunk. "When?"

"Couple months, soon as they get my relief here."

His voice was flat, and even as he relayed the information, she saw the sadness in his eyes. He was staying in San Diego, as he had requested more than a year ago, but his principal reason was gone. His pain was still intense, like a deep open wound. Her throat tightened with pity.

He picked up his small duffel bag. "This is all I need right now. I'll get the rest of the stuff later. Let's go home."

That night, he slid his hand around the back of her head and buried his fingers in the silky coolness of her hair, nuzzling her lips softly and stroking her responsive points.

She shivered as his mouth forced hers to open while his hands caressed her body. His touch sent a surge of heat that spread through her quicker and more powerfully than the wine she had just sipped. It was almost annoying how easily he could reduce her to a creature of tingling nerves. She felt she might shatter into a thousand pieces.

Her naked breasts pressed against him, and the hardened tips were like points of fire against his chest. Hunger, in the form of pure raw desire, quickened in him. Shuddering in a mutual release heightened by months of deprivation, he whispered, "I love you."

"Oh, Matt, I've waited four years to hear you say that. Umm," she murmured, nestling even closer, "I'd like to be like this always."

They lay for several minutes, locked together. Finally, he raised himself and propped his head on one hand. "My staying power has shrunk," he laughed softly. "Come on. Let's take a shower. I'll scrub your back if you'll scrub mine."

The next morning, he announced, "I'd like to fly up to Frisco this weekend to see Debbie. Would you mind taking me to the airport? I'll only be gone a couple days."

When he returned, he seemed in high spirits.

"How's Debbie?" Sandy asked as she drove him home from the airport.

"Just fine. She really likes her job. She's dating a couple of guys from what I gather. She says there's no one really special, but she did a lot of talking on the phone to this one guy who called every night."

"That's nice."

"I hope you don't mind, but I'd like to go see Bobbie this next weekend, maybe take her out to dinner. I'd like to see how she's doing." Matt looked intently at Sandy.

"You don't need my permission to do whatever you feel you ought to do." It was true, but she couldn't shake off a gloomy pre-monition.

"Thanks," he said, "I appreciate your understanding."

Sandy didn't hear from Matt on Monday. She called and left a message on his machine. By Thursday, he still hadn't called. Her mind was running wild with concern. The warm fuzzies of a few days earlier disappeared; and her cold fears returned.

Thursday evening, when he finally called, she was a bundle of nerves, besieged by a sense of impending doom.

"Sorry I haven't called sooner," he stated as soon as she answered. "I spent most of Sunday with Bobbie. Then we were out all this week on sea trials. The new XO reported aboard, so we're getting ready for the turnover," he continued in a dull voice.

She held her breath. Were her worst fears going to be realized? Deep down, she'd always been afraid that Matt had not entirely let go of his prison dream, as unrealistic as it seemed. Did the loss of their son bring them back together? She waited.

"Have you eaten?" he asked.

"No."

"Why don't you come over, and I'll rustle something up."

This was the moment of truth. Good news or bad, she wanted to know, once and for all where she stood. As she drove west on Interstate 8 and turned north onto 805, her imagination ran wild. Bobbie had lost almost everyone that mattered to her—first Tom, then Hank. She needed a man, pure and simple. It stood to reason she'd pull out all the stops to get him back. Was he foolish enough to take her back? Had his reluctance to marry her been his subconscious need or wish to get back with his ex-wife? She'd heard of soul mates. Did Matt consider Bobbie his one true love, leaving him no capacity to love someone else? The idea squeezed her heart like a vise.

She couldn't discern what was going to happen from his kiss— not long and hard and passionate, but tender and loving nonetheless.

"What's that I smell?" she asked, sniffing, trying to conceal her nervousness.

"I ordered pizza and fixed a salad. That okay?"

After dinner, he got out a deck of cards and the cribbage board. "Wanna play?"

"Sure." But after a few hands, she could control her curiosity no longer. "Well? Are you going to tell me what happened?"

"Bobbie's getting married," he announced quietly.

"I'll be damned." Her face must have betrayed her shock and surprise, and probably her relief. "To whom?"

"A guy she met at work—one of the construction superintendents."

She eyed him carefully. "And how do you feel about that?"

"I'm glad," he said simply. "She needs someone. We had a nice talk. She seems to have come to terms with Hank's death, perhaps better than I have. I think we made peace with each other. We probably shared a little more of what you call honesty than anytime since I've been home."

He stared into space and was quiet for several moments, shuffling the cards repeatedly. "Lots of things might have been different if we'd tried that starting in 1973, but we didn't and we reached a point of no return a long time ago, because of failings in both of us. I didn't want to admit it and I tried to deceive myself for a long time, but I really knew better. We couldn't have made it work, even before Tom's death, probably never after I got home."

"Why?" She really wanted to know the answer, to perhaps once and for all free herself of her guilt for not having kept her mouth shut back in 1973.

Matt shut his eyes, as if probing deep inside himself for an answer. "It was hard to let go. Until it happened to me, divorce wasn't an option I'd ever considered. Mom and Dad are still together. Dad drank too much, and Mom ended up an invalid with MS, but they stuck together. Bonnie and Ray have been married since right after she got out of high school. Even my brother, who drinks as much as Dad ever did when he was that age, and his wife are still together. Both of Dad's sisters, who live back in my home town, outlived their only husbands of almost fifty years. I can't think of any of my close relatives who are divorced."

He put down the deck, and looked across the table. She smiled and nodded her understanding and encouragement. He rose, stood by the chair and stuffed his hands in his pockets. "It isn't a religious thing. None of my family is overly religious. It's a commitment thing. You make a commitment, you live up to it. You make a vow, you keep it. That's why I was never unfaithful to my wife." He flung one arm upwards. "Oh, sure, I'd go out with the guys in the PI and Hong Kong, and we'd drink too much and party, but I was never one to take the dollies to bed."

Again, he looked her way. "When I realized Bobbie hadn't kept her vow, I knew here," he pointed with one hand to his head, "it wouldn't work, before I could accept it here." He placed his right hand over his heart.

"The ironic thing is Bobbie knew it wouldn't work before I did. She knew me well enough, I guess, to recognize what had happened had destroyed us. Trust—it's a fragile commodity, and once shattered, it's like trying to put a smashed eggshell back together."

Whew! That's about as profound as I've ever heard him, thought Sandy. She said simply, "I can see you've given this a lot of consideration."

"Yeah, but it probably took me too long to figure it out." He grinned and shook his head ruefully. "I met her new beau when I took her back to the house Sunday evening. Seems like a nice enough fella. I wished them well." He sat back down as she dealt a hand.

Sandy could not believe the weight she felt had lifted. Now, with Bobbie safely out of the picture, and his feelings out in the open, the road should be clear for their marriage. *Maybe we can have a double wedding.*

"What are you thinking about?" he asked as she uttered an unintentional giggle.

"Oh, nothing," she fudged. "I just have a really good hand." After the hand was played, she laid down twenty-four points. That, plus a good crib won the game and relieved her from having to explain her devilish thoughts.

He put away the cards, took her hand and headed upstairs. She followed willingly. Time to dynamite out any remaining obstacles. Except for the first night the ship was back when he uttered those three important little words, he hadn't said anything or taken any actions that would indicate he was ready to change the status quo. She was, and the timing had never been more opportune, in her opinion.

Upstairs, she puffed a couple pillows against the headboard and leaned against them. "So what about you and me? You're about to report to two or three years of shore duty, right here in San Diego. You won't have to be going off and 'leaving a wife' as you used to say. But you haven't said a word about us getting married."

She saw him flinch and compress his lips. "I could still be in line for another sea job in a couple of years."

Sandy braced herself against the pillow, slowly counted to ten, and when she was calm enough, said quietly but firmly. "I really resent that. How long are you going to carry that pole on your back? You really play your role as a martyr to the hilt. You aren't the only man in the world whose wife cheated on him. Nor is that occurrence exclusive to men who are out to sea. If I wanted to cheat on you, I could do it whether you were here or off on some cruise. And, if I don't cheat on you when we're not married, why should you be afraid marriage would change that? It's time to get on with your life and leave your bitterness in the past. I know Hank's death was devastating, so I backed off last summer. And I know Bobbie hurt you, and I've tired to make allowances for that. I've tried to make it up to you, by loving you, by helping you where I could, but you seem to enjoy wallowing in your self-pity."

He rubbed her thigh with the tips of his fingers. "Jesus, you're a stubborn woman. What's wrong with things the way they are?"

"Was that a trick question?" she asked, glancing sideways at his face.

He laughed in spite of himself. "No. I mean . . . . What's wrong with the relationship we have?"

"When I was a teenager, proper mothers taught their daughters that men don't buy the cows if they can get the milk for free. I am fast coming to the conclusion that as long as you can get sex free, you have no intention of making a permanent commitment. I understand now the importance you place on commitment, but do you think it's a once-in-a-lifetime event?"

Then a thought occurred to her. "Or, maybe there's another possibility. Maybe you think a woman who doesn't hold out for marriage, like your precious Amy, isn't worth marrying."

"Oh, honey, you know better than that," he scolded, rubbing her arm.

She ignored him. "Maybe my strategy was all wrong, I thought honest and open love was what was important. I should have known by the way you dealt with Bobbie and with Hank that you didn't know how to give or receive unconditional love. But I cared enough about you to send the very best, and you're an idiot if you think otherwise."

"Honey, come on, let's talk about this later. We don't have to decide this tonight." He propped himself on one elbow.

"Yes! We do. You're not taking me seriously. You know what, you're a damn fool. You can deny it till doomsday, but you love me and you need me. I know you do. That's what's made me hang in so long, not what you *said*, but how you *acted*. I looked below the surface and saw a man I could respect and honor, but one who was suffering. I was willing to make some sacrifices, to put in the extra effort, to give you some extra time to allow your wounds time to heal. But you won't let them."

"Honey, come on. I'm tired, it's been a hectic week. Let's not spend it arguing. We'll talk this weekend."

She shoved his arm away and sat up on the edge of the bed.

He rolled over on his back and exhaled loudly.

"Matt, you have a black belt in procrastination, and I'm not waiting any more. I was so happy to hear about Bobbie, because frankly, I really thought *she* was my most formidable competition for your love, but it's *you*. My friend, I think you're going to find the Navy isn't a very warm mistress, nor is she going to provide you very much companionship in your old age, after she's through with you."

He tried once more by scratching her back.

She pulled away. "It's almost like you might be happy with me, and for some reason you're not entitled to happiness. You work harder at being unhappy than any person I know. God, Matt, I just don't understand you."

He exhaled again and dropped his hand back onto the bed. "Dammit, I don't want to talk about it right now. I'm tired. If you don't want to make love, fine. Let's just go to sleep." He rolled over, turning his back to her.

She ignored his bad humor, stood up and put on her underclothes. Holding her slacks, she continued, "Matt, we both took a lot of forks in the road to get us to this point—here in your bed. You know what they are better than I. I'm going to go home now. I've been neglecting my dog for you. If you want some freedom to check out what else might be out there that's better than what I'm offering, it's yours. I won't be bothering you. We've reached another one of those damn forks. If you choose one way, it means we get married, for better or for worse, the whole nine yards. If not, then I simply give up. I'm not prepared to wait another four years—not even another year—for you to decide when or if you're ready to marry me."

She slipped into her slacks and blouse, and sat down in the chair beside the bed to put on her shoes. Fully dressed, she walked into the bathroom before Matt realized she was up.

He put on his shorts, and waited for her to come out. He'd

promise something to get her to stay.

She came out of the bathroom and not looking in his direction, picked up her purse and keys from the dresser and headed for the stairs.

Matt quickly stepped between her and the door and grabbed her hand. "Honey, I'm sorry . . . ."

Her legs were weak and shaky, but she pulled free of his light grasp. "I'm sorry too. But I'm not a beggar and I'm through selling myself short. After this much time, I'm either worth the marriage commitment from you, or you choose the other fork—wherever that may lead you. You know I love you, but it's not my decision. The ball's in your court. Goodbye, Matt." Her eyes were full of tears and steely determination as she quickly moved down the stairs and out the front door, closing it quietly.

For two weeks, Matt busied himself with work on the ship and at home. He'd been gone a long time; there was plenty to do. He cleaned the garage, oiled all the oak furniture and door trim, dug up the old plants on the patio and planted new ones, bought himself a new ladder and washed all the windows inside and out. During the week, with his relief aboard, he simply couldn't find enough work to fill more than about twelve hours a day. He managed to find racquetball opponents for a couple hours on the weekends, and he took advantage of the swimming pool in his development for the first time since he'd lived there.

Starting about the third week after Sandy left, he found it more difficult to fill the void in his life with busywork. It had never registered before how much time he spent with her, how many things she did with him, how much he enjoyed her company. Time started to weigh heavily. He really hated to go home to that empty house. There were several evenings, on his way home from the ship that he drove over to Harbor Island and just sat in the car watching the boats. That little man-made island hadn't even been there when he left in 1965. They'd dredged it up out of the bay while he was gone—one of the nicer changes he'd noted on his return.

For a man who normally enjoyed cooking at home, he ate out a lot, but dining alone, whether at a restaurant or in his silent house, was still distasteful.

Sitting alone one evening the phone rang. *She decided to call.*

It was John. Matt felt the same tinge of disappointment as he did when he got that first letter in prison and it wasn't from Bobbie. "What's happening?" he asked.

John sounded excited. "I wanted you to be the first you know— I made captain, and we just picked up the cutest little boy you've ever seen from the adoption people."

"Congratulations," Matt said.

"Hey, you and Sandy gotta come up soon and see the little guy."

"Yeah, maybe after I report to Miramar; should have a more predictable schedule then."

John ended the conversation with another announcement. "Jim's still outdoing me. He called a few weeks ago and said that Julie was pregnant again. Oh, he said Amy was engaged—getting married the end of this year."

After hanging up, Matt fixed a sandwich although he wasn't hungry. He watched television until the eleven o'clock news ended, but still had trouble falling asleep. He kept thinking . . . analyzing.

He'd perfected mental gymnastics in prison, but that was mostly limited to remembering, reconstructing his life's history up to that point. This was different—now he was analyzing relationships—his relationships—something he'd not only never perfected, but hadn't even practiced very often.

So, what in the hell did he want? Freedom? That had been a precious word at one time, a coveted prize, but it brought a different result now. This emptiness he was feeling—the way he was missing Sandy—were good indications, even to him, that he loved her. But was it enough?

What was love? He certainly thought he loved Bobbie, but obviously not enough to suit her; certainly not enough to hold her when he was in Vietnam. He'd sure as hell loved Hank, but for a while there, it seemed like his son hated his guts. It was painful to love someone and lose them. He'd probably subconsciously fought falling in love with Sandy because being in love made him vulnerable, and if he was vulnerable, as he had sorely learned, he could be hurt. Well, he was hurting now, anyway, so what did that tell him?

It had been more than four years since he came home—and he was no closer to getting back to a "normal" life—whatever the hell that meant—than when he had moved into the BOQ.

John's call reminded him of his prison buddies. If they were haunted by the prison experience, it didn't show much. Few of them had been afraid to risk another commitment.

Mike Hastings, a bachelor when he was shot down in 1966, had married his Navy nurse within a few months of returning home. In late June of 1973, Matt had been Mike's best man at his and Rachel's wedding in the chapel on the grounds of the Naval Hospital. Later they bought a condo in Del Mar and Matt and Sandy had gone to their open house. Last year, they had a son. Every time he saw Mike at a get-together, it seemed like prison was far behind him. He'd found a job with the Navy in San Diego. It wasn't flying, but it allowed him to go home every night to his family. It was obvious he was happy.

Both John and Jim had quickly moved on. In less than a year, both had met and married nice girls as soon as their first marriages were dissolved—while he'd screwed around trying to put back together something that was hopelessly smashed.

They had been in about the same predicament as Matt when they came home, except their wives didn't even try to hide the fact that they had found someone new. Would he have reacted differently if Bobbie had told him in the limo, or at the hospital or in the car going home? Would learning about her affair a month or so earlier have made a damn bit of difference? Probably not. When he came home, he wanted his family together. He'd dreamed too many godforsaken nights of returning home and picking up where they left off—as if he'd just been gone on a long, long cruise—to let go easily. Now he realized that was probably about as unrealistic as expecting things to magically work out by themselves after they started to fall apart.

Even Steve, who would suffer the physical reminders of his "tour" in Vietnam for the rest of his life, who had retired from the Navy when he couldn't fly anymore, and who, like Matt, had wanted so much to keep his family together, had now gotten on with a new life. Steve had called shortly after Matt got back from the first cruise to offer his condolences; he had attended Hank's funeral. He had also announced that he and Jennifer had bought a condo in Encinitas and flown up to Vegas the previous weekend and tied the knot. If Matt wanted something to do, he had a standing invitation to go up there for a visit, but without Sandy it didn't sound like fun. Usually when they got together in the past with Steve and Jennifer, they drank a lot of Cold Duck and played bridge which wasn't a three-handed game.

But John and Jim had moved on at what Matt believed to be a considerable cost. They had essentially lost their first families. As far as he knew, Jim had little contact with his nearly-grown children and John had almost none. They were starting over, and they would both be near sixty when their "new" families were out of high school. Maybe that would keep them young—or, he suspected, turn them grey even sooner.

But Steve, despite having tried damn hard to keep his family together, was also still unsuccessful in having much contact with his children.

Why were many of the kids so alienated from their POW fathers? Did they somehow blame them for getting shot down? Did they feel, since their mothers were getting divorces, that they could be loyal to only one parent? Would they, when they were adults, see things differently and want to re-establish that parent-child connection with their fathers—or were those relationships for some undefinable reason—irreparably severed? If so, why?

It had to have been tough on the children of all the POWs while the men were in Vietnam. It probably was doubly confusing to have the family break apart as soon as their fathers returned. Divided loyalties—he'd seen that with Debbie. No wonder some of the kids were screwed up. Maybe his trying so long and so hard to get back with Bobbie, for all its down sides, had a positive aspect too. At least he felt he had salvaged a decent rapport with his daughter, and he probably would have had a terrific bond with Hank, after the truth came out, had he only lived.

The next evening Matt drove out to the cemetery.

After a weekend visit to Nebraska, the first time he'd been back since that Christmas when they moved his parents in, his townhouse was just as quiet, just as lonely as when he left. He renewed his analysis pilgrimage.

So—if all the other guys who were in at least as bad shape, family-wise, as he had been, had been able to move on, why in the hell was he sitting around feeling very much like he did when he was in prison—bleak, hopeless, miserable and very lonely? Next to the torture, solitary confinement had been the worst. Being alone wasn't any fun—then or now. There might have been a time, before he ever married, that he would have been satisfied with the "gay bachelor" lifestyle. But, at this stage of his life, after everything that had happened to him, he wanted a lifetime companion. He was about to report to a job that would probably require a lot of entertaining; he wanted someone there beside him. He'd reached a point in his career where most things were done with couples—he wasn't flying a single-seat jet anymore.

Without a doubt, Sandy was, in many ways, the most exasperating woman he had ever met, but she was also the most loving and the most supportive. He missed her terribly. He would gladly trade the silence of his quiet house for her laughter, or even for a spirited, fiery outburst from her.

When he left home in 1965, the speed limit was fifty-five miles per hour, and people drove fifty-five. When he came home, the speed limit was sixty-five but few drove less than seventy. The world had sped up, but he hadn't quite caught up. It was time he quit trying to drive fifty-five. If he wanted to survive in today's world, he was going to have to drive the damn speed limit, even if he thought it was a little dangerous. Sandy was a sixty-five or even seventy mile-per-hour kind of person. If he sat on his butt much longer, she'd be gone, and then he could sit around for as long as he wanted and cogitate on things he'd never understand and couldn't change even if he did.

The more he thought about it, the angrier he got—at himself. He was not going to be a "lifer." The shackles that had been holding him back since 1973 were not the French-made ones in Vietnam; these were his own design. So what if he couldn't have what he'd had before—maybe he could have something better. Perhaps what he had before wasn't as great as the illusion he'd created in prison.

If only Hank could be a part of the future, whatever it held. On the previous occasions, being alone had not really been his doing, and it certainly hadn't been his choice. But this time he was alone and it was his doing and he did have a choice.

He'd had no control over what was happening to him, around him, for too damn long. When he was shot down, he had no say-so. Oh, he could resist some, but essentially what happened—even whether he lived or died—was in someone else's hands. He'd expected that when he returned home, he'd be back in charge—both of his life and his family. Well, it hadn't worked out that way, much of it because of his own surrender. He could have taken control when he learned of Bobbie's affair, but it was like he didn't know how anymore. He'd just let things happen *to him*. It was time *he* started making things happen. It was time he took control of his own destiny, and he needed to do something about it right now.

Sandy was home, sitting on the patio, enjoying a travel-poster San Diego evening, Ratman in her lap. She leaned back, resting her head against the chair cushion. Looking up, she saw the nearly full moon framed perfectly between two tall queen palms. She studied the twinkling stars, locating Orion. There was another constellation, but she couldn't remember the name. Instead, she sat up and focused on the city lights below; she was more familiar with them than the heavens. There was the Coronado bridge, the El Cortez, even the stadium was all lit up for some reason. She patted Ratman, who responded by licking her face, his cold nose nudging against her cheek. *A beautiful starlet night, and I'm cuddling with my pooch.* It would be a great evening to sit in the Jacuzzi, drink wine and make love.

It had been a desolate seven weeks since she more or less delivered her ultimatum to Matt. At first she was sure he cared enough that he'd come around, but as the hours turned into days, the days into weeks and now months, it appeared she had sorely misjudged him. As much as she ached to have him back, even on his terms, some part of her refused to give in. She wanted the wedding ring, the commitment he so prized. If he really cared so little, it was better she accept that now and try to forget about him and a future with him. Or, if he didn't know after almost four years that he loved her, he'd probably never realize it. But, the silence was hell. And trying to find someone else like him would be impossible. Oh, well . . . *shit happens.* She'd been alone before she met him; the world wouldn't stop.

Time to come out of mourning and get on with life. Maybe she'd take a cruise. She'd never been on a cruise. Maybe she would meet Mr. Right, like in those shipboard romance movie scenes. She laughed at herself, patted Ratman and drained the wine glass.

She jumped at the shrill sound of the phone. Ratman leapt down, and cocked his head toward the phone.

"Can we get together and talk?" It was Matt, not even bothering to identify himself.

Her stomach felt like she'd just taken a swift elevator ride. She was so startled she was speechless for several moments. Finally, she murmured, "Sure."

"Fine. About thirty minutes. I'll pick you up, okay?"

Matt's knock on the door was answered by an outwardly-calm appearing Sandy. Ratman, close to her side, snarled, the hair on the back of his neck standing up. He sniffed Matt, then wagged the stub of his tail. Matt reached down to pat him.

"Hi. Give me a second and I'll get my purse. Ratman, come."

They walked toward the car in silence, side by side, not touching.

"Is my favorite hamburger joint okay?"

"Sure."

Throughout the drive and the meal, Matt kept up a steady stream of chitchat. He updated her on the turnover, told her about Steve and Jennifer's marriage, John and Liz's new baby, and Julie's pregnancy. He told her about his trip back to Nebraska. "Bonnie said to tell you hello." He asked how had she'd been, how her real estate office was doing. Finally, he announced, "I'll be reporting to Miramar in ten days."

After dinner, when they got back in the car, Sandy cut to the chase. "You said you needed to talk to me. I get the feeling you haven't said what's on your mind. So let's hear it."

He pulled off Mission Gorge Road into a vacant lot and shut off the engine. Turning toward Sandy, he said simply. "I missed you."

She sat quietly, watching him.

Still searching for words, he proceeded cautiously, "You know how I felt about getting married . . . ."

Sandy moved toward him, her anger rising, "If you called me tonight to explain that you're still not ready to get married, you could have saved us both a lot of time—if you'd simply told me over the phone—or not calling at all would have sent the same message. I told you, I'm . . . ."

Matt grabbed her shoulders with both hands. "Will you shut up for five minutes."

"I beg your pardon!" She jerked angrily out of his grasp.

"That's not what I wanted to tell you. Dammit, I love you. I don't know what else to call it. I've really missed you, and I don't want to lose you. If marriage is the only way you'll have me," he held up a white piece of cloth and waved it, grinning, "then I guess we'll have to get married."

There was a long silence. Her eyes widened. In seconds, that familiar twinkle had returned to her eyes. "Was that a proposal?"

"Hell, no!"

Her shoulders sagged ever so slightly, but before she could respond, Matt continued. "As I recall, you proposed to me within the first six months we were dating. And you've continued to do so with great regularity ever since. That wasn't a proposal—it was an acceptance!"

"Oooh. Well . . . okay. You certainly took your damn sweet time."

Shortly after the Vietnam POWs were released in 1973, the Joint Chiefs of Staff were to be given a formal debriefing as to what went on in North Vietnam during the men's captivity. Colonel John Peter Flynn, the SRO, was to be the briefing officer. Flynn called Hervy Stockman, one of the POWs and asked him to design an emblem to represent the group. The idea for the design of the emblem was Hervy's. He finally settled on the current design with the flag colors of the United States of America, South Vietnam and Thailand. The ideas were of the "4th" referred to the 4th war . . . WWI, WWII, Korea and Vietnam. "Return with Honor" was the Code of the prisoners - We all go home with honor - or no one does. Hervy faxed the design to Colonel Flynn, who had it reproduced to be added to his briefings.

Although the emblem was designed before the NAM-POW organization was formed, the original emblem was painted and is retained in the NAM-POW organization's files.

The emblem represented, in the first briefing before high ranking U.S. Government officials, a solemn symbol to honor and commemorate the men and women who served as POWs in China (5); North Vietnam (472); South Vietnam (262); Laos (31) and Cambodia (31).

ABOUT THE AUTHOR

Karen Black is an estate planning, trust, probate and elder law attorney practicing in California. Her diverse background includes: legal secretary, a construction estimator and office manager, Suzuki motorcycle dealer and truck bumper salesperson.

Karen's husband, Cole Black, spent almost seven years as a Prisoner of War in Vietnam.

Karen has four children and Cole has one son from previous marriages.

Code of Conduct is her first published novel.

BIBLIOGRAPHY

Alvarez, Everett, Jr. and Anthony S. Pitch, *Chained Eagle*. New York: Donald I. Fine, 1989.

Alvarez, Everett, Jr. and Samuel A. Schreiner, *Code of Conduct.*

Anton, Frank with Tommy Denton, *Why Don't You Get Me Out?* Arlington, TX: Summit Publishing Group, 1997.

Bailey, Lawrence R., with Ron Martz, *Solitary Survivor: The First American POW in Southeast Asia.* Washington, DC: Brassey's, 1995.

Brace, Ernest C., *A Code to Keep;* The True Story of America's Longest-Held Civilian Prisoner of War in Vietnam. New York: St. Martin's Press, 1988.

Carey, Dave, *The Ways We Choose;* Book Partners. Wilsonville, OR, 2000.

Cayer, Marc, *Prisoner in Vietnam* (English version). Marc Cayer; Prisonnier au Vietnam (French version), Asia Resource Center, Washington, DC, 1990.

Chesley, Larry, *Seven Years in Hanoi; a POW tells his story.* Salt Lake City; Bookcraft, 1973.

Coffee, Gerald, *Beyond Survival: Building on the Hardtimes-* A POWs Inspiring Story. New York: Putnam, 1990.

Day, George E., *Return With Honor*, Mesa, AZ: Champlin Fighter Museum Press, 1989. Excerpts appear as *Promises to Keep*, Reader's Digest (December 1991), pp107-111.

Dengler, Dieter, *Escape from Laos*, San Rafael, CA: Presidio Press, 1979.

Denton, Jeremiah A. with Ed Brandt, *When Hell Was in Session.* Washington, DC: Morley Books, 1997. Originally published: New York: Reader's Digest Press, 1976.

Dramesi, John A., *Code of Honor*, New York: W. W. Norton, 1975.

Dudman, Richard, *Forty Days with the Enemy.* New York: Liveright, 1971.

Gaither, Ralph, as told to Steve Henry, *With God in a POW Camp.* Nashville, Broadman Press, 1973.

Gragg, Rod, **Bobby Bagley**, *POW.* Van Nuys, CA: Bible Voice, 1978.

Guarino, Larry, *A POW's Story: 2801 days in Hanoi.* New York; Ivy Books, 1990.

Hubbard, Col. Edward L., *Escape From the Box: the wonder of human potential.* Edited by Art Nicolet. West Chester, PA: Praxis, International, 1994.

McCain, John with Mark Salter, *Faith of My Fathers.* New York: Random House, 1999.

McDaniel, Eugene B. with James L. Johnson, *Before Honor.* Philadelphia: A. J. Holman Co., 1975.

McDaniel, Eugene B., *Scars and Stripes: the Red McDaniel Story.* Published by friends of Red McDaniel, Philadelphia: A. J. Holman, 1975.

McGrath, John M., *Prisoner of War: Six Years in Hanoi.* Annapolis, MD: Naval Institute Press, 1975.

Mulligan, James A., *The Hanoi Commitment.* Virginia Beach, VA: RIF Marketing, 1981.

Nasmyth, Spike, *2355 Days: A POW's story.* New York: Orion Books, 1991.

Plumb, Charlie as told to Glen DeWerff, *I'm no Hero.* Independence, MO: Independence Press, 1973.

Plumb, Charlie, *The Last Domino?* Independence, MO: Independence Press, 1975.

Purcell, Ben and Anne, *Love and Duty.* New York: St. Martin's Press, 1992. Random House, New York, 1973.

Risner, Robinson, *The Passing of the Night: My Seven Years as a Prisoner of the North Vietnamese.* New York: Random House, 1974, 1973.

Rowe, James N., *Five Years to Freedom.* Boston: Little, Brown, 1971.

Rutledge, Howard and Phyllis with Mel and Lydia White, *In the Presence of Mine Enemies. 1965-1973: A Prisoner of War.* Old Tappan, NJ: Revell, 1973. Also, Boston: G.K. Hall, 1974.

Stockdale, James B. and Sybil, *In Love and War: The Story of a Family's Ordeal and Sacrafice During the Vietnam Years.* Annapolis, MD: Naval Institute Press, c1990. Harper & Row, 1984.